The Garden and Jerusalem

Volume 1: By the Waters of Babylon

by A.L. Porter

APORTER PUBLISHING
Chicago, Illinois

Copyright 2023 © by A. L. Porter

ISBN (Print): 979-8-89282-209-1

Also by A. L. Porter:

Seeking a Distant Shore

Contents

The Garden and Jerusalem

Volume I: By the Waters of Babylon

By the waters of Babylon we wept,
Wept for lost Jerusalem.
Sing! our captors said,
Sing a song of Zion.

We could not sing the Lord's songs
In a land become so strange,
Only weeping and memory
could sustain our hope,

We shall not sing the Lord's songs
unless the Lord break these chains,
Unless God himself judge our oppressors,
until Jerusalem is ours again.

Introduction: Babylon's Child

Some said he was a rascal, some said he was clever - too clever for his own good, or anyone else's. His father, they said, was at wit's end with the boy - his second son, so unlike the firstborn. Still, the elder brother would inherit the family business in any case; it would be left in safe hands. The second son's foolishness would be on his own head.

Not everyone shared the common opinion. Young Roger, they said, was more than clever — he had gifts that were underappreciated. Most notably, he had a knack for languages

— more than a knack — an uncanny ability to absorb, digest, and master the speech of strangers. It had something to do with his congenial approach to life, his eagerness to please, his innate empathy — the easy-going nature of many second-born sons. But there was more to it than that; beneath the pleasant mien was a voracious intelligence that devoured whatever life sent his way.

It seemed at first that this would be his undoing. As a youngster, he was wont to escape the watchful eye of his mother and rove the streets of London with a gang of like-minded companions: mischievous, cocky, irreverent — though not really threatening the public safety. There were plenty of boys doing the same things in London in those days — whenever they could contrive to escape the supervision of their elders on some "errand" or other. Roger and his friend Alfred Fitch had a few dodgy scrapes, but nothing that rose to the level of criminality.

It was when Roger started school that his life seemed to turn a corner. He had learned to read at home before he was five. His familiarity with the Bible was remarkable (there weren't that many other books available at home). His teachers were impressed, then a little alarmed at how rapidly he grasped things. He was easily bored. They remedied this by giving him extra work — Latin at first, then Greek. Sometime after his tenth birthday, they discovered that he was studying Dutch and French on his own initiative: He had taken up the habit of attending Sunday services at the Stranger's Church at Austin Friars, where the services were conducted in Dutch and French — for the expatriates that had fled to London from across the sea. This was not an entirely welcome discovery: most Londoners knew very little about the doctrines preached to these foreigners, but it was supposed that their theology must be radical, if not heretical — why else would they have been forced to flee their homes?

The suppositions were not wrong. Roger was exposed to some of the most radical of Reformation theologians. The pastors of the Stranger's church were evangelistic in their zeal and happy to loan the young Englishman books and pamphlets that explained their beliefs. Roger was eager to explore them. Within a year or less, people began to notice a change in him. The carefree and mischievous boy was gone. In his stead was a sober, serious youngster with a piety beyond his years — opinionated, overconfident, possibly radical to the point of heresy, but always certain of his beliefs. It led to conflict with his friends and family. At length, it was said that his father had stopped speaking to him . . .

Part 1: The Chief Justice

London, 1616: St. Sepulcher Without Newgate

London was bursting at the seams, as so often in its past. Political turmoil notwithstanding, it was now a thriving city of more than 200,000, double the number it had been a generation ago. The plague that occurred in 1603, the year of King James's coronation, and killed tens of thousands of Londoners (widely considered to be a warning from God at the time), was only a memory. There was no room within the ancient city walls for the newcomers, so they collected like waterborne flotsam, jammed into grubby settlements outside the walls. There were a few well-built structures outside the city walls, such as the Church of the Holy Sepulcher, which had stood since the Saxon kings ruled England, and then been rebuilt more than a century ago. During the Crusades, it was customary for English knights en route to the Holy Land to stop there, as the church was dedicated to its namesake in Jerusalem. The Crusaders journeyed no more; the Turks now ruled Jerusalem.

St. Sepulcher, as the church was now called, had one more distinction that lived in the memory of its parishioners — the legacy of John Rogers, the heretic. Rogers had been among the bible translators who assisted William Tyndale while in exile during the reign of Henry VIII, had returned during the reign of his son Edward, and became vicar of St. Sepulcher, where his preaching was much admired and celebrated. He was the first to be convicted of heresy by "Bloody Mary", and was burned to death at Smithfield, just over a furlong from St. Sepulcher — a convenient proximity, one may suppose; at least his parishioners could attend his execution. John Rogers' teaching was vindicated after Mary's death (which not a few attributed to God's judgment upon her), and the congregation enjoyed that sense of satisfaction that comes from being on the side of martyrs, without actually having to face the fire.

The last heretic burned at Smithfield was a man named Bartholomew Legate. He and his brothers were street preachers who rejected all churches as irretrievably corrupt. One of Legate's brothers died in Newgate prison, just inside the city walls from St. Sepulcher. Legate himself survived long enough to be publicly executed; the bells of St. Sepulcher were rung to commemorate the event. That was the last year that any heretics were burned in England. The old ways were passing; the new were embraced.

There were a few famous men in the congregation at St. Sepulcher's. Notable among them was Captain John Smith, adventurer and colonizer of the Virginia Plantation, surveyor of Virginia and New England, and celebrated author of popular books about the riches and opportunities of the American continent. His adventuring days were over, but Sundays found him in regular attendance at St. Sepulcher's.

Another prominent citizen who could be seen in attendance was Sir Edward Coke, once Speaker of the House of Commons, later Attorney General for England and Wales, then Chief Justice of the Court of Common Pleas, and more recently Chief Justice of the King's Bench. Coke was sixty-four years old now, retired from public service -- or not, depending on the King's pleasure. Just now, it was the King's pleasure that Sir Edward be in the royal presence. But that could change . . .

Coke (he pronounced his name "cook") was a wealthy man with numerous estates he could have lived in, but he preferred to stay in London, near the political drama that was unfolding in England. St. Sepulcher's, just outside the city walls, was a good place to meet and converse with other men of his class and convictions. Of course, the bulk of the congregation was men, women, and children of lesser rank. Sir Edward and his peers found seats near the front of the sanctuary; their lessers sat in the back.

On one particular Sunday in April, Sir Edward's attention was caught by one of the lessers, as he left the service. It was a boy, perhaps thirteen or fourteen years of age, who appeared to be unaccompanied. Not much to look at, but the lad was carrying something unusual: a book that appeared to be a bible, and some sort of tablet, or board, such as a scribe might use for taking notes. Curious, Coke directed one of his servants to find out who the boy was and what he was doing. Once outside, Coke greeted the vicar and waited for his servant to bring the boy to him. It was a pleasant sunny morning.

The boy was introduced as "Roger Williams, Sir. At your service."

"Do you know who I am?"

"Indeed, Sir," the boy replied, with a deferential bow, "You are Sir Edward Coke, the great jurist."

Coke liked the sound of that. "And how do you know me?"

"Why, Sir, for your many famous judgments, for your defense of our rights against the royal prerogative. For your integrity. For your courage against the tyrannies of the archbishop and his High Commission."

Coke was accustomed to flattery, as powerful men are, but it was unexpected from such a source as this. The lad was not poorly dressed; no doubt the son of some skilled tradesman or merchant, but nothing suggested that he traveled in the circles that Coke did. What could this boy know of judgments and rights?

"What have you there?"

"My Bible and my writing materials."

"Writing materials?"

"Aye, my paper and pencil." He produced a fat, wooden cylinder, one of those newfangled writing sticks.

"You write without a quill?"

"Aye, if I use an inkwell, I could spill it — too risky in a crowd."

Coke nodded. "And what have you been writing?"

"The sermon." Here, the boy opened his notebook to display what he had written. Coke found it undecipherable. "What kind of scribbling is this?"

"It is called shorthand. A manner of writing that is faster than ordinary writing."

Coke looked skeptical. His servant, on the other hand, smiled and nodded, as if the boy was making sense.

"Read some of what you have written."

The boy straightened himself and began to read: "It is not enough that we be obedient to the laws of the Church, nor is it sufficient that each of us live orderly and righteous lives. God is about a work greater than those things. The atoning work of our Lord Christ worketh mightily among us, to the building of a righteous city, a New Jerusalem, that shall excel the old one as the glorious sun excels the pale, blotchy moon. Our inheritance is the Garden of the Lord, and he intends to lead us to that paradise if only we have the courage and discipline to follow him there."

"A pretty passage. Most inspiring", said Coke.

"Indeed, I thought so, myself," said the boy. "Although some supporting scripture would have made it more persuasive, I think."

"What scripture would you have cited?" The boy's cheekiness amused Coke. *Give the cocky pup enough leash, and he'll soon realize he's out of his depth.* Coke smiled as he thought of some of his own youthful braggadocio.

"I think I would have spent more time in the epistle to the Romans, where the apostle speaks of Our Lord as the "second Adam". If we are to return to the Garden of the Lord, we must lay down our old lives, and take up new ones, even as Our Lord did, else we shall corrupt that paradise if such a thing is possible. The New Jerusalem we seek is the one that comes down from heaven."

Coke looked hard at the boy. The boy gazed back at him. Nothing impertinent in those eyes, just the open gaze of a child who spoke with words beyond his years . . . "Is that what you think?" Coke paused to collect his thoughts. "Do you often have such 'thoughts' about the sermons of your betters? Have you ever offered your wisdom to these men, so that their preaching may be improved?"

"I have thoughts; that I readily confess," admitted the boy. "As for offering them as improvements, I fear that such eminent men of God would as likely cuff me about the ears as thank me for expressing them." The boy grinned.

Coke chuckled. At least the boy was no fool.

"You say your name is Roger? Where is your dwelling?"

"In Cow's Lane, sir. With my family. My father is a merchant tailor."

Ah. Cow's Lane. So named because it was once used to drive livestock to the market at Smithfield, less than a mile from St. Sepulcher. That was many years ago. People had built houses along Cow's Lane so tightly that there was hardly any room between them. With no more space at ground level, they had built higher, adding stories above ground, and even cantilevering the upper floors over the street — until they met the cantilevered rooms of the house across the lane. Cow's Lane was a tunnel now: dark, crowded, and none too clean. This was how the humbler sort lived in London. That said, the people who lived inside the walls of the old city were mostly worse off.

"I should like to meet your father," said Coke. "Will you take me to him?"

"Certainly, sir. He will be home from church by now."

"How is it that he was not at church with you?"

"Oh, he was there; the whole family was. We just don't all sit together anymore."

Coke wondered at this but decided not to ask. "Which way, then?

"Follow me, Sir," the lad strode off to the north, in the general direction of Smithfield and Old St. Bart's. Coke and his servant followed. Coke left his carriage behind at St. Sepulcher, with the driver and one of the coachmen; he signaled the other coachman to come along. It was a pleasant Sunday, but one couldn't be too careful in the warren of narrow streets and alleys that they would be entering.

Soon enough, they arrived at the door of a tall, thatch-roofed house, crammed into a narrow lot between its neighbors. There were more than a few stares from bystanders in the street as Coke's servant knocked on the door. "Who's there?" came the question from within.

"His Lordship Sir Edward Coke, of the King's Privy Council," was the reply.

The door opened slowly. More stares from the bystanders. One look at Coke's clothing and the matching livery of his companions was enough to open the door wider. A maid stood gaping in the entry, then turned quickly inside. In another moment, she was back, accompanied by a tall, well-dressed man — evidently the master of the house. He sized up the group, then his eyes fell on the boy. Coke could see the family resemblance: this must be the boy's father. Recovering himself, the man bowed, "Welcome, Lord, to my humble house. How may I be of service?"

"I would speak with the father of this boy," said Coke, pointing to Roger.

"Why? What has he done now?" The man gave the boy an accusing look.

"My business is better conducted within," said Coke

The man bowed again. "Please, my Lord, enter."

The doorway led into a long hallway that led all the way through the house to the back. A nervous-looking woman stood there, with several children and the maid, all of whom curtseyed or bowed as Coke and his companions entered, then disappeared into the rooms on either side of the hallway.

"James Williams, at your service," said their host. "We can speak in the garden if it please you."

Coke nodded his assent. James Williams led him back through the hallway to the rear of the house, where there was a small yard, a privy (better here than indoors), a couple of fruit trees, and a vegetable patch. Servants brought chairs from inside the house. Coke sat down first and gestured for his host to do the same. Coke's servants stood within eyesight at the back door. James Williams directed Roger to go back inside. "How can I be of service to you, Lord?"

Coke settled into his chair. "I am of a mind to take your son into my service," he said, "with your consent, of course."

James Williams was surprised at the suggestion. "I can hardly object to such an opportunity on behalf of my son, though I fear you may be disappointed in him." He lowered his voice and leaned forward. "He occupies his mind with impractical matters. I can scarcely imagine that he will make a reliable valet or even a footman."

Coke nodded. "I have something else in mind for the boy. I think he is a clever lad."

"Clever. Aye, clever he is — clever to a fault! No head for business, preoccupied with 'spiritual' things." James shook his head.

"A disappointment, then?"

"I had hopes he might follow me into my business," said James, "but I do not think a man of such 'spiritual' sensitivity can thrive in my business. The boy has become 'converted', as he says. He's a Puritan now, by my lights. A lot of strange and troublesome opinions, and a habit of talking about them at any excuse. I account myself a religious man; I attend church every week. That's good for business, and good for the soul. Disputing about religious questions is a waste of time."

Coke smiled and nodded. The sentiment could have been his own, but he had many Puritans among his friends and peers, and he knew about religious disputes. "Still, I have a use for cleverness. I think your son could serve me very well. I have in mind to use his 'shorthand' as my personal secretary. He seems to handle language well enough."

"Aye, he speaks and writes well enough — in English, French, and Dutch. (I encouraged him in that.) His teachers say he has a 'gift' for languages — did very well in Latin, or so I'm told. When he is interested in a thing, he concentrates his mind admirably. When he is bored, his attention wanders."

"I do not think he will get bored in my service," said Coke with a chuckle. "What I propose is this: I shall take Roger on as a kind of apprentice. He will work for me for seven years. I will supply his food and lodging; he will wear my livery. At the end of that time, I will arrange for him to be placed in a position that will provide a modest living, such as a man would need to marry and establish a family of his own. I will charge your family nothing for this 'apprenticeship'. What say you?"

James Williams bowed his head. "My Lord, that is a most generous offer. I am more than joyful that your favor has fallen upon my son. Let it be as you have said."

Coke and his companions returned the way that they had come; his coach was waiting at St. Sepulcher's, where he had left it. On the way home, he imagined the hubbub that his visit had probably introduced into the Williams household.

London, 1616: Hatton House

Sir Edward Coke maintained a large house in the city, in addition to his many estates in the countryside. It had come into his possession through his marriage to Lady Elizabeth Hatton. Hatton House, as it was known, stood outside the city walls, in a neighborhood near the old palace of the Bishop of Ely, not far from St. Sepulcher's church, west of the crowded warrens of Cow's Lane. The house was large enough to accommodate Lord Coke's family and staff — his wife Lady Hatton, two daughters, and 30 or so servants. He sent one of the servants to collect Roger Williams on the following Monday and introduce him to life in the service of one of England's wealthiest men.

For Roger, it was a new and fascinating life. He had new clothing, including shoes. He slept in an attic space with several other servants and ate with a great many other servants in the lowest levels of the great house. The house buzzed with activity. There were rules to learn and customs to observe. There was a hierarchy among the staff, and he had to learn which of them to defer to, and when. His own rank, of course, was near the bottom, though not quite — he was somewhere above the scullery maids and the stable boys because of his close association with Sir Edward, though it was always safest to bow and be deferential — and it didn't cost anything.

The first afternoon, he was summoned into Sir Edward's library. Coke was there, with another man who was dressed in black, among more books than Roger had ever seen. "I have summoned you here to note our conversation," Coke began, "It is my wish that our conclusions be recorded. You will find writing materials there," — he nodded to a small desk. It was so — paper, ink, and a quill. Roger sat down.

Coke's companion was introduced as John Endecott, a "lawyer of some ability, a scholar, useful to me, at times." Coke laughed as he introduced the man. Endecott smiled at the jesting and nodded (what choice did he have, thought Roger). The two men talked of various things, all of which raised more questions than answers in Roger's mind. He noted what was said, all the while trying to piece together what they were actually talking about. There was a matter of charters, and what they should contain. There was also a rich Baron involved, or was the Baron named "Rich"? They spoke of Virginia, which Roger had heard of, and New England. Also, some mention of "things at court", which Roger decided meant the Royal Court of His Majesty the King. It was dizzying, almost intoxicating, to hear such matters discussed in such a casual way. Roger tried to focus on his notes.

After an hour or so, Endecott stood, thanked Lord Coke for his time, and excused himself. Coke turned to Roger and began to explain: "When men speak of weighty matters, or matters they imagine to be weighty, they may misremember what was said, and by whom — stop writing now; none of what I am telling you needs to be recorded . . ." Roger put the quill down.

Coke continued, "As I said, men may disremember their words, especially when weighty matters are discussed. Master Endecott and I may have different recollections of that which we spoke, a year hence. Your record will serve as a means of restoring our memories, should that be necessary. You should note the date of your writing, but do not sign it (neither shall I); it is for my personal use alone. I do not need a word-for-word account; a true relation of the facts will suffice. Read back to me what you have written."

Roger began to read from his notes. He was frequently interrupted by Coke, with "That last part is unimportant. Leave it out," or "Are you certain that he used that exact word?" Coke explained, gradually, what had transpired and what it meant:

Robert Rich, the 3rd Baron of Leez, was a wealthy and influential man, much interested in foreign trade and in the plantations in the Americas. He was one of the major investors in the Virginia Company and hoped to establish more plantations in North America and the Caribbean. The business of obtaining royal charters for such plantations was a ticklish one. The King would not issue such charters willy-nilly, for he understood their potential value, and there was more than one party of investors "in the game". The terms of the charter needed to be favorable enough to attract investors in the first place, but also include incentives to attract immigrants. There had to be a promise of profits for all parties — the King, investors, and the plantation. The Virginia plantation had not yet returned much profit. Lessons needed to be learned and applied. Lord Rich had money (and friends with money), as well as influence. But Lord Coke's support would be important, too. Endecott was speaking on behalf of the Baron.

"This is but the beginning of a courtship," said Coke. "In time, there will be contracts and compacts, and real money will be forthcoming, and men will bind themselves by oath and by signature. Now is the time for speaking of dreams and possibilities. Your notes will help us hew to today's conclusions when next we meet — which might be a year from now."

"But Master Endecott does not have the notes."

"Quite so. Nor shall we give them to him. Information is power. His patron may well wish to shift his ground when next we meet. Your notes will help me pin him down. Endecott is no fool — he'll make his own notes, and shape them to his client's best advantage."

Roger nodded. "There was something else I heard, that sticks in my mind, some coloration or tone . . . "

"What's that?"

"It seems to me that both of you are anxious that the affairs of these plantations not be entirely transparent to His Majesty, or even his Privy Council."

"I do not recall saying any such thing."

"You didn't say it, and neither did Master Endecott. But I can't ignore the feeling that the both of you, as well as the Baron, would like to see the governance of these places outside the King's purview, or perhaps out of the reach of his tax collectors?"

Coke looked at Roger intently. "Whence this *feeling*?"

Roger met his gaze. "More than once, you agreed that some matters relating to the business of the plantations would be 'of no particular interest to the crown', but seemed to mean that it should be none of the King's business. I can imagine that the King would think otherwise, given his reputation as a ruler who puts his finger in every pie, so to speak, especially where money is involved."

"His finger in every pie? Where did you hear such talk?"

"It is an expression common in my neighborhood, especially when the royal tax collector appears."

Coke laughed out loud. "Aye, that describes the tax collectors! But I would caution you about referring to His Majesty with such a coarse expression."

"Blame it on my youth or my humble upbringing, then. But am I wrong to suppose that the wealthiest of men (like these investors that you speak of) have a similar way of describing things?"

Coke smiled and shook his head. "No, you are not wrong. In private, such men use language that is very coarse indeed when it comes to paying taxes. I merely caution you to be careful what you say. In Cow's Lane, a man may speak as he likes; only his neighbors will hear him, and they are all in the same boat when it comes to taxes. In this new world that you are now part of, a careless word could be construed as treasonous — and such constructions could cost a man his freedom, even his life."

The boy's eyes widened. "Truly? The casual words of a mere apprentice?"

"Hear me carefully. It is not the apprentice who matters, but rather who the apprentice serves that counts. You have entered a world of great rewards and greater risks — my world. As long as you work for me, my enemies are your enemies — and I have powerful enemies. Those who would pull me down will use you to do it if they can."

"I did not realize my situation was so perilous." Roger's shoulders slumped a little.

Coke felt a little sorry for the boy: a lot to absorb on his first day. "Not so perilous as I made it sound. Those who wish me ill have many avenues to attack me — most of which are more likely of success than going through my private secretary. Be of good cheer; you are in the service of a patron of great power, well able to do battle with his foes."

"I hope I shall never give you cause for disappointment, Sir. And may I never become the witless tool of your enemies."

Coke saw something in the boy's face that spoke of simple sincerity, and it touched him. "I may have been too free with you," he offered. "It will all be well in good time. What else did you *feel* about what you heard?"

The boy was silent for a moment as if thinking. "I hesitate to compound impertinence with folly, but it occurred to me that there could be another reason that the investors might prefer that the King be not too involved in their endeavor."

Coke cocked his head, raised his eyebrows: "And what reason might that be?"

Roger started slowly, then the words poured out: "It is said that a struggle . . . is underway in England, between the King and Parliament. It is also said that the struggle is partly about religion, but also about the ancient rights, which the King, so they say, does not fully respect and is loath to honor. These struggles are tangled with one another — it is not always easy to tell when the battle is over religion, as the Puritans say it is, and when it is over the law (as you yourself have said). It occurred to me that some men might wish to use these plantations as a kind of haven from the storms that rage here — a place out of the King's purview, a place where men could order their lives according to their particular preference."

Coke looked hard at the boy. "There certainly are some men who would imagine such a use for a new plantation," he allowed, "but they are not very numerous. This is not a matter for public conversation. The main interest is profit — that is reason enough." *The lad has a wit beyond his years*, Coke said to himself; *He could talk himself into a world of trouble. He will need guiding and watching. But he intuits what others miss and notices details that others overlook.* . . "You would do well to hold such questions close. You may ask me anything you wish, but do not confide what I tell you, or what you hear, or what you *feel* with anyone else."

Roger nodded his agreement. "May I ask another question?"

Coke nodded.

"Have you read all these books?" His eyes roved around the library.

Coke relaxed and nodded, "Some at least, of all of them; all of most of them."

"I have not seen so many in one place before."

Coke saw a hunger in the boy's eyes. "Would you like to read them?"

"May I, Sir?"

"Since you are in my employ, it would serve me well if you did. I can recommend some volumes that might make you more useful to me."

Roger's eyes shone. "Thank you, Sir. I will apply myself with vigor!"

Coke chuckled, then grew serious. "I insist that you remove none of them from this room without my specific permission. You can read in here whenever you are not needed elsewhere. There may be times when I will exclude you from this room, for some private matter, but most often you will be with me when I am here, taking note of whatever transpires."

Roger nodded.

Coke continued, "I intend to use you, Roger Williams, like an extra set of eyes and ears. It suits me best if those eyes and ears are honed and trained. I do not need an extra tongue, so it is not necessary for you to speak your mind unless I ask you to. Most of the men with whom I do business are accustomed to ignoring servants; you will be practically invisible to them if you remain silent; all I need you to do is observe and record."

"It sounds as if you wish me to act as a spy." Roger's face suggested that the idea was not entirely unwelcome.

Coke shook his head. "I did not say 'spy', I said 'observe and record'. That is all I need you to do. We will not be concerned with what other men hold secret—unless they blurt it out in my presence. You will be surprised at the things a gentleman may say when he thinks that nobody is listening. And a servant is a nobody in the eyes of most of them. If the day comes when I need to dispute some past conversation, your record will witness to <u>my</u> version of what was said. Two witnesses are better than one.”

Roger's evening was free that first day, and he spent what time he could in the library. He slept in the attic of the great house, with half a dozen or so young male servants, rose at dawn, dressed, and gathered for his breakfast with the other servants near the kitchen.

There was a strict hierarchy at breakfast — pride of place was given to the most senior staff members. Roger sat at a bench along one side of a table, which seated half a dozen or so of the younger servants on each side. Other tables were reserved for the chief butler, the valets, the ladies’ maids — people who actually spoke to Lord Coke or Lady Hatton in the course of their workday. Kitchen servants, stable hands, and cleaning staff sat at other tables, like Roger. Everyone’s clothing was inspected for conformity to the household standard before eating. There was some confusion about where Roger should eat: as a newcomer, he would ordinarily take a place near the bottom of the hierarchy, but as it became clear that he would spend much of his day in the company of Lord Coke, it seemed proper to move him up to a better table. If he had been a grown man, he would certainly rate a place at the head table, but he was only 13 . . . On the first morning, Roger found himself seated with the middling sort of servants — some old, some almost as young as he; one in particular was a girl of about his age, seated across from him. She introduced herself, “You’re the new one, aren’t you? My name is Isabel. Isabel Glover. I serve Lady Hatton.” She was dressed like a servant, with a small cap covering her hair, and an apron over her kirtle and blouse — all very neat and clean.

Isabel was a personal servant to Lady Hatton, the mistress of the house. She was the daughter of a middle-class family in the city, who had placed her in Lady Hatton's service, in hopes that she might make a career there. In return for some years of service, it was expected that Lady Hatton would try to find a husband for her (and supply at least a small dowry to seal the deal, which Isabel's family could not afford). Failing that, Isabel could remain in service for the rest of her life and receive a salary much more generous than the average woman of her class. Her present duties included doing whatever Lady Hatton needed at the moment. "She takes me with her whenever she goes out," explained Isabel. "I go shopping with her and carry her parcels. I've even been to Greenwich Palace, and seen the Queen herself!" There was an expression of satisfaction on her face, but not arrogance. Her blue eyes said *You should take me seriously, even though I am young.* She smiled at Roger as if daring him to impress her with the importance of his own position. Roger smiled back, said nothing. Truthfully, he wasn't certain of what his position entailed, much less how important it would seem to the other servants. Her eyebrows were raised now, expecting some response from him. He noticed that a wisp of blonde hair had escaped from under her cap; his eyes stayed there just long enough for her to notice it and tuck it back in. She gave him a wink and a wrinkle-nosed smile. Roger tried to think of something to say.

At length, he asked a question: "How is it that Lady Hatton is not called Lady Coke?"

It was not a question that Isabel was expecting, but she rose to the challenge: "Hatton was the name of her first husband. She did not wish to change it when she married the second time — she remembers her first husband with great affection."

Roger must have looked surprised by this assessment, because Isabel hastened to add, "Do not misunderstand me. Lady Hatton has great affection for Lord Coke, as well. But Lord Coke has six living sons and two daughters from his first marriage. The union with Lady Hatton has much to do with the combining of two great fortunes. Lord Coke is twenty-six years older than Lady Hatton; he is not her first love, nor she his."

Several other servants were looking sideways at Isabel now; some appeared to agree; others seemed to regard the topic as unsuitable for the breakfast table. Roger had heard a great deal more than he was prepared to digest. He nodded.

Isabel had not finished yet. "Some say that Lord Coke pursued Lady Hatton out of rivalry with his old foe Sir Francis Bacon. Lady Hatton 'passed the bacon and married the cook,' they say. Both are powerful men, but Lord Coke has the greater wealth, and Lady Hatton knows best how to spend it." There were a few chuckles from the other servants at the table. A bell rang. Breakfast was over. Time to get to work. Isabel rose and excused herself, with another wink at Roger.

"I believe the maid fancies you," said someone else, as the rest of the servants chuckled and laughed. Roger was at a loss for words; he went upstairs to the library, looking for his master.

He did not have to wait long. Lord Coke swept in, wearing a dressing gown, ready for a day's work. He waved Roger to a small desk, then rummaged around in his papers and pulled out a document. "Copy this. Do not use shorthand. I want to see a sample of your best penmanship."

Roger's penmanship had been well-regarded at grammar school; he undertook to use his best skills at copying what was evidently a short letter. He added a few curving flourishes, hoping Coke would be pleased with his efforts.

Coke grunted. "This will do. You should learn to write in a plain style, easily read. Fewer flourishes, next time. If we need flourishes, we'll call for a scrivener." Roger bowed his head.

Coke began speaking, gesturing with his hand that Roger should be taking notes. He paused from time to time, consulting some book or other, as he gathered and honed his thoughts. Coke was famous for writing books (among many other things), in particular, books about the law. Beginning in 1600, he had published a review of important cases in English law. His *Reports*, as they became known, eventually came to eleven volumes over fifteen years. Here, Coke had selected the most important precedents and decisions, presented them in full, and commented on their significance.   It was an immediate success with the legal profession, and by this time had acquired the status of an authority in its own right. Coke was still preparing more volumes.

Coke looked up from his reading and leaned forward, his dark eyes focused on Roger. "Attend to what I am about to explain. I do not like to repeat myself."

Roger nodded. "Yes, sir."

"There are four courts that you will encounter while working for me. Each of them claims to have final say in some matters of the law. All of them must serve the subjects of this realm by serving the Law of this land, England. The legitimacy of these courts depends on how well they serve the Law and the people who are under the Law. Do you understand?"

Roger nodded again.

"The first of these courts is the Court of Common Pleas. This is the final court of appeal for all matters relating to the Common Law, the most ancient and traditional law of this kingdom. I was once Chief Justice of that court."

"There is also the Court of Chancery, presided over by the Lord Chancellor of England."

"The third of these is the King's Bench, where felonies or other violations of the King's Peace may be tried, under the prosecution of the Attorney General. I am currently Chief Justice of the King's Bench. These first three courts meet in the same place — Westminster Hall, as you shall shortly see for yourself." Roger had some familiarity with these facts — his curiosity had carried him to Westminster on more than one occasion; he said nothing.

"The fourth, you have heard of. It is called Star Chamber. Members of the King's Privy Council preside there. Some say that Star Chamber is the ultimate court of appeal since it is closest to the King himself. But they mistake the importance of the Law if they think that the authority of the King could ever overrule it."

Roger interrupted, "But surely the King is supreme in his prerogative?"

"The King sits secure on his throne, because the Law protects him, just as it protects the lowest of his subjects. Without the Law, we would all live in anarchy or tyranny. The King cannot rule without the Law, nor can the people prosper without the rule of just laws, administered by a just ruler. The Law is more ancient than any king, and will remain when kings and kingdoms are only a memory."

"I doubt it would please King James to hear you speak thus."

Coke laughed. "I doubt the same. Our King is most jealous of his "supremest" vocation. But he is from Scotland, a place where lawlessness is all too common. England is a realm of laws, and English kings must submit to them."

Roger wondered what the King would say if he heard such talk. Better if he never did. Best they should never hear his answer.

Then it was back to work. There were letters to answer; Coke dictated, and Roger wrote in his "plainest" script. Occasionally, Coke needed to reference some book or other in his library, to clarify his thoughts; Roger was impressed that he almost always knew which volume he wanted, and where the citation could be found in the book — to the point that he could direct Roger to the location of the book on the shelves. Once, he told Roger where the book was, and had him open it himself, and read out the relevant passage — in Latin, of course, since it concerned a case from the reign of Edward V. Roger struggled to keep up. They were interrupted at midday by a servant who brought their dinner. A short break, and then back to work. They spent the afternoon on Lord Coke's personal matters — he was writing some books concerning the law. He directed Roger to retrieve various volumes from the shelves, rummaged through notes, collected his thoughts, and refined his arguments. Roger struggled through it. As the light from the high windows faded, Roger realized that the day must be fading, as well. They lit more candles. There was a knock at the door.

"Enter!" said Coke.

"Papa?" A young woman, not much older than Roger, stuck her head in the door.

Coke beamed, "Yes, dearest. What is it?"

She stepped into the room. Roger was looking at the loveliest young woman he had ever laid eyes on. Her image swam in his vision — he forced himself to look away, and it felt like something was tearing inside him. She was looking at her father, then turned her gaze to Roger. She smiled as if expecting him to do something. Something, anything that might please her . . . what? He collected his wits and his manners, stood, and bowed. That broke the spell. She curtseyed in return, with a knowing grin — it occurred to Roger that he was not the first young man to be dazzled by this beauty.

"This is my dearest daughter, Frances," said Coke, with more than a little pride. To Frances, he said, "This is my servant, Roger. He is assisting me today. No doubt you will be seeing him about the house."

"Mama wants to know if you will be eating with us this evening," said Frances.

"She knows I could never refuse you," replied Coke. "Is it time for supper so soon?"

"It's nearly 7:00. I trust you will change for supper?"

Coke looked at his dressing gown and nodded. To Roger, he said, "That will be enough for one day. See to your own supper, and report back here in the morning."

Roger felt as if his feet were nailed to the floor. Frances smiled at him again. He fixed the image of her in his mind — the poise, the sense of being in command (who would not yield to the commands of such a one?), yet no trace of arrogance, certainly no hint of cruelty. She gazed upon the world with gentle eyes, eyes that cut to the heart of a man. Eyes that accepted the world's awed admiration as merely her due, graciously — it is not false pride for a goddess to receive such adulation from her admirers — and goddess she surely was . . .

"Roger?" Coke interrupted his daze.

"Yes, Sir," Roger replied, bowed, and excused himself.

It turned out he was late for the evening meal in the servants' quarters: it was full dark outside, now. But when he explained where he had been all day, the cook took pity on him and produced a meal. He wasn't that hungry, long as the day had been: visions of Frances Coke filled his mind. She disturbed his sleep that night, as well. Memory of gentle eyes and a calm, curious expression glowed in his mind. If he had thought of something to please her, to make her laugh, surely it would have been as if the sun had risen on a summer morning, and all the flowers of the earth opened to bask in the radiance. He was suddenly and poignantly aware of his station in this house, in this world. He felt small, shabby, common in the presence of such radiance.

This feeling was unfamiliar to Roger Williams. He was well aware that his world was one of privilege and power for the very few, and comparative obscurity for the rest (like himself). However, the obscure majority might scuffle and wrangle for some advantage that might allow them to rise above the rest (to however trivial a degree), it would not really change anything. This had never bothered him. His betters might have their fine clothes, their great houses, their privilege and titles, but Roger had always felt that his cleverness and curiosity gave him advantages that set him apart somehow from the rest of the world. The fact was that when you got close enough to the privileged and powerful, they looked pretty much like everyone else — the clothes were just pretense, the fawning acolytes were only mummers in a play. They were likely to be as dull as anyone else. Frances Coke was evidence of a higher state of being, a state to which people like himself could aspire, but in vain. He realized that cleverness might never be enough to lift a man to that level, even in his own eyes, never mind hers. Any such aspirations seemed somehow shameful, like swine dreaming of becoming angels.

At breakfast the next morning, Isabel noted his rumpled, tired appearance. "Missed you at supper last night," she said as if expecting some excuse.

"Lord Coke kept me busy," Roger replied.

"What did he busy you with?"

"Writing."

"Writing?"

"And reading."

"Reading." Her brows furrowed in mock confusion. "Reading what?"

"Books."

Isabel gave him an exasperated look. "I hardly thought you were reading the stars. What books? What was in them? Why did you read them?"

Other servants were looking at Roger now with curiosity. "Law books. I read law books."

"To what purpose?"

"I cannot say," Roger replied (although he certainly had speculations of his own). "Lord Coke told me which books to fetch and what parts to read. We were at it all afternoon, until after supper."

Isabel cocked her head. "You make it sound as if Lord Coke is simply too weary or lazy to fetch and open his books for himself. Is that all you are to him, a fetcher of water, and a carrier of wood? Does he not value your advice?" She was baiting him, daring him to brag that his employer relied on him for *something* significant.

Roger declined to rise to the bait. "I have been led to believe that the job comes with pay and benefits, such as this excellent breakfast. As for advice, Lord Coke has not asked for any. I could, of course, offer advice if someone — you, for instance — asked for it."

"And what advice would you offer to *me*? Her tone was just a little sarcastic.

"Why, to finish your excellent breakfast, before the bell is rung!"

At this, the other servants at the table laughed. Isabel colored a little but shook her head and joined the laughter.

Roger felt that he had established himself as a man who would not stoop to bragging or gossiping just to impress his fellow servants but could be trusted to protect the confidentiality of his master's business, or anyone else's, for that matter. No doubt he would be tested again. He intended to be found worthy.

It was two days later that he saw Frances Coke again. She was with her mother, Lady Hatton, and a small crowd of servants, including Isabel. There was another young woman with them — possibly Frances' sister. They were dressed for an outing of some sort. Lady Hatton, Frances, and her sister were dressed in long silken gowns with broad skirts that reached nearly to the ground. Roger knew from his familiarity with tailoring that underneath the skirts was a farthingale — a supporting framework of hoops that kept the skirts filled to the point that getting through a narrow doorway was impossible. Their torsos were encased in "stays", tight-fitting undergarments stiffened with whalebone, to give them the desired shape. Around their necks, they wore stiff, lacy collars, or ruffs, which stood out from their necks like some elaborate dog collars. When they walked, they appeared to glide, since their feet were covered by the hems of their skirts. The overall effect was that of chessmen with unusually wide bases. (Appropriate, as it turned out, because they were bound for the Queen's palace, where a certain kind of chess match would be played — or so Lady Hatton intended.)

Isabel was dressed up, too, but without the farthingales or the ruffs. She caught Roger's eye and winked at him as he bowed to the ladies. The rest of the party were dressed for court as well, according to their status. One manservant's job appeared to consist of carrying Lady Hatton's lapdog — for this, he was allowed to wear his own collar (or more properly a ruff).

Isabel whispered something to Lady Hatton and pointed at Roger. Lady Hatton looked at him and spoke: "Boy! You There! What is your name?"

Roger bowed again. "I am called Roger. Roger Williams, at your service, my Lady."

"They tell me you work with Lord Coke, nearly every day. Is that true?"

"Aye, Lady."

"Then tell him we are off to Greenwich, to see the Queen. We shall not return until evening."

Roger bowed again. "Yes, my Lady."

With that, she turned and glided out the door, followed by her retinue. There was a carriage outside, with footmen and armed retainers. Isabel smiled and winked at Roger as she followed her Lady outside. Then Frances caught his eye as well, and smiled pleasantly, devastatingly — Roger's heart jumped for joy and ached in the same moment.

Lord Coke was late arriving at the Library that day. He seemed distracted by something. He fussed a bit over some papers at his desk for a few minutes. "I will explain a case to you," Coke said after a while. "This case will serve as an example of how great crimes are uncovered, how prosecuted, and how punished. It is not as simple as you imagine. You may take notes if you wish." Roger nodded.

"A certain man named Sir Thomas Overbury died a few years back. He had been committed to the Tower of London, based on his refusal to accept a promotion that the King offered to him, possibly at the behest of his friend, the Earl of Somerset. This in itself is not remarkable. Prisoners in the Tower have died before and will do so again. Last August, an apothecary's servant made a deathbed confession that he had delivered poisons to the Tower and that Overbury had been murdered thereby."

Roger nodded and blurted out, "Indeed, it is a famous scandal. I have heard of this. The conspirators have been convicted and hanged for their crime."

"You do not grasp the nub of this case; no one does," Coke corrected him. "Consider what I am about to say. The King has instructed me to pursue this case without regard to privilege or title. He called down curses on me if I fail to ferret them out, and God's curse on himself and his family, if he pardons any involved in this crime."

"How far does the investigation lead?"

"There's the rub. It may lead as far as the King's bedchamber."

"But why would the King want to murder Thomas Overbury?"

"You have put your finger on the key question in this prosecution. Who had motive to kill the man? Not the apothecary who provided the poisons, not his servants who delivered it, not his jailer who poisoned his food, not the Governor of the Tower, who was responsible for his safety. These were merely the pawns in a much larger game. Who benefited from Overbury's death?"

"Surely not the King! How does this matter touch him?"

"It was the King who committed Overbury to the Tower, where he was held for the convenience of his murderers."

"And why did the King send him to the Tower?"

"For refusing a preferment urged upon the King by the Earl of Somerset, the King's favorite, and Overbury's close friend. It is supposed that the Earl wanted Overbury sent abroad or imprisoned for some dispute among them."

"He had a falling out with a close friend and had him killed?"

Coke shook his head. "That seems far-fetched. To find motive, we must look deeper. There is another player in this drama. The Earl's wife, Lady Frances Howard, Countess of Essex, has been named as the coordinator of the conspiracy — paying for the poison, persuading the jailer to administer it, and the Governor of the Tower to look the other way."

"But why would she wish Overbury dead?"

Coke sighed. "Why, indeed? Did she consider Overbury a competitor for her husband's affections? (If that were true, the King himself might have motive.) Or did she have reason to fear him? We may never know. The examination methods that were used on the other conspirators cannot be used on her, due to her sex and social rank. She is a member of the Howard family, and her relatives stand high in the government of the kingdom."

"How, then, is she in the Tower, now, if such a powerful family is behind her?"

Coke sighed again. "That is a question that troubles me. Or rather, why is the King so bent on prosecuting her so relentlessly? Does he wish to remind the Howards that he is sovereign? Does he think to cleanse himself of all suspicion by championing justice with vigor? Or does he secretly hope that the Countess and the Earl will be acquitted?"

"Surely the King's secret hopes are outside the scope of the prosecution?"

"If you believe that, you know nothing of prosecutions, especially prosecutions in which the King has taken a personal interest. All depends on whether the King is pleased with the result. Conviction or acquittal, the most important result is whether the King is satisfied that justice has been done. Failing that, my position on the Privy Council is forfeit."

"So you are at risk, then?"

"I have been at risk before. There are no great victories without risk. Besides, there is a bright spot. The King has made Francis Bacon my co-prosecutor in this matter. If I fail, I will drag him down with me." Coke chuckled. "What say you, Master Williams? Do we soften the prosecution to shield the King as we suppose he wishes, or do we do as he says?"

"Are you asking for my opinion?"

"Why not? What harm could it do?" Coke seemed more relaxed, now, almost jovial. Perhaps unburdening himself improved his mood.

Roger thought for a moment. "It seems to me that separating the crime from the King is a prudent approach . . . "

Coke nodded. "Go on."

"But people are unlikely to accept the verdict if the Countess, the 'coordinator' as you call her, is not called to account."

"True." Coke nodded again. He appeared to be at ease, now, leaning back in his chair, his hands folded in front of him.

"So, the Countess should be the focus of the attack. Perhaps she resented Overbury for some reason. Perhaps she feared that Overbury would somehow alienate the King's affection for her husband?"

Coke nodded. "Perhaps."

"If the rumors I have heard are true, the Countess needed an annulment of her first marriage to marry the Earl. Did that happen while Overbury was alive?"

"No, in fact, it was granted some months after Overbury's death. What is your point?"

"Did Overbury know something that would have prevented the annulment?

Coke leaned forward. "He certainly did. He knew that the Countess and the Earl had been conducting an adulterous affair for years prior. Overbury published a poem titled "A Wife," which praises the virtues of marital fidelity. The Countess is said to have taken it as a personal insult. I acknowledge your point about making the Countess the focus. But that leaves her husband, the Earl. Would you argue that he duped the King into assisting him in his murderous plan? That argument reflects poorly on the King's judgment."

"Then, argue that the Earl was duped. Duped by a ruthless woman who lured him into adultery, and then made him an unwitting accomplice in the murder of his friend."

"You have the mind of a lawyer," grunted Coke. "Pray that it doesn't get you into trouble." He was smiling, but Roger took the hint and said no more.

"There are facts aplenty that could be used to support such a prosecution. But it is not that simple. I have been advised by Bacon (and thereby also the King) not to dwell too much upon the tawdriest matters, but rather to temper my accusations, only to what will see justice accomplished. Some matters best left concealed, or so they say."

"What sort of matters?"

"To name but a few," replied Coke, "the fact that the Countess obtained her annulment from her first husband under false pretenses. She contrived with a certain 'astrologer'(I might as well say 'witch') to make the man impotent, through the fashioning of a little wax figure of a man, into which she thrust thorns from a barren tree. His supposed impotence was the grounds for her annulment; the King and Queen attended her wedding to the Earl. She turned to a famous physician for aphrodisiacs and other potions: a man whose services were employed by nearly every woman affiliated with the palace (and who kept records of their numerous dalliances and adulteries). This cries out for exposure: Who else might have been poisoned? To what extent are papists involved?"

"Papists?"

"There are known to be many recusants among the Howard family. Some are believed to be in the pay of the King of Spain. Perhaps Overbury knew things that they wished to remain secret."

"But that would be treason!"

"Aye, you're a clever lad. We're at peace with Spain, now, but that is not to say that Spain is our friend, or that it seeks our welfare. This case has tentacles that reach everywhere."

Coke was silent for a moment. Roger spoke, "So the King might want to send a warning to the King of Spain, by way of the Howards, through a conviction of the Earl."

Coke nodded. "He might. But the King has not said so, and I dare not ask the question."

"I am surprised that the Howards have not contrived a more vigorous defense of one of their own. This trial cannot be to their advantage, whatever the verdict."

"The Howards have been at this game for a very long time. You may recall that two of Henry VIII's wives were Howards."

"Two? I know of Katherine Howard, but who was the other?"

"Anne Boleyn was cousin to Katherine Howard. Both married to the King, both beheaded for reckless conduct. It appears to be a family trait. Katherine Howard took full responsibility for her behavior, thus sparing the others of her family, who were held in the Tower on the day of her execution. A noble sacrifice. Whatever their carelessness, the Howard women know how to die."

"Do you think that the Countess will do the same?"

"We shall soon see," Coke said,

"But if she is to be sacrificed, for whose benefit? Her family? The King? The whole court? The King of Spain?"

"That," said Coke soberly, "is the kind of question that can get you into trouble." He turned his gaze to the papers on his desk. "We have work to do."

It was not long before a servant brought their dinner. Then it was back to the notes on Lord Coke's book. He seemed to enjoy this work more than the other things they did. He relished pointing out little details that made one precedent or case particularly important, or one error that proved fatal to another case . . .

The doors to the library swung open suddenly to make way for Lady Hatton. She appeared to be in a hurry; there was an emphatic bounce to her farthingale as she glided into the room, followed by her maid, Isabel. Roger rose to bow. Sir Edward rose more slowly and said, "Welcome home, dear wife. How fare you?" He signaled to Roger to cease taking notes.

"I am just returned from Greenwich," she announced, "where I have attended the Queen. I have heard some distressing news."

"Is Her Majesty ill again?" Coke's attention was keen, focused. If the Queen's health were in jeopardy, this could have implications. . .

"Queen Anne is plagued by gout and mourns for her son, Prince Henry, as always. The news I have is not about her."

"What then? Some gossip from the ladies?"

"It is not mere gossip. I learned that Lady Compton has decided that our daughter Frances should be wed to her eldest son, Sir John Villiers, and is negotiating the dowry, even as we speak!" Her voice rose with indignation. "And I knew nothing of this!"

Coke looked at her, said nothing.

"It is humiliating to be kept in the dark on a matter so close to my heart. How much more to think that my youngest daughter could be sold to such a feeble-minded pretender as John Villiers!"

"Feeble-minded?" Coke spoke. "Did his mother call him so?"

"Of course not. She thinks that the sun rises and sets for him. But everyone says he is nothing like his younger brother, George, the Viscount. Not only feeble-minded but old — far too old for our Frances."

Coke gestured dismissively with his hand."I have met the man. He is twenty-five years old and seemed healthy enough to me. As for feeble-minded, he speaks well enough to keep up a pleasant conversation. He is not so 'blessed' by the King's attentions as his younger brother, but that could make him a better husband — he will spend his nights at home rather than in the palace. I hear that he has expressed great admiration for Frances, to the point that he would marry her without a dowry — 'in her smock', I believe was the expression."

"Lady Compton would never stand for that! She sees Frances as nothing but a source of revenue for her greedy purse!"

Coke nodded. "I believe you are right. She has demanded £10,000, plus an additional £1,000 each year, for the rest of my life. It is not enough for her to plunder my treasury; she would have me live out my days as if I were her tenant, indebted to her and her family."

"I forbid this 'match'. I will have no part in it. I will fight to protect my child from the avarice of the Villiers family."

"Take care, Madam, of how you speak of that family. George Villiers is a man dear to the heart of the King, dearer than any other; dearer than the Queen, so they say. He promotes him to greater and greater power at every opportunity. It will not do to insult them."

"I am well aware of how the King adores his 'Steenie', and how he neglects his wife. It does the King no credit, and fosters gossip that does me no credit to repeat . . . they say that things are done in the Royal bed chamber that cannot be spoken of . . ."

"Then do not speak of such things, prithee. No good can come of it." Coke raised both his hands as if to fend off her words.

"We cannot let our daughter marry into such a family, to be immersed in such a sea of avarice and immorality!" Her voice was now shrill.

"My dear wife," began Coke with a faintly ironic tone, "The both of us have labored long together to ascend the pinnacles of power in this kingdom — you in befriending the Queen, I as I have sought to win the King's favor. Now that we have succeeded, it is vanity for us to complain about the company we must keep."

Lady Hatton made a face. "I hold to my point."

"The point is a moot one. I have indeed received communication from Lady Compton on behalf of her son. I have refused her offer. I do not expect that we will come to terms."

"When did you refuse her?"

"I sent a letter some few days ago."

"But today, at Greenwich, she spoke as if the wedding was imminent."

"I sent the letter to her estate in Leicestershire; she probably has not seen it yet."

"Why Leicestershire? She lives in London most of the year, these days."

"Her letter came to me from Leicestershire. It seemed best to follow her example."

"Why did you not tell me about this? Had I known that you had refused her offer, I could have told her myself, this very day!"

Coke chuckled. "Aye, that would have made a scene to gossip about for a week, at least. But a public confrontation would have given greater offense — and I do not wish to offend the Villiers family."

"But Lady Compton has already set the stage for her embarrassment in speaking of the matter so publicly."

Coke nodded. "That was her decision. I have tried to be discreet in this matter. I am not at fault."

"You mean that you hope the King's favorite will overlook the matter." Her tone was accusatory.

Coke nodded again. "I have often found that men are more reasonable in disagreements of this kind."

"Still, you could have told me that you refused the match when I first mentioned it. Why force me to pour out my heart in this way?"

Coke smiled. "I enjoy the heat of your words, the passion in your speech. I love the way your cheeks are flushed when you are angry — it touches my heart."

Lady Hatton's cheeks flushed even more, but she was out of words. She turned and glided out of the room, followed by Isabel, who shot Roger a wink as she followed her mistress.

London, 1616: The Arena

The next weeks and months were the most exciting of Roger Williams' young life. He was caught up in a dizzy whirlwind of meetings, sessions, trials, and conversations. Most days he spent in the company of Lord Coke. Some days, there was business at St. Paul's Cathedral, where the powerful and influential often met (outside on the great steps, when the weather was fair, under the eaves when it was not), to conduct their business. Sometimes it was in the great hall at Westminster, where Lord Coke presided as Chief Justice of the King's Bench. Less frequently, there was need for Lord Coke to attend King James in his palace at Hampton Court. In all these places, it was as Lord Coke had said — Roger was treated as if he were invisible.

Sundays were work days for members of the King's Bench, though there was usually time for Lord Coke (and sometimes Lady Hatton) to attend church services in the morning — along with their servants, of course. Often they attended St. Sepulcher's, though St. Bart's and even St. Paul's were also options. "You may sit with your family when we are at St. Sepulcher's," Coke offered to Roger.

"I think my place is with you, Sir," Roger replied. (In truth, he would not have been comfortable sitting with his father, nor would his father have been; the pew that Lord Coke occupied was nearer the front of the sanctuary, in any case.) Sometimes Roger imagined that he could feel his father's eyes on the back of his head, but he put that thought aside. He was usually able to greet his mother with a smile or a brief hug after the service, before following his master out and on to the business of the day.

Travel to these places was usually made in the comfort of Lord Coke's carriage. Roger noticed immediately that the view of the city was different from inside a carriage. On foot, the city streets were a gritty or slimy (or both) network of cobblestones and mud, strewn with the inevitable chunks of animal manure. Add to this the crowded bustle of the main streets, or the dank gloom of alleys and side streets, and a pedestrian had to be alert at all times. In a carriage, though the ride was bumpy, Roger was separated from all that — literally and emotionally above it all. Even at a modest pace, there was a sense of voyeurism, of watching the world slide by from inside a kind of cocoon. The men and women who rode were not living in the same city as those who walked.

On days when Lord Coke was to preside in court at Westminster, he might take a barge from the landing where the River Fleet flowed into the Thames. This involved a procession — Lord Coke in his scarlet robes, accompanied by at least four men-at-arms (they carried rapiers at their sides, and who-knew-what-else concealed in their garments), marching down to the landing, with Roger (clad in black) bringing up the rear. The trip upriver to Westminster was propelled by rows of oarsmen, who strove against the current with no small effort if the tide happened to be on the way out. From the barge, the sense of living in a different city was even stronger. There was a fascinating view up and down the river, unobstructed by buildings — downstream to London Bridge, with a glimpse of the Tower of London beyond; the spires of St. Paul's Cathedral to the north, and dozens of other church spires within and without the city walls, visible in every direction. As they made their way upstream, first west, and then following the curve of the river southward, other sights came into view: Lambeth Palace, where the Archbishop of Canterbury lived, then the mass of Westminster Hall and its tributary buildings. All of them looked clean and lovely from a distance; none of the grime and decay of the ages could be seen. The same was true of the rest of the city when viewed from the river. It reminded him of a painting by some Dutchman that hung from the wall in Sir Edward's library.

The Great Hall at Westminster was the largest building of its kind in all of England. It was more than 500 years old now. Once the residence of Kings, it had been turned into the nation's largest courtroom. So large was the chamber that three courts could meet within it at the same time, and often did. If that was not enough busyness for the old building, there was a constant stream of foot traffic in, across, and out of it — both houses of Parliament met in adjacent chambers with connecting passages and doorways, and the Court of Star Chamber (the King's Bench) was located across a courtyard immediately to the south. On a busy day, the place was crowded by magistrates, plaintiffs, lawyers, clerks, and the simply curious. For a lawyer like Lord Coke, this was the center of his universe. Here he had first risen to fame and fortune; this was the arena where he had won great victories and suffered stinging defeats. Here he was either adored or reviled, never regarded with indifference. Men sought his opinions, whether to learn from his wisdom or to find some pretext to pull him down. Roger Williams heard all this, noted it, digested it. As time passed, he began to understand it.

The world that Roger had entered was like a great arena, where the rich and powerful battled each other daily. There were more than two or three combatants in this contest, and the alliances between them were subject to change. First among these was the King himself. Ordinarily, the lesser competitors would all be competing for the King's favor, and all of them were doing so. But in England, there was another dimension to James Stuart's rule — he was regarded by many as a foreigner. His tastes and ideologies were distinctly different from his predecessors, his personal habits . . . peculiar. Prominent among his peculiarities was his cultivation of "favorites" — young, attractive men upon whom he showered titles and privileges. These men were regarded with resentment or jealousy (or both) among the most prominent aristocratic families since they often came from the lower ranks of the nobility, but many opted to play the game by grooming their sons to appeal to the King. It was not a vocation for the faint of heart — men who got close to the King were covered with caresses and kisses in public places ("lasciviously", according to some observers); more than a few young men gave up courting the King's favor, because they could not endure his "slabbering".

Easier to curry favor with the King's favorite than with the King himself, perhaps. The most successful of the King's favorites was George Villiers. James called him "Steenie," a shortened form of "Stephen," after St. Stephen, who, according to scripture, had the face of an angel. Everyone agreed that he was indeed a very good-looking man; his beard was the envy of the court — naturally curly (his rivals had to use curling irons to achieve the desired effect). He was also a very good dancer (something he had picked up during his time in the French royal court), which endeared him to all the ladies — and allowed him to shine at all the fetes, balls, and masques that the royal court hosted. He brought glamour and style to the court — something that counted for a lot with the aging King. James showered Villiers with favors — money, titles, gestures of affection. Just this year, he had been awarded the titles of Viscount Villiers, Baron Whaddon, and Royal Horsemaster — each of which came with an annual income. Most importantly, the King relied on Villiers for advice — advice on foreign policy, religious policy, domestic affairs, including royal appointments. It was generally understood that all promotions and appointments had to go through Viscount Villiers. He was able to obtain titles and offices for his relatives and friends — for the right price (the selling of titles and monopolies was a major source of revenue for the King, and the Viscount naturally was entitled to his share).

Then there was Queen Anne, a princess of Denmark, and mother to one (surviving) royal prince and a princess. Her influence on the King was less these days than it had once been. Her eldest son, Henry, had died suddenly at age eighteen, and she never completely recovered from the loss of her firstborn. Her health was in decline now, as well. But she still held court, attended by many of the wives of England's most powerful men. There was more than one pathway to the ears of the King.

There were other players in the game, as well. Men like Robert Rich, Earl of Warwick. Lord Rich was a Puritan and a high-ranking member of the nobility; his family had served the crown in key positions since the reign of Henry VIII. Lord Rich was a merchant adventurer, founder of plantations in the New World, and trader across the seas of the world. He and other men of his class were determined to maintain their families' historic position and privilege in England. He and his allies were also determined to complete the reformation of the Church of England, or, barring that, to obtain toleration within the Church for their Calvinist (Puritan) beliefs and practices. For them, the King's claim to absolute rule was pretentious, not to mention un-English. Their ancestors had taught hard lessons to ancient English Kings about the limits of royal power, and they waited for the right time to repeat those lessons.

The scourge (sometimes literally) of the Puritan faction was the Court of High Commission, directed by the Archbishop of Canterbury. The High Commission was tasked with maintaining orthodoxy and discipline within the Church of England. This included the power to seek out, arrest, torture, and even execute persons found to be practicing their religion in non-conforming ways. Roman Catholics were persecuted most vigorously since they were presumed to be loyal to the Pope, and therefore treasonous. (Attempts to assassinate the King and Parliament, like the "gunpowder plot", were sufficient to put them all under suspicion). The High Commission was also very keen on pursuing the various sorts of non-conforming Protestants — Anabaptists, Baptists, separatists of all sorts — all of them heretics in the eyes of the Church, all of them potentially treasonous in the eyes of the King. Strongest of all these worrisome elements were the so-called Puritans, who had resisted the High Commission for decades and tried to abolish it through Parliamentary action more than once. Many, sometimes most, of the members of the House of Commons had Puritan sympathies. The High

Commission was able to threaten certain members with fines or imprisonment, though its harshest treatment was reserved for men of lower social rank — execution of even the lesser nobility was a rare event, unless convicted of outright felonies.

Other bases of power were chary of the King's prerogative. Prominent among them was Lord Edward Coke, Roger's employer. Coke was no Puritan; he was uninterested in theological debates. He shared the King's fear of all things Catholic and supported the High Commission's determination to hunt them down. Coke had personally prosecuted the members of the Gunpowder Plot and secured death sentences for all of them, even the nobles. He did, however, object to what he saw as the High Commission's overreach in pursuing Protestants of all varieties. Coke was the leading figure for a significant number of like-minded men who were more concerned about rights than religion. With so many contestants in the arena, it was only natural that they would form alliances and factions, and that they would shift their allegiances as circumstance and opportunity presented themselves. . . . .

The King, for his part, presided over all this with an air of parental indulgence. He was not particularly alarmed by the maneuvering and wrangling. On the contrary, it pleased him to rule over a certain amount of "hurly-burly" because it fell to him to impose order upon it. Pitting one group against another brought out the strongest arguments on both sides, and he would ultimately declare the winners. Advisors came and went, factions rose and fell, but he — the King — would have the final say. Every expression of this royal prerogative buttressed his confidence in himself, his wisdom, and his rightful power. More troubling was the attitude that some matters in his kingdom were not properly under his control: the idea, for instance, that some laws, traditions, or institutions were outside his purview. The English held stubbornly to some peculiarities about these things; he was determined to reshape the kingdom into a more favorable image. In this, he had help; he surrounded himself with advisors who seized every opportunity to enhance the royal power and reduce that of any competing interests. Chief among these at present was Lord Coke's nemesis, Sir Francis Bacon.

Francis Bacon was the son of Nicholas Bacon, Lord Keeper of the Great Seal during the reign of Elizabeth, a member of the Privy Council. His son Francis was ambitious to rise at least as high as his famous father. The pathway to that success was obvious enough to him — help the King in his quest for absolute power, whenever and however he could. The strategy appeared to be working: Francis Bacon persuaded the King to remove Edward Coke from his position as Chief Justice of Common Pleas by "promoting" him to Chief Justice of the King's Bench, and, coincidentally, appointed Bacon to the position of Attorney General. Coke was humiliated by this "promotion", but could do nothing to defy the King. It may have been a measure of revenge for Bacon, or maybe Coke was merely an obstacle that had to be overcome on Bacon's path to power. Coke took it personally; he would answer in due time.

May 24, 1616: Trials

The day for which the city had long waited had arrived. Lady Frances Howard, Countess of Essex by her first marriage and Countess of Somerset by her second, was to have her day in court. The trial was to be held in public, in the Great Hall at Westminster. The King himself would attend. Crowds of spectators surged into the Hall. Those wealthy enough had purchased seats well in advance; the rest had to stand, to strain their ears and eyes, jostle for a better view. The King, naturally, was seated on a temporary throne, surrounded by his attendants along with his Attorney General, Sir Francis Bacon. On the main floor sat the lead prosecutor, Lord Edward Coke, facing the dock where the accused would stand during the trial. Behind him, nearly invisible, sat Roger Williams, clad in black, with his ink, quill, and paper. Roger realized he had the best view in the hall of what was about to transpire. Further back, on a raised dais, sat the magistrates who would decide the case.

The accused was ferried up the river from the Tower under guard. She was brought into the hall and led to the dock. She was dressed in black and held a fan in her right hand, which she used to cover her face (though it was not hot that day). The court was called to order, and those who had a seat sat down. A few preliminary remarks, and Lord Coke was given leave to speak.

From where Roger sat, he saw the 64-year-old frame stiffen as if called to attention. There was a gleam in his Master's eyes that spoke of a bird of prey, seeing everything, seeking out that telltale move that would call him to attack. Coke began reading the charges, in lurid detail, his voice rising to fill the hall. When he finished, he was a little out of breath. The Countess seemed to wilt under his words.

It was the defendant's turn to enter a plea. "Guilty," she replied. "Guilty on all counts." The crowd murmured with surprise, or maybe disbelief.

Coke's shoulders slumped a little. "I should have seen this coming," he muttered to Roger, "she has been advised to sacrifice herself, and she has done so."

"But surely the evidence against her is overwhelming?"

Coke nodded, "It is. There is no doubt about her guilt. But strange that a woman so shameless in her life should now become the meek, trembling creature you see before you."

There was nothing now but to await the verdict and the sentence. It did not take long. The Countess was guilty; she would hang. A gasp of surprise swept through the crowd. Hang? A countess? Surely a countess would be given a more honorable death — beheading was the privilege of aristocratic criminals. Would the King grant her a more honorable end?

The King said nothing. He rose from his seat and left the hall, surrounded by his entourage. The Countess lowered her head and appeared to be weeping.

Several men stepped forward to congratulate Coke on his great victory. "Count it a victory for justice," he replied. Sir Francis Bacon approached. "It is well done, well done. The King sends his regards." Then he was gone.

Others wished to greet Lord Coke as he pressed his way through the crowd; it took them a good while to get back to the landing on the riverbank. The royal barge had just loaded and was pulling away, loaded with the King and his attendants. Roger saw Francis Bacon standing next to the King, speaking. As the oarsmen pulled away, Bacon saw Coke and pointed in their direction. The King waved, and everyone ashore bowed. There was another barge at the shore, this one for the condemned Countess, on her way back to the Tower of London. "We'll wait for them to leave," said Coke, "It can get crowded on the river." So they stood, while Countess and her guard were loaded and departed. Still, Coke was not yet ready. "Is something wrong, Lord?" asked Roger.

"I feel the need for solid ground beneath my feet today," Coke replied. Turning to one of his retainers, he said, "There is a stable not far from here, is there not? I mean, one where I may rent a horse?"

"Aye, sir."

"Go, then. I will need six horses for the rest of the morning." To Roger, he said," How is your horsemanship?"

"I can't say, sir. I've never sat on the back of a horse."

"Never? It's about time you learned!" The other retainers chuckled.

It turned out that Lord Coke was an expert horseman. His retainers were all comfortable in the saddle as well. For Roger, it was bumpy and awkward. "Don't sit there like a sack of barley, use your knees, like this," he was advised. "You have to move with the horse." Roger did the best he could. It was a revelation to travel so far above ground level — a different view of the world. No wonder that Lords and Ladies rode, while the lesser sorts walked — riding gave a man a sense of power, of privilege . . .

They headed out of the village of Westminster, into the open country that lay between them and London. It was only a few miles, but Roger had rarely been outside London and never viewed it from such a perch. It was late May, nearly summer, and the fields were lush and verdant. The horses settled into an easy walk. Roger rode next to Sir Edward, two retainers in front, two behind. "I went hawking hereabouts when I first came to London as a young man." Coke recalled, "Those were some times! It was less crowded then, here and in the city. Room to ride and hunt and breathe. All the houses you see near the road — " he gestured with a sweep of his arm" — have sprung up since those days. No more hawking — too many people."

Roger tried to imagine Edward Coke as a young man, carefree in a city full of possibilities. "Did you come here often? When did you stop?"

"No, not often. I discovered early on that success in the law requires rigorous study. Some of my colleagues failed to learn that lesson and did not apply themselves. Now they envy my success and wonder why I have been so 'lucky' in my career. I do not deny that I am a fortunate man, but 'luck' has little to do with success."

By now, the houses along the way were becoming more numerous. Larger houses were set back from the road, with manicured grounds in front of them. There were also farm cottages here and there, but the larger places spoke of money — money earned by men of commerce, who did their business in the city. Soon enough, they approached the edge of London proper — or at least the edge of the sprawl that crept slowly westward, outside the city walls around Newgate. This was familiar territory to Roger, though he was not accustomed to seeing it from this perspective. It was messy and chaotic, in stark contrast to the countryside they had just passed through, yet lively, vigorous, garrulous, and grubbily cheerful. Home.

They arrived at Hatton House near noon. Coke ordered a stable hand to take one of his own horses and to lead the rented ones back to Westminster, then ordered dinnerr to be brought to the library.

"We have work to do," said Coke. "I must prosecute the Earl of Somerset in the morning. I was not expecting things to go as they did with the Countess. I must reconsider my approach."

He was silent then for several moments. He looked up and spoke: "The Countess, however scandalous her character, is not one to surrender without a fight. What we saw today was a sham."

"Do you mean she was performing the role of a penitent, like an actor upon a stage?"

Coke nodded. "Exactly. And a fine, great stage it was, with none other than the King himself in the audience. I was merely a player, performing my part. The question is, what is the legend of this play? Who is the playwright?"

"Could it be the King himself?"

"If not the King, then Francis Bacon and the Howards, of that I am certain."

"But, how did they persuade the Countess to act her part, if it means that she must end at the gallows?"

"She has been given expectation of clemency, no doubt."

"But the King said . . ."

"Aye. The King said 'no pardon'. The word of the King must stand." There was more than a trace of bitterness in his tone. "The Great Ones are not bound by words or promises. For them, the Law is a tool, a means to accomplish their purposes and ensure that 'law-abiding folk' will not oppose them. They consider themselves above the law, free to use it as it suits them."

"Do you suppose that the Earl of Somerset has been given expectation of clemency, as well?"

"I am certain of it. Tomorrow will be another sham, for the satisfaction of the people, just like today."

There was a knock at the door. "Enter!" barked Coke.

A servant opened the door. "Sir Francis Bacon, Lord Attorney General, is here."

"Show him in," said Coke.

Coke and Roger rose and bowed as Bacon stepped into the room. "Please be seated," said Coke.

Bacon smiled and seated himself — a gracious, charming man; pleasant, unassuming. "I am here on behalf of the King," said Bacon, "and the opinions I shall express are His Majesty's, not necessarily my own."

Coke nodded, said nothing.

"First, His Majesty is pleased with your prosecution at the trial this morning. It was straightforward and plain, without unnecessary details that would titillate or confuse the case. The people understand that justice has been served. You have done honorable service to the kingdom."

Coke's eyes narrowed slightly at the words 'honorable service', but he said nothing, waited for the next shoe to fall.

Bacon continued, "His Majesty hopes that tomorrow's trial may be conducted with the same efficiency and decorum, without unnecessary digressions and speculation. That the defendant's reputation not be tarnished more than it already has been by his odious crimes, that he not be pressed to the breaking point (as you are famously wont to do, my Lord, truth be told), nor baited and harried. Such a performance would not serve the interests of the King's justice." Bacon paused, inviting an answer.

"Does the King have an opinion on whether Earl Somerset might be acquitted? Would such an outcome suit him?"

"The King does not intend to influence the trial in any way whatsoever. But he and I both agree that acquittal is unlikely." Bacon's face displayed benign disinterest, but Roger detected unease beneath that placid exterior.

"Please tell the King that I am grateful to hear he is pleased with my service. I shall do my best to prove myself worthy on tomorrow." Coke smiled at Bacon. Bacon acknowledged with a nod and smile of his own.

Bacon rose to his feet. "It will be a relief to all of us to put this scandal behind us, at last. It has gone on entirely too long. Reputations have been damaged; none of us has been untouched by it (here he nodded knowingly at Coke), and all because of an adulterous affair that ran to murder."

Coke rose to his feet, as well (Roger remembered himself belatedly, and stood also). More bows, and the Lord Attorney General excused himself.

Coke sat back down. Roger could tell that he was unhappy.

"So, young Roger, what did you learn from our visitor?"

"I imagine that the Earl has been urged to plead guilty, in return for a promise of clemency, but that he refuses to do so."

"You may be certain of that which you imagine. What else?"

"He will plead not guilty tomorrow, and you must examine him while he stands in the dock. The King expects him to be convicted. He also desires that you treat the defendant more gently than you might treat a man of lesser rank if that were possible, but not so gently as to allow the possibility of an acquittal."

Coke snorted. "Aye, that is what the man said. But what did he *mean* ?"

Roger shook his head. "I cannot be sure of what he meant if it was not what he said."

"The man said one thing only that was completely true — that the King would be relieved to put the scandal behind him. Everything else was to serve some covert purpose." Coke's tone grew heated, "The King expects that the Earl will be convicted; no doubt Lord Bacon has already paid a visit to the magistrates, to ensure that outcome. He as much as admitted that just now, when he encouraged me to be gentle in my prosecution tomorrow: he already knows the verdict is a forgone conclusion, he simply wants to avoid airing the lurid details of the case, because it would embarrass the Howards to have their private peccadillos made public, and it might remind people just how intimately the Earl was involved in the King's personal affairs, before he fell from favor. Bacon was here to remind me that I am merely a player on the King's stage, and to ensure that I speak the lines assigned to me and no others."

"But he also said that the King has no intention of influencing the trial. Why not take him at his word?"

"As I said, there was only one thing he said that was true. That was not it. The King considers that the Law exists to serve him and his authority. He does not hesitate to meddle in the courts if it serves the cause of justice—his justice, justice for him and his friends."

"If the King is certain of the outcome, why send Bacon to speak with you?"

"Lord Bacon is a lawyer. Thorough. Checks every list twice."

"Does this change what you will do tomorrow?"

Coke sighed and thought a moment. Then, "No, no, it must not deflect me from my duty."

"How would it deflect you from your duty to the King?"

"Not my duty to the King. My duty to the Law! The law must be impartial and must treat every man the same, else justice is corrupted. My duty is to treat the Earl as I would any other man in the dock."

"And if your duty makes enemies of the King and the rest of his government, will it be worth the danger? For a verdict that is already decided?"

"Justice is a harsh mistress. Those who would woo her must have stout hearts."

The following day began much as the previous one had. The trial was held in the Great Hall at Westminster, attended by the same officials, minus the King (who remained in his palace at Greenwich), and a crowd as large as the day before. It would not end in the same way. The Earl of Somerset stood defiantly in the dock and proclaimed his innocence. Sir Edward Coke began his examination slowly, methodically, building in intensity with accusation after accusation, like a pack of wolves pursuing their prey. The essence of the argument was that the Countess, now unequivocally guilty, could not have contrived the murder by herself — too many others had been drawn into the plot, a network of criminals so broad and diverse that only a mastermind would have known how to select them, direct them, lead them to success. And who stood most to benefit from Overbury's death? No one more than the Earl himself, who stood to be exposed as an adulterer. Who could be the mastermind of such a project? The very image of the Earl, standing in the dock, dressed in black velvet, resolute, implacable, unrepentant. (A clever move, thought Roger, to use the Earl's very appearance against him.) Lord Coke was in his element here, displaying the excellence that had burnished his reputation.

Many in the crowd appreciated the risk that Coke was taking in assailing such a powerful figure in such a reckless manner; people sensed that Coke was attacking not just one man, but all the privileged and corrupt courtiers that inhabited his world. The courtiers and the powerful understood it also and resented it.

When Coke had finished, Roger could see that he was spent; the fatigue showed in his sagging posture. The magistrates took their time in reaching a verdict. It was past sundown before they reported their conclusion: Earl Somerset was guilty and sentenced to hang.

By this time, people were hungry; the crowd dissipated rapidly. A few lingered to congratulate Coke on his success, but Coke's party had little difficulty getting back to the barge they had arrived on. Francis Bacon, in his scarlet robe, passed them in the gathering gloom with his own attendants. He had no words of congratulation.

At Greenwich, the King awaited news of the trial with some anxiety — unable to eat, so they said. As more news trickled in of Lord Coke's performance, the King seemed disquieted, uneasy. The Viscount Villiers tried to cheer him up: "At least the matter is finished. Lord Coke was perhaps excessive in his zeal, but that is his reputation. The crowd would have been disappointed with anything less. Now they have had their show, their 'pound of flesh', and they will soon forget the whole matter."

The King smiled at Villiers, "Aye, that's my Steenie, always ready to move on. Tomorrow will be a better day for the man who is quick on his feet."

Within a few weeks, the consequences of Edward Coke's successful prosecution were played out. The King decided to pardon the Countess on condition that she leave the country. Leave she did — to France, where her family had property and housing suitable for a woman of her station. Her husband, the Earl of Somerset, was pardoned as well, but with the proviso that he remain in the Tower of London. Neither of them would keep their appointment with the hangman, but they would live separately; the King was adamant. Some thought the pardons scandalous — another example of the way in which the nobles of the realm could commit crimes with impunity. Others saw it as the stuff of tragedy: Two lovers overwhelmed by passion that led them to adultery and murder, now denied the union they truly yearned for, separated by walls of stone for all time — a punishment worthy of the Greek Gods. Poems were written about them. Lord Edward Coke had a more cynical take on the decision: "The King doesn't want the blood of his old favorite on his conscience, but the only way to guarantee that the Count and Countess won't begin telling tales is to keep one of them in custody."

Lord Coke had another legal matter to resolve. If the King had been disappointed with his prosecution of the Earl, he was likely to be frustrated by this one. It started several weeks before, as a small lawsuit over a benefice that the King had granted to one of his bishops — the right to receive certain revenues for performing certain duties. The benefice was granted *in commendam*, which meant that the bishop could assign the duties to a deputy and still be paid. The trouble began when two plaintiffs said the benefice (and the revenue) were rightfully theirs; their lawyer asserted that the King had no legal right to issue this or any benefice *in commendam*. Precedent was not on the plaintiffs' side — Kings had been doing so for centuries. The case would almost certainly have been decided in favor of the bishop, but King James (goaded by his Attorney General, Francis Bacon, it may be supposed) reacted hastily, commanding Lord Coke and the other 11 magistrates of the court to suspend hearing the case until he (the King) could advise them how to proceed.

This created a thorny problem for the magistrates. The King was anxious to suppress any argument in any court that might seem to infringe on royal prerogative. It was a tempest in a teapot, really: the King's right to issue benefices was well established. What was not well established was the King's right to throw any case out of court that did not please him, or offended his sense of royal prerogative. If the King had the power to prevent this case from being heard, where would it stop? Coke and the other magistrates decided to hear the case anyway and informed the King that they were bound by oath to follow the law, and the King's demand to stop the trial was unlawful. The King did not take it well. Roger, in the background, was witness to all these events. He would have a front-row seat to their sad conclusion.

On June 6, all twelve of the magistrates were summoned to account for their letter before the seventeen Lords of the King's Privy Council. Among them were archbishops and bishops who had clashed with Edward Coke in the past, nobles from the Howard family, who were still stinging from the conviction of the Earl of Somerset, and, of course, Francis Bacon, Coke's longtime rival. It quickly became apparent that the King was seething. The case was read, then the letter from the magistrates. He stood, tore the letter up, and threw the pieces on the floor. All of the magistrates, including Coke, fell to their knees begging for pardon. Roger, seated at the back of the room, had never seen anything like it. His companions in the back of the room were crawling from behind their desks to their knees, as well. Roger belatedly followed their example — not a prudent time to sit taller than anyone else in the room.

The King declared that the magistrates had no right to conduct a hearing after he had ordered them to suspend it; that his royal prerogative gave him the right to delay or terminate any case that impinged on that prerogative, that it was the duty of the magistrates, indeed of all his subjects, to honor that prerogative above all else. Anything less was tantamount to treason.

Only Edward Coke spoke in defense of the magistrates. When he did so, Francis Bacon, Attorney General, sprang into action. Roger realized that Bacon had prepared for this moment and was only waiting for the chance to attack his old rival in the presence of the King and his council. Each of the twelve magistrates was forced to answer whether they agreed to honor the King's prerogative in all such matters in the future. One by one, each did. Only Coke answered differently, saying, "When the case should be, he would do that which should be fit for a judge to do."

The court was dismissed, and the magistrates excused. Lord Coke's face was a mask, frozen, unreadable. It was not until they were back in the library at Hatton House that he said anything about the hearing. "The King is drunk with the wine of his 'prerogative'," sighed Coke, "and Bacon is the cupbearer who whispers in his ear and urges him to drink more. If this stands, the Law is corrupted, and the corruption seeps from the throne. Unless a means be found to stanch it, there shall be no justice anywhere in this kingdom."

Roger could tell that he was weary; he looked suddenly older.

Two weeks later, the King had his say. It was a "Star Day", one of the days of the week when the Court of Star Chamber met, so called because the ceiling of the courtroom was painted dark blue and decorated with small, gold-leaf stars, as it had been since the reign of Henry VIII. Plaintiffs before the Star Chamber had their cases heard before the highest authorities in the Land — the Privy Council. Decisions of this court were final — no higher appeal was possible. By tradition, the most important seat for the panel of judges was held for the King, though it was never occupied by the sovereign — the empty chair symbolized the authority of the King *in absentia*.

The place was full of plaintiffs, lawyers, and general lookers-on. The court rose to its feet as the magistrates entered and were seated. And then King James entered and took the seat that was never occupied. There was an audible gasp in the room: no sovereign had sat in that chair for a century or more. Clearly, the King was changing the rules in Star Chamber.

He was changing the rules elsewhere, as well. The prerogative of the crown was "absolute," he said, and promised to punish anyone who said otherwise. He decried the "new Puritanical strains that make all things popular," by which he put himself on the side of tradition, and against most of the lawyers in the room — "It is a presumption and high contempt in a subject to say that a King cannot do this or that . . ."

His meaning was clear enough; no subject of the King could protest any action he decided to take, nor could they appeal to the law — it was, by definition, impossible to call the King(or his servants) to account under the Law, because the royal prerogative was higher than the Law. Anyone who said otherwise would be punished, according to the King's wishes. There was despair, then anger, among the assembly. Some looked to Lord Coke, but he said nothing. From where Roger sat, the mood of the room was palpable. King James seemed oblivious to anything but the sound of his own voice.

That evening, and all the following day, a parade of lawyers, magistrates, and parliamentarians appeared at Hatton Hall and passed through the library. Roger was kept busy with his notes. Some came to bemoan the King's speech, some were urging Lord Coke to take some action or other to mitigate the King's policies, some came with warnings: "Look to yourself, Lord Coke. The King's wrath is not yet cooled, and Francis Bacon has said openly that he intends to humble you, till you grovel at his feet."

Coke merely raised his eyebrows at this last report. To the others, he replied that he had never disobeyed a command from the King, and would not begin now. "If the King is dissatisfied with my service, he may dismiss me from my office. That truly is his 'prerogative.'"

The warnings were not idle. Five days later, Lord Coke and Lady Hatton were in court again. This time, criminal charges were laid. It was claimed that Coke had contrived with Lady Hatton, and with her father (Chancellor at the time), to divert funds that were due the crown to his own profit; that the previous Spring he had abused his power from the bench; that he had contradicted the King's Attorney General in the presence of the King and his Council ("indecent behavior").

Coke answered that he had not profited from the business with the late Chancellor's supposed debts, that everything he had done, he had done openly — with the full approval of King and Council. Lady Hatton had a good bit to say on the subject, as it was her inheritance from her father that was in question. She vigorously insisted that nothing improper had occurred. And she declared that she would stand with her husband to face whatever the Court should decide.

On the other charges, Coke was apologetic — he had erred, as judges sometimes do. He had meant no disrespect to the Attorney General when he spoke in the King's presence.

Roger wondered if the words felt like sand in Lord Coke's mouth. Francis Bacon for his part, seemed to savor the words of apology. Perhaps the sight of Lady Hatton, who had once spurned his offer of matrimony, sitting in the dock was satisfying as well.

The Cokes gave their defense and went home to await the decision.

Four days later, they had it. The King was dissatisfied with Lord Coke's apologies, and he was henceforth suspended from his position on the Privy Council. Neither would he serve as judge in any local court. Instead, he was ordered to spend the summer at home, reviewing the 11 volumes of his *Reports*, identifying any errors, and reporting such errors to the King himself for correction. That was it. Coke was no longer a magistrate, nor any longer an advisor to the King. The implication was that he was expected to refute his life's work, the *Reports*, to mold them to the King's own opinions on royal prerogative.

"Why review the *Reports* ?" asked Roger that afternoon in the Library.

"The King knows that the *Reports* are the basis of law practiced by every lawyer and judge in England. It is cited as an authority in every brief, every decision. If His Majesty can change it into a voice for his views, he can control the findings of every court in the kingdom."

"He hopes to overrule the minds of men by changing some books? Is that possible?"

"Not in the short term. The King hopes to win the battle for men's minds over time, perhaps a generation."

"Is there nothing we can do to prevent him?"

"We?" said Coke with a sardonic laugh. Then, "We will do as the King commands," said Coke, "though I do not expect it will please him, in the end. He does not grasp the stakes in this struggle; he has misread the times. "

"How so?"

"He sees only his personal power at stake in this struggle; he wants to enlarge it, at the expense of all others, and rule this nation as a benign despot. If he has his way, we shall all become little more than servants: ignorant, compliant, obedient. He intends to pass that legacy on to his son, Charles. But this realm is changing. Ignorance is waning. Men are learning to think for themselves. Men who esteem their own judgments are not quick to yield obedience unless compelled to. The King fancies himself the greatest mind in the kingdom and believes that all men are persuaded by his reason and eloquence (and none dare contradict him). This struggle will not be won in his lifetime (or mine either, for that matter), it will last for generations to come."

"Who, then, can be certain of the outcome?"

"Nothing is certain, but the wind blows strongly in our favor. In battles like this, it matters much what the contestants strive for. He is fighting for power and privilege; We are fighting for a nation."

July 1616: Summer of Discontent

There was a great deal of bustle at Hatton House for the next two days: Lord Coke's personal effects, including all his notes and a good portion of his Library, were moving to his country house at Stoke Poges, in Buckinghamshire, along with Coke himself and a fair number of his servants. "Fair" was a sticking point — Lady Hatton had decided to remain in London for the summer, and Hatton House thus needed to be fully staffed to meet her needs. In the end, only half a dozen servants, including Roger Williams, would be traveling to the manor at Stoke.

"I advise you to visit your parents in Cow's Lane before we leave," Coke said to Roger, "it may be months before we are in London again."

Roger could walk the distance to Cow's Lane in less than half an hour, without hurrying. But the distance seemed greater, now. On foot, at street level, everything was familiar — he had wandered these lanes and alleys freely just months ago, the vendors and passers-by recognized him, greeted him, noted that they had not seen him about lately — and yet it was not the same; the smells of the streets was familiar, but not as welcome to his nose — they seemed stronger, even overpowering, now. Also, the look of the places — smaller, coarser, humbler. Something had changed in them, or maybe in him. This had been his world, only 3 months ago — he knew it and inhabited it the way a fish inhabits its river — but it was no longer comfortable.

So too, his family home; once amply large (except when his father harangued him for his deficiencies), now seemed cramped and suffocating. His mother was delighted to see him, of course, and his younger siblings crowded around to admire his clothing, the youngest clamoring for a place in his lap. His father eyed him soberly and took in his clothing with a tailor's eye. "You've gained a bit of weight," he remarked.

"Aye. They feed me well." His mother's face showed concern; "Is it rich food, such as Lords and Ladies eat?"

Roger smiled. "Not as pleasant as your cooking, Mama, but there is always plenty to eat. I eat with the servants, in the lowest part of the house. Once or twice, some delicacies that the folk upstairs could not finish found their way down to us, but mostly the fare is plain and filling."

"Delicacies?" His oldest sister wanted to hear more.

"Lady Hatton likes to give banquets for her friends. Once they brought down the remains of a great bird — a peacock, so I am told. I got a bite or two of it."

"How did it taste? Heavenly?"

"Much like a goose, as I recall." His sister looked disappointed. His father grunted.

"I hear that your master has been disgraced. Has he terminated your employment, then?"

"Nay. But he is retiring to his manor in Buckinghamshire for the summer, and I am to go with him. It was his idea that I visit you before I leave."

"Are you with him often?" his mother wanted to know.

"Nearly every day, often all day long. I take notes for him."

"Notes? What sort of notes?" His father sounded skeptical.

"Notes of his conversations, thoughts, legal matters."

"Tell me an example." All eyes were on Roger now.

"An important part of the job is discretion. I am not supposed to speak of what I hear, indeed not to speak at all, unless it is requested of me." That much was true, though Roger and Sir Edward spoke more freely behind closed doors than many would have supposed.

"Aye, that's a good answer. If you learn when to hold your tongue, this employment you have will do you good." His father's opinion, in a nutshell.

"Do you go where his Lordship goes, even to court?"

"Most of the time. I have been to the palace a few times, to Westminster Hall, and Star Chamber."

"You have seen the King, then!" his mother's voice was excited. "Did he speak to you? What do you say in the presence of the King?"

Roger chuckled. "I say nothing in the presence of the King. I pray that the King will not notice me; I seek to be invisible in the presence of the King." His mother looked disappointed. "Look," Roger continued, "every magistrate who presides in court or appears before the King has a lackey with him unless it is some private audience. We — for we serve together like a flock of starlings: the Brotherhood of the Lackeys Invisible, you could say - are kept out of sight, somewhere in the back of the room, or behind some screen, where we listen, waiting for our masters to summon us to some service. The Great Ones ignore us to the point that we must always be watchful of their movements — to make way for them without being stepped on. The High and Mighty clamor to be noticed; we seek obscurity. I dress like this" — here he gestured to his dark attire — "to escape the notice of my betters."

"If you have learned proper humility, as well as discretion, you have indeed profited from this employment," his father quipped, with more than a hint of sarcasm.

Roger realized that the needling did not annoy him as it once would have. He had changed, and it was precisely the things that he could not talk about that had changed him. He was a different person now after little more than three months away from them. His mother put out some food, and he ate with them before returning to Hatton House.

At breakfast the following morning, Roger ate one last time with his usual tablemates. Isabel sat across from him and offered her opinions freely, as usual: "The manor at Stoke is large, larger than this house," she offered, "I've been there more than once — it can be a bit boring. I'm sure you'll be alright if you can stand Lord Coke and his moods."

"Moods?"

"Lady Hatton says he is getting moodier in his dotage. 'A right cranky old curmudgeon,' those were her words." There was nervous tittering from some of the other servants at the table. This was a bit overly frank, even for Isabel. She leaned forward and said in a lower voice, "They're at odds again, you know, fighting like a pair of old cats in the alley. That's why she's staying, and he's going."

Roger didn't know. Lord Coke did not discuss his marital relations in the library or anywhere else that he and Roger were together. Apparently, Lady Hatton was less discreet around her servants.

When the bell rang, Roger rose to excuse himself. As he turned to leave, he felt Isabel's hand on his forearm. "Come back to us safe, and bring Sir Edward with you," she whispered. Roger didn't know what to say; it hadn't occurred to him that his efforts could affect events at all. She smiled at him and kissed him on his cheek — now he was completely at a loss for words. She turned away, and he stood there, numb. Another servant slapped him on the back with a chuckle. "Well, if you can't do anything else, at least move out of the way!" Roger came to himself and headed upstairs. Time to pack his things.

Packing his things did not take long; the whole of his possessions would not fill a good-sized trunk. A few changes of clothes, his Bible, his writing materials — that was it. He did have a sewing kit (including needles and thread) that his mother had pressed upon him when he first left home, a penknife (for cutting the points on quills), a comb for his hair, and a brush for his teeth. None of this was particularly bulky or heavy. He stuffed it all into a rucksack and gave it to the servants who were loading a wagon downstairs for the trip to Stoke Poges.

Lord Coke appeared astride his favorite horse; two retainers were mounted, as well. Roger found a spot in the back of the wagon. "Ye'll have a rough time of it back there," volunteered the driver, "Better if ye sit with me." Roger complied. The first part of their journey westward was over cobbles — noisy and jarring — because the wagon had none of the springs that a carriage would have. Once they were well away from the city, the cobblestones gave way to dirt and gravel — not as noisy, but not much smoother.

The driver's name was Wilkins; he had made the trip from the manor at Stoke just to transport Lord Coke's luggage to his country home.

Their route lay north and then west, up the high road toward Oxford. "How far are we going, then?" asked Roger.

"Twenty mile, not much more," replied Wilkins.

Twenty. Twenty bone-jarring miles. Roger wondered if he could walk alongside the wagon, but decided he wouldn't be able to keep up for very long — and Lord Coke and the others were already pulling away . . . Better to stick with someone who knew where they were going.

Once on the High Road, they picked up speed — four strong horses and a pleasant morning — it could have been worse; the wagon load wasn't all that heavy. Lord Coke and his riders were far ahead now. Roger concentrated on the scenery. It was early July, the height of Summer. To Roger's untrained eye, it seemed the world had slowed down. Birds sang. Dragonflies zoomed back and forth across the road in front of them. Some of the fields they passed had flocks of sheep, others herds of cattle, and still others appeared to be planted with row crops. He could tell that different crops were grown in different fields, but he realized that he wouldn't know barley from wheat or oats — until after they were harvested. . .

They arrived shortly before sunset, up a curving, graveled drive to a large manor house. They were met by servants, who were evidently expecting them, and quickly unloaded the wagon. Roger was glad to be on his feet again, sore and aching from the journey. He fetched his rucksack from the rear of the wagon.

He paused to view the great house: red brick, 3 stories tall, with its clusters of chimneys. The house faced southward, across a large grassy expanse. Westward, to his right, was a small lake or pond, its bank lined with trees. To the left, he could see a church steeple rising from behind another line of trees. Quiet, notwithstanding the bustle of the servants unpacking the wagon. He heard the call of a bird from somewhere across the water.

Roger turned to enter the house. "You there! Identify yourself!" an old man stood in the doorway, blocking it.

"Roger Williams, sir. At your service." He bowed.

"And what service might that be?" The tone was challenging.

"Why, whatever service my master may direct."

"And who is your master?"

"Lord Coke, of course. Is he not within?"

"Lord Coke's whereabouts are his own business. What have you to do with him?"

"I am his secretary, come this day from London, with Lord Coke. Is this not his house?"

"Who vouches for you?"

"Why, Lord Coke himself. Is he not within? Ask for him, he will vouch for me."

"Lord Coke cannot be bothered with strangers at his door. Who else could vouch for you?"

"I rode here on the wagon with the luggage. The driver can vouch for me."

The old man snorted. "On the wagon? A wagon boy, then, or a stablehand. I thought as much. Don't put on airs, boy. I have known Lord Coke for many years. He has no 'secretary', and if he did, it would be a job for a grown man."

Roger was embarrassed and hungry. He didn't feel like arguing. Just then, Wilkins appeared and beckoned him. "If you want some supper, come with me — around back, to the servant's entrance." Roger shouldered his rucksack and followed Wilkins around to the back of the house, through a narrow door, down to the large room where dozens of servants were eating. Wilkins, of course, was known to them and was cordially greeted. Roger was a stranger. "He rode in with me from London," said Wilkins, "Name's Roger."

Roger was directed to a table with a dozen or so young servants — a stable boy, a kennel boy, a scullery maid, a chambermaid. He was at the bottom rung of the ladder, here. Supper was a mutton stew with bread and cheese. His table companions looked at him with curiosity.

"You came from London? Today?" the tone was skeptical, coming from one of the maids.

Roger nodded, his mouth full.

"Where did you come from, before London?"

Roger swallowed. "I was born in London. Lived there all my life. I entered Lord Coke's service this spring." He hoped that would answer their questions; he took another bite of stew.

"Is it as beautiful as they say?" This question from Mabel, the chambermaid.

Roger swallowed and took a breath. "Some parts of it are. Others are dirty and run-down." Better to tell the truth than feed any country notions of life in the big city, he thought.

"My Pa went to London once," volunteered the stable boy. "Said that the rats were big as cats, and the streets had a foul stench."

"He must have been in one of the better neighborhoods," said Roger. "Where I was born, the rats are as big as dogs. They say that the King captured one, put a leash on it, and made a gift of it — to the Spanish ambassador."

Mabel's eyes grew large. "He didn't! What did the ambassador do with it?"

"What could he do? He couldn't insult the King by refusing such a gift. The ambassador's valet walks the animal every morning in the streets outside the old Ely Palace, where the ambassador lives. He has taught it to sit, beg, and roll over." He winked at the kennel boy, who covered his mouth with his hand.

A bell tinkled. "Psst! It's old Cedric, back already!" whispered Flossie, the scullery maid.

Roger looked up to see the old man who had denied him entrance at the front door. Old Cedric was scanning the room, looking for someone. "I am looking for a man called Roger Williams," announced Cedric. "The Lord Coke needs him."

Roger stood. Cedric did not look happy to see him. "Come with me," he said and turned on his heels. Roger scampered to keep up. They ascended a flight of stairs and wound up in what was a large dining hall. Lord Coke was seated at one end of the table, along with the two retainers he had ridden with, and several other servants — all men. Coke looked up and smiled. "Roger! I thought we had lost you on the road!" He laughed. "Come, sit near me. Have some supper."

There was consternation among the servants at this gesture, particularly for Cedric, who could not resist saying, "I found him downstairs, Lord, eating with the lesser servants."

"Thank you, Cedric. From now on, Mr. Williams will be eating with me. We will take our midday meal in the library most days; suppers will be here at this table. Since we have so few ladies with us this summer, it will be a stag affair most evenings."

"Very good, sir," Cedric replied, a little stiffly.

Coke turned to Roger. "How was your journey?"

"A little rough, to be honest. I rode on the wagon with Mr. Wilkins."

"You could have ridden a horse if you had asked for it."

"I didn't know who to ask. And, remembering my last ride astride a horse, I think I may be less bruised by the wagon."

Coke laughed and was joined by his retainers. He seemed more relaxed than Roger had seen him — almost jolly. He cracked jokes, teased his servants, and told stories into the evening. Perhaps living in London was stressful; perhaps it was living with Lady Hatton that weighed on him. Here, he was like a younger man, carefree, or even careless.

Roger discovered that he would not be sleeping in the attic with the other servants. Lord Coke had arranged for him to sleep in a small room — little more than a closet, really - on the second floor, near Coke's own bed chamber. "It will be more convenient," explained Coke, "I will know where to find you."

In the morning, he was roused by Old Cedric. "Lord Coke orders you downstairs for breakfast," he was told. He rubbed his eyes, dressed, and combed his hair. How early was it? Very early, as it turned out — the sun was barely up. Coke was in an ebullient mood. "Eat quickly, Roger. We have work to do."

After breakfast, they went to the library. It was larger than the library at Hatton House, with more books. The books they had brought from London were still packed — Roger busied himself with unpacking them and finding them places on the shelves.

"The King has set us a pretty task for the summer," said Coke, "We must review all the cases in the 11 volumes of my *Reports*, find the errors, and report back with them in the autumn, with suggested corrections. This is no small task. I happen to know that there are no errors in my *Reports*. Nevertheless, we shall have to find some. It could take us all summer, but I do not intend to spend my entire summer in this library. More important matters must be addressed. For instance, your poor horsemanship. We will correct that, starting tomorrow. We will need to do some hawking — maybe some hunting as well — if we are to think clearly enough to find these 'errors'. I also find that bowling concentrates the mind wonderfully. Archery helps, too, I have found."

With that, Coke handed him a book. "Volume 1 of the *Reports*," he said, "read it and be prepared to explain it to me by tomorrow evening ." With that, he rose and left the room.

Roger set to work, reading and taking notes. He was relieved to find that Coke had presented his commentary in a very organized way. There were several technical terms whose meanings he had to deduce from their context, but he was able to note down an outline of each case and outline the commentary as well. This was far from understanding everything he was reading, but he could go back to review his outline, time permitting. He had worked his way through several cases in this way when there was a knock at the library door.

It was Cedric. "Lord Coke has left instruction that you will eat your dinner here, in the library," he pronounced. He opened the door wide, and in stepped another servant with a tray, and a meal — mutton stew (same as last night's probably), bread, cheese, some dried fruit, and a mug of ale. A bit more rustic than what he was accustomed to, but welcome all the same. He thanked the servant, then asked Cedric a question: "You said that Lord Coke had 'left instruction'. Does that mean he has left the premises?"

Cedric seemed annoyed at the question, but replied, "I believe the master has gone hawking this morning."

"Ah. Thinking then. Please thank him for this meal when he returns." His tone was dismissive, and Cedric was unsure how to respond, but he bowed and excused himself. Roger thought he had probably laid claim to a little more respect than Cedric was inclined to pay him, but that was just the first step in establishing his position in the household.

By late afternoon, Roger had outlined more than half the cases in the first volume. He debated whether to stop and begin reviewing his notes or to press on to finish the reading. What was it Coke had said? He was to explain it the following evening. Would he be allowed to refer to his notes for the explanation? He decided to review what he had already written down. There were similarities in the way Coke laid out the cases, he noticed; certain patterns of analysis that were repeated again and again. The details varied, but he began to get a sense of how Coke approached a case. As an experiment, he read the text of the next case in the book without reading the commentary, then he outlined on his paper how he thought the commentary might be organized, and compared his outline to the actual one. He got about half the points correct — not that impressive, but not as far off as a wild guess, either. He decided to try the same approach with the next case . . .

He heard the sound of voices — loud voices, coming from beyond the library doors. The doors flew open, and Lord Coke breezed in, accompanied by another, younger man. The younger man was taller than Coke and a good deal huskier. The two were laughing about something; Coke appeared to be in a very good mood. He pointed at Roger, "Clem, this is the lad I told you about. Goes everywhere I go, nowadays."

Roger stood and bowed, "At your service, Sir."

The younger man nodded. "Clement Coke."

"My baby boy," added Sir Edward.

'Baby' did not do justice to the man, though Roger could see the family resemblance. Clem Coke was brawny and carried himself like a man who usually got his way — not a man to cross, or even annoy. A bruiser, more than likely. He carried a rapier at his side and a large knife sheathed on his belt.

"Clem will be staying with us for a few days," said Sir Edward. "In fact, I think he could help with your education, while he's here!" he laughed again.

In the morning, Roger discovered what sort of "education" his master had in mind. At breakfast, he was presented with a pair of riding boots — a little worn, but still serviceable. "These should fit well enough," said Sir Edward, "They were Clem's when he was about your age."

Clem looked at them and nodded as if remembering his childhood.

"Clem will be teaching you to ride this morning," said Lord Coke, "I'm sure you'll pick it up quickly."

The boots seemed to fit; Roger was able to walk around in them without discomfort.

The stables were behind the manor house, to the north. Servants had already saddled and bridled two horses; one was Clem's — a large, big-boned chestnut stallion. The other horse was a smaller gray mare. Evidently, this would be Roger's mount.

"Always mount a horse on the left side — the horse's left, not yours," said Clem. With some effort, Roger got on the mare. "Check to be sure that the stirrups are the right length. When you stand in the stirrups, there should be about a hand's breadth between your arse and the saddle. Like this." Clem demonstrated.

"The first thing is, don't pull on the reins so much. Don't rely on the stirrups to hold you in the saddle, either. Grip the horse with your legs — not your knees, your lower legs — then lean forward a little, to move with the horse."

Roger tried doing all these things at once. It felt awkward.

"Give the reins some slack, and nudge her a bit."

Roger did so, and the mare began walking around the yard.

"When you want to pull up, pull back on the reins, and sit up straighter — not so hard, you'll hurt the horse's mouth!"

After several starts and stops, Roger felt he was getting the hang of it. It was hard to read Clem's expression.

"Now watch me," said Clem. He started his horse at a walk, guided the stallion through a series of turns, then began to trot around the yard. The second time around, the horse broke into a canter, and Clem eased him back to a trot, then a slow walk, stopping in front of where Roger sat on the mare. Very impressive.

"Show me what you can do," said Clem. Roger tried the same series of gaits. Walking wasn't so bad; trotting was jarring, so much so that Roger didn't dare let the mare into a canter.

"Watch me again," said Clem, "this time pay attention to how I move when the horse is trotting. It's called 'posting'. You have to move up and down, in rhythm with the horse. Use your legs to grip. Like this." Clem was already moving as he spoke, and the stallion trotted gracefully around the yard. Clem pulled up. "Now, you try it. Don't lean back, move forward. Roger urged the mare into a trot and struggled to match his rhythm to the horse. It seemed like he got it right on every third or fourth stride, then bounced in the saddle. "Keep moving forward," said Clem, "Relax. Let it come to you."

And then somehow, it did come to him. For a moment, at first, just a few strides, then he lost it, then he got it back. He began to feel like he was part of the horse, or the horse was part of him.

"That's enough, " said Clem, "Don't wear the horse out."

Roger had lost track of time. When he dismounted, his legs felt wobbly and weak. Clem noticed. "Aye, you'll be sore in the morning. Takes time to learn to ride. I'm told you're needed in the library."

Roger found his way to the library, walking stiffly. Lord Coke was waiting for him. "I see you're learning the ways of horses," he said, with a knowing smile. "We have some work this morning. How are you doing with the *Reports* ?"

Roger told him that he had made it more than halfway through the first volume.

"Did you understand it?"

"I believe so. My French and Latin are stretched a bit, but the English parts are clear enough."

Coke grunted. "Let's find out how much you really understand."

"May I refer to my notes?"

Coke nodded, then posed a question about one of the cases. Roger answered as best he could. Coke peppered him with more questions. This went on for the rest of the morning. A few times, Coke dismissed his answers with a wave of his hand. More often, he followed Roger's answers with follow-up questions. When he was satisfied with an answer (or maybe just tired of the case), he grunted and moved on to another case. Roger was scrambling through his notes, trying to keep up. Finally, Coke asked him about a case that was not in his notes at all.

"I don't believe I am familiar with that case, Sir. Is it possibly among those in the latter part of the volume?"

Coke thought for a moment. "Perhaps it is. Find it in the volume, and read it to me."

Roger complied. The case itself was in Latin, the commentary in French (a Norman dialect, not exactly his forte).

"Now, explain it to me," Coke demanded.

Roger did his best. He relied on his recall of other cases, as he identified what he hoped were the salient points, and laid them out in an order he hoped would please his master.

Coke grunted again. "Truthfully, I did not expect you would make as much progress as you have. I am pleased. This bodes well for our summer. At this rate, you will manage a volume in less than a week. I am satisfied."

"I did find one error," Roger offered.

"How's that?!" Coke appeared to be irritated

"It's a typographer's error, I think. A misspelling."

Coke relaxed and nodded. "Make a note of it. The King shall hear of it." He laughed.

It was time to eat. Sir Edward led Roger to the dining hall, where Clem was waiting for them. A couple of Coke's retainers joined them, and dinner was served — a platter of baked trout, a meat pie, bread, ale, and roasted vegetables; it occurred to Roger that this was probably how Lord Coke dined most days, though he never would have known it, eating his midday meal in the library. Roger had an appetite after the morning's exercise and dug in.

The conversation at the table was dominated by Lord Coke and Clem, both of whom had a lot to say about the state of the realm. Roger listened. Clem was apparently in communication with a great number of the gentry in the countryside — men who would serve in Parliament, the next time the King called for a Parliament. They were alarmed at the King's extravagant claims to royal prerogative, unsure what to do about it. "People keep asking me what <u>you</u> will do about it," said Clem to his father.

"I? Why am I the oracle in these matters?"

"It is understood that you are close to the King. They imagine that you have some influence with him."

Coke snorted. "If that were true, I would be in London, not here." He took a gulp of his wine, emptied the goblet, and refilled it. "Explain to your friends that there is only one institution in this kingdom that can implement a law that the King is bound to obey, and that is Parliament. Parliament is not in session now, and the King will not call a new one if he has his wits about him. The King considers that Parliament has only one purpose -- to provide money for his enjoyment of the throne. As long as he has enough money, Parliament is an unnecessary thing." He took another gulp of his wine, for emphasis.

Their conversation went on in this vein for a while. No one, not even a Parliament (should one be called), had the courage and the will to constrain the King in any way; the hard-fought balance of power that had served England so well was out of balance, and there seemed no way to restore it. Coke finished his wine. He looked across the table at Roger and nodded. Something about his expression said he had drunk more than enough wine today.

"I have a taste for the longbow," said Lord Coke, "an itch to feel it in my hand. What say we teach young Roger, here, about the archer's craft?"

"Right now?" asked Clem.

"Yes. Now would be a good time."

Orders were issued to servants; before long, they had retrieved three longbows and a few dozen arrows from the armory. The servants set up a couple of targets for them.

"I will show you how it's done," said Lord Coke (none too steadily, thought Roger), "See? You don't pull on the bowstring, you hold the bow close to your body, then hold the string with your right hand, and push the bow away from your body with your left." He let fly, and the arrow sailed wide and far beyond the target. "Too close," mumbled Coke, and he began to walk in the opposite direction from the targets until he was twenty yards farther away. "Watch me," he said, as he aimed toward the targets. Clem grabbed Roger by the arm and pulled him out of the line of fire, and waved all the servants well away, too. Coke let fly again, and his arrow found the target. "See? Nothing to it. Clem, show the lad how it's done. I think I shall take a nap." With that, Lord Coke ambled off in the direction of the house.

"He demonstrated the technique well enough," said Clem, "but do not follow his example. Always be sure that no one is anywhere near where the arrow could land unless you actually want to kill someone. Stand beside or behind the archer, never in front."

After an hour or so, Roger was able to hit the target at forty yards about half the time. "Not bad, for a beginner," said Clem, "you should practice more." Then he asked, "Does my father often drink wine these days?"

"Only in moderation, until today. Of course, I don't eat in his presence when we're in London, but I've never seen him like he was today."

Clem nodded. "It's not good for him to be alone so much. And that woman isn't doing him any good either. At least he has your companionship — he is quite fond of you, I think. This business with the King will be his ruin."

Clem left the following day. Lord Coke's spirits seemed to sink with his absence. At supper, he turned to the wine again. By the end of the meal, he gave Roger a mournful look and began speaking, "You see before you an old man," he began. "A man at the end of his career. *Better is the end of a thing than the beginning thereof: and the patient in spirit is better than the proud in spirit,* or so the preacher says. I confess I have not much patience; perhaps pride will be my downfall. I do not foresee an end for me that is better than my beginning."

"Sir?" Roger wasn't sure what his master was talking about.

"I have friends," said Coke, "who urge me to repudiate my own words, apologize to the King, and hope for mercy. They say that the right must triumph in time and that this situation calls for patience. Perhaps when we have another king, the time will be ripe to reassert the ancient rights; perhaps the King will mellow, and bestow again the rights our forefathers knew." Coke shook his head, "I say that a right that is granted is a right that can be taken back. Rights belong to us by Law — they can neither be bestowed nor denied."

He continued, almost in a whisper, "Lady Hatton is convinced that this business will result in my downfall, and hers. She blames me for putting our family's fortunes at risk, for nothing more than foolish pride. 'Who do you think you are?', she says, 'Do you think your learning puts you above the King? See to your family, they are your chief responsibility!' His whisper was higher-pitched now as if mimicking a woman's voice.

"I suppose a woman will always think of family before all else," offered Roger.

Coke sighed and nodded. "It was not always so, between the Lady and me. When we wed, she was as eager as I was — we were both so hot for that union that we were married in Lord Burghley's house without banns, at night. I had to grovel to the Archbishop for leniency, lest he declare the marriage null and send us all to jail." Here, he laughed. Then suddenly he was somber again. "I don't suppose she got what she had bargained for; she would have been happier with a younger, carefree man — a man who dances, who charms; the sort of man who is at home at the theater, or a masque, a courtier — but also a man with a great deal of money, willing to spend it all on her!" he chuckled, a little ruefully.

"Yet she chose to marry you," Roger pointed out.

"Aye, she did — chose me over a multitude of eager suitors, many of them titled, some wealthy. But those were all unsuitable — for her family. They needed allies who would strengthen them against the Earl of Essex and his allies. I was one of theirs: they knew me to be loyal. This is the way a man takes care of his family — he forges the alliances that lead to power and influence. It requires constant vigilance — the higher you rise, the farther you can fall."

Roger considered this for a moment. He wondered if people like these could untangle their affections from their ambition; and if ambition was thwarted, did affection suffer as well? "Do you suppose that Lady Hatton understood the bargain that was made when she married you?"

"She understood it at least in part. She has dedicated herself for nearly twenty years to the service of the Queen; she has done her part in raising our family's fortunes. Sadly, the Queen's favor does not count for what it once did and never did for what it should have. The King heeds his favorites more than his advisors or his Queen. Lady Hatton might say that she has borne more than her share of the burden, and my efforts have been less effective than hers."

"Do you fear that her affections for you are diminished by this setback in your career, then?"

"I fear that they are. She is not a woman of mild disposition. Her passions can be enchanting, but once her heart is set on something, she worries it like a dog with a bone. It takes a great effort to shift her attention elsewhere, and usually a good deal of money as well . . . I think it will require more than jewelry and parties to put me back in her good graces, this time."

Coke changed the subject again. "Do you bowl?"

It took Roger a second to catch up with him. "I have seen other men at bowls. I know how the game is played. My father had little use for such pastimes; he preferred to occupy himself with profitable matters."

"It is a sport for gentlemen," Coke allowed. "In fact, a commoner caught bowling is subject to fines. It used to be allowed on Christmas Day only; Queen Mary outlawed it altogether for any but the gentry. How would you like to try your hand at it?"

Roger hesitated. "You said fines were involved?"

"Aye," said Coke with a twinkle in his eye, "but only if you win a game. It would be my duty as Lord of the manor to fine you if you should happen to beat me."

"So... my best strategy would be to make sure that you win."

Coke laughed. "I see you've mastered the game already! Come with me to the green." Coke gave orders, and his servants scurried around to fetch the balls for a game of bowls. Coke's retainers were summoned as well; men who appeared to be very familiar with the game. They whispered among themselves as the green was laid out — Roger realized that they were making wagers with each other.

The game was fairly simple. A small ball, called the "jack," was pitched or rolled to the middle of the green. Then the bowlers tried to roll larger balls toward the jack; the ball that stopped closest to the jack earned a point. Each of two bowlers was given two bowls at a time. The bowler whose bowl ended up closest to the jack was awarded 1 point. If that bowler's second bowl was also closer to the jack than either of the opponent's bowls, a second point was awarded. The first bowler to reach 21 points won the match. There was a catch: the bowls were weighted to be lopsided — they did not roll in a straight line, but curved as they rolled, in unpredictable ways. This led to hilarity and frustration, which the bowlers expressed loudly. Even when a bowl stopped near the jack, there was always the possibility that it would be knocked out of position by the next one — either deliberately (or so it was claimed when an opponent's bowl did the deed), or by accident.

Last to go were Lord Coke and Roger. When Roger's turn came, all of the treacheries of the game were on full display. His pitches swerved in every direction possible — except toward the jack. At the end of the first ten games, he trailed twenty-nil. Lord Coke found the whole of his efforts hilarious, roaring with laughter, and slapping his thighs. Roger tried to keep smiling; no reason to show his humiliation. The retainers were whispering among themselves, placing side bets — against him, most likely. Roger supposed that anyone betting on him must be demanding very favorable odds. Then, almost miraculously, his next bowl corkscrewed its way around Lord Coke's two other bowls to rest directly against the jack. One of the retainers whooped with glee — evidently, he had gotten very favorable odds, indeed. So twenty to one, then. Not a complete washout. "A lucky pitch," said Coke. Roger's next bowl was better than most — good enough, he thought, to show that his previous one was not a fluke. Lord Coke's next bowl landed a little farther away. Roger's second bowl curved all over the green and stopped less than a foot from the jack on its far side. The retainers were whispering furiously, now, wagering on the next shot, the outcome of the game, the outcome of the match.

Lord Coke stepped up to the line and released his bowl, which struck Roger's first bowl, then glanced off on a path that struck Roger's second bowl, driving it away from the jack altogether. The winning shot — 21 points, match over.

"A lucky pitch," offered Roger. *An unbelievable pitch,* he said to himself.

"Bowling is like politics," said Coke. "Everyone seeks to be close to the center of power, but the pathway is crooked, and setbacks come from unexpected directions."

Roger bowed, conceding the match. The retainers all cheered Lord Coke's victory and sought to ease the sting of defeat for Roger.

"Better stick to archery," he was advised, "That's the sport for a commoner." Roger took their advice. His archery improved as the summer wore on.   He bowled only when Lord Coke couldn't find anyone else to play against him.

News from London trickled in from time to time. Sometime in July, came word that George Villiers had received another promotion from the King — he was now Earl of Buckingham. Clearly, the King had overcome his disappointment in his old favorite, the Earl of Somerset; "Steenie" had filled the vacancy in his affections.

In Stoke Poges, things had settled into a more leisurely routine. Most mornings, Roger was invited to go riding with Lord Coke and his men around the estate, or sometimes through the neighboring villages. Sundays, they attended services at St. Giles church, less than a mile from the house. Lord Coke's presence was received with the usual bows and curtseys from the rest of the congregation — they didn't often share the chapel with so prominent a patron. The local priest was delighted to have a member of the King's Privy Council sitting in the front row; he made what Roger supposed were extraordinary efforts to inspire the piety of his congregation and impress Lord Coke with his erudition. Perhaps, Roger reflected, this was the best chance for promotion that had come the vicar's way — perhaps the best that ever would . . .

Other visitors came and went throughout the summer; three of Lord Coke's other five sons visited for a few days each and brought their grandchildren with them. This seemed to lift Lord Coke's spirits a good deal. For Roger, the workload was light enough to allow time for recreations like riding or bowling. Roger was comfortable on the back of a horse, now, and the other exercise he got was good for him — he put on some muscle and was noticeably taller. His clothing was a bit small for him, now; nothing major — he could do the alterations himself (there was advantage in being a tailor's son, after all.) Roger got into the habit of swimming in the pond to the west of the manor in the late afternoons — it relaxed him. Always in the back of his mind was the fact that Lord Coke was expected back in London in the autumn to answer for his writings. Roger had seen nothing that would give him reason to expect a warm welcome for Lord Coke in London.

One particular case in the *Reports* became the topic of an afternoon. It concerned Coke's opinions on the use of oaths in trials, particularly on trials conducted by the Court of High Commission. English courts had long proceeded by administering an oath to defendants, referred to as the "oath ex officio". Defendants were presented with the charges that they were facing and then entered a plea of guilt or innocence, followed by an oath to answer all questions from the magistrate truthfully. It was an efficient way to proceed with most kinds of cases. A defendant who lied under oath was guilty of perjury, which the magistrate could punish appropriately. However, the questions a magistrate could ask were limited to the charges specified, and decisions were to be based strictly on evidence presented in court.

The Court of High Commission was administered by the Archbishop of Canterbury and other clergy. Its purview was (supposedly) limited to matters of church discipline. But the Commission had gotten into the habit of requiring the oath ex officio of men suspected of religious nonconformity and then questioning them about all manner of their personal opinions, without any specific criminal charges. Any answer might lead to the "discovery" of some heretical or ignorant notions (particularly since the inquisitors were skillful and relentless, and had means of torture at their disposal), at which point the defendant could be convicted of a crime he had never been charged with. Once the defendant had taken the oath, he was required to answer any question that the magistrates could come up with. Refusal to answer was itself a crime; a mistaken answer might be heresy or even treason. Sir Edward Coke had been asked for an opinion on the use of the ex officio oath in situations like this, and his opinion was harsh — no man should be required to incriminate himself in a court of law, especially when it was about a private opinion that he held. The Court of High Commission had no right to require such an oath; no defendant was obligated to take it. Coke had been overruled by the King; the Archbishop now regarded Coke as an enemy of the church.

"It is grotesque," said Coke, "a gross violation of an Englishman's liberties. There is no place in the common law for an institution like the Court of High Commission. Many are urging the abolition of that Court. It may take an act of Parliament to do so, but God willing, I shall live to see the day!"

Roger had heard of the Court of High Commission and the fear that it struck in the hearts of Puritans — people like himself. Still, the threat of Catholic recusants and "Popish" ideas was real enough. "How should we protect ourselves from heresy and Popish plots, if the Court is abolished? What other legal protections would remain?"

Coke snorted. "Evidence! Actual evidence! Conversations! Letters! Barrels of gunpowder! Those are the basis of criminal proceedings. The imaginations of a man's mind are not treason. The things he mutters to himself when taxes are due are not treason, either. We should stick to evidence!"

Emphatic as he was, Roger did not ask him any more questions.

Roger wrapped up the last volume of the *Reports* in late August. He spent the afternoon going over them with Lord Coke. Together, they had identified enough "errors" to fill one page of paper — most of them trivial, none of them the sort of change that was likely to satisfy the King, or his Attorney General, Francis Bacon.

"It is not what the King hopes to see," admitted Coke, "perhaps his anger has cooled, but I think Bacon will fan the fire — he is determined to pull me down, and humiliate me. I will not lie to please Bacon or the King. I do not expect this to end well."

It was a somber tone for the end of Summer. The day was hot; Roger decided to go for a swim. He laid his clothes on the bank before getting in the water. It was a private place, screened from view of the manor by a line of trees and shrubs that grew along the shore, their roots reaching down to the water. The water was warm by this time of the year, and he surrendered himself to it, floating on his back for a time, enjoying the embrace. He wasn't a particularly strong swimmer, but he was confident in the waters of a small pond like this one. After a while, he felt refreshed and clambered to the bank to pull on his cotton breeches. He waited to let his skin dry for a moment or two — pulling on a tight-fitting garment over wet skin was extra work, and this garment, like so many others, was a bit small nowadays. He turned to pull on his shirt, which was cut loose, and it was over his head when he heard a sound. He looked up to see two women standing on the bank above him. They were both holding parasols, which partially obscured their faces.

"Good afternoon, Sir. Enjoying your bathe?" The voice was familiar — Isabel, Lady Hatton's servant. The other woman was . . . could it be? Frances Coke. They both giggled.

Roger was embarrassed, blushing. They giggled at that, too.

"Pardon me, ladies," he said, "I did not expect to see you here at the manor. Have you been here long?"

"You mean, how long have we been standing here?" said Isabel, with a sly grin. "I would say it's been quite a while, wouldn't you, Lady Frances?"

"Yes, I would say quite a while. The scenery is fascinating from this spot." Frances was grinning, too. Roger had his shirt on by now, and pulled his hose up over his upper legs, to his waist, then started on his stockings and shoes.

"I should have asked how you came here from London, and whether you had a pleasant journey," he offered. He wanted to change the subject, forget all about the scenery they had found so 'fascinating'.

"We left London this morning, in Lady Hatton's coach. The ride was pleasant enough," said Isabel.

"Lady Hatton?"

She is up at the house, conferring with Lord Coke about some matter. We decided to stretch our legs and take in the . . . scenery." Both of them giggled again. Roger nodded and smiled. This joke wasn't going away; best to ride along with it. He had his shoes on now and was ready to walk back to the house.

A servant ran up, puffing. "Lady Hatton says that Isabel is needed at the house, forthwith. You should hurry." With that, Isabel scampered back to the house.

"Lady Frances, shall I escort you back, as well?" the servant asked.

"I did not hear you say that Lady Hatton wanted to see me right now. I think I shall remain here for a while." The servant bowed and trotted away. She turned her eyes to Roger. Dazzling. He was tongue-tied.

"Come, walk with me," she said. He felt like a puppy, helpless and clumsy. She looked into his eyes intently, as if searching for something. She began to walk southward, along the shore of the pond.

"Isabel tells me that you are an honest, truthful fellow. Is that true?"

"I hope so, Lady." It was an odd question. Odder, he thought, that Isabel would have mentioned his name to Lady

Frances at all. Something twitched inside his chest at the thought.

"Then answer me this. I have noticed that many men, young and old, behave as if they have lost their tongues when I am around. Why do you suppose that is? Is it because they find me attractive, pretty . . . beautiful?"

Roger nodded. "Beautiful, certainly. Transcendently lovely, I suppose."(No supposing about it, really, she was utterly exquisite.) Roger was a little surprised with himself, blurting out such a remark. Frances appeared not to notice: maybe people said such things to her all the time?

"But why does it make them act like fools? Is it all because of my face? Why my face, rather than Isabel's, for instance?"

"Isabel has a very pretty face," Roger allowed, "But she is not the daughter of a great Lord, and she does not carry herself like a great Lady."

"So it is a matter of carriage and clothing? What does that have to do with who I truly am? For all that any of them know, I am a shrew, a harpy, a harridan. Where is the beauty in that?"

Roger was completely taken aback by her question. Forgetting himself for the moment, he said, "I do not believe you are any of those things — the way that you ask that question tells me that you would not act like one. It speaks to character."

"Character? What do you know of my character?"

"I know that you are a young woman of curiosity, who fishes for compliments."

She stared at him for a moment, giggled, then laughed out loud. "Isabel was right about you," she laughed again.

Roger was encouraged to think he had amused her.

"I think I envy you," she said.

"How so, Lady?"

"You can go swimming when you like. You can tell the truth when called upon to do so. You can admire whom you please; no one clamors for your attention because of who they think you are. You are not some prize that men of doubtful character vie for. You are free."

"None of us is truly free, Lady."

"Still, I envy you. Consider my state. I am destined to be 'bestowed' upon a man of my parents' choosing. Whoever he may be, he will expect a large dowry from my father. It is advantageous for my family if I am esteemed beautiful, for that may mean that the dowry demanded will be a little less than it would be for a plain-looking woman. It is profitable that my face be attractive, my carriage noble, my conversation pleasant. In any case, my parents expect that the dowry will be down payment for an alliance with some other powerful family, whose favor will contribute to our prosperity. All of my siblings, including my step-sisters and brothers, wish for a 'good match' for me because it augurs good fortune for them."

Roger was moved by her frankness and her cool assessment of the social landscape surrounding her situation. He was touched by a sense of pity, or protectiveness toward her; a flash of gallant impulse to rescue a lady in distress from a perilous fate.

"Don't look at me that way," she said. "I said I envy you, I didn't ask for pity."

Roger nodded and decided to put a brave face on it. "I don't suppose we could trade places. Your clothing would not fit me."

She giggled, snickered. "I think it would amuse me to see you in a farthingale, stays, and ruff."

"Lady, I have spent a good deal of time with your father. I believe he loves you dearly. I do not imagine that he would bestow you on a monster, no matter how modest the dowry. Have faith that you will find happiness in wedlock." The words sounded silly to him, but the sentiment was genuine. She appeared to take it as such.

"It grows late. We must return to the house," she said.

At supper, Roger ate with the other servants in the basement again. People were friendly; a little curious about his status in their world. They knew that he spent a lot of time with Lord Coke, doing whatever-it-was in the library, but also the riding, the bowling, the meals together. He had no title, other than 'secretary', but apparently it was a high rank in Lord Coke's estimation. He sat at the table he had occupied the first evening of his arrival, with Mabel and the others. "Are you eating with us because you are disgraced?" was the first thing out of Mabel's mouth.

"Nay, I always eat supper in the basement at Hatton House, just like all the other servants. I was only eating upstairs because Lord Coke was on his own this summer. Now that Lady Hatton has arrived, it is back to the usual routine."

"But we saw you riding with Lord Coke and bowling — all sorts of things. Is this usual in London?"

Roger shook his head. "No, not in London. I imagine that Lord Coke was bored and wanted some entertainment. He certainly found my bowling amusing."

"Ah." The supper was mutton stew. Roger wondered if they ate anything else in the servants' quarters at Stoke Hall.

That night dreams overtook him; dreams of Frances Coke, faced with a life of misery, promised to a cruel, stupid man — then rescued at the last moment, by a gallant young fellow on a fiery steed, who swept her off her feet, and onto the back of his great horse, where she clung to him, her arms around him, while they sang and laughed. He did not sleep well that night; he woke feeling tired — as if he had been singing for hours.

In the morning, Lady Hatton and her companions made ready to leave. Lady Hatton did not look happy. Isabel took Roger aside and whispered what was going on: "Lady Hatton is very put out with him. Says he is stubborn, inflexible, and foolish. He will not grovel to the King or his Chancellor, and the whole family will suffer for it. She says she will take steps to protect her own fortune, even if he is determined to throw his career away!"

For once, what she was telling him made sense. The only surprise was that Lady Hatton appeared to be surprised that her husband had decided to make a stand. Or perhaps she was feigning outrage to protect herself and her wealth. . .

That evening, Roger was invited to supper with Lord Coke again.

"You never explained to me why you didn't sit with the rest of your family in church before we met," Coke said.

Roger was surprised and cleared his throat. "It has to do with my religion," he said.

"Your religion?"

"My father and I disagree about the nature of true religion. He is satisfied with the outward forms — the liturgy, the sacraments. I believe that none of that is sufficient: the heart of a man must be devoted to God, else he is no true Christian. I spoke with him about this, but he would not hear me. He said that if I truly believed my worship to be genuine and others counterfeit, I should separate myself from him and the rest of my family on Sunday mornings."

"You told your father that his religion was false? Did you also suggest that his soul is damned?"

"Not in so many words. He took it like that, I suppose."

"That's a harsh thing for a son to say to his father, not to add disrespectful!"

"I meant no disrespect. I meant only to challenge him to take his religion more seriously. I do not judge him, nor any man. I cannot claim to know who shall be saved and who condemned on the day of judgment. I do believe that it is my Christian duty to strive to live a holy and upright life, and I fear for those who treat their religion as a pastime or a hedge against eternal suffering."

"You talk like a Puritan," said Coke.

"My father says the same. He does not intend it as a compliment. If I have offended you, I am sorry. But you did ask the question."

Coke chuckled. "I am not offended. I have many friends who are Puritans — men I respect, though they aren't much fun at a wedding feast. Just so you don't try to convert me to your way of thinking."

"No, Sir. You are the master, I am the servant. I know my place."

Coke looked at him, searching for a hint of sarcasm, but found none. "That is true, but you are more than a servant to me. I have enjoyed your companionship, especially here at

Stoke, and your service to me has been more than that of a simple servant. You are useful to me, but I am determined to be useful to you, as well. You have earned my respect; I hope that I have earned yours."

Roger flushed a little. "There is no man that I respect as I do you, Sir. May I never give you cause to be disappointed in me." He rose from the table and bowed.

"Please sit down," said Coke. This conversation was becoming awkward. "I mean that I value your service and your person very highly. I do not know what I would have done this summer without your companionship. I do not know what awaits me in London, but the day will surely come when I am no longer your master, nor you my servant. When that day comes, I hope that we will still be on . . . friendly terms."

Roger nodded but said nothing for a while. Then, "I hope so too, Sir. May it please God to bring it about."

Coke changed the subject. "Do you know what they call my son, Clement?"

"Clem?" There was another nickname Roger had heard, but he didn't wish to offend.

"They call him 'fighting Clem', as I think you well know," said Coke.

"I admit that I have heard him dubbed so, though I must say I have found him an agreeable enough fellow."

Coke grunted. "Aye, he's pleasant enough in polite company. Has a temper, that one - not an asset for a lawyer. Of all my sons, I had hopes that Clement might follow in my footsteps, but the subtleties of the law did not appeal to him — he quit his studies after only a few months. He is loyal to our family, and especially to me — and I am grateful for that, but I wish that at least one of my sons was prepared to take up my mantle when I am gone."

Roger did not know what to say. He wondered why his master would speak so openly of his personal life to a mere secretary, but then it occurred to him that with Clem gone, there was really no one present to whom Lord Coke was closer than himself. Odd to think that great men should be so lonely at the peak of their careers . . . but he understood why Lady Hatton would not be a suitable confidant for her husband, under the present circumstances. As for the rest of Lord Coke's peers, they had rejected him, almost to a man. Roger felt the man's vulnerability. For the first time in his life, he looked at the life of an older man with a sense that it was a picture of his own future — not just prosperity, success, and respect, but also the grinding struggle against the relentless assault of years, the accumulation of enemies, the doubtful hope of a legacy. He thought of his own father, and his feelings softened a bit.

Coke was looking at him, he realized. "Clem was kind to me, as you have been, and I will always remember that, with gratitude," he said. Sounded lame. He added, "Sir, if I have learned anything in my service to you, it is that there are many men in this kingdom who are willing to pick up the mantle when you are ready to lay it down. Perhaps the loyalty of a son is a legacy in its own right."

Coke was silent for a moment. Roger felt he had to say more.

Roger spoke, "Studying the *Reports* these past months has persuaded me of this much: the Law is indeed the foundation of all government, regardless of what the King and his lackeys imagine. Men of reason and integrity — and there are many of them — recognize this fact. As long as men will defend the Law, the tyrants will not rest easy."

Coke smiled at this with his eyes closed, nodded, then looked at Roger with a hint of a tear in his eye. "And that is why we cannot yield to the King's demand. Whatever the cost, we dare not yield." *We*, he had said. Roger realized that his destiny was now linked to that of Lord Edward Coke. He felt a surge of energy as if he had suddenly received a touch of divine fire.

Before Roger knew it, September had come; it was time to return to Hatton House. This time, he rode to London — on Maggie, the mare he had been riding all summer. Coke and his retainers rode alongside, and they kept up a brisk pace, trotting most of the way, leaving Wilkins and his wagon far behind.   The heat and humidity of summer were past; a refreshing breath of cooler weather accompanied them on their way. Fields were ripe for harvest now, indeed, some had already been mown.

The court was in no hurry to give Lord Coke his hearing; perhaps they preferred to let him dangle for several weeks. Roger thought it might be a good sign: maybe they intended to treat him leniently, once they had made their point. It was October 2 before Lord Coke was summoned to appear before Chancellor Bacon and a panel of senior magistrates. He presented them with his one-page list of "errors" in the *Reports* and requested an audience with the King.   Bacon forwarded the paper to the King but warned James that granting an audience would suggest that a reconciliation had been accomplished.   The magistrates warned James that a summary dismissal of Coke would be unwise, given his reputation, and that arguing over opinions in the *Reports* would be fruitless — contending with Coke on his own ground might backfire.   James replied that he wanted Coke gone, and gone quickly.   Bacon responded with a 17-point indictment of Coke's past statements and decisions, but none referenced anything in the *Reports*.

On November 14, 1616, Roger was working with Lord Coke over some notes for a book he was working on. There was a knock at the door. "Sir George Coppin, with documents from the King", said a servant.

"See him in."

Roger felt the tension in the room. A communication from the King could not be refused; this was what they had been waiting for. Or maybe what they had been dreading.

Sir George held a scroll in his hand, unrolled it, and read it aloud: "For certain causes now moving us, we will that you shall be no longer our Chief Justice to hold pleas before us . . ." It was a hammer blow. Coke held himself erect and showed no emotion.

". . . and we command that you no longer interfere in that office, and by virtue of this presence, we at once remove and exonerate you from the same."

Exonerate. Not the usual meaning of the word, thought Roger. Still, the meaning was clear enough.

Edward Coke, Lord Chief Justice of the King's Bench, was no more. From now on, he was merely Sir Edward Coke, weeping for his loss.

December. 1616: Christmas in the Countryside

Roger half expected that the dismissal would drive Sir Edward to wine and despair, but it was not so. Many friends came to visit him over the next few days with words of encouragement. All his friends seemed to agree that the Law was on his side and that it was the King who was at fault.

Lady Hatton, of course, took it differently. From her point of view, Coke's dismissal was a disaster, a complete overthrow of her life's work. The Cokes had been partners for nearly twenty years, often squabbling, but always agreeing on their joint mission — to gain advancement and wealth through earning the King's (and Queen's) favor. As far as Lady Hatton was concerned, Sir Edward had failed in his duty to their marriage. This was a breach that could not be mended. Sir Edward was no longer welcome in Hatton House and went to live with his daughter in her manor near the village of Standon, some 30 miles north of London.

"Standon Lordship", as the manor was called, was immense — a mansion, really. It had been built during the reign of Queen Elizabeth by Sir Ralph Sadleir. The house reflected the wealth and status that Sir Ralph had acquired for his service to the crown — Elizabeth herself had been his guest. In due time, the house had passed to Sir Ralph's son Thomas (namesake of Thomas Cromwell, Sir Ralph's mentor during the reign of Henry VIII) and afterward to his grandson, also named Ralph, who was married to Sir Edward Coke's daughter, Anne. The Sadleirs had hosted King James in 1603, on his way to London for his coronation. Anne was only eighteen years old at the time, but managed the hospitality of their royal host so well that her reputation was firmly established for years to come. Ralph established his reputation as the very model of a country aristocrat: a generous host, an enthusiastic sportsman, celebrated for his benevolence to the poor. He did not involve himself much in political matters. His wife became known as a patron of the arts. The Sadleirs were considered reliable allies of the King;

Edward Coke's residence in their house was viewed with favor: perhaps his daughter could bring him to his senses.

It was late November. Autumn was nearly spent. A cold, windy drizzle blew in from the Northeast, spattering in the faces of Roger, Sir Edward, and the handful of retainers that accompanied him. It was a far cry from the pleasant rides of a summer morning he had enjoyed at Stoke Poges. Even Maggie seemed to find the weather daunting. When the bulky mass of the manor of Standon Lordship appeared ahead of them at last, they were all a bit chilled.

They approached the house through a gateway and into a large walled courtyard. The house itself was festooned with crenelated towers on its corners and on either side of the great doors. Chimneys sprouted everywhere. They drew up to the great double doors and announced themselves. The doors swung open, and they rode directly into the gatehouse, out of the rain. "Welcome, Lord Coke! Welcome to Standon Lordship. It has been too long since you graced these halls," said the chief steward. Other servants scurried to take charge of the horses and lead them to the stables.

"Call me Sir Edward," replied Coke. "I am Lord no more."

The steward nodded. "A grave injustice, I think. You shall always be a 'Lord' to me."

Other servants took charge of the parties' baggage and led them deeper into the great house. Roger shouldered his rucksack and was following one of the servants toward the servants' quarters when Sir Edward spoke: "Wait. The lad comes with me. Make certain that his room is near my own."

The butler looked surprised but took it in stride. "Very good, Sir. I shall make arrangements." He led them into the house and into the Great Hall, where a roaring fire was set in a large ornate fireplace. Ralph and Anne Sadleir waited there to greet them. Roger and the other retainers bowed. Sir Edward was greeted with a handshake from his son-in-law and a hug from his daughter. "The servants will show you to your rooms. You should all get out of those wet clothes. Supper will be served soon," she said.

Coke looked weary; the weather and the journey had taken their toll. Anne Sadleir gave him a concerned look.

"I am tired," admitted Coke. "A good meal will restore me." He turned to Roger and said, "This is Roger Williams, my personal secretary. I want him near me while I am here."

Anne looked surprised and gave Roger a looking-over. Roger bowed. "Do you mean that he is to eat with us?" she asked.

"Yes. I would have him sit at my right hand."

She curtseyed. "It shall be as you say."

Ralph Sadleir's table was everything it was reputed to be. After they were seated, servants carried in an entire roast pig on a large platter, followed by a goose, several ducks, and a haunch of beef. The side dishes were too numerous to count; there was ale and wine (Roger stuck with the ale) aplenty, and an array of sweetmeats and pastries. Roger was reminded of a proverb: "*When you sit down to eat with a ruler,*
consider carefully what is before you; And put a knife to your throat if you are a man given to appetite. Do not desire his delicacies, for they are deceptive food."

Sir Edward was constrained in no way; he made merry — so merry that Lady Anne directed her servants to help him up to bed and tuck him in.

Roger was on his way to bed when a servant approached him. "The Lady Anne would speak with you privately," he said, and led Roger downstairs to a sitting room, or parlor, with a fire in its ample fireplace, and a few candles for light. Anne Sadleir was seated in a large chair beside the fireplace. Roger bowed and, because there was no other place to sit, remained standing. The Lady looked him up and down.

"My Father has taken a fancy to you," she said, "and I cannot see why. Where are you from? You do not appear to be from a well-established family; at least your clothes do not say so. Your table manners are not those of a gentleman. What have you done to earn a place at my father's side?"

Roger was surprised at the directness of her questions. Where to start? "I am a tailor's son," he began. "My father is a prosperous businessman, though no more prominent than his peers. I have an uncle who was once Lord Mayor of London, though I do not think my master took me into his service for that reason. As for the way I am dressed, what you see is what Lord Coke has supplied me with. I am, as you observed, neither a gentleman nor the son of a gentleman. As far as why Lord Coke has taken me into his service, you would get a better answer from him." The expression on her face suggested that she found this last remark a little impertinent.

"And what service do you perform?"

"I take notes of meetings that he attends or thoughts that he wishes to have written down."

"Where do these 'meetings' occur? What are they about?"

Roger hesitated. Even though she was Coke's daughter, he did not suppose that he owed her a detailed account of Coke's personal affairs. His obligation to discretion might get him into trouble, but he would honor it. "Mostly they take place in his library. Sometimes also at court. Mostly they are about matters of the Law."

"Are you trained in the Law?"

Roger shook his head and smiled. "No, my Lady. I merely take note of what the greatest lawyer in the kingdom has to say." He could tell that she was a little pleased to hear her father praised so. She smiled, despite herself.

"Where else?" she persisted.

"As you surely know, Lady, Lord Coke's position (until recently) often placed him in the Court of Star Chamber. He has also been a member of the Privy Council and met from time to time with the King himself."

"And you were with him? Dressed like that?"

Roger tried to conceal his irritation. "Dressing like this, especially in the presence of the King, is merely a way to show that I know my place. My duty is to know my place, and avoid drawing attention to myself — so that greater men may conduct their business without distraction."

"That's a good answer," said Lady Sadleir, "you're either a wise and humble servant or a clever and ambitious one. What advancement do you expect from your service to my father?"

The question surprised him. Evidently, she supposed that he regarded his service as the first step in a lucrative or distinguished career, as any member of the gentry might. "Lady, I am no gentleman, as you have noted. Lord Coke took me into his service with a promise to my father that he would help me find some employment suitable to my class when I am old enough. I have yet to serve out my first year — I have six more years to go, at least, before any such 'advancement' will occur."

"Another good answer. Tell me, how do you rate my father's health? His state of mind?"

A change of subject. Good. he paused a moment. "He was very fatigued by this journey, as you saw for yourself — mostly because of the weather, I think. The King's rebuke lies heavy on him, but he is not in despair: the King's favor changes with the wind. He was in good spirits this summer at Stoke; I believe he will recover from this disappointment in time."

"I hear that woman has put him out of his house."

She could only be referring to Lady Hatton. "I am not privy to any conversations on that topic."

"No notes then?"

Roger shook his head firmly. "Lord Coke does not discuss such matters with me."

"But surely, in a house full of servants . . . ?

"A house full of servants is a house full of gossip. I avoid speaking of matters that are none of my business."

"Spoken like a man of integrity," she said with a nod, "or maybe just a man of cleverness." Roger did not reply.

She changed the topic again. "I am worried for my father's well-being. There are threats that I think he chooses to ignore. He is not a young man anymore. I fear that others may try to persuade him to take foolish risks, risks that will damage his career — all for vanity, or for their own advantage, not his. I would be grateful if you could keep me informed about any such influences that you notice."

Roger looked at her hard. Was she asking him to spy on her father?

"I would be willing to reward you, of course," she added.

Roger replied, "I already have a master who pays me fair wages for my service. I would not know how to serve two masters; it is enough if I am found worthy in serving the one."

She looked at him with a trace of annoyance. "My father is not the only one in a position to secure your future. If he is led into some further folly, he may not be able to help you. Do you wish to wager it all on one man?

Roger stood erect. His eyes were bright; "There is no man in England that I would rather wager on than your father. He has been like a father to me, and I will stake my life on him, and serve him as best I can."

She gave him a disapproving look. "Words well spoken. Time will tell whether you can live up to them. My father has a way of inspiring admiration and loyalty in other men. He also inspires hostility and enmity in others. I do not understand it, but I fear that it will be his ruin."

Roger nodded. He was well aware of Sir Edward's influence on people.

"You understand my concern, then?"

"I understand that your father is a great man and that others look to him for leadership. I also know that he has enemies, mostly men who are envious of his abilities or who see him as an obstacle to their ambitions. I think it must be the destiny of men like your father to attract enemies and inspire followers. I think he has one advantage that his enemies do not appreciate — his mind is governed by principles, not by mere ambition or overweening pride. In the end, I believe that principle will triumph over self-seeking." Roger was surprised at the words coming out of his mouth, but they rang true.

"Triumph? What triumph? My father is out of government, disgraced, put out of his own home!"

"I do not think that will be the end of the tale. He still has many friends, both in and out of government, and I have not observed that Lady Hatton's feelings are the same from one week to the next."

"You have made a fair assessment of that woman," Anne Sadleir conceded, "but his friends have not proven strong enough to protect his position."

Roger nodded again. "Not yet. Perhaps not this year, or the next. But sooner or later, his integrity will speak for him, and other men will rally to him."

"That is small comfort to him now," she replied. "I would rather see him reconciled to his king and his government. What would prevent that, besides his stubbornness?"

"I believe that Francis Bacon, the Lord Chancellor, will prevent that, with all the resources at his disposal. There will be no reconciliation while Lord Bacon has the King's ear."

She looked intently at him. "Well, you are not the simple lackey that you pretend to be, as I suspected. You see and hear more than you admit, and you keep your own counsel. I believe you are loyal to your master, as well you should be. Take care that you do not open your eyes to things that you should not see, nor entertain notions that have no place in any man's heart." It sounded like a dismissal. Roger bowed and left the room.

They stayed at Standon Lordship through Christmas. Sir Edward received a string of visitors, mostly from London. Clem Coke visited briefly as well. Roger sat in on most of these meetings and often took no notes. But it was clear that Sir Edward was not going to simply disappear into a quiet retirement in the countryside. People brought tidbits of news from the Royal Court, or London more generally; much of it gossip, as far as Roger was concerned. One visitor was the exception — Sir Ralph Winwood, the King's Secretary of State, and member of the Privy Council. Winwood was the one member of the Privy Council who still expressed loyalty to Sir Edward Coke. It became clear why this was so, as the two spoke together in Roger's presence (Coke had signaled him not to take notes). Winwood shared Coke's mistrust of Spain, his distaste for the

Howards' pro-Spanish policies, and the general corruption of the Court. He was also alarmed at the King's assertions of "prerogative" at the expense of traditional rights. None of this was mentioned to Lady Anne, of course, who saw in Winwood's visit a hopeful possibility that Winwood could move her father toward reconciliation with the King. She was not entirely wrong — though Sir Edward was far from softening his position to mollify King James. Rather, the two men were plotting to return Sir Edward to the King's favor by another route — a route that led through George Villiers, Earl of Buckingham, or more precisely, through his mother, Lady Mary Villiers Compton. Lady Compton's appetite for money had not abated, and it was reported that her eldest son, John Villiers, was still enamored of Sir Edward's youngest daughter, Frances. A marriage into the Earl of Buckingham's family could lead to Coke's return to royal favor.

Roger took all this in with a mixture of sadness and disappointment. He could not imagine Francis Coke married to anyone without a sense that some vague hope had been dashed, some dream extinguished. He understood, of course, that she must be married to someone eventually, and that it would not be to a man like himself. But she had taken on the dimensions of an ideal in his imagination, a paragon of womanly virtues, tantalizing and untouchable. Anything so crass as a matrimonial negotiation seemed unworthy of who she was. But of course, not everyone saw her as he did; she had many admirers, each with his own idea of who she was. Something in him withered at the thought of her as someone's wife — a harsh reminder of how humble his estate was, how young, how powerless he was to make his own dreams reality. It tasted a little bitter to be reminded in such a blunt way of his insignificance.

Sir Edward Coke's feelings were mixed as well. Frances was his youngest child, and he doted on her. He felt a sense of pride when her charm and beauty were lavished with praise. But he had a duty to find a good husband for her and to do so in a way that enhanced the power and influence of his family. The present opportunity simply raised the stakes a little. Coke was not merely playing for his own career; the future of his nation was at stake. Coke had one card left to play in his contest with Francis Bacon, and Frances Coke was that card — a high card, by his estimation, high enough perhaps to win the pot, if it were played skillfully enough.

Lady Hatton, of course, was likely to prevent the match if she could. The negotiations would have to be kept secret. Success, if it came, might well spell the end of his marriage. High stakes indeed.

At breakfast one morning in December, Lady Anne Sadleir decided to direct Sir Edward's attention to Roger. "Papa, look at your secretary. Do you not see how shabbily he dresses?"

Coke looked a bit surprised and directed his gaze to Roger, who was definitely surprised at this invitation to everyone at the table to inspect his clothing. He felt self-conscious, a little stung with humiliation.

"He dresses thus because it serves my purpose when others overlook him or underestimate him," Coke replied at last. If I dressed him in a gentleman's attire, I would have to dress myself more lavishly as well, lest people become confused at which of us is which!" Coke laughed at his own joke and added, "It is convenient for me that he dresses the way he does." Roger said nothing but felt the eyes of the whole room upon him. He was blushing, he realized.

"It is not convenient for me," said Lady Anne. "He looks like he belongs with the other servants. If he must dress like them, he should eat with them." There it was. Lady Anne was offended by Roger's position in her house — he was out of place and should be put back where he belonged.

Coke stood up. "Very well, you are the mistress of this house. It shall be as you say." He turned to Roger and said, "Come, master Williams. We must find our way to the servant's quarters if we are to finish our breakfast." Roger stood. The rest of the room was silent. Lady Anne looked confused; a multitude of emotions played across her face.

"Papa, don't be unreasonable," she protested. "It would only embarrass me if it got out that I made you eat with the servants."

"Embarrass you? Rather, you might be embarrassed to be known as a woman who humiliates other men's servants publicly. It does not speak well of your breeding. You should have spoken to me privately if this situation truly offends you."

"Please, both of you, sit down," said Lady Anne. To the whole room, she said, "My father and I will speak of this later."

Roger had lost his appetite. Sir Edward whispered to him, "Dig in. Eat as though this house were your own," and followed his own advice.

Roger was not privy to the discussion of his attire that occurred later that morning. When Sir Edward summoned him, he informed Roger of the outcome. "We have reached a compromise," said Coke. "You will eat with me, as you have done. However, something must be done about the way you dress, as long as you are a guest in this house. I have called for a tailor, who will outfit you as befits your station. Once we return to my house, you will dress as I see fit."

The tailor appeared that very same afternoon. He looked at Roger, took some measurements, inspected his clothing, and clucked his tongue a little. There was some discussion with Sir Edward about colors and fabrics. In the end, a kind of compromise was agreed upon. Roger was presented a few days later with two complete sets of clothes, including underwear and stockings. One set was dark brown — hose, doublet, and jacket, with a new shirt that sported a broad, flat collar such as a low-ranking clergyman or a shop owner might wear, folded down over the front. The collar had only modest ornamentation, but it was an upgrade over his other clothing.

The other set of clothes was more flamboyant. The doublet was blue, with embroidery at the cuffs, and puffed out at the upper arms. There were slits in the fabric, called "jags", to reveal a russet lining. The hose were of the same material, but cut fuller, and gathered at the knee. The stockings were russet, to match the sleeves on the doublet. There was a good bit of lace in the collar of the shirt, and it was ruffled. "Something to wear to a party," chuckled Coke.

"What party?"

"My daughter is hosting a Twelfth Night gala this year. Can't have you looking shabby. Wear the brown to supper and dinner, save the blue for Christmas."

At least the clothes were comfortable; Roger realized just how constricting his other clothes had become.

Lady Anne expressed her approval of Roger's new clothing at supper that evening. She addressed her remarks to Sir Edward, rather than Roger, as was proper: "He doesn't look that shabby when he is properly dressed," she said. Then, "Papa, I think I shall have use for him. Will you lend him to me?"

"What use?"

"We are hosting the other families on the manor for Twelfth Night, and we shall have dancing. Sadly, there are more young women available than young men. I would make a dancer of him so that the ladies will not be idled for lack of partners."

Sir Edward looked at Roger. "Have you ever danced?"

"I know some reels and country dances. I am no courtier."

"Nor should you wish to be. But I think it could be to your advantage to receive some instruction." He looked at Lady Anne. "You can have him for an hour or so, for the next few days." She smiled as she bowed her head.

The dancing instructor was a lean, gangly old servant named Clifton. He proved to be quite nimble for a man of his years and expected younger men to be as graceful as he was. Roger quickly recognized the reason that Lady Anne had drafted him: there were more than a dozen men of various ages and physical condition in the ballroom, but they were outnumbered by an array of female servants, who cast decidedly skeptical looks at their potential partners. A glance at his companions told Roger why: they were a motley collection — a few looked as if they were comfortable on a dance floor; most showed evidence of years of Ralph Sadleir's reputed generosity in matters culinary. Still, Roger thought, all of them must have grown up with the dances proper to their class. How likely was it that they had somehow forgotten the dances of their youth?

The answer came from the dancing master, "Lady Sadleir is hosting a ball for the gentry of our district, come Twelfth Night. She has decided that there will be dancing — not only the country dancing that you are familiar with but also courtly dancing, as befits the nobler among her guests." He lowered his voice a little, "Truth to tell, there are not that many of her guests acquainted with the court, but she is determined that her Twelfth Night will be none the lesser for that. It will not do for her guests to be denied a minuet or a gavotte, simply because there are too few dancers to fill the ranks. The ranks, in short, must be filled by all of you." There were raised eyebrows among the men, and a few excited whispers from the women.

"To begin with, each man must take a partner," said Clifton. "For this first lesson, women may partner with women — the steps are the same . . ."

He stepped them through a pavane—a slow, dignified processional dance. The men got rather the sharpest of his corrections: "Lightly, lightly on your feet!" he proclaimed, "Point the toes! Point the toes!" The women seemed to understand him implicitly, giggling or snickering at the men's quest for grace of feet.

They also learned a minuet — partners in rows, none too quick. The galliard was more lively and required more energy. The faster tempo concealed some of the men's awkwardness, and Roger thought he was doing pretty well. Clifton begged to disagree. He appeared to be exasperated. "It's no good to simply hop up and down. You have to be *light* on your feet!" Clifton demonstrated. He was indeed light on his feet — surprising for a man of his years, thought Roger.

There were more lessons as the days passed, and Christmas approached. At some point, the whole 'lightness" business began to feel natural to Roger. Some of the others still struggled. The women seemed to have noticed this and often preferred Roger as their partner. Among them was Bridget, a short, plump young woman with red hair and a confident air. Clifton decided that she and Roger made a good couple and began to use them to demonstrate his technique. "There! See that? That's what it's supposed to look like!"

Clifton, it turned out, was looking to winnow out a few couples to learn a more difficult dance. The Italians called it "La Volta", or "the vault". It was a long-established crowd-pleaser, said to be a favorite of the old Queen Elizabeth. The signature move of La Volta involved a turning lift: the man grasped his partner's middle with one hand on the small of her back, and the other on her waist or belly. Then, turning clockwise on his right leg, he lifted her off the ground, using the upper part of his left leg to support her . . . bottom. The lady steadied herself by resting her right hand on the man's shoulder while arching her back, her feet pointed gracefully at the ground, and her left arm sailing free, like the wing of a bird. It was necessary, of course, that she land lightly and gracefully, as well.

The first time Roger tried it with Bridget, it was awkward, but she was game to try it again, and soon they were doing it smoothly, Bridget smiling and squealing just a little as she soared in the air. Then other young women lined up to take their turn as well. Roger began to tire. Clifton noticed and came to his rescue. "That is enough for one day," he said. "We'll practice more tomorrow."

As Christmas approached, Clifton had four couples that he deemed skilled enough to perform La Volta; the rest of his trainees would perform the other dances.

Roger kept bumping into Bridget — nearly every day — despite his duties and the size of the house. It was clear that the Twelfth Night feast was much on her mind.

"Did the ladies tire you?" she asked.

Roger nodded. "Aye, a little. I think that Twelfth Night will be a challenge for my stamina."

Bridget smiled. "Be at ease. You have had many partners, but on Twelfth Night you shall be mine. I will not push you beyond your limits."

Roger wondered what she supposed his limits might be. He wondered what hers might be.

Christmas came, and with it the merriment and foolishness that the season demanded. Sir Ralph Sadleir was generous to the wassailers and the roving mummers, tolerant of the Lord of Misrule when he appeared at the gates of Standon Lordship. There were fewer public demonstrations of generosity, as well: servants were dispatched to all the poorest families of the nearby village with bundles and baskets of food to aid their celebration of the season. This typically took place in the afternoon, without fanfare. On one occasion, Roger was told to report to the kitchen to help with a delivery. When he arrived, Bridget was there. "I asked particularly for you to assist me," she said. "It's a large family — more than I can carry by myself." It was true. There were two large wicker baskets with covers and a rolled-up bundle of fabric.

Roger went to fetch his coat, then had a thought. He walked to the stable and asked a stablehand to saddle Maggie for him. Then he went back to fetch Bridget, now wrapped in a cloak. "I thought you might prefer to ride," he said, as he led her back toward the stables, "since you so clearly enjoy vaulting."

She giggled and blushed a little. "Just how do you think we shall ride, with all of this to carry?"

"I didn't say that *we* would ride, I said that you might. We can tie the bundle on the horse's back. You can ride with one basket, I will lead the horse and carry the other."

"Aye, a lady should ride," she giggled. It took a stepladder for her to get into the saddle, where she sat sideways. Roger tied the bundle behind the saddle, handed one basket to Bridget, and lifted the other — which gave him one free hand to lead Maggie into the village.

The place they were headed was on the other side of the village. The cottage, if it could be called that, was small, with a dirt floor. There was a fireplace and a fire. The air was smoky, the room not much warmer than the outside. The woman inside appeared to have at least five children; there could have been others who were old enough to be at work, somewhere.

"Sir Ralph Sadleir sends greetings at Christmas tide," said Bridget.

"Thank you, Lady," replied the woman, with a curtsey.

Bridget looked around the place. "Have you enough wood for the fire?"

"Bless you, Lady, we do — thanks to Sir Ralph. Please thank him for us. God bless him and you for remembering us."

Bridget bit her lip. "I shall ask him to send more. It is cold at this season."

The woman bowed again. "Thank you, Lady."

With that, they excused themselves. The cold was noticeably sharper outside now.

"She called me 'Lady'", observed Bridget. "Lady Anne would have taken exception if she were here, but it seemed rude to correct the woman. She meant no harm."

Roger nodded. He helped Bridget back onto Maggie's back. Then he took the reins and started back through the village.

"Must I ride alone? There is room up here for another." She smiled a crooked, mischievous smile.

Roger nodded again and got up behind her. He was seated behind the saddle, but the reins were long enough to reach back to where he was. Bridget was still seated sideways, with his arms on either side of her. She smiled and leaned on him slightly. "That's better. We'll make more progress this way."

Roger kept the horse to a walk, just to ensure that neither of them fell off. It was better than walking — for one thing, the body heat from Maggie took the edge off the cold.

On the way back through the village, they encountered several people who knew Bridget. Of course, she had to exchange greetings with them, to be sure that they saw her on the horse, in the arms of a strange man . . . she would be talked about this evening, for sure. "You know," she said quietly, "I was born and raised in a cottage no bigger than that one." She was looking into his eyes for some hint of surprise or acknowledgment, her face close to his.

"Was it in this village?"

"Nay, but not far away."

"Are your parents still living?"

"My father lives. Mama is dead now five years."

"I am sorry to hear that." The horse was exhaling clouds of steam in the chill. Roger couldn't think of anything else to say. Bridget's life had been a hard one — nothing like his own.

"What of your family?"

"My mother and father still live in the city — or rather just outside it. I have three brothers and two sisters. My father is a tailor and does well enough to support them all. *But we always had wooden floors*, he thought to himself. He didn't say so.

"Are you the oldest?"

"Nay, my brother Sydrach is three years older than I — eighteen by now, soon to be on his own."

"Wait. Are you telling me that you are only fifteen years old?" She sat up in the saddle, as if startled, or as if Roger had said something crude.

Roger nodded. "Tall for my age, they say," he smiled sheepishly.

"I took you for older," said Bridget. There was disappointment in her voice. She asked no more questions until they arrived back at the manor house.

Twelfth night came at last — the final day of Christmas, and the most celebrated. Lady Anne had busied herself with preparations for her ball to assure success. The great hall was decorated, the musicians hired, and the food prepared. Guests began arriving in the late afternoon (some traveled a good distance, and dark fell early at this time of year) and continued to stream in until it was full dark. A bell rang, and Lady Anne announced the beginning of the entertainment: "Let the dancing begin!"

Roger and Bridget were waiting in the next room with the other dancers. A few of Lady Anne's guests were familiar with court dances — or claimed to be — so they were waiting to make their entrance, as well. When the music began, they took their turn entering the Great Hall to the measured tones of the minuet.

Roger was wearing his blue doublet with the russet hose. Bridget was dressed up; she had done something with her hair, and there was a noticeable aroma of some fragrance about her. Her movements seemed a little stiff — nervous, maybe? Or perhaps she was simply moving as she thought a 'Lady' should . . .

The musicians moved from the minuet straight into a gavotte. The transition was not as smooth as Clifton would have liked, but Lady Anne's guests had more difficulty than her trained servants did. It took a few measures for everyone to get back in step, but there was scattered applause, as well as laughter when they managed it.

The *piece de resistance* of this performance was supposed to be 'La Volta'. It occurred to Roger that Lady Anne's guests might be at a disadvantage here — they probably hadn't been practicing as much or as recently as he and Bridget and the other servants had. Had to make the best of it and hope that no one got injured.

At the opening strains of La Volta, three pairs of Lady Anne's guests smiled and withdrew from the floor. The audience chuckled sympathetically. That left two guest couples and the four servant couples. Roger looked at Bridget. She was flushed, smiling, winking once at him. At the vault, she moved confidently to him, then soared upward with a little squeal; the audience heard her and tittered at her enjoyment of the moment. Something felt different to Roger. She was stiffer, somehow; he had to adjust his grip on her midsection. One of the guest couples nearly took a fall and withdrew before it was time for the next vault. The rest soldiered on and completed the dance to cheers and applause from the rest of the guests. Roger, Bridget, and the rest acknowledged the applause with a bow. Lady Anne appeared to be pleased. Then it was time for the rest of the crowd to join in — circle dances and reels now, simpler but safer.

Bridget, Roger, and the rest of the servants retreated to the back of the room so that the guests could dance nearer the musicians. "I nearly lost you on the first vault," said Roger. "I don't know why it felt so different."

Bridget feigned annoyance. "I'm wearing stays," she said, "like a proper lady. That's why it feels different."

There were other servants inviting him to dance, now, but Bridget spoke sharply to them. "I said you would be mine on Twelfth Night, and I intend to keep my promise," she said. Some of the dances, like the allemande, involved changing partners as it proceeded, but Bridget stuck with Roger as closely as she could. Among the household servants, a sharp look from Bridget was usually enough warning. Servants who had accompanied Lady Anne's guests needed more persuading. "I told that hussy you were only fifteen, but she wouldn't back off until I threatened her," Bridget whispered to him.

Roger was confused as to why his age mattered, but he resolved to enjoy the dancing while his stamina lasted.

The guests who lived nearby began to leave, taking their servants with them. Some of those from farther away would be staying the night. Sleeping arrangements would have to be adjusted to accommodate them — guests and servants both. And of course, everyone had had plenty to drink. It was a recipe for . . . irregularities. It occurred to Roger that Bridget may have something of the sort in mind. As the crowd dwindled, she approached him with a purposeful look on her face.   "Roger Williams," she said, "thank you for a most memorable evening. It was not the evening that I imagined, but that is not your fault. Would to God you were eighteen years old, as I am, or even better, twenty. I had hopes for us, but I cannot promise you I will wait until you are grown."

Roger realized then how close he had come to . . . what? Something he was unprepared for, in any case. "I will remember this evening with fondness, as well," he replied. He couldn't think of anything else to say that would do justice to the situation.

January 1617: Much Ado

It was the second week in January when a rider appeared at Standon Lordship with a message for Sir Edward. Roger and Sir Edward were going over some notes for the next edition of the *Reports* when the messenger arrived. He was not from London, but rather from Stoke Poges. Coke opened the letter with a curious frown. "It's from old Cedric, the butler," he stated, then read some more. Roger watched as his face expressed surprise, then anger, and finally resolve. He put the letter down and exhaled slowly. "We must go to Stoke today," he told Roger, "Pack your belongings, and . . . no, first take a letter to my son Clement. He must have a part in this adventure, also."

It took more than an hour to pack their things, prepare the horses, and say their farewells. Sir Edward was engaged in a long conversation with his daughter, the Lady Anne. She did not appear to be pleased with what they discussed. It was midmorning before they got on their way — Sir Edward, Roger, and six retainers, all mounted, plus several pack animals with their luggage. It was a chilly day, but not much wind. The previous night's frost had melted away under the feeble sunlight that found its way through high, thin clouds.

"Stoke Poges is nearly fifty miles away," Coke explained, "It will take most of two days to get there, and this day is nearly half spent." They proceeded at a slow trot to get the most out of the horses. As the day warmed a bit, Sir Edward shared a few details of their mission. "I have received troubling news about events at my manor at Stoke," he said, "I must verify for myself whether this news is true. If even half of what Cedric has written is true, it will require all these men" — he tossed his head in the direction of his armed retainers — "and more to make things right."

By noon, they reached Hertford and stopped to eat and rest the horses. Then it was on to Hatfield, southwesterly. The roads were not crowded, which was a good thing, since Sir Edward was becoming impatient. Roger still didn't know what was in the letter from Cedric. Had the government made some move against Sir Edward by seizing some of his personal property?

It grows dark early in January. They stopped to spend the night in Watford, much to Sir Edward's reluctance, because the weather was turning against them — rain mixed with sleet, driven by a northerly wind. "Extra oats for the horses tonight," Sir Edward ordered, "we'll be pushing them hard on the morrow."

In the morning, there was a light dusting of snow on the ground, but the weather was clearing. True to his word, Sir Edward pushed the horses hard — a few miles at the gallop, followed by a few miles at a walk, then back to the gallop again. Noonday came and went, but Coke was unwilling to stop to eat. An hour or so after midday, they arrived at their destination.

Roger had not seen the place in winter. It appeared a little exposed to him, like a man stripped of his outer clothing, shivering a little in his underwear — the thickets and groves around the place were without their leaves; the pond to the west was clearly visible from the house.

At least he had no trouble at the front door; Cedric admitted him along with the rest of the party and even had a nod of recognition and a smile for him. Perhaps it was the new clothes.

Sir Edward proceeded to walk all through the house, accompanied by Cedric. He appeared to be looking for something — going through the cupboards and closets in room after room. Cedric spoke to him in lowered tones from time to time. Roger and the retainers found their way to the kitchen for a late dinner. Flossie was there and smiled when she recognized Roger. "You have missed Lady Hatton," she murmured. "She was here not two days ago, but is now returned to London."

Roger was surprised at that bit of news. Could Sir Edward's hasty return have anything to do with it?

Sir Edward appeared in the kitchen, accompanied by Cedric. "I have been robbed," he declared, "the victim of a great embezzlement, inflicted upon me by my wife!"

Lady Hatton's visit to the manor at Stoke turned out to be a kind of fishing expedition. She had cast a great net to catch as much of the household furnishings at Stoke as possible, and carried them off — anything of gold or silver, anything that could be removed. Two wagonloads, according to Cedric. In their place, she had left some cheap replicas of her catch, as if to hope that no one would notice what she had accomplished. It was a raid worthy of a buccaneer.

Cedric, of course, had detected the substitutions immediately: he had spent a lifetime polishing and cataloging these things. And he had done the only thing he could think of to inform his master of the raid, by sending a messenger.

"My Lord, I am sorry for the loss, but I did not think it proper to oppose my mistress with force," he said with a shamefaced expression.

"You were quite right," replied Coke. "The woman is a monster. She might have had you arrested — or worse, scratched your eyes out — if you had opposed her openly. The matter is in my hands now, as it should be. Roger, come with me and bring your tablet. We must take inventory of everything that has been taken and every counterfeit that has been left in its place."

The "inventory" took all afternoon. It turned out that Sir Edward had kept records of everything he had purchased for the house over the years, as well as most of the gifts he had received. Lady Hatton had not thought to destroy those records, and Sir Edward's memory turned out to be exceedingly precise about the value of his property, in any case. Gratefully, none of his books or notes were missing; Lady Hatton had not seen the value in them.

The evening meal was quiet, as if Sir Edward were digesting more than his dinner. Roger could only guess why Lady Hatton had raided the place; apparently, she saw the family fortune as a sinking ship and was determined to salvage as much of the cargo as possible for herself. He could also only guess at Sir Edward's next move; he was certain that there would be one.

Roger slept soundly that night — cozy room, familiar bed. Shortly before noon on the following day, there was a commotion outside. It was "fighting Clem" with a dozen armed companions. Sir Edward was delighted to see them. He embraced Clem and greeted the rest of the men with a shout: "Well come, stout fellows. Welcome to my home!"

Sir Edward and Clem sat before the fire in the library, with Roger off to the side. Sir Edward explained what had happened.

Clem shook his head. "Treacherous woman. She has outdone herself."

Sir Edward nodded, then chuckled. "I have to admire her audacity. She is a woman who knows what she wants and does not dither about seizing it."

"Where has she taken this 'loot', do you suppose? Back to London?"

Sir Edward shrugged. "We shall certainly search for it there, but I think she is cleverer than that. We may find what we seek in her castle, in Dorset."

"Corfe Castle? It may be hard to retrieve it from there."

Coke shook his head. "Not so. It has not been garrisoned since Christopher Hatton bought it from Queen Elizabeth. The fortifications are in disrepair. It is just a big, damp house with a wall around it, now."

"In that case, I can take it with the men I brought with me."

Sir Edward nodded. "First, we'll go to London. If Lady Hatton has not been there lately, we can make a fair guess as to where she and my treasure are."

They left for London early next morning, in a drizzling mist. The party was twenty-strong now, and turned the road into a wet, muddy mess with their passing. They arrived at Hatton house in the late afternoon, mud-spattered and chilly.

The servants seemed surprised to see Sir Edward at the house, but they scurried to take the horses in charge and see to their guest's hospitality. "Where is your mistress?" Sir Edward demanded.

"Alas, Lady Hatton is not here. She left more than a week ago, and did not say where she was headed."

Coke snorted, "I supposed as much. Tell the cook that we will be feeding an extra score of guests this evening, and find lodging for them wherever you can under my roof."

"Welcome home, Papa."

Roger turned at the sound of the familiar voice. Frances Coke, curtseying and smiling at her father. Isabel stood just behind her and smiled at Roger with a wink.

Coke's face lit up, "Dearest daughter! Come greet your Father." He embraced her and asked, "Did your mother leave you here all alone, then?"

"Hardly alone, Papa. You forget that I am nearly grown now. Mary is here. The house is full of servants."

He held her at arm's length. "Aye, I forgot. I remember when I carried you on my shoulders . . . Did your mother say where she was going?"

"Nay," Frances replied," she said she had some financial matters to straighten out. I supposed she was going to visit you at Standon or Stoke. Mary, myself, and her maid, Isabel, were left here. What is going on, Papa? Why all the coming and going? Has some misfortune befallen Mama?"

Sir Edward sighed and smiled. "Nothing that should worry you, my sweet. Your mother was at Stoke a few days ago, but she left before I arrived. I need to speak with her. If she is not here, I am sure she will be found elsewhere. Let me get out of these wet clothes, and we shall speak over supper."

Roger, by now, had retrieved his baggage and was lugging it up to the servant's quarters in the attic. He was waylaid by Isabel, who had questions and news, as usual: "Tell me the truth. Have they quarreled again? How bad is it this time? Lady Hatton was in high dudgeon when she left here, that I can tell you!"

Roger shook his head. "I know of no quarrel. I have not seen Lady Hatton since last I was in this house, and neither has Sir Edward, as far as I know. We were at Standon until four days ago, then rushed to Stoke, and now here." (He deliberately left out the details about the missing household items at Stoke and the inventory he had compiled; that seemed a matter for discretion.)

"Did Sir Edward travel to Stoke expecting to meet Lady Hatton there?"

"I think he may have. He was certainly disappointed to learn that she was not there when he arrived. (This was mostly true, though Roger, without adding any awkward details.)

"And then he rushed here, with a body of armed men, hoping to find her safe at home, or barring that, prepared to rescue her from some peril?" Isabel was excited at the thought, Roger realized.

Roger shrugged. "I cannot say more than I have said. The situation is delicate."

Isabel's eyes were bright. "A bold and gallant deed. A man rallies to defend his lady." Then, "Oh, I hope that she has not met with some misfortune. I am sure that Sir Edward and his men will soon put things aright."

Roger nodded. "I am sure that they will."

"And you have a part in this adventure, too. Don't try to deny it."

Roger shrugged. "Any part that I play in this matter is a small one. I serve Sir Edward, that is all."

"You are too modest, as always." She took his arm, pulled him close, and kissed him.

Roger excused himself, blushing a little. She noticed and giggled. He had no sooner stowed his belongings in the attic than he heard a summons from downstairs. Sir Edward had a job for him.

"We must do here what we did at Stoke," said Sir Edward, "I have already noticed that a few items of silver plate appear to be missing, and I expect that there are more. Get your tablet, and walk with me."

By suppertime, they had made the rounds of all the common rooms on the main floor of the house, as well as the bed chambers of Sir Edward, Lady Hatton, and their daughters. Once again, Sir Edward's recollection of the value and provenance of his personal belongings was clear and exhaustive. They didn't check the servant's quarters: "Nothing of value there," said Coke.

Sir Edward noted that nearly all of Lady Hatton's gowns were still hanging in her quarters and ordered the servants to remove them all, along with any other personal items that she might have left behind. He had them locked up in a storage area in the basement, with strict orders that no one allow her to get to them. For good measure, he kept all the keys to the area on his person.

They ate late that evening. The dining hall was full with Sir Edward, Clement, Roger, and the seventeen armed retainers that they had brought with them. Frances Coke and her sister Mary took on the role of Ladies of the House in their mother's absence. Sir Edward was generous with the wine, which the retainers appreciated, and things got raucous before the meal was finished. Clement sat next to Sir Edward, and Roger overheard him say, "It must be at Corfe. You can add four of my men to your party. You know what you have to do." Clem nodded.

The following morning, Clem and his men left early, with a great commotion. Roger noted that they had added two large freight wagons to their cavalcade; apparently, they were confident that they would find what they were looking for.

Roger was wearing the blue doublet with fancy sleeves since his brown suit had gotten muddy on the journey. More than one servant in the house commented on his changed appearance over breakfast. "I hope you're not dressing up on my account," said Isabel with a wink; "if we had known this was a formal occasion, we would have put on airs of our own." Roger smiled and said, "These old rags? It's the best I could do until the laundress has cleaned my work clothes." Several people chuckled at his jest, but he sensed an undercurrent of doubt: if his clothing was indeed a sign of some promotion, then the hierarchy of relationships among the servants would have to shift in response. Changes, even minor ones, introduced an element of uncertainty.

Later that day, Roger was on his way to the laundry in the basement to fetch his newly cleaned clothes when he heard his name called.

"Roger Williams." It was Frances Coke, standing in a doorway, simply dressed yet looking gorgeous as ever, if not more so. The sound of her voice and her utterance of just his name stopped him in his tracks; something clutched in his chest, delightful and terrifying at the same time. "Yes, Lady?"

"Come. I would speak with thee." Her eyes were luminous, lovely, compelling.

Thee was an archaic word that was used by a social superior to address someone of lower status; it also suggested intimacy — an intimacy bred from affection, or just the intimacy that every master exercised over the personal affairs of their servants. Roger could not refuse her, nor did he wish to. Something in the back of his mind warned him that she was using her charms quite consciously to bend his will to hers. He was willing to be bent.

He followed her into the next room. She turned to him and looked into his eyes — imploringly, now, as a frightened child. Roger was stirred with feelings of protectiveness.

"You must tell me what is going on with my parents," she said. "Has something happened to my mother? What is all this 'inspection' you have been doing? Where is Clem bound with all those men?"

"Lady, your parents should speak for themselves in such matters."

"They do not speak to me at all. I am asking you — because I think you will tell the truth, however unflattering it may be."

Roger hesitated. "I can tell you only what I know for certain. We left — Sir Edward, his retainers, and I — Standon Lordship four days ago after Sir Edward received a message from Stoke. I do not know what the message was; I did not read it." (That was true enough in the narrow sense of the term, though Roger had a pretty good idea of what the note said.)

Roger continued, "When we got to Stoke, Sir Edward directed me to conduct an inventory of his household goods. He says that some of them are missing, and others have been 'embezzled' — substituted for similar items of lesser value. Clem arrived at Stoke on the following day with his men. The next day, we journeyed here, and I was directed to conduct another inventory. Sir Edward believes that 'embezzlement' has occurred here as well — though I suppose you would know more about that than I." Her eyes flickered a little as Roger tossed the narrative back to her.

She was not satisfied with his answer. "And where is Clem headed now?"

"Lady, I was not informed of his plans."(strictly true, no one had mentioned Corfe Castle to him directly; he had been eavesdropping).

"And what is this business of locking up Mama's gowns?"

Roger shook his head and spread his hands. "Lady, you know as much as I do about that."

"You dress as a man who knows things. Has my father promoted you in some fashion? You look like a man who has come up in the world."

"I am dressed this way because my other clothes were soiled on the journey. I am on my way to fetch them from the laundress now. In future, you will see me clad in sober brown, not this . . . getup."

"The 'getup' flatters you. You have a good-looking leg. How did you come by it?"

Her frank remarks about his appearance flustered him a little. "Lady Anne Sadleir convinced Sir Edward that I should be more . . . gaily clad. She thought me too shabby for her house, especially at Christmas."

"My step-sister did you a favor, I think. You could pass for a young gentleman in that garb."

Roger chuckled despite himself. "Lady, I do not wish to pass for anything more than what I am."

"And what exactly are you, Roger Williams? My step-sister seems to think that you are more than what you appeared to be just months ago. Who can say what you may become?"

The question cut him, inside. It was not a question he dared ask himself, not one that he wanted to consider with Frances Hatton standing there, radiant in her youthful beauty, those mesmerizing eyes . . . Thankfully, she changed the subject: "You say you prefer to dress in brown?"

"Aye, it seems more suited to my work."

"Then why would you wear the other? Did Lady Sadleir have some occasion for you to wear it?

Roger nodded. "It was for the dancing, I think. She wanted me to look the part."

"Dancing?" Frances' eyes narrowed a bit.

"Lady Sadleir needed some young men to learn court dancing for Twelfth Night — not enough of her guests were skilled enough for the performance she had planned, so I and a few others were 'recruited' to fill the ranks, so to speak."

"Court dances? Which ones?"

"The allemande, the minuet, the galliard. Oh, and the volta, as well."

"You danced La Volta." It was not a question, more like a challenge, with a dose of skepticism.

"It was only at the beginning of the evening, as an entertainment for her guests. Afterward, it was country dancing, and everyone joined in."

"Sounds like a merry party. How do I know you are telling the truth?"

"What would I have to gain by a lie?"

She pursed her lips. "I have a way to find out." She walked across the room, opened a door to the hallway, and called for a servant. "Find Isabel, and tell her to come to me. Tell her to bring Nigel and his tambour, and a recorder."

It took only a few minutes for the others to arrive. Roger was too curious to be bored; besides, he could not simply walk away from his Master's daughter without an explicit dismissal. And the nearness of Francis Coke was delightful and terrifying at the same time.

Isabel walked in, saw Roger, and smiled. She gave Frances a quizzical look. "This fellow is handsome enough, don't you agree?"

Isabel grinned and replied, "Handsome is as handsome does, my Lady."

"Quite so. he *says* he can dance. We will prove him today with your help."

Isabel smiled and curtseyed. "At your service, Lady."

The servant named Nigel entered with a small drum and a recorder. Roger could guess now what was coming. He was going to dance for the ladies.

Frances took the recorder and blew a few notes to warm up. Turning to Nigel, she said, "You know the tempo for La Volta, don't you?" Nigel nodded. "Then play," she said. She gestured for Isabel to join Roger in the center of the room.

"Do you know this dance?" he asked her.

"The question is, do <u>you</u> know it?" she replied with an impish grin.

Once the tempo was established, Frances began to play the tune. Roger took Isabel's hand and began the familiar steps. When it came time for the vault, she placed her right hand firmly on his shoulder. He placed his hands about her waist. She was wearing no stays — he could feel her supple muscles in his hands as she arched her back and soared, with a little squeal of excitement, her free hand soaring, her feet walking on air, spinning wide. When she landed, she landed softly, her eyes bright, a little flushed. Three more lifts and the song was over.

"What say you, Isabel? Can he dance?" Frances' tone told Roger that she had already made up her mind on the question.

Isabel was a little short of breath. "I believe he'll do, Lady. I believe he'll do."

Roger thought he had proved his point, and made as to leave.

"Wait!" said Frances. She handed the recorder to Isabel, walked up to Roger, and looked into his eyes. "My turn," she said.

Nigel began on the tambour, Isabel joined him on the recorder. Once again, the familiar steps. Frances gave Roger what he supposed was intended to be a flirtatious, seductive look: he realized that she was play-acting a role, as she might well do at a court ball, but it tugged at him nonetheless. When the vault came, he could feel her muscles flexing under his hands (why couldn't she have worn stays?) as she arched her back and soared, a brief smile of ecstasy on her face - this part was no act, he sensed: she was like a dove soaring above a shabby, broken world; a young woman freed, however briefly, from the cares of family, position, duty. Her soul was in it, straining against the chains of mortality, tasting freedom in the moment. He was enraptured, helpless in the instant, all his defenses overwhelmed. And then he brought her gently back to earth. Still, three more vaults to go. He would make them last as long as he could, savor the vision that she was, remember it as long as memory would last.

When the music stopped, he bowed, and she curtseyed in return. She appeared to have recovered her composure. Isabel was looking at both of them with an odd expression on her face.

"Lady," said Roger, "with your permission, I will return to my duties."

"Dismissed," she said with a polite smile and a nod.

Roger made a point of not wearing his blue doublet in the house after that. Most days, he wore his old clothing. Sir Edward seemed to approve.

Lady Hatton's coach arrived at Hatton House two days later. She was not pleased to discover that her husband had taken possession of the place. She was less pleased when her coach and horses mysteriously disappeared from the stables the next morning. She had friends and relatives living nearby — she was forced to appeal to their hospitality while she planned her next move.

Clem and his men appeared another two days later, their wagons full of household goods. Sir Edward was able to identify much of it as having been removed from the house at Stoke, and some from Hatton House, as well. There was a good bit that seemed to have come from neither place.

Clem shrugged, "We took what we could; no time to distinguish between what was embezzled and what belonged in the castle. We dared not linger long — we caught the servants by surprise, and they went into hiding, but they would have rallied, sooner or later."

Sir Edward grunted in satisfaction. "Well done, son, well done. We'll sort it all out in time."

It was not certain exactly when Lady Hatton learned that her castle in Dorset had been plundered, but according to rumor, she did not take it well.

1617: Riot and Reconciliation

In March, the King resolved to visit Scotland, the land of his birth. It was a major logistical undertaking — much of the court would travel with him. Someone had to stay behind and run the government, of course. Sir Francis Bacon was 'created' Lord Keeper of the Seal (or Chancellor) on March 7, 1617. Bacon was elated; he had at last ascended to the highest office in the land — a post held by his father under Queen Elizabeth — and now his triumph was complete. King James was disinterested in the minutiae of running a kingdom in most cases, anyway. Getting him interested in particulars was usually a matter of convincing him that his royal prerogative was under attack, somehow. Francis Bacon had done so more than once and had earned the King's trust. With James gone to Scotland for several months at least, Lord Bacon would conduct English affairs according to his own judgments.

King James would not travel so far without his favorite, the Earl of Buckingham. With Buckingham gone, the key conduit to royal favor was none other than his new Chancellor, Francis Bacon. There was a great shifting of the rivalries and alliances at court (or what was left of it); everyone wanted to be in the Chancellor's good graces.

One of Bacon's first acts was to order the construction of a new prison for the Court of High Commission. It was announced that the jailers in the new prison were not obliged to honor writs of habeas corpus — suspects could be arrested, tortured, or held indefinitely, and most importantly, secretly, without interference from lawyers and magistrates. It was a great victory for the Archbishop of Canterbury, who became a vital ally of the Chancellor in his quest for dominance in government. It was very bad news for Catholics, Separatists, and Puritans generally, and although the Court of High Commission was supposed to concern itself exclusively with religious offenses, who could be sure who they were holding, or why?

There were other, unexpected matters to deal with. It seemed that Sir Edward Coke and his wife, Lady Hatton, were engaged in some sort of feud. This would ordinarily have been of only passing interest to Lord Bacon: Coke himself was no longer any threat, and Bacon was not a vindictive man. There was history with Lady Frances Hatton, of course (it was humiliating to recall her rejection of him), but Bacon had no desire to revisit all that; upon reflection, Frances Hatton's rejection of him might have been a blessing in disguise . . .

But the Cokes would not go away. They were disputing the division of their property, and it was acrimonious. Worse, their rank and reputations were such that their conflict wound up in court - before the King's Bench, in the presence of the whole Privy Council. This was Lord Bacon's problem, like it or not.

Lady Hatton fired the first broadside. She appeared before the Council in late March, supported by a posse of her powerful friends and relatives. She scarcely needed to mention that she was on intimate terms with the Queen, but she did. She told a hair-raising story of harsh treatment from her husband, and did it with such passion that one of the Council members remarked that it was a "performance worthy of Burbage" — a reference to the famous actor Richard Burbage, who was then at the height of his career. She complained that her husband had forcibly removed her coach, her horses, and even her clothing from Hatton House; his son "fighting Clem" had raided her house at Corfe, bullying and terrifying her servants to the point that they went into hiding, and could not be found.

Sir Edward made his rebuttal immediately afterward. He had his own tale of marital abuse. Lady Hatton, he claimed, had "embezzled" all his gold and silver "plate" from Hatton House and Stoke Poges, replacing them with similar-looking brass plate, to conceal the substitution. He and Clem were merely trying to locate his missing property. In all of his argument, he emphasized the natural prerogative to which a husband was entitled, in domestic matters. (Clever approach,

Bacon thought, - had the King been present, Coke would have won his case on those grounds alone). The implication was clear — a decision in favor of his wife would undermine the authority of husbands everywhere. All of the members of the Privy Council were married men. Point taken.

All of this was problematic and annoying for Francis Bacon. He had no particular interest in the resolution of the Coke's case one way or another; the main question was which of their respective allies could strengthen Bacon's position if their side won or weaken him if they lost. It was the same for the other members of the council; all of them had ties to one faction or the other, and most of them had ties to both. For Francis Bacon, the vital thing was to get some settlement before the King returned from Scotland — if this mess were unresolved upon the King's return, it would reflect poorly on Bacon's ability to manage the King's affairs.

In the end, the court tried to wash its hands of the whole matter. Parties were urged to effect a reconciliation. Everyone on the Privy Council hoped never to see the Cokes again.

Roger was never sure how Sir Edward and Lady Hatton patched up their differences. Despite all their acrimony, there was evidently a tie of affection between them, more than that, a passion — a passion that could drive them apart, and then draw them back to each other again. Before long, Lady Hatton moved back into Hatton House, and Roger was eating in the basement with the other servants. At breakfast the first day back, he was seated at the usual table, across from Isabel, who had questions, but also news.

"Lady Hatton says that a couple of her best gowns are still missing — and that she won't give back the silver until they are returned to her," she offered. She gave him a challenging stare.

"I decided not to keep any of the gowns," Roger replied with a breezy air, "They made me look fat."

Chuckles round the table: the servants were mostly relieved that the Cokes had reconciled - a permanent separation could have put their jobs in jeopardy. The stories of their tit-for-tat antics were, of course, well known and had grown with the telling; that the Lord and his Lady could get away with such behavior surprised no one; class had its privileges, including the privilege to act like fools in the public square.

Actually, Roger had played only a minor role in all the drama — "fighting Clem" and Lord Coke's armed retainers had done most of the work. Now, however, all was forgiven and (temporarily, at least) forgotten. He wondered if Sir Edward knew anything about the missing gowns.

Later that day in the Library, Sir Edward received another visit from Sir Ralph Winwood. There was news: Lady Mary Villiers Compton (mother to the Earl of Buckingham) had agreed to accept Frances Coke as wife for her son, John, in consideration of a dowry of 10,000 pounds. It was understood that her younger son, the Earl, would use his influence with the King to restore Sir Edward to the Privy Council. It was all that Coke and Winwood could have hoped for.

Roger listened to all this in silence, stunned. The news was no surprise; he just wasn't ready for it. Frances Coke had taken up residence somewhere inside him, and he wasn't ready to let her leave. She lived in his memory as she had been when dancing La Volta - soaring, reaching joyfully for the heavens like a bird at first flight, aching to be free of the earth altogether. Except that it would not be so; she must return to earth, and to duty, and to an all-too-human destiny. It seemed an outrageous injustice for a soul so precious, so delicately beautiful. He heard his name being called . . .

"Sir?"

"I said, draw up the marriage contract according to the terms in this letter. Make a copy; we'll send one back to Lady Compton through Sir Ralph."

"Yes, Sir."

"Once we have finished, send someone to fetch Frances and Lady Hatton. It is time they are made aware of my decision."

Roger did as instructed. The terms of the contract were already spelled out, so a little standard language of introduction, and the date were all that he needed to add. Sir Edward and Sir Ralph continued to converse as he did so.

It was clear that their attention was on the political consequences of this contract, how best to leverage it to the greatest influence in affairs of state. Sir Edward would be Lord Coke again once he was restored to the Privy Council. It was unlikely he would ever serve as any sort of magistrate while the King lived, but he would still have a voice in government, and his views were still widely respected. Francis Bacon would use all his powers as Lord Chancellor to prevent this, of course — that battle had just begun. But with the Earl of Buckingham on his side, Coke was confident of success. Sir Ralph Winwood was already in correspondence with the Earl, and through him, the King - both of them were still in Scotland, not due to return until the end of summer.

More strategic matters were discussed, also. Both men agreed that any formal alliance with Spain was out of the question because it would require an official policy of toleration for English Catholics. This meant that they would be at odds with the policy priorities of the Howards and their allies, clients of the King of Spain. They would have to make the Earl of Buckingham their patron and ally; a strategy that was well underway. Confrontation with the King and his pretensions to 'royal prerogative' would be avoided. This was a bitter pill for Coke to swallow, but the ground rules of the game had been changed - nothing could be accomplished from political exile; better to stay in the game until an opportunity presented itself.

Roger heard all this with a sense of rising excitement. He realized that the game they were playing was a risky one. He also realized that Frances Coke's marriage was the price of admission. She had told him that day at Stoke that she expected no more than to be used as an item of commerce in the business of her family's fortunes - almost a sacrifice on the altar of prosperity, and seemed to be resigned to it. But was she? And if she were not, would she feel differently if she understood that the stakes were much higher than personal wealth or influence? The future of the nation might be at stake here - whether despotism would triumph over the Rule of Law, whether Spanish Papism would overwhelm the Protestant cause, whether the Court of High Commission would finally crush religious dissent in England. Would she understand the importance of her sacrifice? Sacrifice - a chilling word in this context . . .

Roger realized that his feelings were carrying him away - feelings about the cause that Sir Edward had come to represent in his mind and the justice of it, feelings also for Frances that led him to see her as a victim of other men's ambition, or worse. It was only a 'sacrifice' for Frances if she didn't wish to marry John Villiers; perhaps she would actually prefer him? A weighty decision for a young woman of fifteen years to make, probably better that her parents take the matter in hand . . .

Parents. Roger remembered what Lady Hatton had said months ago about John Villiers and his family. He wondered what she might do when she got wind of the contract he had just copied.

He was about to find out what Lady Hatton might do. His copying finished, Sir Ralph took one in hand, for delivery to the groom's mother, and left. The wheels were in motion; no stopping now. Roger went to summon Frances and her mother.

He found them both in the Drawing Room, with several other servants, and bowed as soberly as he could. "Lady, Sir Edward wishes to speak to both of you in the Library."

"Right now?" Lady Hatton seemed a little annoyed at the interruption.

"As soon as is convenient, Lady," Roger replied and bowed again. Frances caught his eye and gave him a quizzical look. Something in his face must have betrayed his inner struggle.

"What is it about?" asked Lady Hatton.

"That is not for me to say, Lady. I am merely the messenger, here."

She snorted, "You know more than you will tell me, I can see it on your face. It is some matter that you think will displease me, and you do not wish to feel my wrath. Very well, tell your master that we will come shortly."

Roger bowed again and left the room. He did not return to the Library. He didn't see the need to be present for the imminent conversation; he wasn't sure he would behave properly if he were to witness it.

Shortly, Lady Hatton and Frances emerged from the Drawing Room, headed in the direction of the Library. They passed him in the hall; Frances shot him another look. Isabel trailed behind them and stopped to speak to Roger.

"Something is happening. Don't deny it - it's written all over your face," she said in a low tone. "Is it bad news? Has some disaster befallen the family?"

Roger shook his head. "It is not for me to say."

"You know, you make a terrible liar. This matter touches you in some way; I can see that much. Lady Hatton thinks that every servant is afraid of her wrath, but I think it must be something else. Am I right?"

Roger said nothing. Isabel looked intently into his eyes as if the answer was written there. Finally, Roger said, "If this were a matter personal to myself, Sir Edward would hardly discuss it with Lady Hatton and his daughter."

"Right," said Isabel. "And there is no reason for Frances to be there unless it touches her in some way. I understand it now. Something is about to happen to Frances!"

Roger was dismayed that she had hit so close to the truth and bit his tongue to avoid a reply.

"You have feelings for Frances; I have seen it. No, do not deny it - there is no shame in it; all men have feelings of one sort or another for Frances. You have behaved honorably, as far as I can tell: done your duty as a servant, refrained from seeking advantage. Frances has feelings for you, too. You have been a friend to her — a kind of friend that other men cannot be."

At the mention of Frances' feelings, something lurched in his stomach. It must have shown on his face, for Isabel spoke again: "It is the lot of masters and servants. Feelings are our daily bread; our destinies lie elsewhere. So long as we remember that, we can go on; we live out what is possible, not what we dream."

It was an astonishing thing to come out of her mouth. Roger realized that she was speaking from her own experience: "We live out what is possible, not what we dream?" What impossible dreams did Isabel cherish? What was possible for her? The two of them were cut from the same cloth, chained to what was possible, dreams notwithstanding. It was the same for everyone he knew - master and servant, man and woman — dreams crashing like waves against the implacable rocks of possibility. He felt the cold touch of cruelty. He felt tears welling in the corners of his eyes. Isabel saw them, placed her hand on his cheek, and kissed him on his forehead.

July 1617: An Abduction and a Rescue

Lady Hatton made her objection to the marriage contract quite loudly - loudly enough to be heard in the hall outside the library. Soon, the news was all over the household: Lady Frances Coke was to be married — to the brother of the Earl of Buckingham, no less! Everyone understood that this was an important match - that it portended good things for the career of Sir Edward, and for Lady Hatton as well. Apparently, she came to understand this; when she emerged from the Library, she appeared to have calmed down.

The quiet lasted for more than a week. There was a flurry of visits and messengers: arrangements for a wedding as prominent as this one were likely to be were necessarily elaborate. Then Sir Edward woke one morning at Hatton House to discover that Lady Hatton and Frances were nowhere to be found. Inquiries were made; no one could account for their whereabouts. Servants reported that the two had slipped out of the house the previous evening through the garden and entered a coach that was waiting for them. They had not taken much in the way of luggage with them - it didn't appear that they planned on being gone long. Isabel had not gone with them.

Sir Edward sent servants to the likeliest locations, such as Corfe and Stoke. Inquiries were made at the houses of all her good friends and relatives, as well. It became obvious that Lady Hatton did not intend to be found. "She thinks to prevent the marriage by abducting the bride," concluded Sir Edward. He undertook a more vigorous search.

It was impossible, of course, to keep the matter a private one. London had spent the past few months gossiping about the Cokes' scandalous (or comical) antics ("embezzlements, raids, suits, and countersuits"), and this was more grist for the mill - though kidnapping a bride was their crowning achievement (so far, at least. Who could put a limit on what foolishness these two were capable of?)

Francis Bacon was aware of the scandal now, as well. He recognized at once that the impending marriage was simply a vehicle for Sir Edward Coke to return to government. Here was an opportunity to thwart Coke's ambitions and take down Winwood in the bargain. He sent an urgent letter to the Earl of Buckingham in Scotland. In it, he denounced Winwood for conspiring to marry the Earl's brother into a "disgraced house", reminded the Earl of the Coke's scandalous behavior, warned him that Sir Edward's unpopularity would drive away all the Earl's friends, and possibly threaten his relationship with the King. He waited for a reply, believing that he had made a compelling case.

Meanwhile, Sir Edward used his contacts and influence to discover that his wife and daughter were hiding at a place called Oatlands, some twenty miles west of London. He acquired a warrant from Sir Ralph Winwood to search the place and made plans to retrieve Frances. "You'll be coming with us," he told Roger. "We shall leave around sundown."

Clement was there, with a dozen or so armed men. Roger supposed they were expecting a fight. "Should I go armed, Sir?"

"Nay, if it comes to fighting, I want you out of the fracas. Someone must live to tell the tale!" He laughed; Clement and the rest laughed along with him.

Roger was mounted on Maggie, the grey mare he had ridden since last summer. Their company made quite a racket on the cobblestones as they headed westward. Most people were in their homes at supper by this time of day. They trotted at first, but Sir Edward was eager to fulfill his mission and soon broke into a canter. Once they were well away from the city, he was galloping. "Best spare the horses, Sir," shouted Clem, "We will want them fresh for the return trip."

Sir Edward had to admit that Clem was right — they would be riding as far as Stoke Poges if everything went well. They pressed on, a half-moon high in the sky.

Roger was comfortable in the saddle by now, but this was the first time he had ridden with a sense of urgency and adventure. It was exciting. He was part of a rescue - a rescue of a lovely young woman from - what exactly? Did her mother intend to marry her off to some other man? It was hard to imagine that Frances was in any physical peril; though her mother was willful and abrasive, she must surely have made arrangements for her safety. A crisis of state, then. They were rescuing Sir Edward's career. Didn't have the same romance to it, but he truly believed that Great Matters were at stake . . . He thought of Frances. He wondered how she was feeling about all this. Perhaps she was frightened; perhaps she was distressed to be the point of conflict between her parents; perhaps she needed to speak of these things with a friend, someone she trusted who could comfort her . . . Sir Edward had broken into a gallop again. Roger had to spur Maggie to keep up.

It must have been nearly midnight when they arrived at a substantial manor house. The house was dark, but Sir Edward's party soon roused the occupants. There was bantering from the upstairs windows and shouting from below. Sir Edward announced his intention to search the house and declared that he had a warrant to do so. The occupants were not impressed. Clem and the armed men searched the outside of the house, looking for a way in. Roger was detailed to hold the horses. At length, the men found a large timber, which they used to batter in the front door, and rushed in. There was a great deal of shouting and screaming, but Sir Edward emerged at last, with Frances in his firm grip. Roger scanned her face in the fading moonlight. She looked confused and a little distressed. Clem was on his horse now and swung her up behind him, where she clung to him. Roger recalled that he had seen something like this in a dream—but no, it was not the same.

"I have a job for you," said Sir Edward. "We are headed for Stoke, where my daughter will be safe. I need you to return to London and report to Sir Ralph Winwood that she has been rescued. Do you think you can find your way?"

"I will, Sir," Roger replied. No chance to speak to Frances, then.

Once out on the main road, Roger turned eastward. The rest of the party was westward bound.

The moon had set, and he had only starlight to see by. Roger slowed Maggie to a walk - he was in no particular hurry, now. They had proceeded on their way for perhaps an hour when he heard noises on the road behind him. Someone or something was in a particular hurry. He guided Maggie off to the side of the road to avoid a collision in the dark. Soon enough, the bulk of a coach appeared, drawn by six horses at the gallop. A voice was shouting, urging haste. A familiar voice. It was Lady Elizabeth Hatton, bound for London, hurtling through the dark, with a posse of armed men behind her. Roger waited a while before resuming his journey; he had no desire to speak with Lady Hatton, and he knew for a fact that she was going in exactly the wrong direction to catch up with Sir Edward and her daughter.

He let Maggie find her footing in the dark. No hurry; Sir Ralph would be at home in bed for some hours to come. He had time and space to reflect on the night's events and his place in them. Nothing heroic, but he was the bearer of an important message, a message that could be part of some Great Matter. A story to tell his children and grandchildren, if he ever had any to tell. What was it that Isabel had said? 'We live out what is possible.' He had a sense that his possibilities might be not only exciting but important; his life might be one of significance. It was a heady thought. He prayed that God might make him worthy of a life of significance.

Before long, the sky in the East got lighter. Soon, the twilight was sufficient to let Maggie trot. He calculated he would be back in London in time to catch Sir Ralph Winwood at his breakfast.

The Lord Chancellor was roused from a sound sleep by the sound of someone trying to break through his bedchamber door. Alarmed, he called for his retainers. When they opened the doors, a woman burst through, demanding to speak with him. It was Lady Elizabeth Hatton, rumpled and desperate. The story she told was too incredible; she and her daughter had been violently attacked at the home of Sir Edmund Withipole, and her daughter had been abducted. She demanded that a warrant be issued for the arrest of her attackers and that her daughter be returned to her custody. It took Bacon some time to collect himself. When it became clear that the "abductor" was none other than the girl's father, things became clearer in his mind. The fact that Sir Ralph Winwood had issued the search warrant on his own was a windfall, really. It dovetailed perfectly with his plan to stymie Edward Coke and disgrace Ralph Winwood. First, lay a sound foundation - no careless omissions. The warrant for the return of Frances Coke must be issued by the entire Privy Council - something that Winwood had failed to do. This could be the thing that would bring him down. He informed Lady Hatton that he would support her suit, but that she must bring it before the entire Privy Council, the following Sunday. When she left, he paused to catch his breath. The woman was ruthless. To think he had sought to marry her. And now, she could well be the instrument by which he would finally triumph over his rival Edward Coke and his allies. It was almost too ironic, too good to be true.

Roger caught Sir Ralph Winwood before he had finished his breakfast and reported that Frances was now in her father's care. Afterward, he headed toward Hatton House. Riding through the streets of the city by himself gave him a sense of freedom that he was unaccustomed to. Also, a taste of power — the power of those who sit above the masses, and look down upon them. He felt like his own man, astride a horse (even if the horse belonged to someone else). It occurred to him that returning to Hatton House on this particular morning might be awkward- Lady Hatton would likely be there, but Sir Edward would not; he might find himself in an uncomfortable position. He decided to visit his family in Cows Lane before returning to Hatton House - at least he could say that he had been visiting them if anyone demanded to know where he had been. It was still early in the morning; they would likely be at home.

Cows Lane seemed narrower than he remembered it, and his family home smaller. Part of it came from riding on horseback, he supposed. His mother embraced him with delight, though she was shorter than he remembered her — no, he was taller now, that was it. He was nearly as tall as his older brother Sydrach now — and Sydrach, at eighteen, was a grown man, working in the family business. His younger brothers, John and Daniel, had also changed. His father acknowledged his visit with a grunt and looked at his clothing — with the critical eye of a tailor.

"We hear of your master nearly every day," his father said. "He seems to be a man of many troubles."

Roger nodded. 'Troubles' was a fair description of Sir Edward's life over the past several months. Still, "He perseveres. He is not a man easily discouraged. I expect his fortunes will soon improve."

Roger's father snorted. "It is hard to imagine how they could get any worse. Is it true that his wife so disrespects him that she has absconded with their daughter and is nowhere to be found? A man who must endure that kind of foolishness in his own house must be at wit's end - if he has any wits at all!" He laughed, and Roger's younger brothers laughed as well.

Roger held his tongue for a moment. He felt he should be defending Sir Edward, but he didn't want to contradict his father, especially in front of the whole family. He had done enough of that when he lived under this roof.

His mother spoke, "I think his wife is most of his trouble. She seems determined to ruin him. Is he such a monster as she says? Or is she the one to blame?'

Roger smiled. "Lady Hatton is a woman accustomed to having her way. She is wealthy and beautiful — few men dare deny her what she wants. Her husband does not always bend his will to hers." There. That was true, and general enough to avoid sounding like common gossip . . .

"They say that she stole away with her daughter in the middle of the night, just to prevent her from marrying into the Villiers family. Is that true?"

Roger nodded.

"And that the marriage was proposed as a ploy to restore Sir Edward Coke to the King's favor, though why the King should care is a mystery to me." Roger's mother had been listening to gossip, apparently. She left the remark hanging, hoping that Roger would try to explain the matter and give away more juicy details. His father was silent, waiting for some response as well.

"I believe that the marriage is sought by John Villiers through his mother because he regards Frances Coke with . . . affection, or at least supposes she will make him a good wife. She is a very beautiful young woman." It twinged him a little, that last remark.

"He that marries for love hath evil days and good nights," said his father, reciting the old proverb. It was surprisingly apropos, if applied to the Coke's marriage - though it seemed that the evil of the days had taken over their nights as well, by now. It might turn out to be the same for John Villiers, he realized. Frances was like her mother in many ways. . .

His father was looking intently at him. "Are you offended by what I have said?"

Roger shook his head. "No, I think you have put your finger on the source of the problems in the marriage of Sir Edward and Lady Hatton. I hope that their daughter does not learn the meaning of the proverb."

Roger's father relaxed and sat back in his chair. He had not expected his son to agree with him, to concede to his wisdom. He was enjoying the moment.

"But there won't be a marriage if the daughter cannot be found," his mother pointed out.

"Oh, she has been found. She is under her father's roof, in Stoke." Roger had not intended to give that much away, but the word would be on the street before the end of the day anyway.

"When did this happen?"

"Last night. Sir Edward discovered where she was, and applied . . . some force, to bring her into his custody."

"That's more like it!" said his father. "Men have been mocking him as a man who cannot keep his own house. A man can only forbear so much." He smiled as if Sir Edward's actions had somehow validated his own husbandship.

"But if your master is at Stoke, how is it that you are in London?" his mother wanted to know.

"Sir Edward sent me here to deliver a message. I'll be returning to Stoke when I have some news for him."

"A message? To whom?"

Roger started to answer, then thought better of it. "I think that is a matter for discretion."

His mother looked disappointed. His father seemed to agree with him, for once. "Aye, Sir Edward's affairs are none of our business. Best his servants remember that."

Roger smiled at the back-handed compliment. He nodded and said, "Many of them are none of my business either. I should remember that as well."

His father nodded. "The tailor's trade is the same. A man may blurt out surprising things when he is being fitted for a new set of clothes. An honorable man ignores the things that he is not supposed to hear; a practical man forgets them."

Roger nodded in return. An honorable man, his father; a practical man. A man who lived within the confines of his class and trade. A man who had learned to ignore what must be ignored, to forget what was best forgotten. A man who survived; a success among his peers, a nobody in the eyes of his betters. A man who could offer his sons only the chance to become as he was, and felt rejected when the offer was not taken up. Roger got a glimpse of how much his ambitions had disappointed his father, and he felt a pang of sympathy for him. Now, at least they could agree on something . . .

His thoughts were interrupted. He realized that his mother had said something, and was waiting for a reply . . . what was it?

She repeated herself. "I do not understand the behavior of these people. It seems like great folly to me. What advantage do they seek in these turmoils?"

Roger shook his head. "No advantage that I can see. Reason has been cast aside, passions seem to have taken control of their minds."

Roger's father grunted in agreement. "Everyone sees the folly except the fool himself."

Roger returned to Hatton House at mid-morning and left Maggie at the stables for the stablehands to care for. There were stares and whispers aplenty at his return, though no one demanded to know where he had been. The fact that he was on horseback seemed to grant him a kind of immunity from accounting for his whereabouts.

Inside the house, it was much the same, until Isabel saw him: "Have you come from Stoke? Where is Sir Edward? And what of Lady Hatton and Frances?" She pulled him aside; others were straining to hear what he might say.

So, evidently, Lady Hatton had not arrived yet. He assumed she was on her way to London when last he saw her, but maybe he was mistaken . . .

"Well?" Isabel was expecting an answer. She looked anxious but determined.

"I am come from my father's house this morning," he replied. "I wished to see that my family were well."

"And were they?"

"Yes, thanks be to God. Very well."

"But you arrived here on horseback."

"Aye. I thought to make my mother proud, to visit her astride Sir Edward's mare." He gave her what he hoped was a sheepish smile and shrug.

"You have not told me everything I need to know." Her expression was accusatory, her eyes searched his.

"You are right. I have not told you all that I know, nor what you need to know. The two of us are in a tight spot here. The master I serve and the lady you serve seem to be at cross purposes just now. Neither of us can assume that speaking of what we know would not betray the confidence of those we serve. Neither of us can assume that speaking freely would not bring harm to ourselves or to the other. Anything that I tell you must be kept in strict confidence, no matter how unwelcome the news."

She moved closer to him, whispering now. "Tell me. Whatever it is, tell me. I can keep a secret."

Roger believed she could keep a secret, but he did not trust that she actually would - not if she saw some advantage in telling it. It occurred to him that most, perhaps all of her "indiscretions" were deliberate — calculated to achieve some response or to elicit some information that she sought. He would have to assume that anything he told her would be shared with someone else, sometime, whenever it seemed to her advantage.

"All of us saw you leave with Sir Edward and his men yesterday, and here you are, alone. We have a right to know whether our positions are in danger," she murmured in an undertone.

So that was it. Apart from the typical appetite for gossip, Isabel and the others were worried about their jobs. Understandable.

"This much I will say," Roger began. "When last I saw Sir Edward and Frances, they were safe and sound, headed westward. They may be at Stoke, but I cannot be certain. When last I saw Lady Hatton, she was also well but headed toward London in her coach. She had an escort of armed men with her, so I think it unlikely that any harm could befall her. I assumed that she would be here when I arrived. (Since she has not, I would appreciate it if you would contrive to conceal my absence from the house last night and my arrival this morning from her. I would like to keep her attention away from my family." That last bit supported his story of his whereabouts that morning and offered a personal reason for his request for secrecy.

Isabel seemed a bit relieved. "I am glad to hear that they are well," she said, "but what of our positions? Are they confirmed enemies now? Do they expect us to war against each other also?"

Roger shook his head. "I cannot say that I have seen any sign of reconciliation between Sir Edward and his wife. I can only guess what the future holds for their servants. If Lady Hatton returns and discovers that I was with Sir Edward last night, I will probably be thrown out on the street that very hour. I hope that you will keep your promise to be discreet."

That last remark, come to think of it, was probably as true as anything he had said. He could sleep at his parents' home in a pinch, or perhaps with Sir Ralph Winwood. . .

"But you said you saw her last night. Surely she knows you were with them?'

"I heard her voice in the darkness, as she drove past me on the road. I do not think she saw me."

"Oh." Isabel nodded as if she could envision it. "So you separated from Sir Edward and the rest after Frances was found. No doubt Sir Edward sent you back here for some special task."

This was closer to the truth than Roger had intended to go. "The less said about that, the better," he said. He was surprised that she did not press the issue.

"You must promise me that you will tell me anything you hear concerning my position in this household," she whispered.

Roger nodded. "And you must do the same for me. Do not worry; this dispute will be settled by persons far above our station, if at all. There is safety in obscurity; ignorance is our friend."

She looked at him with a hint of annoyance. Ignorance was never a friend to someone like Isabel, merely a barrier to be overcome. Then she nodded as if conceding his point. "We shall speak again soon," she whispered.

There was a great deal of wrangling over the two conflicting warrants that Sir Edward and Lady Hatton had obtained regarding custody of their daughter, Frances. They agreed to have her reside at a "neutral" location, pending trial before the Privy Council. Under Bacon's supervision, the Council heard Lady Hatton's plea first, then demanded that Sir Edward appear in Star

Chamber to answer charges of using "riot and force" to break the King's peace — a very serious charge.

Roger sat to the rear of the chamber with the other secretaries and sized up the Council. None of them appeared to have friendly feelings toward their old colleague, except Sir Ralph Winwood. Lord Chancellor Bacon looked like a cat with its gaze fixed on its prey, alert to the point that he could not take his eyes off the accused. The charges were read pretty much as Lady Hatton had made them, he supposed; they had a lurid quality that echoed of her speech and idiom. It looked as if Sir Edward had overreached himself: a conviction might well cause the Villiers family to renounce the wedding; not only would he face imprisonment or fines, but his possibility of returning to government would be gone for good. And Frances — what of her? Would she now be considered damaged or tainted to other suitors? It was surprising that Lady Hatton had not foreseen this possibility. Or had she? Was she really so willful that she was willing to damage her daughter's reputation in that way (to say nothing of her own social position - what could she have been thinking?)

Coke responded by charging his wife with a breach of the King's peace. He noted that she had also forged a marriage contract for Frances with the Earl of Oxford, who was known to be in Italy at the time that he purportedly signed the contract. And in any case, it was his exclusive right as father to decide whom his daughter should marry. This last point should have carried some weight — it relied on the solid basis of a father's prerogative, something that the Council had already found persuasive. Roger looked for some indication that the argument had hit home: nothing on the faces of the Council appeared to be cause for optimism. Sir Edward would have to answer these charges in Star Chamber, they said. They would convene the trial in a week or so, they said. Sir Edward would have to wait for his day in court. Francis Bacon seemed to relish that last bit.

When they returned to Hatton House, Sir Edward had Roger write a letter to the Earl of Buckingham, explaining his actions. He had acted aggressively, he admitted, in part to avoid the impression that he was somehow complicit in his wife's actions to prevent the marriage, or (worse?) that he was unable to govern his own household.

Next, it was Winwood's turn. The Council met the following week to consider whether his granting of the warrant to Coke was treasonable. Lord Chancellor Bacon was on the threshold of triumph.

But Winwood had a letter. A letter from the King, in which all his actions in the affair were approved. The Council was stunned into silence. If the King was involved, they would take no action against Winwood until they could be sure of where James stood. Two days later, the King's reply to Edward Coke's letter arrived, and they saw the light: Coke was vindicated, Lady Hatton rebuked. Bacon was left to clean up the mess as best he might. Worse, he received his own letter from Buckingham, scolding him for "overtroubling" himself in the family affairs of the Villiers.

Bacon defended himself in letters to the King: He had only been trying to protect the King's interests - Edward Coke was a troublemaker who would foster disunity in the government, should he ever get back in; imagine how much trouble he could make if the King decided to call for another parliament . . . It was to no avail. The Earl of Buckingham was determined that his brother would marry the woman that he and his mother had chosen. And Sir Edward Coke would be restored to the Privy Council, if only just to remind the Chancellor of who held the power to make such decisions. Francis Bacon, on the other hand, might lose the King's trust if he persisted in this nonsense.

Lady Elizabeth Hatton saw which way the wind was blowing and announced that she was delighted at the prospect of John Villiers as her son-in-law. To prove the point, she doubled the dowry, with 10,000 pounds of her own money.

In August, the King and his court returned to London. The King professed to be delighted with the match and the promise of unity among so many of the noble families of the realm. The wedding would be held at Hampton Court Palace

— that splendid example of Italian architecture that Cardinal Wolsey had built for himself more than a century ago, then gifted to King Henry to save his career. King James and Queen Anne would attend the wedding, naturally. Lady Elizabeth Hatton would not — Sir Edward had obtained a warrant to have her held under house arrest until after the wedding; he wasn't taking any chances.

September 29, 1617: A Palace Wedding

The wedding was set for a Monday, September 29th. Frances Coke had been living at the home of her half-brother Sir Robert Coke, in Kingston-upon-Thames, southwest of London, since her 'rescue'. Hampton Court Palace was across the river, a few miles away.

The day before the wedding, there was a great stir about Hatton House - Sir Edward was taking a fair number of his servants with him to Kingston, along with all the clothing that a wedding would require. They would spend the night in Kingston, at his son's home, and travel the few miles to the palace from there, clad in their wedding finery - an adventure for many of the servants, (it was said that the King would be there!) Sir Edward and his retainers would go on horseback. Roger would ride too — on Maggie, the gray mare that had become like an old friend over the past year.

Kingston was on the opposite bank of the river. The shortest route lay eastward, through the congestion of the old city, then across London Bridge and westward to Kingston. Sir Edward was not deterred by the congestion. They set off with a clatter of horseshoes on the cobblestones and pressed their way through the crowds as fast as traffic would permit. The day was sunny and cool; Sir Edward was in an ebullient mood - and why should he not be? Tomorrow would be a day of triumph. He had spent much time with the King in the past several weeks; the King seemed appreciative of his counsel (as long as Francis Bacon was not around to contradict him).

Roger and Maggie struggled to keep up as they dodged their way through the streets. This was not particularly worrisome: He knew the way to London Bridge, and once across it, the traffic would be lighter. He could find the way to Kingston by himself if need be.

It did need be. By the time Roger was clear of the bridge on the south side of the river and well out of town, Sir Edward and his men were out of sight. Roger supposed that if he galloped Maggie for a mile or so, he might catch them, but maybe not — and anyway, what was the need? He urged Maggie into an easy trot, posted to match her gait, and enjoyed the weather. He felt confident in finding his way to Kingston, confident of finding his way anywhere he decided to go: that was how a man on horseback felt - independent, master of his destiny, free.

Free for as long as it took him to get to Kingston. He arrived around noon at Robert Coke's manor. The place was all a-bustle with preparations for the wedding and the guests who were expected. Roger took Maggie to the stable, which was crowded with animals. Clem Coke greeted him there: "Williams! I see you're riding — same old mare!"

Roger bowed. "Yes, sir. A very dependable mount."

"That's good; we're going to need her tomorrow — one of our family guests came in on a lame horse. Give her to my care — I'll find a good use for her."

"How will I get to the wedding then?"

"Eh?" Oh, I see. I supposed you would be riding in one of the family carriages, but let me confirm that. Don't worry, I'll make sure you get to Hampton Court, even if it's only on a dickey seat." Someone else interrupted him just then, so Roger went into the house to look for his dinner. The house was aswarm with activity. Servants and their masters and mistresses were everywhere — unpacking luggage, assigning the guests to their rooms, greeting long-lost relatives and acquaintances. Most of the newcomers were from the households of Sir Edward's children; all came to spend the night in the house of their brother Robert because of its proximity to the wedding venue. Roger found his way to the great kitchen, where dozens of servants were working to feed the throng upstairs. Once he identified himself, he was given a corner to sit in, where he could eat his dinner, out of the path of the kitchen staff. Roger sought out the steward, who directed him to the attic of the manor, where he would sleep that night. He did not need much space; he had packed only one change of clothes — he would be wearing his blue doublet with the russet stockings tomorrow.

In the morning, the household was in even greater uproar than the day before. Everyone was rushing to get some breakfast and then get dressed for the wedding. Sir Edward had provided no less than nine coaches to transport his friends and family (and the bride, of course) to the palace. They would be escorted by more than two dozen mounted retainers — a regular cavalcade of Cokes.

Clem Coke was in charge of assigning the guests to their respective coaches. Roger found him outside, in the courtyard near the main gate. He noticed Roger, smiled, and said, "I have not forgotten you. I shall find a seat for you on one of the carriages. Come see me just before the procession leaves."

The coaches pulled up before the great doors one at a time to receive their highborn passengers. Everyone was dressed to impress — satin and velvet, ruffs and farthingales. It was no simple task for the ladies to get into the coaches, but they managed it.

Roger waited by the door for Clem to tell him where he would be riding. Clem gestured to the fourth carriage in line: "There's a dickey seat on the rear of that coach, between where the coachmen are standing," he said, "that's yours!"

Roger started in the direction indicated when he heard his name called. "Roger Williams! Over here!"

It was Lady Anne Sadleir, in the fifth coach. He answered her summons with some trepidation.

"I see that my father's fortunes are restored," she said when he was close enough for conversation. "To what mechanism do you credit this success?"

"The credit, if credit be due, must be given to Lord Coke's friends, and his own abilities and resourcefulness. My part has been to follow my master's instructions," Roger replied.

"Well spoken, as always," said Lady Anne. "You may go far if you keep to such humble-seeming replies. But I know that you have been his close companion through all of this, and I am certain that you knew more of his affairs than you were willing to tell me at Christmastide. I was annoyed at your reticence, but I think you have proved that discretion is a faithful companion for a man like my father. All is well if he is restored to government, as I suppose you expect that he will be." She was fishing for some inside information again, with that last remark.

Roger bowed his head ever so slightly. "My Lord Coke keeps his own counsel, but he seems to be in the King's favor, these days."

"And do you suppose that he has learnt how to stay in the King's good graces, or will he return to his old ways, and fall from favor again?"

Roger smiled faintly, looked her in the eyes, and said, "Let us hope that Lord Coke will always have a place in the King's affection and in his government."

"Which can only advance your fortunes, you mean," replied Lady Anne. "It is well. Your interests and my father's are aligned. I think you are clever enough to see that, with just enough integrity to seal your loyalty to him. He has chosen well. I am content."

Roger noted the backhanded compliment ("Just enough integrity?") and excused himself with a bow.

The carriages were pulling round and out the main gate of the courtyard, bound for Hampton Court, a few miles away. Roger had to run behind the fourth in line and scramble up onto the dickey seat. Two coachmen, standing at their stations on either corner at the rear of the coach, noted his breathless arrival and smiled at him. Roger nodded back and hung on as best he could.

Their course lay through the town with its cobblestoned streets (bumpy and clanging), and across a great wooden bridge (rumbling and humming under the wheels of the coach) — the only bridge across the Thames until one reached London Bridge itself. From there, it was only a mile or so to the great courtyard of Hampton Court Palace. The gatehouse was built of red bricks, with crenelated towers on either side. They drove through the gatehouse from the West and into the great courtyard (the 'Base Court') beyond. Here, crowds were already assembled, with horses, coaches, and a colorful swirl of festive clothing. They passed through another gateway to the East, where the carriages stopped. Roger hopped off the dickey seat and looked for a familiar face, someone who could explain where he was supposed to go or to do. The occupants of the carriages were greeted with bows as they stepped down, and were directed up a broad flight of stairs to the Great Hall, thence to the chapel beyond. Roger followed a stream of lesser folk to his left, past the entrance to the Great Hall, and then into a smaller courtyard which formed the north wall of the chapel itself. Here they would stand and wait for the ceremony. The chapel at Hampton Court was large enough for a few hundred, at most. Since the King and his retinue of courtiers were present, the servants had to stand outside, straining to hear what they could. The wedding ceremony itself was splendid, or so they said. The King had taken Frances Coke from her father's hand and presented her to Sir John Villiers himself.

When the couple walked out of the chapel, through the courtyard, and toward the banquet in the Great Hall, the servants greeted them with cheers. Roger caught a glance of recognition from Frances and saw the hint of a tear in her eye, but she was smiling her devastating smile. Her husband was a handsome man, he decided, and seemed to be as dazzled by her as any man might. *May she find happiness, as well*, he prayed silently.

The wedding feast was set out in the Great Hall of the Palace. The King and the wedding party sat at a great table on a raised platform at the head of the room, the important guests at tables that stretched the length of the hall. Roger found himself seated among other servants at the far end, more than one hundred feet away. He could see Sir Edward, the King and Queen, and the rest of the guests at the head table; servants stood behind them to attend to their requirements. Roger saw a familiar figure standing behind the bride - it looked like Isabel. Perhaps she was standing in for Lady Hatton, in her absence? Rumor said that the King had sent an invitation to Lady Hatton, suspending her house arrest, so that she might attend the wedding, but she had refused. Perhaps that explained the tear in Frances's eye?

The questions crowded into Roger's mind, confusing him. Everything looked splendid and glorious, but just under the surface was turmoil, avarice, and bitterness. It was not just the occasion; Roger had seen enough of these people over the years to understand that all their pretensions to power and glory rested on the frailest of foundations. It would collapse one day, and when it did, it would crush everyone in this kingdom, high and low. He took no comfort in that thought — he counted himself among the low who would be crushed. Best enjoy the spectacle while it lasted: drink the wine, savor the delicacies — tomorrow will have time for regrets.

After they ate, servants appeared to remove the tables. There would be a splendid masque ball later in the evening, with courtly dancing. Guests left the Hall to prepare. When they returned, the noble ladies were covering their faces with elaborate masks (or 'masques'), feathered and bejeweled. It was supposed to conceal their identities from the men, whose task it was to identify them. The whole business was a fabrication, intended to spark flirtation or outright seduction, under the premise that the parties had no idea with whom they were flirting, so could not be held accountable for what they said the next morning. It was the sort of event that Queen Anne (and Lady Hatton) reveled in. No other nobleman's wife would have missed it to save her life.

Roger, like the other servants, stood aside while the courtiers danced. The ladies' gowns were splendid, the men's attire scarcely less so. Frances and her husband led the dancers, of course; Frances wore no mask (it wouldn't have concealed her identity from anyone else anyway — who else would be dancing with the groom?)

Roger noted that John Villiers was a pretty good dancer. Not as accomplished as his younger brother, the Marquis, perhaps, but his breeding showed. When they called for "La Volta", he lifted Frances gracefully into the air, soaring like a bird, a look of joy on her face, then lightly back to earth, to the applause of the crowd. A bird. A bird in a cage.

Roger decided not to think about that, nor to dwell on how it had felt to dance La Volta with Frances that day at Hatton House. John Villiers looked like a happy man; he had reason to be.

Roger felt the closeness of the room and turned back through the crowd to one of the side hallways off the Great Hall, hoping for some fresh air. Someone clutched at his arm. It was Isabel, who had somehow found him in the press. She was wearing a gown and held a feathered mask in front of her face. "It's me, Isabel," she hissed. She needn't have done so, but Roger pretended to be surprised. He led her further down the hallway, where there was some privacy. Some other couples had hit upon the same idea - not all were servants. Through the hall, it opened into another room; not large, but not crowded yet.

"I fear we may not see each other again, after tonight," said Isabel.

"You mean, until Sir Edward and Lady Hatton are reconciled again?"

Isabel shook her head slightly. "Lady Hatton has decided that I am to attend Frances henceforth. She says that there should be at least one person in her new home who will be familiar to Frances and loyal to her. I won't be returning to Hatton House, even if Lady Hatton does."

Roger understood. Frances Coke, at age fifteen, was a member of the Villiers family now; a family with its own history, its own rivalries, its own internal politics. She would need a friend - more than one, if she could find them. . . "I think Lady Hatton has made a wise choice."

Isabel's voice had a tinge of sadness in it.

"Of course, I will miss your presence at Hatton House," he added lamely. "You will be living in London, will you not? I travel quite freely in the city these days. We shall probably meet again."

"If you wish it, you can make it so," she replied. Her tone suggested skepticism or a challenge to his willingness to seek her out in her new lodgings. He resisted making a promise to do so; the events of the day were crowding his mind, scrambling his feelings.

The musicians struck up another tune. "Dance with me," said Isabel. That much he could do. They made a good couple, as far as dancing was concerned. They danced a galliard, then a minuet, along with several other servants, in a room just off the Great Hall. The honored guests and courtiers, of course, did their dancing at the front of the Hall, near the Royal Presence and the musicians, but the music was loud enough to be heard where Roger and Isabel were. When the strains of La Volta were heard again, Isabel held out her hand with a knowing smile. The other servants in the room were not prepared to attempt this, so they made space in the center for Roger and Isabel to dance. Isabel gave him her most seductive look (so he supposed - some of the other servants whistled), and laughed out loud when she soared through the vaults. The other servants clapped and cheered. Isabel curtseyed when they finished, her face flushed. Roger bowed in return, then whispered, "You're wearing stays this evening."

"Of course I am, you naughty fellow." Then she winked and kissed him. More whistles and whoops from the bystanders . . . Roger smiled and bowed again. More couples drifted into the side room where they were. There was more music, more dancing. Outside, in the Great Hall, things were getting raucous. The wedding party at the head table had an unlimited supply of wine available, and some of them were testing those limits.

A familiar-looking servant entered the room, fastened his look on Roger, and beckoned him over. "My mistress, the Lady Anne bids you come with me, at once," the man said.

Roger looked back at Isabel, whose face showed disappointment. He bowed, blew her a kiss, and followed his summoner.

He was led down a passageway to the rear of the Great Hall. Lady Anne Sadleir was waiting restlessly for them. Clem and Robert Coke stood nearby. "We must get my father out of this place," she said in a low tone. "He has had too much wine. I fear he will make a fool of himself, or insult the King, which is the same thing. The wine has loosened his tongue. So far, he has ridiculed nearly everyone at the table except the King. They laugh, to show that they know how to take a joke, but everything is in peril if we let him continue."

"What do you want me to do?"

"Approach him from behind the dais. Whisper in his ear that there is some urgent or secret matter that you must speak with him about. Lead him back here."

"Why wouldn't Sir Robert or Clem be better suited to this task?"

"They have already tried. He just waves them off. Father trusts you; he will follow you."

It was worth a try, and Roger was in no position to defy the demand, in any case. Lady Anne's servant showed him the way to where Coke sat, roaring with laughter at one of his own jokes. Yes, he had definitely been overdoing it. Roger bent to whisper something in his ear. He turned with a smile and said, "Roger, my boy! Come sit! Share my joy today!"

Drunk as they were, the others seated on the dais recognized that this was a serious breach of decorum. Roger bent again and spoke more into his master's ear. Coke's face grew serious, and he nodded. "Excuse me, Lords and Ladies, but duty calls," said Coke as he rose unsteadily to his feet. There were chuckles and titters all around.

Roger led Sir Edward back to where Lady Anne was waiting. Roger and Clem took charge of him there and hustled him away, still giggling.

"That was well done," said Lady Anne to Roger. "How did you persuade him to come with you?"

"I whispered to him that Lady Hatton had arrived and was purloining the silverware in the kitchen. I explained that if she were caught at it, it would be a great embarrassment to Frances on her wedding day. I suggested that we should take care of the matter as discreetly as possible. I said that Sir Robert and Clem were waiting to assist him."

Lady Anne looked at him with amusement. "So you do know how to lie when the situation requires it! No, do not deny it. I am not reproaching you; you did what was necessary. The best liars are the ones with a reputation for telling the truth. What will you tell him in the morning, if he remembers any of this?"

"I will tell him the truth. He was in peril of losing all he had gained, and I thought a good joke would amuse him."

Lady Anne shook her head slowly. "And he will forgive you, I do not doubt. Come, we are returning to Kingston tonight, and Clem has a carriage waiting."

October 1618: Recovery and Resistance

The day after the wedding, Sir Edward was restored to the Privy Council. He was Lord Edward Coke once again. He took the news with satisfaction and admitted that his recollection of the previous evening was incomplete. He had no memory of the ride back to Kingston when he awoke. Later that day, he and Roger returned to London.

In Council, observers noted that Lord Edward was a changed man. He was careful not to contradict the King in anything; he appeared to harbor no ill feelings against Francis Bacon. At the age of sixty-six, it seemed the old man had mellowed, at last. The King was delighted to have peace and unanimity among these advisors — he was getting older, too.

Roger had a different view of things. Lord Edward still had private meetings with his friends and allies, and Roger was usually present, whether or not he took notes. Lord

Edward and his friends were no less determined to defend their liberties against royal prerogative, no less intent on guiding English foreign policy away from a Spanish alliance, and no less desirous to eliminate the Court of High Commission and the *ex officio* oath. They were biding their time, garnering support, waiting for an opportunity - some scandal or failure that would force the King to call a Parliament - the only remaining institution in England that could checkmate a despotic king.

The scandal was not long in coming; it came from an unexpected and ironic direction. Sir Walter Raleigh, now sixty-five years of age, had been living on borrowed time since his conviction for treason in 1603, the year of Queen Elizabeth's death. He had been convicted of participating in a plot to deny the throne to King James, even as he was journeying to London from Scotland. The evidence was slim, but the prosecutor had done a brilliant job of convincing the magistrates of Raleigh's guilt; he was sentenced to death by hanging, disembowelment, and dismemberment. The brilliant prosecutor was none other than Sir Edward Coke.

Before the order of execution could be carried out, the newly-crowned King James commuted the death sentence - and left Raleigh to rot in the Tower of London. Years later, Raleigh's rooms in the Tower were needed for other high-ranking prisoners - such as Lady Frances Howard, Countess of Essex. Raleigh was paroled from the Tower - delivered, indirectly, by the efforts of the same prosecutor who had obtained his conviction.

"I was pleased that the King decided to release him," confided Coke. "I prosecuted him vigorously because the evidence was not that strong. I did not expect that he would be condemned to death - I assumed that the magistrates would show him some deference, due to his rank and fame. Those were early days - none of us knew how the new King would rule. I did not think him worthy of death - certainly not so worthy as the traitors in the Gunpowder Plot, who would have killed the King and his Parliament, if they had succeeded."

"Isn't it ironic that Sir Walter was released from the Tower so that his rooms would be available to the conspirators who murdered Sir Thomas Overbury?" asked Roger.

"Fitting, I should rather say. They were more deserving of that residence than Raleigh. Raleigh, at least, understands the peril of seeking an alliance with Spain. He is ambitious and holds an exaggerated opinion of his abilities, but his political sense is sound."

Somehow, Raleigh persuaded the King to send him on a voyage to search for El Dorado (the 'City of Gold') in South America. (Raleigh had led many other expeditions and colonization efforts as a younger man — all of which had failed spectacularly. How the King was persuaded to finance such a scheme is a mystery; the promise of gold has led to many foolish adventures.)

Raleigh's expedition failed, as so often before. This time, he compounded the failure with an attack on a Spanish settlement, which was specifically forbidden by the King's terms. Upon his return, the Spanish Ambassador demanded that King James reinstate the death sentence on Sir Walter Raleigh.

James, still seeking an alliance with Spain and still hoping to marry his son Charles to a Spanish princess, complied with the demand. Raleigh was beheaded on October 29, 1618.

"See what folly is revealed here!" Coke exclaimed, "If any man would know the price of a Spanish alliance, here it is, writ large. Spain will not stop with the shedding of one man's blood - her aims are nothing different from 1588 — the conquest of our realm, and the extermination of our religion! They hope to achieve through diplomacy what they have failed to do by force of arms!"

Coke's feelings were echoed everywhere. Popular revulsion swept the country. Raleigh was hailed as a martyr to Spanish appeasement, to 'popish' influence in the government, and to English weakness. Lord Edward Coke and like-minded others had the issue they had been waiting for. Soon, it was risky for the Spanish ambassador, Count Gondomar, to ride in his litter on the streets of London (stones, garbage, and worse might be thrown at him).   King James responded by declaring it a felony to show "irreverence" to strangers, particularly ambassadors, "by look or countenance" — never mind the stones or garbage. This did nothing to cool the nation's anger. Anyone who opposed the alliance with Spain, the marriage of Prince Charles to a Spanish princess, or the foreign policy of the Marquis of Buckingham (promoted just that year from Earl of Buckingham)   and the Howards was emboldened. This included Lord Coke and many others, especially in the countryside. The resentment did not fade — Puritans, conformists, and non-conformists were united in their loathing of all things Spanish. The stage was set for a reform-minded Parliament.

Lord Coke and Lady Hatton did not reconcile after the wedding — it was, from Lady Hatton's perspective, a breach of trust too deep and wide to bridge. The marriage of her youngest daughter over her objections was the sharpest of a long list of grievances. She sought her revenge in countless small ways, making it impossible for Lord Coke to find peace in Hatton House by chipping away at him, until he moved out in exasperation. Once in possession of the place, she left standing orders with her servants not to let him back in. She continued to entertain at Hatton House for a while, even inviting the King and Queen to dine with her.   The King, half-amused at her, suggested she should be reconciled to her husband — to which she replied that if he ever came in the front door, she would immediately leave by the back door.

Lord Coke and Roger took up residence at Serjeants' Inn, a complex of residences that were part of the Inns of Court, the chief residence and training institution for lawyers in England at that time — a university for the law, practically speaking. Residence at Serjeants' Inn was reserved for the highest-ranking lawyers — men like Lord Edward Coke - and their servants, of course. Roger slept in a small chamber that was a little more comfortable than the attic at Hatton House. Mealtimes were usually shared with other men — colleagues and admirers of Lord Coke, lawyers all. Roger found the conversation stimulating and thought-provoking. Mostly, he ate and listened, but when it became known that he had actually read and edited the various volumes of Coke's *Reports*, some became accustomed to testing his memory on the details of the cases. Roger's memory proved reliable, and occasionally he slipped in a remark or two of interpretation. Lord Coke found all of this amusing; he enjoyed showing off his secretary's grasp of the law (the law as interpreted by Lord Coke himself, of course).

Otherwise, Lord Coke was showing the effects of his sixty-six years and the stress of Lady Hatton's endless lawsuits and insults. As husband, he exercised legal control of their joint property, and he had no intention of giving her any more money than absolutely necessary. Rather defend himself against her in court than give anything away. He was leaner, grayer, careworn. He sometimes missed meetings of the Privy Council. People said he was nearing the end of his career.

Roger saw another side of the man. No question, serving on the Privy Council drained him: he was constantly being overruled by Chancellor Bacon or the Marquis of Buckingham, on nearly every question of policy, every legal issue. But when he was away from court, he was energized. In the summer, they returned to Stoke Poges, where Lord Coke was most at home — preparing the next volume of *Reports*, ordering improvements to the estate, and receiving visitors. He still liked to ride in the mornings and indulged in a variety of sports — especially hawking.

Roger's archery and horsemanship improved a great deal; Clem decided to teach him the rudiments of fencing. Roger had the feeling that Coke and his friends were waiting for something. There was a tension, a rumbling of hidden forces lurking just beneath the surface of this bucolic world. The question that nagged at him was . . . when? When did it begin? He took it for granted that he would have a role to play in whatever was going to happen, and he was eager to take his part. But Lord Edward Coke did not indicate that he and his allies were up to anything other than enjoying the fruits of their position. Roger wondered if his master had grown soft, if he would delay until it was too late - how many more years did he have left on this earth?   This and similar questions occupied his mind all summer and into the following winter.

The following March, Queen Anne's long, slow decline ended in her death. They said she had never recovered from the death of her eldest son, Henry, at age eighteen. Three of her other children had died before reaching age two; another daughter had failed to see her 3rd birthday.   The weight of grief, the estrangement from her husband, all of it took its toll on her health.

The King, now fifty-three years old, was also in declining health. His favorite, the Marquis of Buckingham, became more influential than ever. Rumblings of dissatisfaction began to be heard on the streets and in the public houses.   James made an effort to explain himself:

> *"I, James, am neither God nor an angel, but a man like any other. Therefore I act like a man and confess to loving those dear to me more than other men. You may be sure that I love the Earl of Buckingham more than anyone else, and more than you who are here assembled. I wish to speak in my own behalf, and not to have it thought to be a defect, for Jesus Christ did the same, and therefore I cannot be blamed. Christ had his John, and I have my George."*

This explanation did nothing to improve the public perception of the King and his court. It seemed natural enough to James to compare himself to Christ (he was, in his own words, "the supremest thing on earth"), but it sounded blasphemous to his fiercest opponents. And comparing his relationship with his favorite to that of Jesus and one of his apostles was no less offensive, considering the rumored nature of that relationship. The remark served only to remind the public of the scandalous rumors and failed utterly to cast them in a more favorable light. Puritan preachers punctuated many a sermon with general references to the shameful goings-on at court.

Roger was seventeen now, a young man of more than average height, not yet "filled out", but no longer a child. His work for Lord Coke often involved traveling about the city, which he did freely, whether on foot or horseback. He had always been a sociable sort, and now he came in contact with all sorts — lawyers, clergy, merchants. He was known and trusted all across the city. He developed a sense of the moods and attitudes of the whole community, from the King and his courtiers to the bakers on Bread Street. He became keenly aware of the differences between the levels of society: The King had no more appreciation for the lives of his subjects than they did for his. It was a wonder, really, that they all lived in the same city, breathing the same air, feeling the same wind. He doubted that this could go on for very long without some crisis.

He was able to see more of his family. He would often drop by the house or his father's shop when one of his errands took him near the old neighborhood. He was better dressed now, partly because Lord Coke said he was such a familiar sight that he could enjoy the benefits of 'invisibility' without necessarily dressing like a drab, partly because Lord Coke wanted the world to see that he could afford to dress his secretary as the servant of a wealthy master should be — Lady Hatton's servants were all over town, dressed as if to belie her constant complaints of poverty.

Roger walked into his father's shop one afternoon in October. He was greeted by several of his father's employees, who had known him since childhood: "Master Roger!" said a portly, balding man named Alfred, "Well come!"

Alfred bowed slightly and then straightened to look Roger over with a tailor's eye: "Still growing, I see. Time for a new doublet, I think, eh?"

Roger smiled. "Aye, and a few other things as well. My master has given me money to buy new clothing, and I could think of no better place to purchase them than here."

"There is no better place," said Alfred. He was dead serious. "Best tailors in the city, these." He gestured to the other men in the shop.

"Is my father about?"

"He is away for a bit. Buying some fabric. We've been seeing some very interesting fabrics from the East, lately — by way of the Turks. May I show you something?"

Roger smiled. "I'll stick with plainer stuff. My master would not approve of anything exotic or fancy - even if he were willing to pay the price, which he is not. I need a couple of new doublets and trousers and stockings, some shirts also - time for new underwear, too, I think.

"Come with me," said Alfred, and led him to the rear of the shop.

Alfred showed him some fabrics and took his measurements. "I'd advise you to have the doublets cut a bit oversized," he said, "Not as flattering to your figure, but you'll want some room to grow if you expect them to fit a year from now. I don't suppose you'll be getting much taller, but a little more room in the trousers wouldn't go amiss, either."

Roger nodded. It was true: his trousers were too tight, and his doublets were hard to close in the front.

"Can't let these out anymore," said Alfred, "They're heavily worn, anyway. I can make you new clothing for a very reasonable cost — call it a family discount." He winked.

Roger's father returned to the shop about then, looked at the fabrics, and gave his approval. He invited Roger to join his family for the evening meal. On the way home, they spoke of the news:

"I see that your master has recovered his position, and seems to be holding on to it this time," said his father, "you must be relieved about that."

"There is something to be said about stable employment," Roger allowed.

"Meanwhile, the government in which he serves dithers as the Catholic kingdoms wage war on all the Protestant ones, and you can find a corrupt official under any stone. Does your master approve of such?"

Roger sidestepped the apparent attack on Lord Coke. He could not resist a dig at the rest of the Privy Council. "I will tell you a secret," he offered.

"Eh?" He had his father's attention, now.

"There is sentiment in the Privy Council for clamping down on corruption, so long as it does not interfere with the bribes that they receive from the Spanish Ambassador. The Marquis of Buckingham receives much of his income from Spain these days - payment for ensuring that England does nothing to help the Protestant cause in Germany."

"You don't say! Is it as bad as that?"

"I am afraid it is. There are a few honest men in government, like Lord Coke. But they are often outvoted by Buckingham's men. The King listens to them, and — well, you have seen how the King treats advisors who oppose Buckingham."

"Men like your Lord Coke, you mean," said his father. "I am glad to hear that you are on the right side in these matters. Keep up the good work, son." It was the only compliment that Roger could recall hearing from his father. He wondered if he was being sarcastic. At minimum, he realized that men like his father were beginning to see the need for reform — the kind of reform that a new Parliament might bring.

At long last, the Privy Council determined that the King should call for a new Parliament. There simply wasn't enough money to run the government without new taxes (called subsidies), which Parliament alone could authorize. There was a buzz in the air about the injustice of monopolies, the corruption of bribery in the realm. King James was aware of this in theory; Roger heard it every time he ventured out into the streets. He was also aware of a host of other discontents — the increasing influence of Spain, the persecution of Puritan preachers and scholars, and the rumors of corruption at court. The subterranean rumble could no longer be ignored.

King James, to his credit, was well-informed of the country's mood and took steps to ensure that none of these discontents would be addressed by the new Parliament. He needed subsidies and was willing that Parliament investigate bribery, or even terminate the royal monopolies that he had sold not many years ago — but that was all. There must be no discussion of foreign policy or religion.

"Much will depend on preparation," explained Lord Chancellor Bacon.

Lord Coke agreed. "We must put forward candidates who can be relied upon to support the King. In fact, let every member of the Privy Council be nominated to serve either in the House of Lords or the House of Commons. That way we can lead the houses of this Parliament in the proper directions."

It sounded reasonable to Roger when Coke said it, and the King smiled. Roger was a little surprised to hear Lord Coke describe himself as a man who could be "relied upon" to guide the Parliament away from discussions about foreign policy and religious affairs. Perhaps the old man had gone soft; he was sixty-eight years old, now. Perhaps. Roger caught a glance from him - lean, spare, clear-eyed. Didn't see much softness there.

On the way back to their rooms at Serjeants Inn, Roger had questions for his master:

"Can anyone guarantee that all the members of the Privy Council will win election to Parliament in this election?"

"Nay, no one can guarantee who will win an election." Coke smiled faintly.

Roger sensed that he was on to something. "And once a Parliament is convened, can the King or anyone else guarantee what matters they will or will not discuss?"

"Nay. The Parliament sets its own agenda." Coke's smile was a little broader, now.

"But the King may dismiss a Parliament if he is displeased with their agenda?"

"Aye, he may. This is why Parliaments do not approve the subsidies until all their other business is finished."

"Has the King no recourse, then, once a Parliament is seated?"

"Sometimes negotiation is involved. When I was Speaker of the House, the Queen would often commit the leaders of the House to the Tower of London, until a satisfactory compromise could be reached."

"How long could the Queen keep them there?"

"As long as she liked. By tradition and precedent, members of Parliament are immune from prosecution for words or deeds occurring in the performance of their duties, but there was no limit on how long they might be held as her guests in the Tower."

"Does the King understand this?"

"I am sure that the Lord Chancellor has informed him of our traditions. That is why he is determined to place only men who will support him in the Parliament, to weed out 'dissenters and troublemakers'."

Dissenters and troublemakers. Roger thought it probably described most of the people he associated with every day, in the King's eyes . . . "Still, a few might slip through, and create controversy in the House?"

Coke eyed him soberly. "Aye, a few. Could make for some interesting debates."

One September afternoon, Roger received a message that he should return home urgently. He begged leave of Sir Edward and walked briskly the mile or more to Cow's Lane. The house was crowded as he had seldom seen it. Something was amiss.

His mother greeted him, weeping. "Your father is gone," she sobbed, clinging to him. It had happened suddenly, shockingly: one moment he was speaking to a customer in his shop, and the next he was on the floor, unconscious.

"No one saw this coming," said Roger's elder brother, Sydrach, "I am not sure how the family will weather this."

"He prepared you to take his place," Roger replied, "and you are well prepared, even if it is sooner than any of us hoped."

The funeral was held a week later, at St. Sepulcher's. It was well attended by the most prominent members of the Tailor's Guild - James Williams was a man highly respected. His pallbearers were all tailors - impeccably dressed (if only because none of them wished to appear poorly clad before their colleagues) and sober (men of commerce do not have time to dwell on death, as a rule, but all of them were sobered at the reminder of their own mortality). Roger and his brothers were there to greet the mourners and accept their condolences. It became apparent to Roger that the Tailor's Guild would rally around his family and offer their support to Sydrach and his younger brother, Robert, to ease the transition. Several men expressed their confidence that Sydrach was more than capable of running the family business.

"You are welcome to join me in running the business," said Sydrach to Roger that evening.

Roger shook his head. "Nay, Father intended to leave it into your capable hands, and he chose well. I am not suited for that life."

"But what will you do? Be servant to Lord Coke for the rest of your life?"

"I could do worse. The work is interesting, my circumstance is comfortable. I am sure that Lord Coke will keep his promise to our father, to find me a suitable career when the time is right."

"It would comfort Mother and the rest of us if you visited us more often."

"I shall make an effort to come 'round once a week, then, to check on her." Roger reflected that with his Father gone, visits to his family would be less acrimonious. Still, there was something unfinished about the whole situation.

The election was held in November. Few of the King's candidates from the Privy Council were elected. Still, James needed his subsidies. Among those elected were Sir Francis Bacon, the Lord Chancellor, and Lord Edward Coke, one-time Speaker of the House of Commons. The Council decided that Coke would assume the leadership of the King's party in the Commons, while Bacon would take leadership in the House of Lords. Prince Charles insisted on attending sessions in the House of Lords as well — to acquaint him with parliamentary politics, and to dampen down objections to his hoped-for marriage to a Spanish princess. It was expected that the Parliament would prove favorable to the King with the leadership in such capable hands. Parliament convened in January 1621, the coldest January in London's memory.

Part 2: The School of Experience

January 1621: The Charterhouse

Roger was glad for his new coat that winter. It was so cold that the Thames River froze over upstream of London Bridge. The ferrymen were out of business until there was a thaw. A few daring souls took advantage of this by walking from one shore to another across the ice, but this was a calculated risk that he did not wish to take: the tides still made themselves felt above the bridge, and the ice could fracture with the ebb and flow.

This left London Bridge as the only practical way to cross — more crowded than ever with all the traffic that now diverted to it. From its ancient beginnings, the bridge had formed the foundations of a bustling market — houses built on the bridge paid rents that helped pay for its construction. This meant that the bridge itself was like a narrow street, hemmed in by rows of shops on either side with residences above — some of which were cantilevered over the river. You could walk the bridge without knowing you were crossing a river at all - except when you came to the drawbridge at its center. Crossing the bridge could be entertaining if a man could take his time, exasperating if he was in a hurry. Roger knew many of the shopkeepers on the bridge, from years of crossing it back and forth. No time to greet them now; he was in a hurry. At the drawbridge, he was in the open, exposed to the wind. He flinched just a little, wrapped the coat a little tighter, and then felt grateful for the shelter of the houses on the other side. Once across, he turned to his left, westward. He was grateful again to finally reach his destination at Serjeant's Inn; home, at least for the time being.

Lord Coke was waiting in his study at Serjeants' Inn when Roger entered. Coke gestured with his hand to a seat directly in front of his desk. Roger sat. This was unusual - Roger ordinarily sat to Coke's left, behind a table where he took his notes.

"What news, then?"

Roger caught his breath while he peeled off his coat, blew on his hands.

"Go on then, warm your hands by the fire," said Coke. "What news?"

"I met with five men, as you instructed me, and gave them your message."

"And have you a reply for me?"

Roger nodded. "Such as it is. They agree that the subsidies must be approved before other matters can be discussed. But they are most determined that support be guaranteed for the King's son-in-law, and will not officially assent to the subsidies until war is declared."

"Most determined, are they?" Coke's tone was even, his face impassive. "Did you not explain to them that the King will neither seek their advice nor follow it on matters of war and peace? It is entirely antithetical to his philosophy; he will take it as an infringement of the royal prerogative. Better to sweeten him up by promising subsidies than appeal to his sense of justice with a grievance about corruption. He might then show some sympathy for his daughter and her husband; might even ask for money to hire them an army. But he will not raise an army in England to fight in Bohemia. The Spanish ambassador, Count Gondomar, will do what he must to prevent that. Gondomar has the King's ear - flatters him continually as the great Man of Peace. Buckingham, Bacon - all of them are on the Spanish payroll. Don't they see this?"

Roger cleared his throat. "I think I did represent your opinions on this matter to them, though not as forcefully as you would have. They see a great Spanish purpose in this: to return all of Protestant Europe, one nation at a time, to popery, either by diplomacy or conquest. They have already renewed their war in the Netherlands; now Bohemia is overthrown, and the rest of Germany must follow if they have their way. If we do not stand with our allies now, we will have to face them alone, they say."

Coke sighed. "That is a sensible assessment of what the Spanish are up to. But we must focus our efforts on what is possible, what might bring success. The King will not go to war for subsidies."

"I believe you are right," said Roger. "But I am only the messenger here. There was some interest in investigating the prevalence of bribery in the kingdom. One of the gentlemen expressed the opinion that Lord Chancellor Bacon is the worst of offenders when it comes to bribery."

Coke raised an eyebrow. "Did he now? And what remedy did he propose for this state of affairs?"

"It was the general opinion that Lord Bacon should be called to account for his crimes, and if he be found guilty, should be permanently banished from government."

"Aye, if he be found guilty, so he should." Coke leaned forward. "And how many in the house do you suppose have the stomach for such business? Do they understand that the King might commit them to the Tower for something like this?"

"I do not think that they have thought that far ahead. These are new members, inexperienced with the King, or the Tower, or with making laws. They have a mandate from their constituents, and their constituents are looking for reform."

Coke sighed. "Aye, there are many first-timers in this crop. And they have more zeal than experience. Still, something might come of it if the whole House can be persuaded. If Bacon were gone, his replacement might be more alarmed by the Spanish threat; it might affect foreign policy in the long term. For now, the Marquis of Buckingham holds the real power. No attack on him will succeed. But he might be persuaded that Lord Bacon is a liability; if that should happen, Bacon is finished."

Roger had nothing to add to that last remark. He stood to leave, but Coke waved him back into his seat with a distressed expression.

"We have other matters to discuss. Better we do it now."

Roger waited, listened.

"Roger, I believe you are now eighteen years old." Roger nodded.

"It has been five years since you entered my service, five eventful years. In all that time, you have never given me cause to regret it."

"Thank you, Sir. I have no regrets, either."

Coke smiled and continued, "I do not exaggerate when I say that you have been like a son to me, in many ways. You understand my thoughts, as well as any of my natural sons — better than most of them. You have been a great comfort to me, in my latter years . . ."

"And you have been like a father to me, Sir." Roger's mind was racing. Where was this conversation going?

"We have reached the point of parting. We both knew it was coming. It is a sad day for me, but I cannot put it off any longer."

"Sir? Are you dismissing me? Have I displeased you in some way?" Roger was hurt and confused.

Coke shook his head. "I am not displeased with you. Quite the contrary. I would keep you at my side until my dying day if I could. But I must attend to your future, and that future does not lie under my roof."

"My future?"

"You are a man of gifts. Gifts too rare to be neglected. You belong at a university, where your mind can be trained and disciplined for greater work than this," here he gestured to the room around him.

Roger sat back in his chair, caught his breath. "I don't think I'm ready for university."

"You're not. But you're closer than you think. I have arranged for you to attend the Charterhouse School in Smithfield. They will get you ready for university."

"Am I not too old for that school?"

"You are. No doubt you will be the oldest student in the place. No doubt, some will tease or taunt you for that. But I have influence there, and they have agreed to take you on - since I am paying for it."

"And after that?"

"I am also High Steward at Cambridge. You will attend there, upon graduation from the Charterhouse."

Coke continued, "I made a promise to your father, five years ago, that if you served me well, I would see to it that you were set up in some profession or line of work that would allow you to make your own living. I had in mind to make some sort of clerk or scrivener of you. I see now that it would be a waste of your abilities. University will open more opportunities than you can imagine."

Roger swallowed hard. "Sir, I don't know how I would live, apart from your service. I have grown roots here."

"And now is the time for uprooting. It grieves me to lose you, but it is for the best. *'Every branch in Me that bears not fruit he taketh away: and every branch that beareth fruit, he purgeth it, that it may bring forth more fruit.'*

Roger said nothing for a moment. Then, "What about you, Sir? Is it purging you face, or worse?"

"There is indeed a purging coming. Maybe even a hewing down. May God give us grace to bear it. You will do well to be somewhere else for the next few years; a storm is coming, and it may well fall hardest on those closest to me." Then, "You must report to the school tomorrow. They will have all the required supplies on hand there. You had better pack your things." Roger had been dismissed. He rose and left the room.

The tears began almost as soon as the door closed behind him.

There wasn't much to pack: a few changes of clothes and the usual personal toiletries. Surprising, Roger thought, to have so little to show for five years' service. He was eighteen, now, nearly six feet tall - taller than most of the manservants in the house. He had that, at least, to show for his time with Sir Edward, that and the ideas that had filled his head. It occurred to him that this suddenness must have something to do with the new Parliament. Few of the King's candidates had been elected.

Instead, there were a large number of men who had never served before. Countrymen. Puritans. Men with grievances. There would be confrontation and controversy, perhaps even conflict. And Roger would be sitting on the sidelines, instead of taking part in the excitement.

The Charterhouse School was a unique institution. Founded just 10 years earlier on the site of an ancient monastery, it was both a "hospital" for 80 "poor" gentlemen and a school for 40 boys from "poor" families. "Poor" in this case meant gentlemen who had not inherited any property that would provide them with a comfortable retirement and sons of middle-class families that were likewise without substantial land holdings.

At least four of the Carthusian monks who had once lived in the monastery were executed by order of Henry VIII for refusing to accept his headship of the Church of England. After that, their monastery had come into the hands of several private owners. The last, one Thomas Sutton, had endowed the hospital and school in his will. Upon his death, the will was contested before the King's Bench. The plaintiffs were represented by none other than Francis Bacon. Sir Edward Coke ruled that the bequest was valid. The school owed its existence to the efforts of Coke; his defeat of Bacon was just one more item in a growing list of wounds that Coke and Bacon would inflict upon each other over the years.

When Coke nominated Roger to the school, his acceptance was virtually a foregone conclusion - the school's administrators remembered his service to them and were grateful. Besides, Coke was paying, and paying well for his protégé's schooling.

In those days, the Charterhouse School was located in Smithfield, outside the city wall, less than a mile from Roger Williams' family home in Cow's Lane, a similar distance from Hatton House. The neighborhood was entirely familiar to him.

The students were organized by academic level into "forms"; the first form consisted of students just beginning their studies, up to the sixth form, comprised of students who would be graduating at the beginning of summer, and moving on to a university or seminary.

On his first day, he got an impression of his classmates. They were all boys from modest backgrounds; few had families as prosperous as his own. They had been selected because they showed some particular academic merit; it was expected that most were bound for university. He was, indeed, the tallest of them, and nearly the oldest. Due to his age and stature (and possibly at Lord Coke's urging), Roger was placed in the fifth form, which meant that he would graduate the following year if he performed as expected.

In the beginning, his instructors expressed some doubt about his placement, but he surprised them with his command of Latin, particularly technical terms from the law or literature. His Greek was weak, and they concentrated his efforts on catching up to his peers. His French was more than acceptable, if a little provincial. He was adequate in mathematics, excelled in rhetoric, solid in theology. "A credit to the school," was the assessment of several faculty members. He was also congenial: he got on with everyone. Ordinarily, a fifth-former was expected to defer to the sixth-formers as his superiors in the social hierarchy of the school. Roger's size and experience made him an exception, but he didn't press the matter; he would be a sixth former himself, soon enough. He quickly earned the respect of the upperclassmen.

Roger settled into a comfortable routine at the Charterhouse. His lodgings were sparse but comfortable, the food plain but passable, the company was stimulating. Even the youngest boys were clever and amusing. And then there were the hospitallers - retired gentlemen without the means to support themselves. A few were in poor health, but most were simply gentry without land - men who had served their king and country, now nearing the end of their lives. Roger found opportunities to speak with them and listen to their stories; a few were old enough to remember when the old queen first came into her throne and the glories of those days. Several had served during the Great Armada. It reinforced Roger's sense of how much things had changed, and how much change lay ahead.

Because of his age, Roger was allowed to leave the school grounds from time to time. He used those opportunities to visit his family and catch up on news from outside. He didn't seek out his patron, Lord Edward Coke, for a good while. The sting of their parting was still with him, and he wasn't sure whether a visit would be welcome. He resolved to validate Lord Coke's sponsorship of him by excelling at school.

In Parliament, things began as the King's party expected. Large subsidies were voted for the King's support and military support of his daughter and son-in-law in Germany. The final vote on these funds was withheld until other business was completed. So far, so good. The first hint that something might be amiss was when the House of Commons formed its Committee for Grievances; it chose as its leader Sir Edward Coke. Perhaps Coke would use his leadership of the Committee to mute the complaints of the House and move quickly to approval of the subsidies and dissolution of the Parliament? That was certainly the King's desire. But no, the Committee heard complaint after complaint, week after week . . . Somehow, things were getting out of control.

The complaints became attacks. Attacks led to charges. The House of Commons became like a great grand jury, indicting great and small for corruption and bribery. The House of Lords served as magistrates, as conviction after conviction was handed down. The process included some innovations - the accused were allowed to bring legal counsel with them to their hearings, to argue on their behalf. It was a peculiar idea, but made sense to many members of the House of Commons, who were themselves lawyers by trade (in time, the notion of a right to counsel would become established law, but for now it was just another oddity of the Parliament).

In mid-March, things took a more perilous turn. A committee in the Commons reported its investigation of some supposed bribery in the courts. Bribery to obtain financial advantage was one thing; bribery to pervert justice was another - especially heinous in the eyes of many lawyers.

The outrage focused on one man in particular - Francis Bacon, Lord Chancellor of the realm. Called to account, Bacon did not deny that he had taken bribes, only that the bribes had somehow perverted justice. In many cases, he pointed out, he had taken large bribes from plaintiffs - and decided against them ('no harm, no foul', in essence). It was not a persuasive defense. The King himself offered to assist the House in its deliberations, but the House, through Sir Edward Coke, declined the offer, insisting that the House was well able to handle the matter.

By May, Parliament had made its decision. Francis Bacon was fined £40,000, committed to the Tower, and forbidden from serving in the government for the remainder of his life. The King responded by remitting Bacon's fine and releasing him after only a single night in the Tower. He could do nothing about Bacon's exile from government. The subsidies were still not fully approved, so he dared not dissolve Parliament; he ordered it suspended for the summer and imprisoned a few members in the Tower. Time to remind them of who was in charge. A little cooling off might bring them to their senses.

News of these events was widely publicized on the streets of London and elsewhere. Daily broadsides, or bulletins, were printed and offered for sale, detailing the speeches, proclamations, and controversies that were the Parliament's daily business. Not all the reporting was accurate, but that did not make it any less interesting to the public.

Roger heard the news as well as all the added commentary and opinion that everyone seemed eager to add. There was little sympathy for Francis Bacon on the streets of the city, particularly after his fine was remitted and he was released -

he was never a man with the common touch. For most people, it was a rare case of an arrogant and corrupt official receiving his just comeuppance. But Roger had more direct knowledge of the men in the news than most people. He recognized these events as only the first salvo in a larger conflict. No doubt Sir Edward took some satisfaction in the humiliation of his old enemy, but much larger stakes were at play here. He wished he could be part of the action somehow. . .

But he was on the sidelines, now. And he realized Sir Edward must have intended it that way. What had he said? "A purging is coming . . .and a hewing down"? Bacon's fall was certainly a hewing down, but there might well be other trees to fell before this was over. Roger knew the King and his character: recompense would be demanded; the price would be high.

There was a short break in classes in July. Roger was free to visit his family if he liked until classes resumed. Some students left for their family homes at various places in and around the city. Roger was in no hurry to leave; he rather enjoyed the quiet. One morning, he was summoned by the steward: "You have a visitor in the courtyard," he was told.

It was Clement Coke, seated on his chestnut stallion, smiling. He had another horse with him - it was Maggie, the grey mare Roger had ridden so often just a year ago. She looked happy to see him, too.

"I thought you might fancy a ride in the countryside," said Clem. "I brought you a mount."

Roger nodded. "I think I would fancy a ride."

"You'd best fetch a change of clothes, then. I have a mind to visit my father in Stoke today." Clem was still smiling. Roger bowed and ran to grab a change of clothes and other personal items.

It was already warm in the city as they headed westward. They didn't catch much breeze until they were well away from it. But summer was in full force; the fields basked in the July sun unblinking, reveling in the ripeness of the season. It was good to be on the road on a day like this - gazing down on the world from horseback, carefree and confident.

"You have family in the city, I believe. How do they fare?" Clem asked.

"They fare well, I think. My eldest brother, Sydrach, is to be married this year. He is a merchant tailor, as my father was. My younger brother Robert is intent on following him in that trade; the rest of my family is well, as far as I know."

"I am glad to hear it," said Clem. "My own family's fortunes are troubled by this business with the Marquis of Buckingham's family. It has been the occasion for my father's restoration to government, but I am not sure the rest of us are better off for it. No doubt you have heard of the troubles that my half-sister Frances has had with her husband, Viscount Purbeck?"

Roger shook his head. He knew, of course, that John Villiers had been created Viscount Purbeck by the King just two years ago, which of course meant that Frances Coke was now Viscountess Purbeck - a big step up the social ladder, and witness to the success of the match that her father had made for her. More than that, he had not heard: everyone talked about his brother the Marquis, but John Villiers was not in the public eye.

"Madness has befallen the man. He rants, he harms himself, he threatens his family. The Villiers family blames Frances - says that she has bewitched him. Her life is in ruins."

The thought of Frances in danger, fearing for her life at the hands of a madman, shocked Roger. Something in his chest was writhing, twisting. He felt cold, then hot. His face must have shown it because Clem responded, "I know. It grieves me too. She is only a half-sister, but we were part of the same household as children. It is a shame upon our family that she should be treated so. We are powerless to do anything for her while Buckingham rules the King."

It was awkward to hear so much of the Coke family's troubles. If he had still been living under Sir Edward's roof, Roger would naturally have been treated almost as a member of that family, though a subordinate one. But now he was somehow more independent, felt like more of an outsider. He was straddling a line between intimate and servant, and it was uncomfortable. He decided it might be better to think of himself as a distant cousin — concerned but discreetly ignoring matters that were none of his business.

"Is there truly nothing that can be done for her?" His voice sounded plaintive in his own ears.

"She has left him. The Villiers family considers that she has failed in her wifely duties. She has her title, but nothing more - they have cut her off completely."

So she was probably safe, then. Roger felt relief. Of course, for Clem and the rest of the Cokes, her poverty was a great tragedy - greater perhaps than the prospect of living with a madman. But in truth, there was no reason for Frances to live in want - her parents and siblings owned multiple houses and estates with ample room under their roofs, and well-stocked larders. No, she would not starve or go a-begging. On the other hand, he wondered about her state of mind. It surely must be a great loss to lose her marriage so. Did she feel like a failure? Was she the victim of abuse from her husband?

They reached the manor at Stoke Poges by late afternoon. It was a familiar sight by now; Roger could almost feel the place welcoming him like an old friend. Cedric the butler bowed in greeting and saw him in the (front!) door with a smile.

Sir Edward looked older and tired, but was delighted to see Roger. "Come, my boys! Sit!" Roger and Clem both found chairs. Refreshments were forthcoming.

"I have a good report of your academic efforts," said Coke to Roger."You have done me proud. The schoolmaster says you are a gifted student with a bright future." Roger bowed his head briefly in acknowledgment of the praise.

The conversation then turned to Clem and news of the family, then to more serious matters.

Clem had spent two days in the Tower of London in May for striking another member of the House during an argument. It had required an emotional appeal from his father and a full apology from Clem to secure his release. "Exactly the sort of thing we must avoid," said Lord Coke, "it is a distraction from our purpose. When men on the street talk of the exploits of 'fighting Clem Coke', they forget the more important issues of the day!"

Clem bowed his head, then nodded. "Father, I acted rashly. I shall do better."

Roger was hoping they might have more to say about the incident - who was he fighting with, and why? But, they seemed to be finished with the topic. Lord Coke was more interested in Clem's travels among the people.

Clem had reports from across the countryside, as well as London. He spoke with many men on his travels - including a fair number of the members of the House of Commons, now at home, waiting for Parliament to reconvene. The mood was triumphant in many cases, cautious in some others who feared the King's wrath. They felt that they had accomplished their purpose in purging so many bribe-takers from their positions of influence. But there was also talk of unfinished business - old grievances revived, new ones conceived. The Puritans wanted an all-out attack on the Court of High Commission. Some of them thought that Lord Coke should lead the attack. Many wished to pass a declaration prohibiting the marriage of Prince Charles to any Spanish princess, or indeed any Catholic princess at all. Some wanted most of all to raise an army to fight on the European mainland, to defend the Protestants of Germany and Bohemia against the Catholic onslaught that seemed to be triumphing everywhere.

It seems the time is ripe for change in England," said Clem. "Everywhere it is the same. The King is in for a rude surprise this autumn if he thinks this suspension has cooled things down."

Coke shook his head. "This Parliament has discovered its power. They have not yet learned how to wield it. The risk is not that the King will tame them, but rather that they may overreach before they learn how to wield power prudently. These men have returned to their constituents and can claim some success, but that will not satisfy for long. The impeachment of Bacon is a small thing if Parliament goes back to business as usual; a mere triviality if they overplay their hand and are humiliated by the royal power. Our task is to guide and shape their power into a weapon that can do some good without making an appointment with my Lord the High Executioner."

Conversation turned then to news from abroad, and it was not encouraging. The Catholic reconquest of Bohemia and Moravia was complete. Up to a third of the Protestants in those kingdoms were refugees; the rest were forced to convert to Catholicism or executed. The conflict spread westward into Germany, where Protestant princes, such as King James's son-in-law Frederick, received assistance from other states, including the Dutch Republic and Denmark. Spain, sensing an opportunity, renewed their war with the Dutch Republic. France, although bogged down in a civil war between King Louis XIII and his mother Marie de Medici, offered support to the Dutch, rather than see a strengthened Spanish presence on her northern border. Even the Turks got involved.

The war was becoming general. Armies marched back and forth across central Europe, bringing devastation and disease with them. An army on the move ate everything in its path; an army that stood still was an army that starved. On the whole, the Catholic armies won more battles than they lost, but the Dutch Republic's navy was superior to that of Spain, which was forced to supply her troops overland, along a "Spanish Road" that stretched from Genoa, on the Italian coast, along the eastern border of France, through Frederick's German territories to the Dutch frontier. That route was vulnerable to interdiction at every point along its length, and western Germany became a battleground - the nearest to England of any. A successful campaign there would eliminate the Spanish presence on the North Sea permanently. The pressure on King James to intervene was tremendous.

Which was why the Spanish Ambassador, Count Gondomar, was so critical to Spain's success, and so hated by the anti-Spanish elements in England. Gondomar walked a narrow diplomatic line, flattering the King, bribing the Marquis of Buckingham and the Howards, and teasing the possibility of a Spanish match for young Prince Charles. For Gondomar, an active Parliament was a loathsome nightmare that no true king should have to put up with - and he advised King James to that effect. James was all too willing to hear such advice; it aligned very well with his own beliefs. James also understood the waste and pointlessness of war; Gondomar praised him to his face as a man of peace. And the Marquis of Buckingham, indispensable to any diplomatic success in England, was on the side of Spain, not just because of the money: he was charmed with the power and wealth of Spain and saw a great and lucrative future for himself if a Spanish alliance could be achieved. The voices on the Privy Council that opposed the Spanish alliance were few and faint.

In the countryside and on the city streets, the mood was different - fear and loathing of Spain increased with every military success that was reported. The Parliament would surely speak about it, the more so since one of James' advisors had supposedly suggested that an inquisition, following the Spanish model, was the best solution to the problem of Parliament.

Coke found this last remark laughable. "See what fools there be in government! Where <u>does </u>the King find them? That man is our best ally, though he does not know it."

July 1621: The Viscountess

Roger rose early the next morning, found breakfast in the kitchen, and decided to take a walk in the cool of the morning, down by the pond where he used to swim. He was not far from the house when a coach pulled up to the front - some other visitor, no doubt, with some report on the mood of the country, or some matter for the Parliament to deal with. Sir Edward seemed to be the leader of the opposition party in Parliament now. Ironic. The King would not be pleased with his Privy Councilor. Roger reminded himself that none of this was his business anymore - he was just a spectator with a particularly good seat. He turned away from the house and continued walking. It was a lovely morning. He filled his lungs with fresh air, stood on the shore, and soaked in the view.

The figure of a woman appeared, approaching him from the direction of the house. The rising sun was behind her. Something familiar in her gait . . . He realized with a shock that it was Frances Coke-or rather Viscountess Purbeck, Frances Coke Villiers. When she got closer, he saw that she was as lovely as he remembered (lovelier, if that were possible), more somber in the eyes, a firmer set in the chin, perhaps.

"They told me I could find you here," she said. Then, "I have a matter that I would discuss with you. I hope that you are still an honest man?"

"I hope so too, Lady." Roger was feeling a little unsettled, with her so near.

She began walking southward along the shore. "It is a fine view from here."

He caught a twinkle in her eye and laughed. "So I have been told, Lady."

She looked suddenly serious as if sifting through what to say. "I suppose you are well informed about the troubles that brought me to his place?"

"I have heard only rumors, Lady. But if half of them are true, you have led a very perilous life since you were wed."

"I pity my husband in his distress. But I cannot live with him as a wife ought. His family will never permit me to take him under my care, but will only blame me for his suffering. They were prepared to cast me out, so I left of my own accord. I have learned some hard lessons about this world we live in: The woman is always to be blamed, the law favors men over women, and power and title will overrule justice. My mother understands this — it is why she acts as she does."

Ironic, Roger thought, that Frances' experience should drive her to her mother's point of view. How long before her behavior would begin to match her mother's?

"What will you do, then?"

"I shall survive this disgrace. My husband's madness is grounds to annul my marriage; I hope to wed again, have children, a home of my own, domestic happiness."

Frances was, if anything, as lovely as ever, Roger reflected. If she were unmarried, there would be no lack of suitors. The problem was the Villiers family. They would conceal and deny that Viscount Purbeck was in any sense an unfit husband for as long as possible. Madness was recognized as grounds for annulment of a marriage, but no such suit would ever be heard by an ecclesiastical court in England as long as the Marquis of Buckingham was the King's favorite.

"You said that you have some matter to discuss with me?"

"I have yet one particular obligation to fulfill. My mother promised Isabel's family that she would find a husband for her and supply a dowry when she came of age. Since Isabel is my servant now, that obligation falls to me. I am not eager to see her leave me - she was often the only friend I had among the Viscount's household. But she deserves a chance to have a husband of her own, and children - someone like you, I'm thinking."

"Me?" Roger had not seen this coming. It was a sort of compliment, coming from Frances Coke, and it was gratifying to think that he stood high in her estimation. He wondered if Isabel knew that Frances was raising the question with him. "How could I be a husband for Isabel?"

"You told me once that you found her pretty."

"I remember the day, and the place," Roger replied, "it was on this very bank, on a summer afternoon - though I recall the conversation was more about your appearance than hers.".

She chuckled at the recollection. "I was curious about men, then. My curiosity has been sated in the years since." Then, "I was speaking of Isabel and her need for a husband.

Surely you know that she fancies you." Her tone was declarative as if daring him to deny it.

"She gave me signs that she once did. It is years now since I have spoken with her."

"And why is that? Are you completely impervious to her charms?"

Roger smiled a little, "You speak as if you are her matchmaker."

"And what if I am? Is it so unlikely that you could find marital bliss in the arms of a woman who fancies you? A woman you admit to finding attractive?"

It was a question with as many thorns as a rosebush. Some of the thorns were of his making, most not. He measured his reply before he spoke: "Perhaps you remember a day at Hatton House when you accosted me in the hallway and challenged me to dance La Volta?"

Her eyes narrowed a bit. "I recall something of that day. You danced with Isabel; the two of you made a fine-looking couple."

"I danced it with you as well," Roger reminded her, "you were most insistent that I do so." She flinched just slightly, then smiled and nodded. "Isabel and I danced together again, on your wedding day. We did, indeed, make a fine-looking couple," he added.

A look, possibly of sadness, passed briefly across Frances' face, as of a painful memory, or a regret. "So, what is your point?"

"You asked me a question that day. Do you remember what it was?"

She shrugged and shook her head.

Of course, you don't remember, he said to himself. *The mistress asks the questions, and the servant seeks the answers. But I remember; I remember every word you ever spoke to me, every look, every careless gesture . . .* He took charge of his thoughts before he spoke again: "You asked me what or who I was, or what I might become. I took it as a challenge. I have been laboring to answer that question since that day, and some answers I have. I am headed to university - something that I could not aspire to without your father's support. Whatever my life will be, it will be that of a university graduate, a man of education, neither a tradesman nor a gentleman, but a free man, a man who makes his living with his mind."

"Ah," Frances sighed, "another of Papa's projects. A pity that so many of them result in disappointment and pain. It amazes me that so many men are willing to follow him, considering the fruit of his labors."

It was a fair assessment, Roger had to admit, upon the results of Sir Edward's marriage negotiations involving Frances, and indeed, its effect on his own marriage to Lady Hatton. But surely the fruits of success were ripening now; the Parliament was on the threshold of great things . . .

"You still have not explained what this has to do with Isabel," she said.

"Isabel would not be happy married to a man like me," he began, "she needs a husband who can match her sense of humor and her passion, and also provide the comforts that she is accustomed to. I will not be in a position to offer such to her or to any other woman for six years or more. More than that, I expect to be a different man than I am today. I know not what I shall be, but I am certain I will not be the same man."

"You are ambitious," she said with a tone of surprise. "I have not seen that in you before."

Roger started to contradict her, but stopped himself. There was more than a grain of truth to what she had said. He had hopes, or expectations, now that were very different from what he had imagined for himself just three years ago. Might as well call it ambition. Hard to say where it came from: maybe from the Charterhouse School, where everyone seemed to have a career before them? Maybe from Sir Edward and his determination to make a career for Roger? Maybe he was just growing into manhood. Call it ambition, then. He nodded.

"And you think that a wife like Isabel would hinder your advancement." It was a statement. She sounded almost disappointed in him as if his ambition was merely selfishness dressed up as a virtue . . . Truthfully, he had never considered that the choice of a spouse should factor into his aspirations.

That sort of calculation was for men who intended to rise in the world - in other words, men of ambition.

"I wasn't thinking of marriage in that way," he said. "I truly was looking at it as a question of my suitability for her. It did not occur to me that I should consider my career in choosing a wife."

Frances snorted, "If that is true, you are unlike all the men I have known, including my father — my mother is hardly any different, her ambitions are simply different from his. But see what that has cost them — and me as well. It is my father's ambition that brought his marriage to ruin and me to this state of affairs: bereft of a husband but not marriageable, a title with no means to support myself, a whole life ahead of me but without prospects. You might learn from their example."

"And you think I should marry someone like Isabel? Does she know that you are speaking to me on her behalf?"

"No," Frances replied. "I know that she admires you. But the responsibility of finding a husband for her is mine. I am trying to do my duty by her."

Roger shook his head slowly. "So, after pointing out your father's failure as a matchmaker, you have set out to do the same for Isabel and me? Why should your judgment in this matter be any more sound than your father's?"

She was quiet for a moment, thinking. "I am fond of both of you," she said finally. "I thought you might be a good match. Happiness in marriage is not as common as I once believed it to be; unhappiness is a greater burden than I once supposed. I would spare you that if I could."

She is an aristocrat, Roger said to himself. *She assumes that the lives of others are hers to manage and arrange - a 'natural right', she might say. The burden of the ruling class, perhaps . . .* Her attitude was a mixture of benevolence and arrogance. It annoyed him for some reason that he could not quite articulate.

It was the reminder, he concluded after a moment or so. The reminder that whatever happened to him or Isabel personally, Frances Villiers was of a different sort than they, and always would be. A few men — wealthy and ambitious men — might rise to prominence by marrying above their class (trading wealth or achievement for title), and their children could inherit their mother's bloodline, along with their father's money. Apart from that, Roger and men like him were destined to remain subordinates of their social betters. And people like Frances were committed to treating them that way. Roger remembered his first attempts at bowling, years ago on this very manor: Lord Coke laughing at his efforts, while the gentlemen wagered on his chances of failure - they did not intend cruelty, but there was no mistaking where he stood in their estimation . . .

"Why do you look at me that way?" Frances asked. "I can't tell if you are put out with me, or pitying me for some reason. I don't want your pity, and I have done nothing to warrant your displeasure; I'm only looking after Isabel's welfare."

Roger composed himself. "Do not be offended, Lady. I was reflecting on your remarks. It is, as you say, common enough for people to be unhappy in marriage. The fact that you would consider me a fit companion for someone that you clearly care about is a compliment that I was not expecting. Marriage is not something that I have given much consideration to — which is proof enough that I am not ready for it. I am sure that Isabel will find a suitable husband with your help. But it is beyond your power to assure that they will be happy - that must be their business."

Frances gave him a searching look. Then, "Ah. You think I presume too much to suppose I can promote the happiness of others when my own life is a shambles. A fair point — harsh, but fair. Will you not at least speak with Isabel? I believe she would welcome it."

"Is she here?"

"Of course. I take her everywhere with me. She is up at the house, unpacking our things."

Of course. He should have guessed. Who else but Isabel would do the unpacking? Without noticing, they had both stopped walking. They turned to view the manor house.

"Time to return then, Lady?" Roger asked and offered her his arm.

Frances smiled. "Aye, time to return."

Isabel was glad to see him. She smiled as she walked up to him and put a hand on either of Roger's shoulders. "You've caught a good one, Lady. Plenty of meat on these bones. How shall we prepare him?"

Frances chuckled. "Spit and roast him, I'd say. Too big for the pot!" They both laughed. Roger smiled at their teasing. He was comfortable being the butt of their jokes. It was the one seemingly harmless thing that connected the three of them. The rest was riddled with contradictions, complexities, and unspoken feelings.

At supper, Lord Coke invited all of them - Clem, Roger, Frances, and Isabel - to sit at his table.   He was in a sentimental mood. "It is fitting that all of you are with me today," he began, "each of you has shared in my fortunes and misfortunes to one degree or another for several years."(He glanced at Frances as he said "Misfortunes".) "I will tell you freely that this may be the last time that all of this company will sit around a table together."

People shifted in their seats at this remark; they looked at each other questioningly - what was he talking about?

Coke continued, "If you do ever see each other again, it is likely that I will not be among you." More quizzical looks.

"Papa, whatever it is, just say it!" said Frances. Clem nodded his agreement.

"I have been informed that the King is very displeased with me. When Parliament resumes, he expects me to persuade them to grant his subsidies without delay and prevent the House of Commons from discussing any matters of foreign affairs, the Prince's marriage, or any matter concerning the treatment of Catholics in England. "

"No man in Parliament or out of it can accomplish that," said Clem. "The King's suspension has simply given them more time to consult among themselves as to how they may bend the King's will to their own. They will not be docile; they are in a mood to fight."

"And the blame will fall on me," said Coke. "I shall face the King's wrath, and I do not expect to emerge unscathed."

"Papa!" exclaimed Frances, "If that is so, you must resign your seat!"

"The King does not want me to resign; he wants me to bend Parliament to his will. Anything less will earn his condemnation. And there are other reasons why I would not wish to be absent from Parliament this autumn."

"What reasons? What could be worth risking your life?" Frances's voice grew a little shrill.

Coke looked at Clem and nodded. Clem cleared his throat and said, "It would mean deserting his friends in their hour of need. A dishonorable betrayal of their trust. They have implored him to lead them, and he has agreed to do so. If he abandons them now, things could only go from bad to worse - hotheads will take control, and the whole country will suffer for it."

"Why? What has Papa to do with any of this?"

Coke sighed and turned to Roger. "You know more about this than anyone at this table except myself. Explain it to her. She has a right to know."

Roger was caught unprepared. But Coke was right - he had sat in a front-row seat throughout the preparations for this time. "For many years, the King has dedicated himself to taking control of every institution in the country that might place a check on his power. Lord Coke has been there again and again, to assert the traditional rights of Englishmen and their institutions in opposition to the King, but the King has prevailed. Parliament is the only institution remaining that the King does not control. The King understands this and has avoided calling a Parliament for that very reason. Lord Coke and other like-minded men have been shaping circumstances so that the King will be compelled to call for a new Parliament —a Parliament filled with men determined to defend our rights and the rule of Law. Now that a Parliament has been called, they must seize the opportunity that they have created, and make the most of it - or lose everything that they hold dear." Roger hoped that was clear enough . . .

Frances was staring at him. "Is this what you have been doing all these years? Plotting against the government?"

Coke spoke, "We have been 'plotting', as you say, to *preserve* the proper government of this realm against the corruption and avarice of a King who is under the control of dishonorable men—men who have sold themselves to our enemies, and will sell the rest of us as well, given the chance."

"You are referring to my in-laws," said Frances. "Would that you had not been so eager to sell your youngest daughter to such men!" She stood up and made as if to leave the table; Isabel stood, too.

Frances's tone was even, controlled. "I have blamed myself, more than anyone, for the failure of my marriage. Oh, I recognized that my hand was the price of restoring my father to the King's favor. But I have forgiven you for that because I thought you were serving the interests of our family. Now I learn that I was like a sacrificial pawn in some great chess game, of which you kept me ignorant. A game that you now admit you expect to lose. Tell me, is your cause so noble that it was worth my suffering? And what about the rest of our family? Is their ruin to be the price of your willfulness?"

Coke's face showed his distress: he said nothing.

Frances and Isabel left the dining hall hastily.

"I am sorry, Lord, that my 'explanation' has gone so ill," said Roger.

"Nay, you said it as well as I could have done," Coke replied. Clem nodded in agreement.

They finished their meal in silence. The Viscountess and Isabel did not appear the rest of that day; they took their evening meal in their bedchamber. Late in the evening, as Roger was preparing to turn in, Isabel appeared and motioned him to her side.

"The Viscountess has sent me to find you," said Isabel. "She wishes to speak with you in private."

It was not the sort of request that could be refused, even if Roger had wished to. He followed Isabel upstairs to the bedchamber where she and Frances were lodged. The Viscountess sat in a chair. She had been crying - her eyes were red. She appeared to have composed herself. She fixed her gaze on Roger and spoke in a cool, deliberate tone: "I must know the truth," she said, "You have not been entirely honest with me, but I don't think you would tell me bald-faced lies. Please, be seated," she gestured to another chair. Roger sat. Isabel took a chair, as well.

"Tell me plainly, are we all in danger of our lives over this matter?"

"Lady, I do not think so. Lord Coke has contrived to protect his friends and family in all of this."

"How so? How has he protected me? Or you, for that matter?"

"He has dismissed me from his service and enrolled me in school. I would have stayed with him if he would let me, but he was unyielding. I was wounded in my heart to think that he found me unworthy, but now I see that he intended to protect me from what he sees coming. Whatever his fate, he has secured a pathway to university for me, and I am in no way complicit in this Parliament business."

"So you dabble in treason, and wash your hands of it, while my father faces the King's judgment?'

"Lady, there is no treason in any of this! Lord Coke has not failed to submit to the King's authority in any matter, nor does he intend to. He sees which way the wind is blowing and would warn those he cares for to seek shelter."

"Shelter? What shelter is there for me? He is abandoning me to the storm, or so he says!"

Roger shook his head and sighed. "I think that your father regards your match to the Viscount as a mistake and regrets it. Your suffering weighs heavily upon him. The Villiers family took great pains to conceal the truth about your husband before his marriage, and after — as you well know. I do not imagine that your father understood how things would turn out - I am certain that he would never have agreed to the marriage if he had."

"And yet here I am, without home or fortune of my own, begging for food and shelter from my family."

Roger spoke without thinking. "Lady, I know beggars. They sit in the streets and alleys all over London. Any one of them would trade places with you, and praise God in heaven if they could."

Frances was mildly shocked at his impertinence. Roger felt that he had gone too far. But then she nodded. "Your honesty stings, but I asked for it. Explain how you think that my father has contrived to protect my mother and me from the wages of his labors."

"As for Lady Hatton, I think she is in no danger. The King dined at her home just weeks ago, or so I have heard. No one would believe that she and your father agree on anything."

Roger heard Isabel giggle in the background. "As for you, I believe that he has made arrangements for your inheritance. I think that this house will be available to you as long as he lives, and you will have this or some other when he is gone. You also have brothers and sisters who may come to your aid, if need be."

"That is true. I had nearly forgotten. I think I will visit my sister, Lady Anne Sadleir, soon. I must know what she thinks of all this."

"I would advise you not to speak of this with Lady Anne or any of your other siblings."

"Why not?"

"Lady Anne has a reputation for her loyalty to the King. Telling her what you now know can only compromise her position and force her into uncomfortable choices. Who can predict what she might do? Ignorance of these matters, along with her reputation, should be enough to protect her. The same is true of the rest of your family - the less they know, the safer they are."

"Except for Clem?"

Roger nodded. "Except for Clem." Clem would have to take care of himself.

"If that is so, why are you here, in this house?"

"I was invited by your brother Clem to take a ride in the country. I wanted to see my old mentor once again before I returned to school, that is all."

"You did not know that I would be here?"

"Nay, Lady. How could I?"

"I received an invitation, too. I believe he is up to something."

Ah. So it was not just coincidence, then. Roger wondered what Coke was up to, as well. "I must suppose that he wanted to bid farewell to us, as he said," Roger offered.

"If that is the best reason you can come up with, I think this conversation is finished," Frances said. Roger stood and bowed. She appeared to be less anxious. Roger excused himself.

Isabel followed him out into the hallway. She was holding a candle. "Since truth-telling is the order of the day, I would speak with you also," she whispered. The house was dark. They found their way downstairs to a sitting room. There were chairs before the fireplace, which was cold - no fire was needed on a warm July night.

"What have you been up to these last two and a half years?" she asked. Before he could answer, she continued, "Oh, that's right, you've been conspiring against the government, haven't you? It all makes sense now." Her tone was sarcastic, but more teasing than bitter.

"Under the circumstances, you can understand why I could not have spoken with you about what I was doing," he said.

"Protecting me, of course," said Isabel. "I wouldn't have been interested in those things, anyway. I had hopes that I might see you simply because you might have wished to see . . . me. After a few months, I realized that you must have other things on your mind. Now I know what those other things were."

"I have disappointed you. I am sorry." It was lame, but Roger felt that he owed her an apology, somehow.

"Disappointed, yes. Not devastated. Not crushed the way that my mistress has been."

"These years must have been difficult for you as well, though."

Isabel nodded. "That man can be terrifying. And his mother even more so. We are well out of that house. It's enough to convince a young woman that men - all men- are simply not worth the trouble. I would like to hear an argument to the contrary."

Roger had nothing to say.

Isabel changed the subject. The Viscountess was most keen on speaking with you this morning, when she learned you were here; she got me well out of the way. Can you tell me what was on her mind?"

"It was a private matter. Confidential."

"Then let me guess. Was it about me? The expression on your face tells me I am right, even in this dim light. She is about finding me a husband, and she thinks you might fit the bill, am I right?"

Roger smiled sheepishly.

"Well, a girl could do worse. You're not bad looking; a man with prospects, so they say. And I am of an age and a mind to marry — ripe for it, Roger Williams, ripe for it."

Roger looked at her. Even by candlelight, her . . . ripeness was apparent. He smiled ruefully and nodded. "You have grown to be a lovely woman. Any man would be blessed to wed you."

"Any man, but not every man, you mean. I would not have just any man, I wish to be loved by my husband above all others. Absent that, I would not marry at all."

That was plain enough. Roger felt he should say something equally frank, searched for the words . . .

"But I do not think it right to leave my mistress's service at this stage of her life. She is still very fragile. Part of her suggestion to you is because she trusts you, and few men in her life have proved worthy of her trust. She imagines that if you and I were married, she would have two faithful friends in her life. She knows that a part of your heart is still hers to command - don't deny it, even I can see it. She is willing to make what she can of that part of you, to secure my happiness and hers - perhaps, incidentally, your happiness as well. I can imagine such a life for myself, married to a man I care for, an honorable man, a man that would always take care of me, but a man whose heart can never be entirely mine. . . and I can imagine why that might be miserable for you, a test of your self-discipline — a burden to bear over a lifetime. I cannot be part of such a marriage."

Roger realized that he had to speak now. "Lady Frances did indeed speak to me of you this morning. I explained to her that I cannot marry now, nor shall I for several years. I am headed to university; and after that, who knows?   Lady Frances says that I am driven by ambition, and that nothing good will come of it; that her father is an example of the pitfalls of ambition."

He continued, "As for you, let me say that you have grown also, to be a beautiful and desirable woman — ripe, as you put it so well. Lady Frances will have no difficulty finding suitors for you when you are ready to leave her. And I think you are right about her fragility. One way or another, this business with the Parliament will be over by the end of the year. Time then for all of us to pick up the pieces, and move on."

"Do you really suppose that Lord Coke will lose his life over this?"

Roger shook his head. "Lord Coke has never harbored a treasonous thought in his life, as far as I know. He will not say or do anything that would qualify. Members of Parliament are immune from prosecution for things they say in chambers. The worst that could happen is that he will lose his position on the Privy Council. (That is bad enough; Lady Frances has good reason to say that all her suffering has been for nothing.) But any more punishment than that from the King would be overreach - he would be foolish to attempt it; overreach is the root of all his troubles."

"And the rest of the family?"

"Ignorance is their defense. Unless some servant can be induced to testify that they are part of some great conspiracy, they will not be touched."

"And you?"

"I? I am just a student. Who would believe that I had anything to do with this?"

"I am glad to hear it," said Isabel. I was worried for you at the supper table." She rose from her chair. "When last I saw you, I said it might be for the last time. I was nearly right. This time is more likely our last. Give us a hug and a kiss."

He took her in his arms (or was it the other way round?) and held her while they kissed. She moved her body against him; ripe she was. When they parted, she gave him a look as if to say, "See what you are passing up?" Then she was gone, her candle growing dimmer with the distance in the dark house. Roger felt a little dizzy. He decided to clear his head by stepping outside for a while.

January 1622: Reckoning

By the time Parliament re-convened in November, Roger was already immersed in his penultimate year at the Charterhouse School. The studies were more demanding, but he found he could rise to the challenge. He also began to take the measure of his fellow students and realized that there were some parts of the curriculum at which he excelled even the students a year ahead of him. None of them were dullards, but some things just seemed to come more easily to Roger Williams - languages, especially; he had a way with words - grammar, vocabulary, rhetoric - he soaked it in like a sponge, in any language he studied. There was a pliability in his intellect that could adjust itself smoothly to every language he studied; it was a gift, said his teachers. He also had a knack for debating either side of an issue, or even both at once, which the schoolmasters found amusing. "Beware that you do not lose your sense of integrity in the labyrinth of rhetorical devices," warned one of his teachers, "it is advantageous for a gentleman to handle himself well in debate, but unless his heart is anchored in the truth, he becomes the creature of the moment, adrift on the sea of circumstance!"

Roger nodded at this advice. His rhetorical performances were just a way of showing off, really. The counsel of his heart he kept to himself. His instructors would be shocked if they knew what he really believed; shocked and disturbed. He would hold his counsel and play the game that he was being trained for: his confidence was growing that he knew how to win at it.

Parliament resumed on November 20, 1621. It took them just eleven days to earn the King's rebuke. On December 18, James ordered that Parliament be dissolved. The result was predictable, though most observers remarked on how quickly and efficiently Parliament had finished its business.

They began with a fourteen-point petition that the King refused to read (though he was well-informed of its contents; Count Gondomar's informants delivered a copy of the document to him before the Parliament had approved it.) Gondomar warned the King that unless he was willing to punish Parliament for their 'insolence', he would leave England (thus ending the hopes of a Spanish alliance) immediately. In addition to their objection to the Spanish alliance and the possible Spanish match, Parliament insisted that freedom of speech and debate was their absolute right, and that included amnesty for anything said or done as official business - only Parliament had the authority to discipline its members. At first, members of Parliament insisted that the King had somehow been misled by his advisors, or otherwise misinformed about the petition (Count Gondomar was a chief suspect), but when they submitted a revised version of it ten days later, the King responded by ordering Parliament to dissolve. They stalled for several hours and converted the terms of the petition to a "protestation" that would be entered into the official Journals of Parliament, a kind of benchmark for future Parliaments, without the King's approval or consent. It would have no legal force without James' approval, but it stood as a contradiction to everything that James desired from his Parliament. (There would be no subsidies, not even for military aid to James' son-in-law in Germany - although James and Buckingham had already promised Count Gondomar that they would use the money to make war on the Dutch Republic.)

James took possession of the Journals and ripped the offending pages out of them. He vowed never to call another Parliament.

Lord Edward Coke took most of the blame. He was, after all, a member of the Privy Council - expected to represent the King's policies, not those of James' opponents. He was stripped of his office (once again, he was Sir Edward Coke) and escorted to the Tower of London by no fewer than eight guards.

Roger heard the news through the usual channels of gossip and broadside. "Sir Edward's chambers at Serjeant's Inn have been searched, all his books and papers removed," they said. Roger knew that some of those papers were in his own handwriting, and it gave him pause. But of course, he had never signed any of them - Sir Edward's caution was proving prescient.

There were rumors that Sir Edward was about to be charged with treason. The King's agents raided the manor at Stoke Poges, looking for anything incriminating. They sent inspectors to examine the grounds at Stoke, looking for evidence of poaching - whether of deer or of trees. They found none. At length, the Privy Council decided that charging him with treason with such thin evidence would backfire - the public, after all, was known to agree with every one of the points in the petition.

A cooling off was what they needed; a different type of cooling off was what Sir Edward Coke was experiencing. It was an unusually cold winter. The warden of the tower did not much care to spend money heating any of the cells. Sir Edward shivered his way through his seventieth birthday, hoping for an early Spring.

By tradition, the King issued a general amnesty at the end of every session of Parliament. All the members of both houses were pardoned - except Sir Edward Coke. By law, he was ineligible to receive a pardon if some outstanding case against him was pending. The Crown sued him for 30,000 pounds that he was alleged to owe, for mishandling an inheritance from Lady Hatton, his estranged wife (this was the same case for which he had been acquitted several years before). He was denied books, or paper, or any writing instruments; no visitors were allowed.

There were men in the King's circle who urged the King to ease Sir Edward's conditions while he awaited trial. Among them was Charles, the Crown Prince. The King was implacable, at first: "I know no *Edward Coke*," he insisted. More pressure against Coke was applied by members of the Privy Council, who hinted that the King was inclined to treat him even more harshly " . . . if the King desires my head, he knows whereby he may have it.", Coke replied.

At the end of March, the King directed that Sir Edward be permitted to leave his cell, to walk about the grounds in the Tower courtyard. By then, the weather was improving. Later, his daughter, the Lady Anne Sadleir, was permitted to visit him. Gradually, the terms of his confinement were eased. His son Robert was allowed to dine with him. He was allowed writing materials. Ultimately, he was released to house arrest at his estate in Stoke Poges. The trial was set for the Fall.

Since the crime that Sir Edward was charged with involved taxes on inherited property, the case went to the Court of Wards and Liveries, instead of a higher court. This court was empowered to levy fines on the guilty. Only a higher court could have imposed the death penalty for, say, a conviction of treason, but given Sir Edward's substantial wealth, they could impose a fine that would effectively make him a beggar — punishment enough, surely. The King's advisors were hoping for something of the sort — ruining Coke would send a message to others who shared his opinions.

Roger Williams received an invitation to visit his old mentor at Stoke through Clem, who appeared at the Charterhouse School one August morning, as he had the previous year. It drizzled all that day, and they were both soaked thoroughly by the time they arrived at Stoke. The place looked tireder and drearier than he last remembered, and so did Sir Edward - the seven months in the Tower had taken their toll.

After changing to dry clothing, Roger sat in front of a cheery fire in the sitting room. There was brandy to sip. He relaxed, enjoying the warmth inside and out. Clem and Sir

Edward sat with him, chatting about some family business or other.

"I hear good reports about your progress at school," said Coke to Roger. "They say that you will do well at university."

Roger acknowledged the praise with a bow of his head. "I hope I shall not disappoint, Sir."

"Nay. You have exceeded my expectations already. I suppose it may have embarrassed you to be associated with an accused criminal — in school, I mean."

"Not at all, Sir. In fact, my association with you provoked admiration. Nearly all the students and faculty are of the opinion that you and the Parliament were in the right; that the King has fallen under the sway of the Spanish ambassador, and something must be done to put a stop to it."

"Put a stop? How do they suppose to do that?"

"They have no plan. Only a desire to see the government choose another path."

"Ah. Well, Lady Hatton has done her share in that regard, or so I hear." He chuckled.

"How is that, Sir?"

"Well, it so happens that the Spanish Embassy borders directly upon the grounds of Hatton House. Count Gondomar has asked for permission to traverse through Lady Hatton's gardens to refresh himself. You can imagine how his request was received. He must take his walks in the street, like any other Londoner - which he does only rarely, for fear of encountering the public mood." Coke chuckled again.

"I suppose it is some relief to you that she has someone else to set her teeth against," said Clem.

Coke shook his head. "Not much. She has enough vitriol for more than one man at a time. Still, it pleases me to think that Count Gondomar is a little less comfortable these days. If it were any other man, I might feel some sympathy for him. Instead, I am strangely grateful to my wife." He laughed, and Roger saw a renewed light in his eyes - there was still some fight in the old man.

Coke changed the subject. "You say that the sympathies of the students and faculty at the school lie with Parliament? What do you hear of the rest of the city?"

"It is the same, from everything I hear. Even my brother Sydrach, who has often doubted the prudence of Parliament, is a Parliament man now. People say that the King has been misled - bewitched, even - by Count Gondomar. They believe that Prince Charles' marriage to a Spanish princess will be the end of our nation."

"It is the same in the countryside," said Clem. "Every member of the Houses, Lords, and Commons, with whom I speak, is outraged by what is happening, and their constituents even more so. If the King calls for another Parliament, he won't like it any better than the last one. He'll get no subsidies until he changes course."

"The King will not call another Parliament," said Sir Edward. "He is finished with Parliaments. He'll get such monies as he can, borrow while he can, sell some titles - whatever it takes, but no Parliament. His health is poor, his days are dwindling. He thinks of his legacy - the throne that he passes to his son. He is determined to set an example of firmness so that his son will begin <u>his</u> reign in a position of strength. No compromise is possible while he lives."

Roger saw a gleam in Sir Edward's eyes that had been missing before. *He's not beaten yet,* Roger said to himself. *He's already calculating his next move!* It was a relief to know that the Tower had not broken his mentor; daunting to imagine what the next round in this fight would look like.

In the morning, Sir Edward invited Clem and Roger to go riding with him. The rain had tapered off overnight, the world was freshly washed and fragrant. "I am allowed to ride six miles from the house in any direction, no farther," said Coke. "There are spies about, to report on me. A great deal of trouble for the King, don't you think?"

"Can't see the point of it," said Clem. "They're suing you to take your lands. Even if you do ride outside the six-mile limit, it's not as though you can take your property with you. It will still be here for their taking if you lose the case."

Sir Edward laughed. "Now you're thinking like a lawyer!"

Clem blushed a little, Roger noticed. Since Clem had been elected to Parliament, he seemed to have gained some . . . confidence, perhaps. As if he had finally found a position of significance for himself. Sir Edward had always been affectionate with Clem, but now Roger sensed that there was respect as well. "Baby Clem", "Fighting Clem", had grown up in his father's eyes; no longer the failed law student, but now a Member of Parliament, a man to be honored among his peers.

"What of the case, Sir?" Roger asked. "Are you prepared to defend yourself?"

"The King's men asked the same question," Coke replied, "They even offered me the services of several prominent lawyers to prepare my defense."

"And what did you say?"

Coke shook his head. "I should have said that it was a clumsy attempt to discover my defense arguments ahead of the trial, to aid in my prosecution. But I held my tongue and thanked them. I told them I was abler to defend myself than any other man in the kingdom."

"Was that the King's idea?"

"I doubt it. The King is not prone to attend to such details. But the men around him - men whose careers are in jeopardy if I am acquitted — those men might well have devised such a plan. If the Spanish alliance fails, all the bribes that those men live on will dry up; they must hold the government on its course, or face poverty. Corrupting a trial is no great thing for such men - they are trading a whole nation for lucre."

There it was again—the fire within. Roger had persuaded himself that Sir Edward Coke was retiring from the fight after seven months in the Tower. Anyone who thought that was in for a surprise.

Roger and Clem returned to London the following day.

In late August, the Court of Wards and Liveries met to hear Sir Edward Coke's case. Despite the best efforts of the King's Attorney General, Coke was acquitted of all charges.

The government was in no hurry to return his property, but by November, he had his personal effects back and took up his old residence at Serjeant's Inn.

Count Gondomar, the Spanish Ambassador, was recalled to Spain that autumn, a development that was celebrated by the majority of Englishmen. His retirement did not represent a change in policy for either the government of England or of Spain. But it was a sign, for those who were astute enough to recognize it, of a change in attitude. Spain's successes in what would become known as the Thirty Years War had made an alliance with England less urgent. The pro-Spanish party in King James's inner circle resolved to intensify their efforts to secure an alliance by marrying Prince Charles to the Infanta — princess of Spain.

Roger was well into his final year at the Charterhouse School. He turned twenty-one just before the end of the year.

May 1623: Courtship and Cambridge

Negotiations with the Spanish government for Prince Charles' marriage were bogged down. The new Spanish ambassador was less encouraging than his predecessor, less willing to offer assurances (not to mention less generous with his bribes), less interested in closing the deal. The courtiers around the King were getting anxious. It was the Marquis of Buckingham who came up with the idea to break the impasse with a bold move. "If this ambassador is unwilling to negotiate with us, we must take the negotiations directly to the Spanish Court," he said. He devised a plan to do so. It involved Prince Charles and Buckingham traveling to Spain personally, and sweeping the Infanta off her feet, making a marriage inevitable - surely Love would conquer all! Convincing the King to allow this was the greatest challenge. Somehow, Buckingham did it. For this to work, Buckingham explained, they would have to travel incognito - surprise would deny whatever forces within the

Spanish government who opposed the match to prepare their resistance.

They were not gone a week before the King wanted them back. James' wife was dead, his daughter at war in Germany. His only living son and his closest advisor were now at large somewhere in Europe - he was destitute of men he trusted, surrounded by courtiers desperate for favors and attention. He wept over his "onlie sweete Sonne and my onlie best sweet Servant" in front of his courtiers.

Buckingham had completely misread the mood of the Spanish court. Access to the Infanta was denied, except under the most restrictive circumstances. Charles and Buckingham contrived to have Charles surprise the Infanta in her garden by vaulting over a wall, but she fled from him, screaming. The two men were threatened with arrest; Buckingham nearly talked himself into a duel.

At home, when news of the adventure got out (as it inevitably did), the revulsion was intense. For once, the King and his subjects were in complete agreement - the Prince and the Marquis must return immediately. The Spanish alliance was a mistake; time to look for allies elsewhere. The Marquis was created Duke of Buckingham for his efforts and ordered to return.

During his final week of classes at the Charterhouse School, Roger received a summons to the Headmaster's office. When he arrived, he was pleasantly surprised to see his old mentor, Sir Edward Coke. Coke was smiling, chatting with the Headmaster, sharing a laugh about something. When Roger entered, Coke turned to him with a smile: "Well done, my boy! The Headmaster has been informing me of your academic triumphs! I am proud of you!"

Roger bowed and smiled. "It is only because of your sponsorship that I have achieved anything, Sir."

"Don't be overmodest. You have earned your reward."

Reward? He must be referring to my acceptance at Pembroke College, said Roger to himself. He bowed again, since it sounded like a compliment.

The Headmaster spoke. "The governors of the school have awarded you an exhibition, master Williams. For the duration of your stay at Cambridge, you will receive sixteen pounds per year to cover your expenses. Congratulations!"

Roger was speechless for a moment. It must have shown on his face, because Coke chuckled. "That is not all. As High Steward of the University, I am authorized to inform you that you are to receive a University scholarship as well — for your mastery of ancient languages. That's another twelve pounds per year."

Roger spotted an open chair and sagged into it. "That's very generous of you, Sirs. I don't know what else I can say." His mind was racing. Sixteen . . . no, twenty-eight pounds per year! That was more money than he had ever had to his name, more than most craftsmen in England could earn for a year of labor. With that kind of income, a man could live as a gentleman: if he managed it carefully, he could afford a personal servant, a valet. He could dress as a gentleman ought, eat as a gentleman ought . . . In a flash, his life had changed. No doubt there would be wealthier students at Cambridge, sons of the rich and powerful. But he would be able to hold his head up in their presence, because he had means of his own, means he had earned.

In October, the Prince and the Duke of Buckingham returned to London. Bells rang across the city in celebration; bonfires could be seen at night in every direction. The Spanish ambassador appeared before Parliament to demand that Buckingham be executed for insulting the honor of the Spanish royal family or risk losing any chance of an alliance (the ambassador well knew that James would not be willing to sacrifice his favorite on his own). It was an astonishing act of arrogance, and a complete misreading of Parliament's mood.

Spain had gotten its way with the execution of Sir Walter Raleigh, but there would be no repeat of that fiasco. The Duke of Buckingham appeared before Parliament and declaimed the treachery of Spain and urged a declaration of war. King James agreed and called for Parliament to appropriate the necessary funds. It all happened with breathtaking (for James) speed. France was now the alliance to seek: France would support the Protestant cause in Europe, support the King's son-in-law and daughter, and help the Dutch drive the Spanish out of the Netherlands for good. (Never mind that the French government was waging a war against their own Huguenot protestant minority; keep your eye on the big picture.) The French had a bride for Prince Charles, named Henrietta Maria — Catholic, but pretty. She had this penchant for dancing the ballet - a French conceit. At least she wasn't Spanish. Negotiations were soon underway for a royal match - conducted, of course, by the Duke of Buckingham.

July 1623: Cambridge

Pembroke Hall was founded in 1347, the third such college that came to comprise the University of Cambridge. Roger Williams couldn't help being impressed with the grandeur of the ancient buildings, arranged around two large courtyards, with halls, chapels, and gardens attached. The place was designed to be self-sufficient: students and faculty lived and dined on site, kitchens fed them, and gardens supplied the kitchens with much of the food they served.

It was a world apart in other respects as well. There was a standard of deference expected of students toward their teachers, even when the social class of the student was superior to that of the schoolmaster. Students were required to wear a kind of gown over their clothing when in class, which gave them all a superficially similar appearance - difficult to distinguish the son of an earl from the son of a blacksmith (outside of class, everyone could tell who was who, of course;

the wealthy and powerful brought their servants to university with them.) Roger made it his business to get along with everyone. He discovered that not all the sons of noble families were privileged dullards simply looking at the university as a stepping stone toward claiming their entitled destinies (though some were); he also found that more than a few of the young men from middle-class families were out of their academic depth, as well (and plenty of them were brilliant). His self-confidence grew as he measured himself against his peers. Whatever the future might hold, he was more than able to hold his own among this lot.

The academic curriculum was devoted to tradition (not surprising for a 300-year-old institution). The schoolmasters considered it their mission to pass along the learning of the past, which they held to be authoritative, universal, and sufficient for the education of each generation of students under their tutelage. Intellectually, Roger and his peers found it stifling. But he was getting paid to study - no complaints.

For most of the students, the events of the present time held more interest. Outside the lecture halls and tutorials, conversation turned to what was happening in the world beyond the courtyard walls. Opinions were by no means unanimous; vigorous debates ran long into the evenings, in the students' residences, even spilling outside the school grounds into public houses like the White Horse Inn, where students had congregated for untold generations. Some of those students had achieved fame and glory - bishops, archbishops, even a few chancellors - and others could be found on an honor roll of celebrated martyrs and heretics (the difference between heretics and martyrs was also a matter of debate. Could a man be both?)

The Parliament that convened in 1624 included most of the men who had sat in 1621, including Sir Edward Coke and his son, "Fighting Clem" Coke. The issues and grievances that preoccupied Parliament were also the same. The difference was that so many of the disagreements that had prompted the King's outrage in 1621 had now been resolved - in Parliament's favor. The Spanish alliance was dead, and the possibility of a Spanish bride for Prince Charles was gone with it. The King had already declared a willingness to go to war in Europe on behalf of the Protestant cause; it only remained for Parliament to give him the money to do so. The Duke of Buckingham, once reviled for his infatuation with all things Spanish, was now a popular hero for his public repudiation of Spanish treachery. He sat in the House of Lords that year and was an influential advocate for reform.

"See how the fox has decided to run with the hounds," said Sir Edward to Clem, "How long do you suppose it will take for the hounds to turn on him?"

"If they're anything like the hounds I have known, they'll welcome the fox to share their kennel," Clem replied, "they take more pleasure in the chase than in the kill."

There was a heady feeling of unity in England, a burst of patriotic fervor, a sense that things had turned a corner, and would soon get better. There was little interest in mentioning the past failures of the Duke of Buckingham.

For Sir Edward Coke and others in his circle, the deeper conflicts between royal prerogative and ancient rights were still unresolved, but they were reluctant to spoil the national mood by picking a fight with a king whom everyone recognized was nearing the end of his reign. Antagonizing him at this point would serve no purpose — and might get someone a long stay in the Tower of London.

The Parliament did accomplish one goal that had long been on its agenda; it passed legislation that outlawed all royal monopolies. The Duke of Buckingham enthusiastically endorsed the legislation; the King had no objection, since he was going to keep the money he had received from selling them in the first place, and was expecting generous new subsidies in addition.

October 1624: Unto us, a Child is Born

Father Quentin heard the knock at the rectory door that evening, but sent Father Jones, his Curate, to answer it. He was weary and cold; it had been windy and raining most of the day, and he had been outdoors during the worst of it, visiting the sick in his parish. The knocking stopped - he heard voices at the door, and felt a damp draft around his ankles. The voices continued, and the draft, until Father Quentin shouted to his Curate, "If you must speak at length, at least shut the door, ere we all get the chill!"

Father Jones appeared, just as the draft was subsiding. "This is a matter that requires your attention, I believe."

Quentin stood with a groan. The chill was making his joints stiff. "What is it?"

"We have visitors. You should speak with them yourself."

Quentin walked into the front hallway. Three people stood there, their outer garments dripping from the rain. One was a woman, veiled and dressed in black—a widow in mourning, apparently. She held a bundle in her arms. The bundle squirmed a little - a baby, then. The other two stood together, a young woman with blonde hair and a young man who might be her husband. "What service do you require?" Quentin asked in his weary professional tone.

The woman in black spoke: "My newborn son needs to be baptized."

"That is true enough. If you bring him to church on Sunday, we can perform the service then."

"We shall not be here on Sunday, nor at any other parish nearby. My circumstance" — here she stiffened her posture, as if to emphasize her widow's weeds - "sends me to France, where English priests are hard to find. I wish my son to be baptized into the Church of England, not according to some French Catholic rite."

"I explained to them that in such necessity, a child may be baptized in a private house," said the Curate.

"This is a private house. We have no other in the area," added the widow.

Father Quentin considered the matter. "Where is the child's father?"

"Where do you think? Would I be wearing these clothes if he were still with us?" A bit testy, thought Father Quentin. No doubt the poor woman was grieving her loss . . .

"These two others are prepared to serve as godparents," said Father Jones, indicating the young woman and her . . . husband, was it? Father Quentin turned to them and asked, "What are your names?"

"Isabel and Walter Cutler," said the blonde woman with a curtsey. Odd that she spoke first, but "We are indeed prepared to act as godparents," added the young man, and added: "We understand that our request is inconvenient, but surely the soul of this young child is worth some inconvenience? We are prepared to compensate you for this intrusion." He held up a small purse. Father Quentin heard the clink of coins - large coins, by the sound of them. "I am sure that the poor of this parish could be helped, if you had the resources to offer them?"

Father Jones nodded. "You are quite right. 'The *poor ye shall always have with you,*' as our Lord himself said." He looked at Father Quentin.

Quentin thought for a moment. "Very well, I will fetch my vestments. Father Jones, please get water for the baptism from the chapel."

In the vestry, Father Quentin considered the situation. None of these nocturnal visitors was from the area, of that he was certain. That much they admitted. The veiled woman — whether she was truly a widow or not — was at least making a commendable effort on behalf of the child; he could think of no justification to deny the sacrament to an innocent infant. ('Suffer the little children,' Jesus had said.) The identity of the mother was a question. She would give a name, of course, to be recorded in the registry. Since she was a stranger, he would have no way of determining whether the name was genuine. That made no difference to the infant - a sacrament was a sacrament. It was just possible that the baby was illegitimate — that is, that the father of the child was alive, and refused to acknowledge it. In that case, the mother was feigning widowhood to spare her child that stigma. Leaving the country might make sense if the family had money, and all indications were that they did. Even if the child was a bastard, it would not be a burden on the resources of his parish . . . Yes, baptizing the baby was the best thing for everyone concerned — especially the baby.

There was a small chapel in the rectory, which Father Quentin used for his daily devotions. They all managed to squeeze into the space, and Father Quentin performed the service from the Book of Common Prayer - the portion entitled "Of Them That be Baptized in Private Houses In Tyme of Necessity". When it was time for the name of the boy to be recorded, the widow pulled back her veil and said, "His name is Robert. Robert Wright. He is named after his father. My name is Frances." Her expression was firm, almost defiant. Her face was as lovely as any that Father Quentin had ever seen. He heard Father Jones gasp faintly at his right hand as the name was recorded. The godparents' names were recorded as well - both of them wore wedding rings, which persuaded Father Quentin that they probably were a married couple; then the admonishment to the godparents, the prayers, and they were done.

The visitors gathered their things and left the way they had come. Father Jones showed them the door and stood in the entrance for a while. More drafts swirled around Father Quentin's ankles: he reflected that he wasn't looking forward to Winter. "They left in a coach," Father Jones reported, "an expensive one, as far as I can tell."

Father Quentin nodded. It made sense. Something that wealthy people wanted to cover up. Shame about the child, but at least he had done what he could for him. His mother's wealth and her looks would have to answer for the rest. And there was money in the poorbox.

March 27, 1625: Long Live the King

King James' health took a turn for the worse that winter. His physicians expressed optimism that he would recover in the Spring, but it was not to be. He died on March 27, 1625. He was fifty-seven; not old, but long-standing ailments since childhood had caught up with him. He was not mourned long or deeply; other travails took precedence. In April, the plague appeared in London and gradually increased in strength. A chilly May and a rainy June ruined crops all over the kingdom, compounding the misery. In the midst of this, King Charles' bride, Henrietta Maria, joined him in London, with her retinue of Catholic priests and courtiers. Masses were said daily in the royal palace.

Puritan preachers were outraged and declared that the plague was God's judgment upon the apostasy of the Royal court. "We are like Nineveh in the days of Jonah," they said, "We may yet escape the destruction to come, if we repent." Unlike the King of Nineveh, King Charles saw no reason for repentance. Charles and his Queen left London to avoid the risk of infection. Before it was over, 35,000 would die of the plague in London, uncounted more in the countryside. It was an inauspicious beginning to the new king's reign.

Charles called a Parliament, as was customary for the beginning of a new reign, in April. The newly elected members were first convened on June 18th of that year, in London - just as the plague was gaining strength. . . .

Many of the men in the new Parliament were the same men who had served during the years of struggle with King James - men like Sir Edward Coke, and his son, Clem. The national euphoria of the previous year had dissipated, what with the Royal marriage and the plague, and Parliament saw the opportunity to press for reform. The key, as they saw it, was to constrain the revenue that the new king needed. If they could force Charles to call for a new Parliament every year, they would have much greater leverage over his policies.

By tradition, Parliament agreed at the beginning of every reign to "grant" the new monarch revenues from "tonnage and poundage" - duties levied on all imports and exports - for the duration of their reign. These revenues were the financial base upon which the King or Queen would fund the government. Royal revenue agents were in every port, collecting the duties. Others watched the coastlines, looking for smugglers. In theory, this revenue was adequate funding for the most basic government services — the Parliamentary "subsidies" were extra revenue intended to finance the navy, pay for wars, and so on. In practice, King James had always needed subsidies to finance his lifestyle; when those were not available, he sold knighthoods and other titles, monopolies, or even royal real estate to keep himself afloat financially. Charles quite naturally expected that "tonnage and poundage" would be authorized for his reign, as well.

Parliament decided that it would grant King Charles his "tonnage and poundage," but for only one year - Charles would have to call another Parliament the following year, if he wanted more revenue. They also approved a subsidy of £ 140,000 to sweeten the deal — but that money was earmarked for waging war against Spain.

It was a bold move. If the King agreed, it would mark a permanent shift in the balance of power between monarch and Parliament in England. It would also make the monarch's claim to divine right and royal prerogative moot - future Parliaments could always "correct" any royal overreach by tightening the royal pursestrings.

Charles was shocked, disappointed, determined to fight for his position. He moved the Royal Court to Oxford at the end of July to escape the plague in London. Parliament was compelled to follow - once the King had called a Parliament, they were obligated to serve until he dismissed them. Attendance was another matter - fewer and fewer members attended the sessions as the plague intensified. The threat of infection gave Charles some powerful negotiating leverage.

The House of Commons, led by Sir Edward Coke and like-minded members, passed the bills for tonnage and poundage, and the war subsidies, but they failed in the House of Lords; the Duke of Buckingham led the effort to quash them (at the direction of the King, of course). The King saw no room for compromise and dissolved Parliament in mid-August.

The Duke of Buckingham was more powerful than ever. He was not only Lord Admiral of the Royal Navy; he was now the architect of the war with Spain. Alas, his talents as a courtier did not equip him to be a great military strategist. His armies were defeated in Germany, and a raid on the Spanish port of Cadiz was a disastrous failure. He secretly arranged for ships from the English navy to assist the French against the Huguenot fortress of La Rochelle, in the hope of securing French aid against Spain. The French succeeded in taking La Rochelle—the last Protestant stronghold in France —but then promptly signed a treaty of peace with Spain. When news of all these events became public, Buckingham's reputation was ruined. Calls for his ouster reached a crescendo. The King was determined to stand by him.

The King's revenue agents continued collecting import and export duties as always, even without the legal authority of an act of Parliament. There were protests, of course, but Charles and his inner circle of advisors were not looking for compromise. In 1626, another Parliament was called. This time, the troublemakers would not be invited to the party. Sir Edward Coke was appointed ('pricked' was the technical term) to be High Sheriff of Buckinghamshire - a position that not only made him ineligible to serve in Parliament but also required him to collect fines and rents on behalf of the King.

It was an honorable office, and Coke could not refuse it. At seventy-four years of age, his public career appeared to have reached its end. He returned to his manor at Stoke, from which he made the rounds of the towns and villages of Buckinghamshire. It was a pleasant enough conclusion to a life of public service, honored and respected . . . but Sir Edward Coke was not ready to be put out to pasture.

Several other leaders from the previous Parliament were also "pricked". Still others were awarded titles, which made them ineligible to serve in the House of Commons, although they were now qualified to serve in the House of Lords (a body considered more sympathetic to the King). The new Parliament opened in February of 1626, at Westminster Hall; the plague had abated enough to deem London safe. The attitudes in the House of Commons had changed little — if at all. Commons was emboldened by the events of the intervening months.

Sir Edward observed all this from the sidelines, in his manor at Stoke. "They will not dare to criticize the King directly," he said, "but his advisors are in for rough handling. All of the war efforts have failed miserably. The Duke of Buckingham has mismanaged the Royal Navy to the point that it scarcely dares put out to sea. When they do so, they have been sent to aid the King of France against his Huguenot subjects - it is a scandal! No one accounts for the money spent, but everyone knows that the Duke has been filling his treasury from the royal revenue for years."

"So, you think the hounds have discovered the fox in their midst?", asked Clem.

Sir Edward nodded. "And they are no longer afraid of him, because of such familiarity. Mark my words, they will impeach him, given the opportunity."

"The King will never permit that. He will regard an attack on the Duke as an attack upon himself!"

"And so it will be. Parliament will never blame the King, only his advisors. They will plead their intent to rescue the King from the false and corrupt men around him. The King will not believe them, nor should he. But he will have to choose between his Duke and his money before this Parliament is finished."

In the event, the King chose to protect the Duke. He dissolved Parliament before any impeachment proceedings could be initiated—and before any revenues were approved.

Cambridge, 1625: The Lady of Christ's College

R oger Williams returned to university at the end of Summer with a heady sense of excitement at the news from Oxford. Charles had been forced to dissolve Parliament without any subsidies or even his tonnage and poundage. Parliament had stood firm in the face of the plague, and forced the King to release them — not a victory, surely, but a stalemate was all they needed to hold their ground. The next move was up to the King, and Parliament had sent a powerful message: they could not be bullied; the King would have to surrender some of his power if he hoped to gain their support.

Roger was an upperclassman now. Two years at university had polished his manners. He dressed fashionably (for a man of his class) and confidently - he carried himself as a man who was at ease with his place in society and need not bow and scrape to any man. He was not bedazzled by rank or power: He had stood in the presence of Kings, discoursed with the greatest legal minds of his day, and read the works of philosophers and theologians. He knew powerful and influential men - knew what they were thinking, knew their weaknesses: he was not intimidated. He knew, most importantly, that this world was passing away, and with it the old men who called it their own. In its place would emerge a new world, a world that would belong to younger men — men like himself.

Recently, he had read a book written by Sir Francis Bacon, the old nemesis of his mentor, Sir Edward Coke. Roger was skeptical that there would be much of value in it (Coke said that the book was fit only for "fools"), but it was a revelation to Roger. In *Novvum Organum sive Indicia Vera de Interpretatione Naturae* ('True directions concerning the interpretation of Nature'), Bacon described an entirely new way of understanding the world, a way perfectly suited to the new one that Roger saw ahead of him. True knowledge of the natural world, said Bacon, did not come from tradition, or even from simple logic. To understand the world, it was necessary to observe it carefully, to test and verify ideas empirically. Testing could lead to proof, and such proof was the only basis of truth. It was the antithesis of the approach to truth that underlay all his instruction at Cambridge, and Roger embraced it with enthusiasm. He was not alone; Bacon's ideas were the topic of discussion among many of the students that year. For men like Roger Williams, it was validation of what they already believed about the world that was coming into its own - their world.

Bacon was not the only author they talked about. An Italian scientist named Galileo had been conducting a variety of experiments involving the natural world. He had demonstrated, for instance, that falling objects accelerated at a precise mathematical rate — regardless of their relative size or density. He also studied optics and built telescopes — which were ever more widely adopted by sea captains (the greater the distance at which you could identify a nautical hazard, or a foe, the better). When Galileo turned his telescopes to the heavens, he saw things that no one else had ever reported: the moon's surface was rough and barren, not smooth; Jupiter appeared to have moons circling it; the Sun's surface, far from appearing smooth and perfect, had "blemishes" visible - blemishes that moved from one day to the next.

This was heady stuff - none of these things were part of the received knowledge that Roger and his fellows had been taught, yet all of them could be confirmed - a la Francis Bacon - by direct observation (given the right equipment).

These discoveries had broader implications. For centuries, it had been established that the Earth was the center of the created universe, and mankind was the crown of that creation. The sun, the moon, the planets, and stars — all revolved around the Earth. Mathematicians had labored long to explain why their observations of the movements of those things did not seem to quite follow mathematical laws, to no avail. There were other, heretical explanations for this; they involved the notion that the Earth was <u>not</u> at the center, but that the sun was at the center, and Earth and all the rest revolved around the sun! The Church, of course, condemned these heresies, and the books that promoted them were banned.

The movements in Galileo's observations seemed to support the heretical view — that the sun was indeed at the center — but worse, the sun itself was "blemished", imperfect. It defied common sense to accept such an idea. There was resistance to it throughout the academic world. But the proof, said Bacon, was in the observations, not in the theology. Anything else was sentiment and wishful thinking.

The theological implications were not lost on Roger and others of his generation. If the church and the whole of mankind were thoroughly corrupt (Calvinist theology called it "total depravity"), then it was no great surprise that the sun should be "blemished" as well, or that the moon's surface should appear ravaged and desolate. Theologians had long supposed that although the earth was fallen, the "celestial spheres" were somehow pristine, unsullied by human sin. Time to rethink that idea; maybe the Fall of humankind had corrupted everything. Perhaps that was why, in John's Apocalypse, God created "a new heaven and a new earth."

It seemed to Roger that the winds of political change that he had witnessed with Sir Edward Coke and the winds of intellectual change that were sweeping academia were somehow converging. It was exciting (not to say flattering) to think that he was at the forefront of the gale that was brewing.

He was struggling a bit in his study of Hebrew. The alphabet was different from any other language he had studied, and for some annoying reason, it was written backward - you had to read it from right to left rather than left to right. He asked around the university for the name of a Hebrew tutor who might be for hire.

"You should visit the Lady of Christ's College," he was advised.

"What Lady is that? There are no women on the faculty at Cambridge!"

"Well, they do things a bit differently over there than here in Pembroke, newer college, newer ways, I suppose. Founded by a woman, you know. It's not official, of course - just different. If you walk across town to Christ's College and ask for the "Lady", someone will point you in the right direction."

Roger was confused. Asking around the campus of another college for a "Lady" seemed like a fool's errand. It sounded like the sort of joke one might play on a first-year student — a setup for hilarity and ridicule. He thought it over for a while and decided to investigate the matter for himself.

Christ's College was located on the north side of Cambridge, directly through the town center from Pembroke. It didn't take long to walk there. When he entered the main courtyard of the campus, he located the porter near the gate and made his inquiry: "I have been told to seek out a 'Lady' at this college, though I doubt there is such a person here," he said (he expressed mild skepticism to appear less than a complete fool)

"Ah, that would be the 'Lady of Christ's College' you're seekin'," said the porter. "Across the court to that third doorway, up two flights of stairs, the room's on the right."

If this was a prank, it had been meticulously prepared, thought Roger. He followed the directions and knocked on the door.

"Enter!" said a voice from within.

"I am here to see a lady," said Roger.

"And so you have," was the reply.

The "lady" was a man. A pale man with a slight build, but clearly a man. He wore his hair long, but no longer than many other young men of his age. The "lady" moniker was a joke, Roger realized, perhaps a cruel one.

"You were expecting a woman? Your disappointment shows on your face," said the man, with a chuckle. Then he smiled ruefully, "You have been deceived. It is a tired, old joke. Many have fallen for it. John Milton, at your service."

"I am Roger Williams, at your service, sir."

"What service would that be? Surely, you are here to see this . . . curiosity for yourself?"

Roger shrugged. "I admit to curiosity. However, I was told that the "Lady of Christ's College" might be willing to tutor me. I can pay for a good Hebrew tutor."

"Where are you enrolled?"

"I am at Pembroke. Third year: I study for the priesthood."

"As do I," said Milton. "How is it that you need tutoring in Hebrew? Did they not prepare you in grammar school?

"Alas, I was only at the Charterhouse for two-and-a-half years. Not enough time to study Hebrew."

"You graduated from the Charterhouse School after only two-and-a-half years? That is no small achievement. Were you in some great hurry to get out of there?"

"You could say so. I entered the school later than most. I was eighteen; I was only admitted through the efforts of my patron. He also secured my appointment to university."

"Can you tell me who this 'patron' is?"

Roger paused. "It is no great secret, but I avoid mentioning his name, lest I seem to be trading on it. Whatever success I enjoy here, I would like to believe that it is on my own merits, not on another's influence."

"It is Pride, then, that makes you discreet. Curious. Often it is the other way round - Pride makes many men say more than they should." Milton chuckled.

Roger nodded. "The silent Pride is the more treacherous. It lurks in the shade of false modesty, away from the light of other men's discernment."

Milton chuckled again. "So a man may be proud and modest at the same time, and exercise a self-effacing sense of humor. I see, Sir, that you are a true philosopher."

Roger chuckled and nodded. "I see, Sir, that you are a man who recognizes a true philosopher when you meet one."

"You have piqued my curiosity," said Milton, "Tell me more about yourself. Where does your family live? How was it that this nameless patron found you and decided to make a scholar of you?"

"My family's home is in Cow's Lane, near Smithfield. My father is a successful merchant tailor. I was not 'cut out' for the tailor's trade, so to speak (Milton acknowledged the pun with a scowl and a squint), so I needed to find another line of work. I was accustomed to taking notes on the sermons at St.

Sepulcher when my patron noticed me and hired me as his personal secretary."

"An unlikely story," said Milton, "so unlikely that I can believe it. How long did you work as his secretary?"

"Five years."

"After which your patron dismissed you and sponsored you to the Charterhouse School?"

"Something like that."

"That is a strange rebuke for an unworthy servant. What was the reason for your dismissal?"

Roger sighed. "My master said that my talents were wasted in his service, that I needed more education, to make the most of my . . . gifts."

"It was a reward then, not a rebuke?"

Roger recalled the day he left Sir Edward's service. "It did not feel like a reward at the time, but time has proved him right."

Milton was looking into his eyes. "I see that you are an honest fellow; honest with yourself as well as others. Not many in this place would be as forthright about their humble beginnings, nor about the cost they pay to be here. For most, it is pretense and boasting, and inflated reputation."

"You have told me nothing of yourself," said Roger.

"You mean, how I came to be here, and how I have earned my title of 'Lady of Christ's College'. I did not choose that name for myself - it was given me by some half-witted son of privilege, but somehow it stuck. I am, as you see, no great hairy brute of a fellow - perhaps he was referring to that. Mostly, I suspect that it is because of the poetry that I write. Some loutish fellows think that poetry is for women - they resent having to recite it, and lack the sensibility to write any of their own."

Roger nodded. He knew the sorts that Milton was speaking of. "It is well that they do not attempt it, then. What of your family?"

"Born in London, on Bread Street. My father is a prosperous scrivener and musician. Not that far from your neighborhood."

Roger nodded again. "I am very familiar with Bread Street. No doubt I have passed your family home many times."

"On business?"

"Aye. My service to my master took me all over the city. I know many of the shopkeepers on Bread Street."

"We are not so different, you and I," Milton observed.

"No, not so different," Roger agreed, "though I hope your Hebrew is better than mine."

Milton smiled. "I hope so too - please do not take offense, I merely meant that I enjoy speaking with you, and hope that we shall have reason to speak again."

"No offense taken. I think you could be a great help to me."

"What languages have you studied? Latin and Greek, I suppose."

"And French. Also Dutch, which was spoken in my neighborhood when I was young - still is, as far as I know."

"Could you tutor me in Dutch?"

"I could try. It's not that difficult if you know English and French."

"That will depend on the aptitude of the student, I should think. But I will tutor you in Hebrew, in exchange for lessons in Dutch. I have found that after learning two or three languages, it becomes easier to learn new ones."

"How many others have you studied ?"

"All the ones you mentioned, except Dutch, plus Hebrew, Spanish, and Italian."

Roger was impressed. Languages had always come easier to him than to most people, but John Milton clearly surpassed him . . .

"Some might say that I have overreached in learning languages," said Milton. "But consider how useful it would be to travel the wide world, and be able to speak with the inhabitants of every place, without a translator."

Roger reflected that traveling the wide world had never been an appealing prospect to him, but had to agree that for someone determined to do so, a multiplicity of languages would be useful.

"You intend to travel, I take it?"

"Indeed, I do. Studying the world through books wearies me — though it is the only method that my teachers seem to value. I want to see the world for myself, make my own judgments about what is true. There is a man in Pisa who has seen 'moons' about Jupiter. Have you heard of this?

Roger nodded. "Yes, his name is Galileo. I have read of his discoveries."

"Yet you have not seen these 'moons' for yourself, have you?"

Roger shook his head. "I believe it requires a special instrument."

"So I have heard. I hope one day to use such an instrument, to see for myself whether these things are true. It is not enough to read about them in books."

"Francis Bacon would agree with you," Roger offered.

"Exactly so. You have read Bacon, then, have you? How much better to converse with the man personally!"

Roger shook his head. "I have met Sir Francis. I did not find him so congenial as you might imagine. I do not think he liked me either."

"When was this? And where?"

"The first time was at Westminster, then in my master's house, later before the Privy Council. It was years ago before he fell from power. I have since come to appreciate his philosophy, but back then, he considered my master and me as enemies."

Milton looked surprised. "There is more here than you have told me. If you appeared before the Privy Council, you must have attended the King — the old King!"

Roger nodded. "On many occasions, back in the day. I was personal secretary to one of the council members."

Milton's eyes were bright with curiosity. "And yet you have not told me your master's name. Never mind - I think I can guess if you will answer three questions."

"What questions ?"

Milton was making a game of it, Roger realized. Milton thought a moment, then spoke: "Firstly, is your master still in government?" Secondly, does he seek the King's favor? Thirdly, is he a High Steward of the university?"

"If I answer the third question, the other two are moot. Yes, my master is the High Steward."

"When did you last speak with him? Is he as ill as I have heard?"

"I visited him briefly last Summer. He was hale and hearty then."

"I have heard that he was pricked to be the High Sheriff of Buckinghamshire, just to prevent him from serving in Parliament. Is that so?"

"I have heard the same. But the King does not share his inner thoughts with me."

"Still, the King must fear him to take such steps."

"Sir Edward is the most loyal of subjects. He has never disobeyed his sovereign in the smallest matter. The King has nothing to fear from him."

"How do you account for the King's treatment of him, then?"

"The King is misguided — as his father was. He is surrounded by courtiers and advisors who fill his ears and his mind with foolish advice. Two years ago, they were willing to sell this kingdom to the Spanish for bribes, and our religion with it. Now they are all for war with Spain — as long as the money to finance that war finds its way into their pockets. They inflate the King's estimation of his authority, the better to alienate him from his loyal subjects in hopes that he will fear them and men like Sir Edward, to their profit." Roger realized that his tone was growing strident. Moderation would suit better.

Milton sat back in his chair. "I see that you have given this some thought. Who would have thought that a Dutch tutor would speak so like a Parliamentarian?" Then he laughed. "I share your opinion of the King's advisors," he said, leaning forward in a confidential tone. "It is refreshing to hear my own mind reflected in another's — and so eloquently, I might add. I see that your years of service have formed in you a strength of conviction. I admire that. I envy you a little; you have evidently seen things for yourself that other men must take on hearsay. I wish I had such a store of direct experience."

Roger had said more than he intended to say; more than was prudent, to a man he had met less than an hour ago. "I hope you can understand why I am bound to discretion about the things I have seen and heard."

"I will not trouble you for any specifics. I was merely curious. Tell me, if you can, why you were in Bread Street, as you say you were."

"I was buying bread, of course."

"Of course. And?"

"Part of my service to my master, when he served in Parliament, was to walk the streets of the city, and listen to what the people had to say, what their concerns and desires might be — the better that Parliament might consider matters for their welfare and prosperity. A Parliament that answers only to the King is no Parliament at all. The welfare of the people is their true business."

"I've caught a live one!" Milton exclaimed with a chortle. "You really must be careful about saying things like that."

Roger realized he had gotten carried away. "I hope I can count on your discretion."

At this, Milton laughed out loud. "Aye, discretion is the better part of honesty." He leaned forward and spoke more softly. "Just to put your mind at ease . . . 'Ladies' and 'Poets' are famously unreliable witnesses in a court of law; I am both of those things. You have nothing to fear from anything I would say."

Roger looked closely at his eyes. Milton was being humorous — at least by his own lights, but it was difficult to be sure of his meaning . . . "In a court of law, sir, you would be no 'Lady'. I have not heard that the testimony of a poet carries any less weight than that of any other profession."

Milton sat up straighter. "I see that my flippancy has not eased your mind. I apologize for making fun of matters that you take so seriously. But I will tell you something about myself, to balance the scales, so to speak. I share your low regard for our government and our church. They are corrupt and stubborn. But this can only mean that we are moving toward the end of days."

"How so?" Roger was surprised by this change of direction.

"We were speaking just moments ago of Galileo, who is discovering new things in the heavens, were we not?"

"Yes, we were. But what has that to do with the government or the church?

"Heaven and earth are connected," Milton said. "New sights in the heavens are signs of movement in Heaven itself. As Heaven moves, the Earth must move also. These 'discoveries' in the heavens are signs that something is about to happen on earth, as well."

This was a new idea to Roger. He understood that affairs on earth would be affected by new information or new inventions, but he had not considered that God might be behind them, somehow using them to accomplish some hidden purpose . . .

"It is apocalypse," said Milton, "you know — the revealing of hidden things in the latter days. I don't mean <u>The</u> Apocalypse from the book of Revelation, but that one is coming, too, and sooner than most people imagine. You and I are privileged to live in a time when things long hidden are coming to light; we marvel at them, but these things are signs — more things are yet to be revealed until that day when all things hidden will be revealed for what they truly are. And with the truth must come judgment. Kings and courtiers and archbishops and clerics will face that day with trembling, as well they should. More convenient for them to ignore the signs for as long as they can and persecute the prophets who speak truth to them than to repent. These are the days of Isaiah: *"And he sayd, Goe, and say vnto this people, Ye shall heare in deede, but ye shall not vnderstand: ye shall plainely see, and not perceiue. Make the heart of this people fatte, make their eares heauie, and shut their eyes, lest they see with their eyes, and heare with their eares, and vnderstand with their hearts, and conuert, and he heale them. Then sayd I, Lorde, howe long? And he answered, Vntill the cities be wasted without inhabitant, and the houses without man, and the land be vtterly desolate . . ."*

Roger was stirred by the fervor in Milton's voice; he spoke with a poet's cadence.

"I have a poet's insight," said Milton. "Not everyone finds it agreeable — perhaps most do not. But you now know things about me that are at least as scandalous as your political views. I cannot expose you without risk that you will expose me. That should be enough to make it safe for us to be friends, don't you agree?" There was a twinkle in his eye as he said this.

"I am sure that we can be friends," Roger replied, "though if the High Commission compels me to testify as to your personal views, I shall have to reply that they are beyond all human understanding — or in other words, poetry."

"Fair enough," said Milton, "And if I am compelled to testify, I can only say that you have told me nothing that I did not already believe."

Their conversation turned to other matters, like the wars on the European mainland and the state of England. In Germany, the Lutheran King of Denmark was intervening on the side of the Protestant Princes. France, though an emphatically Catholic Kingdom, felt threatened enough by the Spanish and Austrian successes to ally herself with the Protestant cause to cut off the "Spanish Road" to the Netherlands. "This will prolong the war," said Milton, "but I do not believe it will change the outcome. Both sides pretend to fight for a holy cause, but every nation seeks to enhance its power and wealth."

The plague was abating in London by now, but the Londoners who fled to the countryside took the disease with them. More thousands were dying in the smaller towns and villages.

"This is not the first plague, and I do not believe it will be the last," said Milton. "Our suffering is great, but nothing like the Great Pestilence during the reign of Edward III. If plague is a sign of God's disapproval, then every king of England since Henry VII has been under his curse."

"Now you sound like a Puritan fanatic," said Roger.

"A Puritan prophet, don't you mean? Perhaps you do not recall that King James's coronation took place during a plague year. Before that, the year of old King Henry's marriage to Catherine Howard was also a plague year, the year of his marriage to Jane Seymour (also the year that his first wife died, and his second was executed) was another such year, as well as the year that Henry's father overthrew Richard III, and seized the throne for himself and his descendants?"

"I do not recall any of those years, and neither do you — we are not old enough," said Roger. "But there have been other years of plague, besides the ones you mentioned - years in which no Kings were crowned, no royal marriages occurred. If the plagues are a sign from God, how do you explain those?"

"If you look at the events of any of those years, you can find plenty that deserve God's wrath - some martyrdom or other, some high crime that was ignored, some compromise with papism or heresy."

"But you can find such events in all the years without plagues, as well. By your line of reasoning, every year should be a plague year."

Milton nodded. "So they should. I do not presume to know why God would send his wrath among us some years and not others. Perhaps he spares us, lest we perish altogether."

Roger shook his head. "I cannot agree with your portrayal of God — as if his preoccupation with human affairs is to send punishment continually upon us, relenting only long enough to allow us to survive, so that he can resume the punishment when we are sufficiently recovered. Such an image of God is a false one. 'Prophets' who preach such a message are simply playing upon the guilty consciences of their listeners. They seek to terrify the gullible to gain power over them. They are no better than Papist priests who employ the fear of purgatory to extort money from their hapless congregations."

He continued, "The scriptures teach us that love and mercy are the principal characteristics of God's dealing with humankind. We are not the children of fear or wrath; we are the children of love."

"You refer to the 'Elect', I suppose. Surely the unregenerate are but kindling for the fires of Hell, don't you agree?"

"Who are we to separate the elect from the unregenerate? Surely that is for the Lord himself to determine on the Last Day. Let each man search his own heart and refrain from presumptuous judgments about his neighbor."

"But the plague is real, the suffering is great. How do you answer for all that is broken and corrupt in this world, if it is not the consequence of human sin?"

"The entry of sin and suffering into our world is plainly accounted for in the Scriptures. The source of all our woes is in the deceptions of our enemy — that ancient serpent. He is the source of plagues and corruption, not God. Blaming God for our misery is yet another deception, much like the first one. The deception comes from the same source."

Milton nodded thoughtfully. "And you place those 'prophets' among the deceivers. I think you may be right. I must give this more thought. I have often reflected on the disobedience that Adam and Eve chose, and how it finds echoes in my own heart. But the deception that leads to disobedience — that is a fertile field for reflection. I must do some digging in that field."

He shifted the conversation back: "Do you not see signs of the end times in these things?"

"You said yourself that plagues have come and gone for centuries. Why should this one be more a harbinger than the others? And the war, as you said, seems unlikely to usher in a millennial age, whatever the combatants may claim. No, I see no signs that the End of Days is imminent — but that is to be expected. When it comes, it will be as 'a thief in the night', or so I have read."

Milton chuckled. "And you are content to live in the uncertainty of the moment?"

"Uncertainty about those things that other men claim to be certain of. I am studying for the priesthood. I can hardly serve a congregation if I am trying to discriminate between which of them are truly predestined for salvation and which are not. I must serve all of them to my best ability, and live with the uncertainty. All will be revealed on the Last Day. And if, as the apostle says, we see only 'through a glass, darkly,' I must admit that some of my religious opinions are wrong, as well — unless I am the only man on earth who has the whole truth. That will be revealed on the Last Day, as well. Until then, I must hold my beliefs lightly. I do not trust men of absolute certainty, especially because they so often refute each other."

It was late in the evening when Roger returned to his room at Pembroke. When asked where he had been, he replied, "Been to see a lady." That was all the explanation anyone required.

Part 3: The Petition

1627: Pounds and Prerogative

King Charles' financial condition was dire. Two attempts at getting revenue from Parliament had failed. It was clear enough that the mood of the country had turned against the Duke of Buckingham and, by extension, against Charles himself. Charles borrowed money from overseas until the Dutch bankers and the French government would loan him no more. Then he turned to his subjects. There was little enthusiasm among them, so Charles and his advisors hit upon a simple solution — forced loans.

The amounts of these loans were fixed according to the wealth of each subject: the wealthier they were, the larger the amount that they were assessed. Repayment of the loans, of course, would be made whenever Parliament met to grant the King the funds necessary. This created an incentive for the next Parliament to be more sympathetic to the King's needs — simply in terms of self-interest. It seemed quite logical to Charles's advisors. It also meant that the loans would be repaid by imposing new taxes on all of Charles's subjects — but those taxes would be imposed by Parliament, not the King himself. Some of his advisors pointed out that this could very well alienate Parliament from the general population, especially the voting public, thus fracturing the popular resistance to the King. None of them suggested that this would be a bad thing.

The forced loans raised 250,000 pounds — more than Parliament had ever authorized through taxes. Not everyone complied with the King's demands. Seventy wealthy "gentlemen" publicly refused to pay any such loans or even to collect them from their tenants, and were committed to prison, presumably until they produced the required "loans"; this at least was the popular conjecture, since none of the "gentlemen" was charged with any crime. The King and his advisors recognized that the legal basis of these arrests —

indeed, of the whole forced loan program — was flimsy, at best. Charging the "gentlemen" risked losing in court, which might undercut not just their incarcerations, but the loans as well. Better to simply hold them without charges.

Five of the incarcerated men applied for writs of *Habeus corpus*, which would have required the government to either charge them with a specific crime or release them. A panel of judges sided with the King and denied the writs — on the grounds that, since they were not charged with any crime, the offenses must be so serious that it would threaten the security of the kingdom to make them public. The King and his advisors breathed a sigh of relief. They calculated that they had the initiative now and that the next Parliament would prove more tractable.

It was a grave miscalculation. Suddenly, the ground for the conflict between Charles and his Parliaments had shifted: foreign policy and the Duke of Buckingham's incompetence were no longer at the top of the list of grievances. Instead, the key point of conflict was between royal prerogative and ancient rights. This was Sir Edward Coke's bailiwick: he had fought numerous battles with the old King James over the limits of royal power, over *habeas corpus*, over the primacy of Common Law — and lost most of them. Here was the opportunity to enter the fray one last time (He was seventy-five years old now), and turn all those defeats into victory. All he needed was an arena for the fight.

King Charles called another Parliament at the end of 1627. This time, Sir Edward Coke was not excluded from serving; it was reported that his health had so declined that he would not seek election. The reports were false. Coke would have one last chance to argue his case.

Stoke Poges, 1627: Prospects and Expectations

Nothing was going according to plan for Roger Williams. Four years of study had earned him a degree — with distinction, in fact — and an ordination to the priesthood. He had the qualifications and the financial means to pursue a Master of Divinity degree (there were still two years remaining on the term of his 'exhibition'), and he knew that his application would be welcomed at Cambridge. None of which mattered now. William Laud, the new Bishop of London, was determined to suppress Puritanism in the Church of England for good (his predecessors had tried to accomplish the same thing over the last six decades, and somehow failed, but Laud was nothing if not ambitious). To that end, he had instituted a new requirement for all students enrolling at Cambridge: they must swear to agree that all the service and ritual of the Church of England conformed entirely to scripture. This included the prayers in the Book of Common Prayer (which many Puritan priests were using only selectively, if at all), but applied also to vestments and the display of religious artifacts. Roger regarded all these things as holdovers from a 'papist' past, a backsliding toward Catholicism. He had read the scriptures — in multiple languages — and believed those things were without any scriptural basis whatsoever; he would not take any oaths to the contrary.

His thoughts turned to his patron, Sir Edward Coke. If, as it now seemed, all those years of schooling were going to waste, Sir Edward deserved an explanation. And it was an explanation to deliver personally.

Roger rented a horse for the trip to Stoke Poges. He could have walked, of course, but going horseback seemed the most natural way to go, now. For one thing, he could afford it: he still had income from his exhibition and his scholarship. More than that, he had grown accustomed to living above the ordinary, pedestrian folk. He was not a gentleman (technically), but he had rubbed shoulders with gentlemen for enough years that he felt he belonged in their company. A man on a horse sees the world differently — and doesn't often have to soil his boots with manure. Even when he wasn't on horseback, people seemed to accept his newfound status. It had to do with the way he carried himself, probably. Also, of course, the way he dressed now. People were always looking at how a man was dressed for clues about his social rank. Roger was a tailor's son and understood how to present himself in the most favorable styles. He was careful not to dress "above" himself: when men doffed their hats at his approach, or women curtseyed, he doffed his own hat in return and smiled — a gesture of modesty from a man with the common touch. People admired him for his humility and grace.

The journey from Cambridge to Stoke took two days, even on horseback. Roger was in no particular hurry. His route lay southward, toward London, and a little westward, so that he would not have to go through the city. He intended to visit his family on his way back to Cambridge.

He arrived at the manor late in the afternoon on the second day. It was summer, and the old house appeared to him like some great, fat house cat, napping in the summer heat. Things were much as he remembered them: the country church to the east, the pond below the house to the west. So many memories: it felt as much like home to him as any other place.

Sir Edward was delighted to see him. "Your reputation has preceded you," he said, "You have distinguished yourself at Cambridge. I am truly proud of you!"

"I have disappointing news, Sir. I had hopes of serving the Church as a parish priest or a curate somewhere. That pathway seems to be closed to me now. Bishop Laud is determined to purge men like me out of the church altogether. They say that the Archbishop of Canterbury now takes his orders from Laud. I say this with some embarrassment, but all the money that you have invested in my education may go for naught."

"Perhaps it is time we put all that education to practical use," said Coke.

"How so?"

"Your training is not merely academic. You also have experience of law — the law as it is actually administered — and you are well acquainted with the issues of the day. Not many men have such broad experience. You are also a Puritan—no, don't bother to deny it; I am not insulting you. My point is that you understand how Puritans think. It is not a way of thinking that I find congenial, and that is one thing that separates men like me from men of that ilk — men with whom I must find common ground."

"I should think you have plenty of common ground with the seventy men who are sitting in jail cells all across the land for refusing to 'loan' money to the King, be they Puritans or otherwise."

Coke sighed. "The King has overreached himself in that matter, but it serves the agitators and ranters more than anything; it does not lead to real reform, and it does not contribute to unity among the reformers. The seventy gentlemen are certainly brave; noble, perhaps. But men like me who pay the 'loan' are called cowards. It divides us when we should be speaking with one voice."

"I am surprised to hear that you did not protest the matter more vigorously. It seems like precisely the sort of royal tyranny that you have resisted for as long as I have known you."

Coke's reply was measured. "You have never seen me resist the King's policies with open defiance. My loyalty belongs to my Sovereign, even when he is misguided. Some of these agitators murmur of rebellion — treason, quite simply. That I will never agree with."

Roger heard a tremor in Coke's voice and realized that the years had taken their toll upon him. It must be difficult, Roger supposed, for a man like Sir Edward Coke to come to the end of his career with so few victories to show for it. He had played the game by the rules (as he understood them), and his sovereigns had ignored the rules, claimed that the rules did not apply to them. "Please, explain how I can be of use to you, Sir."

"Please drop the formality. As I said, this is a time that demands unity among all those who desire to restore the balance between royal authority and our ancient rights. We must speak with one voice. That cannot happen until we understand each other and agree on our strategy. A man like you can listen to all the factions. Perhaps they can all be persuaded to pull under the same yoke — at least for a little while."

"That seems a tall order for an unemployed priest."

"There are positions aplenty for a priest in England. The ticklish thing is to place you in the right position."

"But Bishop Laud has decreed that no priest can be placed in a pulpit, except he swear that all of the liturgy in the Church of England conforms with the Holy Scriptures. I can never take that oath," said Roger.

Coke gave him a look of mild exasperation. "Then we will find you some employment where the Bishop of London cannot impose such an oath. We must not allow nit-picking over nuances of theology to divert us from our purpose before we even begin."

Roger did not disagree in principle, but "How do you distinguish between 'nits' and vital issues?"

"I distinguish thus: demands for legislation that will never appeal to a majority in the House of Commons are nits. Issues that a majority can agree upon are vital issues."

"But no Parliament is sitting now. Do you really think that the King will call another?"

"I am certain of it. He raised 250,000 pounds from his forced loans, they say. But the Duke of Buckingham has demanded twice that amount, just to pay for a relief mission for the Huguenots at La Rochelle — the same fortress that he tried to help the French capture just two years ago. If the King dares to impose more forced loans on the gentry, he will have to lock up 7000 gentlemen — and he still won't get his money. He can only draw from the same well so many times until it runs dry, and he knows that. He hopes that the next Parliament will be cowed by the threat of imprisonment to grant him his tonnage and poundage permanently, and some generous subsidies as well. If that happens, all will be well in his mind. But he does not recognize that a return to the *status quo* is impossible now. The world has changed. England has changed. No one will ever rule this kingdom in the way that his father did; if he persists on this path, he will lose his throne and his legacy."

It seemed to Roger that Coke's words ventured perilously close to treason. It astonished him. He was accustomed to such talk, of course, among students at the university. But if old men like Sir Edward were thinking such things, England had indeed changed.

"We were speaking of putting your training to practical use," said Coke. "We must prepare for the new Parliament. There is a certain gentleman I know of who requires a chaplain for his estate in Essex. He has served in the last two Parliaments and will certainly be elected to the new one if he seeks the office. He is a Puritan. I think he would hire you as his chaplain with a recommendation from me; the bishops would have no say in the matter. What say you? Would you serve such a man?

"Gladly, sir, if it could be arranged. May I know the man's name?"

"He is Sir William Masham, of Otes Hall in Essex. At the moment, his abode is in the Marshalsea prison: he is among the seventy gentlemen who have refused to procure loans for the King. His reputation has been burnished among the Puritans because of his incarceration. If he will join our efforts and can persuade other like-minded men to do the same, the next Parliament will have an unbreakable majority to oppose the King — he will have to compromise and agree that he is also bound by the terms of Magna Carta."

"Puritans will say that is a far cry from completing the reformation of the Church of England."

"They will be right to say so. But there can be no further reform of the Church until the King is compelled to enforce the laws that Parliament passes. We must establish the principle that the King is under the law before anything else can be done. All these Puritan bills about maypoles and sabbaths, and feast days are a waste of time. Even if they could find the support of a majority in the Commons, no majority in the House of Lords would be willing to give up their Sunday entertainments. We must give our attention to those things that are possible."

Coke produced a quill and some paper. "I will write a letter of introduction for you to Masham's wife, the Lady Elizabeth. She will know how to communicate with her husband. Otes Manor is twenty miles or so outside of London, off the road to Cambridge. Deliver the letter, then settle yourself somewhere in London where I can reach you. I will send you money if you need it."

Roger had some traveling to do. He decided to visit his family in London first, then ride to Otes Manor. After delivering his letter, he could continue on to Cambridge and return his horse. From there, it would be two days walk back to London, where he would wait, apparently for further instructions.

His return to Stoke had felt like a sort of homecoming after four years in Cambridge. He sensed that it was instead the end of a part of his life — the final severing of his connection to any sense of home at all. It was clear that Sir Edward held him in great affection — almost, as he had said, like a son. But 'almost' was the critical qualification. Servants were regarded more or less as family in a house like Stoke Manor, but Roger's connection to Sir Edward was like that of a hireling, now. He was freer than a household servant and thus had opportunities that a household servant would never know, but he could never be at home the way they could. Indeed, there would never be a home for a man like him in a household like Sir Edward's unless he himself were the master of that house. He would need a great deal of money to have a family like that. Unless he could marry into one.

Roger left for London the following morning. Coke wished him a fond farewell, but was a little preoccupied. He was seventy-five years old now, bothered a bit by the aches and pains of his age, concerned about his legacy, and the futures of his children. He had one more battle to fight; "God, give us victory," he prayed.

When Roger arrived in London, he sought out his family in Cow's Lane. His eldest brother, Sydrach, had assumed the role of head of the family; he was doing well: the business was prospering, and Roger's mother was well taken care of.

"I am a priest now," explained Roger. "Though I am still awaiting a suitable position. I thought I might lodge here until something becomes available."

"If all of that schooling has brought you back into the Church of England, then I suppose it was time well spent," said Sydrach. "In times like these, a family needs to be unified. You are welcome to stay here until they find a parish for you."

Roger nodded. Best to leave it there, he decided. No need to alarm his brother with what he knew of the times that were, or the times that were coming. Even less reason to share his religious convictions with him — both of them had had their fill of controversy; nothing would come of arguing.

July 1627: Otes Hall

Roger was on the road north the next day. For the first several miles of the road to Cambridge, it was choked with vehicles and pedestrians, but he was in no particular hurry. He had plenty to think about. His horse walked most of the way, trotting only when a gap opened in the traffic in front. It was a pleasant ride — all the dust and filth of the road was under the horse's feet, not his. The leisurely pace of their journey afforded him time to appreciate the scenery. Around noon, he stopped at a small village to find something to eat. By late afternoon, he had turned off the high road toward the village of Little Laver, in Essex. Otes Manor was a hodgepodge of a building, possibly built over several decades, at the direction of more than one architect. Part of it looked like an ancient fortress, with large square towers and crenellated battlements. The rest looked like a more conventional house, with gables and the usual crop of chimneys sprouting from the roof. A great arched doorway was on the gabled part of the house; perhaps this was the newer part. Roger dismounted before the door, tied his horse up, and announced himself. "Roger Williams, to see the Lady Elizabeth Masham," he said, removing his hat and bowing.

He was, of course, a complete stranger to the servants in the house. But his manners and the fact that he arrived on horseback were enough to get him inside the front door. He stood in the hallway for a few moments. A group of women approached him, the oldest of whom was perhaps thirty-five years or so of age — evidently the mistress of the house. Three younger women stood behind her. The older woman spoke first: "And you are?"

"Roger Williams, with a letter for Lady Elizabeth Masham," he said with a bow. The young women tittered.

"And who is this letter from?"

"From Sir Edward Coke, Lady. It is intended for Sir William, but Sir Edward believes that the Lady Masham would know best how to deliver it with discretion."

"I am she. May I see it?"

"Certainly, madam," Roger pulled the letter from within his doublet and handed it to her, the wax seal prominently intact.

"Where have you come from today?"

"From London, Lady."

"You shall have some refreshment." She turned to the young women behind her and said, "Please show the gentleman to the parlor, and see that he gets something to eat." Turning to Roger, she said, "I will join you shortly. These ladies will see to your needs." Tittering from the other ladies. Roger followed them further into the house to a sitting room. The three sat together on a sofa. Roger sat in a chair facing them.

"I am Mary Bernard," said the eldest. She introduced the other girls. All of them, it appeared, were servants in the Masham household. These young women were not from poor families — quite the contrary. They were daughters from middling families who served "in waiting": waiting to be old enough and refined enough for a suitable marriage. Their dowries would not be large, so their suitors would be men of their own class. The years they spent in service to Lady Masham would train them in the manners and skills appropriate to a lady of the minor gentry. They were trained in all matters related to running a household, from managing servants to managing expenses; from extending hospitality to supervising children. They learned needlework and dancing, and a host of other domestic skills. And in this household, they learned to pray and study their Bibles.

Occasionally, a young woman of this station would marry "above" her class; association with a noble family like the Mashams could lend a tincture of nobility to such a woman, especially if she were unusually good-looking, or unusually charming and agreeable.

There were also cases in which no suitors of the appropriate class presented themselves. Once a woman reached a certain age, her prospects began to wane. The ticklish bit was to neither jump at the first opportunity (unless it was exceptionally advantageous), nor to hold out for too long (overripe fruit does not command a high price). This sort of calculation required the wisdom of years and a certain cold-eyed pragmatism — not the sort of decision to leave to emotional young women or eager young men. Lady Masham would decide which suitors were acceptable and which unions would be approved. It was her responsibility to find suitable matches for all her young ladies.

The appearance of a young, apparently single, young man at her door was a potential windfall, and the other ladies recognized it as such. More information was needed to determine what the young man's potential might be. He was dressed well enough, and his association with Sir Edward Coke spoke well for him. Much would depend on how wealthy his family was. Of course, it was indelicate to ask direct questions about such things; indirection and inference were the polite way to size the man up. All three of the young women had been trained for just this situation.

Mary Bernard launched the first probe: "I believe you said you came from London today? How was your journey?"

"On the whole, pleasant," Roger replied, "We were held back a bit by traffic on the High Road, but it was a fine day to be riding."

"We? You had a companion?"

"The horse, Lady, was my companion. Very good company, a horse. Never gainsays me."

It was a weak joke, and it was suggestive of a man who would rather speak than listen. Naturally, the young ladies were careful to laugh at it.

"Will you be returning to London, then?"

"Not immediately. I am returning to Cambridge. The horse is rented. I must also fetch my belongings from there and transport them back to London."

A rented horse? Not a man of any wealth, then. The ladies exchanged meaningful glances.

Mary was not ready to give up on him completely. "How is it that your belongings are in Cambridge?" She hoped the question was not too intrusive.

Evidently not. "I have just completed my studies there. I am a priest without a parish. I will live with my family in our house in London, while I await a placement."

A priest! A man with prospects. A house in London. This was beginning to look more promising. The younger two ladies shifted a little in their chairs, leaned forward a little.

"I thought you were employed as a messenger for Sir Edward Coke."

Roger chuckled. "I have indeed served Sir Edward in that capacity, and in many others over the years — but that was before my university days. This particular errand is an exception. I am no longer in his service; although I am in his debt, and will serve him whenever he asks it of me."

Roger changed the subject. "You ladies have told me nothing of yourselves. It is rude of me to do all the talking."

There it was. The man had manners, at least. Mary caught glances from her two companions. They wanted her to speak first. "I am the daughter of a priest. Dorcas here is the daughter of a scrivener, and Elaine's father is a merchant tailor in Chelmsford. "

Roger nodded in recognition. "My father was also a merchant tailor," he said, "My elder brother runs the business now. I was not cut out for the tailor's trade" (he paused to let the pun sink in; the ladies caught the cue and giggled), "so I became a scholar." He realized he was still saying more than they were, and directed a question at Mary. "You said your father is a priest. What, may I ask, is his name?"

"His name is Richard Bernard. Perhaps you have heard of him?"

"I believe I have read his books," Roger said. "*The Faithfull Shepheard and His Practice? The Twelve Candlestickes?* Very profitable reading. You must be proud of so accomplished a father."

Mary caught more glances from Dorcas and Elaine. They were rolling their eyes. She felt herself blushing a little. "I suppose I am proud of him," she said.

Just then, Lady Masham entered the room. Roger stood and bowed. "I suppose you know what is in this letter?" She held it in her left hand, opened.

"I have not read the letter, but Sir Edward said it might lead to employment."

"So it might. It praises your character and intellect almost beyond belief. I did not suppose that Sir Edward Coke was a man given to such effusive expression. Is he exaggerating in his praise of you?"

"Lady, that I cannot tell, without reading what is written." Mary, Dorcas, and Elaine were looking at him strangely: they had never heard their mistress address anyone in this tone.

"I shall not let you read it, lest your head swell to the bursting point. But answer me this: what do you know of Sir Edward's *Reports* ?"

"I have read them," Roger replied. "Sir Edward set me the task of reviewing them for errors."

"Errors?"

"It was the King's demand that Sir Edward review his *Notes* for 'errors' and correct them to the King's satisfaction."

"And did you?"

Roger chuckled. "We did not find any errors that would satisfy the King if that is what you mean."

"What did the King do about it?"

"He dismissed Lord Coke from his position as Chief Justice."

"Perhaps your work was of poor quality, then, if you could not contrive to save your master's career? Before you answer that, you should know that I am interviewing you to determine your suitability for a position."

Mary, Dorcas, and Elaine looked at her with surprise, then rose, as if to leave.

"Nay, remain," said Lady Masham, "listen and learn. Someday you may have to conduct an interview much like this one." She turned to Roger, waiting for his answer.

"Lady, the purpose of my work was not to 'contrive' anything. Sir Edward was not interested in contrivances.

Nothing was offered to the King without Sir Edward's full knowledge and approval."

"So it is his fault that the King rejected your work?"

Roger replied with some heat, "The fault was in the King. He thought to bully Sir Edward into compliance with his philosophy. Sir Edward is not a man to be bullied!"

"Not even by a King?"

"Not even by a King."

"Yet it cost him his position. A more prudent man would have found a compromise. A wise and prudent servant might have encouraged that course."

Roger calmed himself. "Not every dispute is amenable to compromise. Some principles must be upheld even in the face of persecution."

Lady Masham nodded. "That is so. What was the principle that Sir Edward upheld?"

"The principle that all men are subject to the Law — the Law of God, first, but also the Laws of England. It did not please the King to hear that, or see that in writing; especially not writing that all the lawyers in England rely on to practice their trade."

Lady Masham chuckled. "It sounds so grave when you speak of it that way. Explain to me how Sir Edward restored his fortunes after his fall from grace. Was there not some contrivance in it?"

"Lady, I am bound by honor to keep some matters confidential. But yes, there was some contrivance in it." Mary saw a change in his demeanor — something here he was not proud of? Some connivance, perhaps . . .

"You disapprove of contrivance?" There was a hint of sarcasm in Lady Masham's tone, as if perhaps this priest were judging his betters, thought Mary.

Roger thought a moment before he spoke: "It is my experience that contrivances often go amiss. I say that, knowing full well that they are the meat and drink of statecraft, as well as the basis for many a marriage alliance, and many a family's fortune. Honesty is a surer path, I think. Or at least I would like to believe so."

"And yet I think you are a man who knows how to contrive, when it suits his purpose."

Roger sighed, bowed his head. "I am indeed such a man."

"By God, I never expected you to be so truthful!" she said. "Are you not ashamed to admit your failings?"

"I have plenty to be ashamed of, but telling the truth is like a cool drink to a troubled soul. It is lies and proud self-deception that make things worse."

Lady Masham found a seat. She had not intended this interview to probe into the man's soul; she was expecting a demonstration of servant-talk: cleverness perhaps, avoidance of the uncomfortable behind a screen of cheerful deference, reassurance that his manners would not be an embarrassment to her household. This one might make an acceptable chaplain, but she wouldn't want him for anything else. "Was there something about this particular contrivance that troubles you? Something that went 'amiss', as you say?"

Roger hesitated. "I suppose that the facts of the matter are public knowledge, and will serve as a parable for the teachable among us . . ."

He was wrapping it up in a homily then, thought Lady Masham. Hopefully, he wouldn't make a sermon of it.

"I think it is generally agreed that Sir Edward's restoration to the Privy Council was accomplished through the efforts of the Duke of Buckingham," he began. Lady Masham nodded; the young ladies pricked up their ears at the mention of the 'Duke'. "And the Duke's support was secured by the betrothal of Sir Edward's daughter Frances to the Duke's elder brother John Villiers. It is not the first time that a man has advanced his career through his choice of son-in-law, nor will it be the last; but contrivance it certainly was, and Sir Edward intended it so."

"That was regarded as a good match on its own merits: the groom from a wealthy and powerful family, the lovely bride from a quality family as well. The parents of the bride and groom can hardly be faulted because the marriage has failed so scandalously." Lady Masham's unease with the story showed in her voice, thought Mary; she must have some other matters in mind . . .

Roger replied, "Our Lord said that we shall know them by their fruits. The fruits of this marriage have proved bitter, indeed. Viscount Purbeck is estranged from his wife; the Viscountess has none of the comforts she had expectation of. Her mother, Lady Hatton, opposed the match so emphatically that she will not be reconciled to Sir Edward. This 'good match' has brought nothing but grief to all of the people involved."

"How might it have been managed to a favorable outcome?"

"That would be no more than my opinion."

"I am interested in your opinion. Please answer the question."

"Sir Edward's daughter was only fifteen years old when she wed. A little more patience from her father might have given her greater chance at success. Also, a little more investigation into the suitability of the groom might have pointed in a different direction altogether. Lady Hatton's objections to the match were declared openly: sending a young woman into a marriage in the face of her mother's opposition created a breach in their relationship that would not bode well for any marriage."

"And yet Sir Edward has no regrets?"

"I cannot be certain, but I think he well may regret it. His youngest daughter was very dear to him."

"Was?"

"They are estranged. She lives with her mother now, I believe."

"Some would say she takes after her mother."

Roger nodded. "I have heard the same."

"So, you think it would have been better to bestow her on someone else?"

"That I cannot say. But if the political considerations had been left out of the decision, at least there would be less cause for regret. The bride and groom have enough to work out between them without the political 'connivances'. Who knows? Given time and space, they might have found happiness together; there might even be children; an heir for the Purbeck dynasty."

"The Viscountess Purbeck has a son."

"When was this?" His face showed surprise, and more than an idle curiosity about the revelation.

"Some years ago, apparently. The boy is three years old, or thereabouts. You must have known her when you served the Coke family."

"I did. I was at her wedding to John Villiers. I am pleased to think that their marital woes have been mended."

"Why would you think that?"

"Surely, if Viscount Purbeck has an heir, there must have been a reconciliation."

"There seems to be some question whether the Viscount has an heir or not. It is a matter of debate in London."

"Do you mean that the Viscount denies that he is the child's father?" Mary saw a look of wounded alarm flash briefly across his face, then he recovered his composure.

"No, it is his brother, the Duke of Buckingham, who denies the boy's paternity."

"On what grounds?" Roger felt a clenching in his stomach. What more harm could the Villiers family do to Frances Coke? Was Buckingham using Frances to attack Sir Edward? An attack on Frances was an attack on her child, as well — his own nephew!"Surely the Viscount would be in a better position to address the question?"

"The Viscount has nothing to say on the subject; he is in one of his 'spells'".

"Spells?"

The Villiers family insists that the Viscount is the victim of witchcraft. His mother says that the boy cannot possibly be his, because he is impotent — and has been for years; how she would know that fact is not explained."

"Nor would I wish to hear the explanation if it were offered," said Roger drily. "What does the Viscountess have to say?"

"She says that if the Viscount were truly impotent, and his mother knew of it, then his family perpetrated a fraud upon her and her family when the marriage contract was signed. Impotence is grounds for an annulment, and her dowry should be refunded."

Roger chuckled. He could almost hear Frances Coke pleading her case. "What is the. Villiers' rejoinder?"

The Duke of Buckingham accuses his sister-in-law of adultery and sorcery, and demands that she be brought to trial."

"Sorcery because she conjured a child out of thin air, and adultery because she produced the child in some more natural way?"

"There is another man in the story."

"Who would that be?"

"Robert Howard, fifth son of the Earl of Suffolk. He has been sheltering the Viscountess in his house. The child was baptized as Robert — Robert Wright."

"And what does Robert Howard say?"

"He says nothing. His mother insists that he cannot be the father of the child, because he, too, is impotent."

"England is in the midst of a plague — a plague of impotent men — or of mothers who pretend to know entirely too much about their son's private lives!" he exclaimed. "And the Viscountess?"

"She says that the child is Purbeck's. Which makes him heir to the bulk of the Villiers family fortune — you know, firstborn son of the firstborn, and all that."

"Which is one very compelling reason for the Duke to have him declared a bastard."

Lady Masham nodded to concede the point. "Also, from the Duke's point of view, legitimizing the boy would mean transferring the bulk of the Villiers estate to the Howard family, eventually. There is already bad blood between the two families, ever since the Duke fell out with the Earl of Suffolk."

"And Frances and her son are caught in the middle of their feud."

"You refer to her by her christening name?"

Roger sighed. "I knew her once. Well enough to know that she had reason to feel betrayed by all the men in her life."

"Including yourself?"

Roger nodded, a pained expression on his face. "Yes, I think so. I certainly disappointed her."

"What could she have wanted from you?"

"Loyalty. A servant's loyalty over a lifetime."

"And?"

"The price was too high. She would have sacrificed the happiness of others in search of her own. I did not love her enough to make the sacrifice that only love could make. She did not love me enough to justify such a sacrifice."

Mary realized that she had stopped breathing at some point in this conversation; she tried to inhale quietly, to avoid distracting her companions. One glance told her that Dorcas and Elaine were mesmerized in the moment as well. There was more here than gossip. The priest was clearly entangled with the lives of the Coke family somehow, and he spoke from personal anguish. He had given away so much of himself — the word 'love' still rang in her ears. A man could love so many things: his horse, his master, his country, his woman, his family. Such love as this was celebrated by poets. This was a man who understood that love could mean pain. She could see it in his eyes . . .

Lady Masham appeared to be relaxed, calculating. "I will have to confirm any decision I make with my husband," she said, "but I am certain he will agree with my judgment in this matter. We will employ you as Chaplain for this house, if you desire the position."

"It would be an honor to serve in such a house," he replied, then stood and bowed.

"Did you bring all your personal effects with you?"

"Nay, Lady. What property I possess — books mostly — are still in Cambridge. I can go there tomorrow and fetch them back."

"Is it a great deal of stuff?"

"A few chests; one for clothing, maybe two for the books."

She chuckled. "A traveling library, then. You will need a wagon to haul all of it."

Roger nodded. "I can hire a carter in Cambridge for that."

"Nonsense! We have carts a-plenty here. I'll send Wallace to Cambridge with you in the morning, with a wagon and a team. With a load that small, he'll have you back here by supper." She rang a bell to summon a servant. "Mr. Williams is to be our new chaplain. Please show him to his room."

The servant bowed. Roger bowed to the servant, then to the ladies, and excused himself.

Lady Masham turned her attention to Mary, Dorcas, and Elaine. "I trust you observed this interview carefully. You can learn a great deal from a servant if you ask the right questions in the right way. Always remember that <u>you</u> are the one in charge; the servant will naturally wish to please you. Beware the slippery answer and the half-truth. Did you notice how I followed the general questions with more specific ones, until his heart was laid open to me? That is the way to be sure of with whom you are dealing."

Heart laid open. Yes, that was what lingered in Mary's memory. It would have seemed a violation of the man's person if he had not exposed it so freely. She wondered if the others had seen the same thing.

"I must arrange to send this to Sir William," said Lady Masham, and left the room.

"He was rather handsome, don't you think?" asked Elaine.

"I suppose so, I hadn't really noticed," Mary said.

"Liar!" whispered Dorcas with a giggle.

Mary's mind was on other things: not the way the man looked on the outside, but what she had seen inside of him in that brief moment of confession. It was the nature of her life that she did not speak with men on intimate terms; even being alone with a man was to be avoided. There were plenty of polite conversations, of course; sometimes earnest, sometimes witty, sometimes suffocatingly trivial. In all such situations, she had learned to be deferential, pleasant, non-committal -

charming above all (you didn't want to put off a potential suitor by seeming . . . difficult).

"I did feel a little sorry for him," said Dorcas, "sort of wanted to comfort him."

"Or just cuddle him like a puppy," added Elaine.

Mary knew what they meant. But what she had seen was more daunting than a puppy. There was more inside that man than the other two could get their arms around. Maybe too much for her, as well.

Elaine was fifteen; sweet, but a bit young to plumb the deep waters. Dorcas was seventeen: as ripe for matrimony as she would ever be. Mary herself was eighteen — not yet destined for spinsterhood, but getting "long in the tooth" for a good match. Of course, there were always old widowers about, who would take a wife for companionship and preferred a bit more maturity; if they were wealthy enough, the second wife might expect a comfortable inheritance — not a bad bargain, really. That was beginning to look like her best chance at matrimony. But now this priest was going to be living in the house. No doubt he would lead the household staff in devotions every day; there would be religious instruction as well: that was the Chaplain's job. She realized that she would be speaking with this man nearly every day. He would serve as her spiritual advisor. The thought was a little unsettling.

L ady Masham decided that the family's new Chaplain was the most sensible conduit for communication with her imprisoned husband. After Roger's personal effects had been fetched from Cambridge, she sent him to London with Sir Edward's letter of recommendation, plus a few others — written by herself, presumably: they were sealed. She said that one of them was an official statement that he was indeed the family Chaplain; he would probably have to present it to the jailers to gain access to Sir William Masham. Roger took the assignment for a test of his competence. He wasn't sure exactly how closely he might be searched or examined by the jailers. It went without saying that whatever was in the other letters, the name of Sir Edward Coke might draw unwelcome attention to his presence. It was best if all of the letters — save his credentials — remain confidential until he delivered them to Sir William. But how to accomplish this? Attempting to smuggle the letters into the jail was risky: if a thorough search discovered them, it would immediately provoke suspicion, and his access to the jail might be denied — and his usefulness to the family would be compromised.

He decided at length on a plan that would be less surreptitious. He would hide the critical correspondence in the open — or rather, among a confusing assemblage of other documents, all tucked inside a large Bible that he would carry with him. He selected a variety of papers from his personal correspondence (letters that had already been opened, some study notes in Latin), and tucked them into the Bible, along with Lady Masham's letters. He was careful to leave corners of the papers sticking out from the cover of the Bible, as if they had been left there in a hurry.

Lady Masham took an interest in what he was doing. "Anyone looking at your Bible would think you a careless, absent-minded scholar," she said.

"I hope you are right," said Roger. "No one expects to find anything intelligible among the rat's nest of paper that a scholar surrounds himself with."

"But the untidiness of it invites attention."

Roger nodded. "An invitation so obvious as to warrant overlooking, I hope."

"But they may search the Bible anyway. And if they find unopened letters . . ."

"It will merely prove that the man carrying them is an absent-minded cleric, who loses track of such things."

"Ah." She smiled, "So that in the worst case, you are merely a careless servant?"

"And who would trust such a careless servant with anything of importance?"

"I knew you for a contriver," said Lady Masham. "God grant you success."

The Mashams provided him with a horse for his journey. He picked out an old, piebald mare: "Such as a careless servant might be allowed to ride," said Lady Masham with a chuckle. Roger thought he had pleased her.

Roger arrived in London late in the day. He put off visiting his family; no reason to involve them in any of this. If things went well at the prison, he could stay the night with them and arrange to inform Sir Edward that he would be living at Otes Hall for the foreseeable future.

The Marshalsea Prison was located across the river from the center of London, a mile or so beyond the south end of London Bridge. Roger presented himself and his credentials to the jailer, "I am here to minister to Sir William Masham," he said. The jailer read the letter and invited him into a nearby chamber. "You must be searched," he said, "I apologize, Father, but it is routine. Alfred, please do the honors." Another guard stepped forward. Then, "Roger Williams, is that you?"

This was completely unexpected. Roger took a moment to recognize the man, "Alfred. Alfred Fitch!"

Alfred nodded. "Aye, it is me."

"But how come you to this place?"

"It is not as bad as it sounds. Steady employment. And I get to go home every night — not like the poor sods inside," he winked, then chuckled.

"But your family?"

"They are well enough, thank you." We lost the shop during the last plague — not enough customers to keep us in business. But I found this job, so the wife takes in some sewing, and I work here. We still live in Cows Lane." He turned to his companions. "Roger, here grew up on the same street. We used to . . . travel together, so to speak, when we were young."

Roger laughed. "Aye, so we did."

"Ye're a priest now, are ye?"

Roger nodded. "Just finished my studies at university. This is my first job."

Alfred uttered a low whistle. "Workin' for the gentry now, I see. You've done well, Roger."

"You've not done badly, either. Bad business, the plague."

Alfred shook his head. "Aye, lost a lot of friends from the old neighborhood." Then, "Don't get ticklish. I have to search your clothing and such. Take off yer boots, please."

Roger did as instructed. They looked inside his boots and trousers; he took off his doublet, and they inspected it carefully. Then Alfred picked up the Bible and opened it. Some papers fell out. "What's this? Latin?"

"Let me see," said Roger. "Yes, those are notes from one of my classes that I left in there."

"Along with a lot of other scraps of paper, I see," said Alfred as he closed the Bible. "How well do ye know Sir William Masham?"

"I have never met him. His wife hired me just yesterday. If I make a poor impression, I could be out of a job by supper time."

Alfred chuckled. "Aye, that's how it is with these gentleman types. Do ye know why he's here?"

"I have heard that he has refused to collect loans for the King."

"Him and a bunch of others. You and I are lucky — not enough money for the King to come after. For once, I can say that I wouldn't trade places with the likes of Sir William Masham." Then, "Ye're all clear. I'll get a guard to escort you to his cell."

Roger got dressed and then followed the guard deeper into the prison. The smell of the place became overpowering: stale urine, chamberpots, and who-knows-what else. Sir William's cell was at ground level — more comfortable than the ones in the basement, probably not as noisome either. He wasn't expecting any visitors, and he was surprised to be told that this stranger was now his Chaplain. Roger found the letters from

Lady Masham amid the clutter in his Bible and presented them to him. He had just one candle to read by. "How is it the seals on these letters are intact? Didn't the guards demand to read them?"

"They must have missed them amid all the clutter," Roger suggested. He explained how the letters were brought into the jail.

"You took some risk, bringing them in so openly," he said.

"Concealing them would have been riskier. If I were caught smuggling something in here, this place could become my permanent residence."

Sir William chuckled. "I see it now. Hide in plain sight, and you can claim that you were hiding nothing at all. The next time we might not be so lucky."

Roger nodded. "The safest way to send a confidential message is by not writing it down at all. Of course, you can only use that method if you trust the messenger."

"And yet, I do not know you. I have no way of knowing whether you are actually a priest, much less whether you are trustworthy."

"I have another letter, which may answer that." Roger pulled Sir Edward's letter from his Bible. "You see that it has been opened — by your wife. I believe that she hired me based on its contents; I have not read it myself."

Sir William read the letter. His eyebrows raised more than once. "This is an unusual letter. Sir Edward Coke is unsparing in his praise of you. Of course, it is possible that you are not actually the man he describes in this letter . . ."

Roger thought a moment. "I have no answer for your last point. There is a jailer here who would vouch for my identity, but I doubt his testimony would settle the issue for you. Sir Edward cannot come here to vouch for me, for obvious reasons. It is possible that we have some mutual acquaintance, but I do not know who that would be."

"What mutual acquaintance could there be?"

"Years ago, when I was in Sir Edward's service, I lived with him awhile in Serjeant's Inn. I met many great lawyers there. Some of them would remember me, I think. I also met many men in Parliament when Sir Edward served there, but that was before I went away to school nearly seven years ago. I am also known to some other prominent men, but that connection is best kept secret. None of them are here in this prison, and that is as it should be."

Roger continued, "I will suggest one thing to you. Since I believe that all the sealed letters I have given you have served their purpose, there is no reason for them to be found and read by anyone else." he nodded at the candle flame.

"Quite so," said Sir William. He set fire to each of the letters in turn. "You are posing as a priest?" he asked.

"No Sir, I _am_ a priest. I am your family Chaplain, until you decide otherwise."

"You have not brought vestments with you."

"I do not believe in vestments. Neither do I use the Book of Common Prayer."

"Then pray with me, at least. That can do me no harm."

After they had prayed, Roger prepared to leave. "Is there any message you would like to send to Lady Masham? It need not be anything confidential; an unsealed letter might ease her heart. If you have anything you don't wish to put in writing, I could memorize a brief message."

Sir William nodded. "An unsealed letter will suffice." He took out the paper, drew his ink and quill, then wrote a short note, and folded it. "Carry it on your person, and let the jailers find it. Tell her that I am grateful for the visit.". Roger tucked the letters into his belt and called for the jailer to release him.

"One more thing, if you please," said Sir William. "My father-in-law, Sir Francis Barrington, is also in prison, for the same reason as I. If you could visit him and simply inform him that I am well, it would be a mercy."

"I will see what I can do," said Roger.

It turned out that Sir Francis Barrington was imprisoned in Marshalsea as well. Roger discovered this by asking Alfred Fitch. Alfred agreed to let him visit Sir Francis briefly.

"His Lady is with him," said Alfred, as they climbed a stairway to the second floor. The smell here was less pungent than the cells below, but hardly pleasant.

"How's that?"

"His wife, the Lady Joan Cromwell Barrington. She joined him in prison, rather than be separated from him; his health is fragile. Also, his daughter is sometimes here."

The Barringtons' cell was notably larger than Sir William Masham's had been. It had two windows, which, when opened, allowed for a cross-draft. The place still reeked, but it was fresher than the corridor outside.

An old man sat in a chair near the windows, his lap covered in a blanket. A woman sat nearby and rose when they entered. "Is this the physician that I requested?" Her question was directed at Alfred Fitch.

"Nay, Lady. My master has not found a physician for Sir Francis, yet."

"Well, see to that he does so, and quickly! My husband's health is failing!"

"Yes, ma'am," said Alfred with a bow. He winked at Roger as he turned to the door and left the cell, closing it firmly behind him. Roger heard the key turn in the lock.

The woman turned her attention to Roger. "What is your business, if you are not a physician?"

Roger bowed. "Roger Williams, at your service," he said, "I am chaplain to Sir William Masham. He asked me to look in on Sir Francis."

"Chaplain? How is it that I do not know you?"

"I am recently employed by Sir William and Lady Elizabeth. She sent me here to minister to her husband, and he asked me to visit Sir Francis, ere I return to Otes Hall."

"What proof have you that you are who you say you are?"

"I have the letter that Lady Masham gave me to gain access to this place." He handed her the letter of introduction he had shown the jailer.

"This is my daughter's handwriting; I recognize it." She handed the letter back to him.

"I also have this note from Sir William, for Sir Francis." He pulled the letter from beneath his belt and handed it to her.

"It is not sealed," she noted.

"Nay, Lady, but no one else has read it. It seems that the jailers insist on reading any written documents that are carried when entering or leaving the prison, but not those that remain inside the walls."

She handed the note to her husband, who read it and smiled. "It is good news," he said, "thank you for delivering it." he handed it back to his wife.

"Do you have a reply for my daughter?" she asked.

"I do, but I am not authorized to let anyone but her read it. I shall, of course, report to her everything I have heard and seen here."

"Can you take a message back to Barrington Hall?"

"Gladly. Although if you wish it to be confidential, I shall have to commit it to memory. The jailers will most likely search me thoroughly when I leave."

"How did you manage to conceal whatever you brought in?"

"I didn't conceal anything. The letter from your daughter was in plain sight. They simply didn't bother to read it."

"Careless of them."

Roger nodded. "Perhaps, but I wouldn't count on them being 'careless' a second time."

"He is right," said Sir Francis. "We can test his memory. Give him a message for our daughter in Otes, and another for the steward at Barrington Hall. Let him memorize them and deliver them. Let each message be written down by the recipient, and return the writing to us. If they are the same as the messages we sent, we will know that his memory is reliable."

Roger wondered if he had overstated his mnemonic abilities. But he had to admit that the test was a fair one. Mercifully, neither message was very long. Lady Barrington read each of them to him a few times, until he thought he had them committed to memory. Then he excused himself.

He was right about one thing; the search that the jailers performed on his way out gave much less attention to his clothing, but more to the papers inside his Bible. It made sense: there weren't that many material objects inside the prison that anyone would want to take home with them; information was another matter.

It was dusk when he left the prison and rode northward across London Bridge to his old neighborhood in St. Sepulcher's parish. He arrived in Cow's Lane in time for supper. His mother greeted him with a delighted embrace; Sydrach, his wife, and the rest of the family seemed happy to see him. He was able to report that he was now employed - a fact that felt particularly satisfying for some reason: perhaps it was proof that his chosen path in life was sober and respectable, after all.

Roger enquired at Serjeant's Inn the following day and determined that one of Sir Edward Coke's old colleagues was maintaining a regular correspondence with him. He composed a short letter on the spot, thanking Coke for his newfound employment, and sealed it. Sir Edward would know how and where to reach him if need be. Then he was on the road to Otes Hall. With any luck, he would be home for supper.

September 1627: The Chaplain Dances

In the months that followed, Roger established himself as the Chaplain of Otes Hall. He led the household in prayer every morning, of course (and usually added a homily for their edification), and preached on Sundays in the family chapel. He avoided using any part of the Book of Common Prayer (which would have meant prompt dismissal from any regular parish church), preaching instead on whatever text he felt led to expound upon. This was only possible because he was unencumbered by the supervision of any bishop or other ecclesiastical office: the power of the Masham family shielded him from oversight — he felt liberated. More importantly, he felt free at last of all the 'popish' traditions he had resisted thus far on his spiritual journey.

It all seemed to work very well. Lady Masham was well pleased with his ministry, and the rest of the household seemed to share her feelings. Roger sensed a spiritual earnestness among the servants at morning devotions; more than a few approached him during the days to ask a question or seek counsel.

He had lived in great houses like this one before, of course, but always as a servant of the lesser to middling sort. At Otes, he was a man of higher status — particularly so because the master of the house was away in Marshalsea Prison. He ate with the family in the dining hall; sometimes he was the "man" at a table dominated by women. They looked to him for stimulating conversation, for a "man's point of view." He did his best; in fact, he charmed them all.

Roger remembered what it was like to eat with the servants in a house like this one. He went out of his way to be polite and appreciative to all of them, regardless of rank. And why not? There was no place for betters and lessers in the Kingdom of God — all God's children were precious in his sight. The apostle James had strictly warned against discriminating between the powerful and the weak, the rich and the poor. The other servants were a little put off by this at first, but soon came to regard him with respect: the man who bowed when greeting the lowliest scullery maid, but dined with Lady Masham and her young ladies could hardly be accused of overweening pride. It spoke to his spirituality, somehow. A modest man. A man to be emulated.

The young ladies were utterly charmed with Roger Williams. In part because he was the only young single man of the middling class whom they encountered on a daily basis. But he was educated, congenial, charming. He had stories to tell that were amusing. He had experience of the wider world, including London — which held a special fascination for young women of their station in life. He had knowledge — or at least opinions — about politics, science, and foreign affairs. His preaching was pedantic, but that seemed to be what Lady Masham preferred. There was no doubting his erudition.

Mary Bernard observed all of this with some detachment. Dorcas and Elaine were bedazzled by him and could spend hours discussing his manners, his appearance, and his conversational charm. One evening at supper, Lady Masham turned the conversation in an unexpected direction: "I don't suppose they have much use for dancing at university, do they, Rev. Williams ?"

Roger shook his head with a smile. "No, ma'am. At least, not the sort of dancing that would suit this house. Students have a great interest in drinking; dancing is of secondary interest, or so I have observed."

"No dancing at all then?"

"Once a young man is full of ale, he may insist on dancing with a barmaid, but it is not a performance that does either of them credit."

"So you yourself are untrained in the art?"

"I had some little training before I entered university."

'Little training'? There it is, lurking just under the surface, said Mary to herself. She had seen him do this before: a self-effacing reply that leaves the door open to a following question, at which he reveals another bit of himself. Always understating his abilities, so that he may exceed everyone's expectations. Setting up another situation where he can surprise and delight people, all the while appearing to be the model of humility. A necessary skill for a man who travels in the company of his social betters, perhaps. Also, the habit of a man driven by a desire to please and impress . . .

"What training was that?" Lady Masham asked the question that the Rev. Williams had prompted. Now for the answer that he was aching to give . . .

"It was at Standon Lordship. Many years ago. Lady Sadleir had a dancing master named Clifton at the time."

Well, thought Mary, that was a surprise. Lady Masham was hooked now; she would go on asking questions until the

Rev. Williams had made his points. Dorcas and Elaine were gazing at him with wide eyes. Clearly, they were thinking about dancing — dancing with the Chaplain.

Lady Masham must have sensed that she was being led through the conversation; she gave him the lead. "Go on," was all she said.

"I was visiting the manor with Sir Edward Coke, my master at the time. Lady Anne Sadleir is his daughter."

Lady Masham nodded. "I know Lady Anne. I have visited her at Standon Lordship."

"Lady Anne was hosting a party on Twelfth Night that year. She wished to have some court dancing for the entertainment of her guests. She tasked Clifton with teaching a few of her servants and myself, so that we could accompany them."

"You are full of surprises, Father. I shall look forward to seeing how well trained you are, come Christmastide."

Thus, she concluded the topic of discussion. She was in control again. Mary was impressed. Lady Masham had learned what she wanted to know, and the Rev. Williams would have to keep whatever else he wanted to say to himself. Dorcas and Elaine looked like they were bursting with questions. Their training prevented them from blurting something out, but Mary could see that it took some effort.

There was another side to Roger's duties that was less public. His reliability as a messenger had been established, and there was demand for his services. Now that his position was established, there was little need for him to travel incognito, so Lady Masham provided him with a faster horse — a five-year-old black gelding named Gondomar. Gondomar was hot-blooded and strong, but Roger found that he could handle him. In fair weather with open roads, they could make very good time, indeed. They made a few trips to London, but most of their destinations were closer to Otes Hall: a half-day's ride or less to some other manor or town in Essex, rarely farther than that. Most of his messages were in the form of sealed letters, but there was almost always one message to be delivered verbally. Roger understood the meaning of those messages well enough to guess what they signified. He had done this sort of work years ago in London, for a network of informants and opinion makers. Now, as he traveled, he comprehended just how large the network had become.

He became familiar with the main roads and some of the back roads, as well. He took no particular care to conceal his movements; a man on a mount like Gondomar was noticed wherever he went — and was usually moving too fast for anyone to follow. And truthfully, a man who rode a horse like Gondomar was assumed to be a gentleman of some importance — not the sort of fellow to trifle with. Roger became accustomed to the deference that strangers showed him and fell easily into the manners of a man of privilege.

The reality, of course, was that he was a gentleman by appearance only. However comfortable his new station, he owned neither property nor title and did not expect any inheritance — nothing in fact, that would earn him a permanent place in this society.

What he did have was a cause. In his travels and conversations, he had come to appreciate just how consequential this cause was. It was the cause of Law, first of all — ancient Law that guaranteed Englishmen certain rights. It was also the cause of justice. It was antithetical to any notion that a King had divine rights that superseded those of other men, or, indeed, that any man's claim to divine authority could supersede them. This last point was not fully grasped by all of the men who now claimed the cause as their own; Roger knew that many would have exempted recusant Catholics from the protection of such rights, but he recognized where this would lead if the principles were embraced. The important thing was to rally the largest numbers possible to the cause: the details could wait.

Roger was also convinced that his was a godly cause. (An opinion shared by many of his Puritan correspondents, though they did not necessarily share his vision of where God was taking things.) As such, he expected that divine power would ultimately be manifest on behalf of their cause. Just as the 'Protestant Wind' had destroyed the Great Armada, he expected that the cause would ultimately prevail. Roger's sense of how and when that would happen was less specific than that of some men he knew.

"All this organizing and debating is well enough," he heard men saying, "but this King will not concede us our rights without a battle. And it will not be a battle of mere words. You must be prepared to take up arms if you hope to prevail. Blood will be spilt before this is over."

Roger shook his head at this sort of talk. He knew that the majority of the country's leaders would hear such words with shock and revulsion. They would not willingly risk the privilege of their positions in a revolt against their sovereign. They hoped to 'tame' him, not replace him. If they expected divine help in their struggle, they must serve a divine purpose: "There is indeed a battle to fight," Roger replied, "it is an ancient one, older than this King or his kingdom, older than all of them. It is the battle for the restoration of our birthright, that communion with the Almighty that was lost when Adam fell. Christ has opened the door to Paradise for us; our fight must be to call men to pass through that door, though the forces of evil would hinder them. I am determined to prepare myself to fight that battle, and share in the victory when it comes."

"Dress it up in religious language, if you please," was the reply, "but the King has religious language of his own. This will not be decided by theologians. The King will have no compunction about employing any weapons that come to hand. A secular ruler will resort to secular means."

There was no point in debating the issue. It was fortunate that only a small minority of the men Roger spoke to held this opinion. Sufficient to recruit them to the cause, for now. Tomorrow would have troubles enough of its own.

In late September, Roger and Gondomar pulled up in the courtyard at Barrington Hall, before the great main door. They had been here once or twice before, and the steward recognized him. "Welcome, Father Williams," he said, "what news have you?"

"I have a letter for the Lady Ruth," he replied. "Is she within?"

"Aye. She is probably at dinner. They have just sat down. Perhaps you would join them?"

Roger was hungry and had only the six or so miles to travel back to Otes Hall before supper. A meal would be welcome. "Gladly, if they will have me."

The steward smiled. "I will announce you," he said. A groom appeared and took Gondomar to the stables. Roger followed the steward into the house.

The household had just sat down for their midday meal. Roger recognized Sir Francis' daughter Ruth Lytton; she had spent some time in Marshalsea Prison with her father. The seat at the head of the table was occupied by a man that Roger had not met before — a cousin, as it turned out.

"Roger Williams, Chaplain, at your service," said Roger with a bow.

"Oliver Cromwell. Please be seated," was the reply. Cromwell gestured to an empty chair along the right side of the great table. Roger found himself seated next to a lovely young woman.

"Roger Williams . . ." he began with a bow.

She cut him off, "Yes, I heard you before. I know who you are." She smiled.

Roger was a little taken aback, looked across and down the table. Everyone else was smiling; some of the young ladies were giggling. He sat down.

"You will have to forgive my cousin's impertinence," said Cromwell. "Her name is Jane. Jane Whalley." He introduced the others at the table one by one. Roger bowed his head to each, and each acknowledged with a nod in return.

"Your name is known to everyone here; you have been of great service to our family," said Cromwell. "What brings you to Barrington Hall?"

"I have a letter for the Lady Ruth Lytton, from her father," Roger replied. "The Steward suggested I could dine with you," he added.

"So he did. You are welcome at our table," said Cromwell. "What is in this letter?"

"I cannot say. I have not read it," Roger replied.

"I shall read it," said Lady Ruth. She directed a servant to fetch the letter from Roger.

"The seal was broken by the guards at the prison," explained Roger.

She nodded. "It says here that my father's health has improved a little. Praise God for that!" There were murmurs of assent from around the table. Turning to Roger, she asked, Have you seen my parents? Is he truly on the mend?"

All eyes were on Roger. "He seemed in better health than the last time I saw them. Lady Barrington tends to him most assiduously."

"And how was my mother?"

"She seems to bear her situation with . . . fortitude. She speaks freely and with conviction. The jailers treat her with respect. Her health appears to be sound."

Jane snickered and gave Roger a dig with her elbow.

"Do not mind my cousin," said Lady Ruth. "She has not visited the prison, as I have. She does not know what it is to endure the reek of such a place, or the boredom, or the humiliation." Roger nodded.

"I merely meant that Aunt Joan is a strong woman, able to bear the burden of her situation — and give the jailers as much trouble as they give her," Jane said. "I am sure that Father Williams meant to say the same thing." She looked at him and winked. Her eyes were blue. Roger nodded again.

Cromwell changed the subject. "What other news do you have for us? You have been to London, I suppose?"

"I have, Sir. There is a rumor about town that the King will soon call for a new Parliament. The Duke of Buckingham is raising an army to go to war with France, but nothing can be done without money."

Cromwell snorted. "After the debacle at Cadiz and the massacres at St. Martin, who but a fool would put that man in command of an army? 7,000 brave lads sailed to France with him, and 5,000 of them are still in France — lying in unmarked graves."

"You are familiar with the views of everyone in London, then," Roger replied. "I have found no one who would trust the Duke to lead so much as a horse to water — except the King, of course."

"Has the King gone mad? Does he not see the folly of trusting this man?"

"The King is surrounded by advisors who depend upon the Duke of Buckingham for their positions and provender. None of them will have anything to say against the Duke's fitness for command. As for madness, there are many opinions spoken on the street, but none that I would wager any money on." Cromwell laughed a little at this.

He felt a hand grip his own, under the table; a woman's hand. Roger paused. "Remember that there are ladies present," said Jane Whalley. "All this manly talk of politics is quite over our heads, I fear. Pray, speak of something that touches the lives of such as we."

She looked into Roger's eyes again with her blue gaze. Roger's hand tingled a little. "I apologize, Lady," he said, "I think it likely the King will release Sir Francis and all of the other gentlemen who have resisted the forced loans before he calls another Parliament — as a gesture of conciliation . . ."

"May it be as you suppose!" said Lady Ruth emphatically, and raised her cup. Everyone else at the table did the same.

After dinner, Oliver Cromwell called Roger aside to ask for more news from London. They spoke for more than an hour. There was a directness about the man that Roger found appealing: a bit like Clem Coke; a man of deeds more than words. Of course, he was young; a few years older than Roger, at most. The sort of man who would inherit the new world that was aborning; a practical man, unencumbered with the customs and traditions that colored the vision of men like Sir Edward Coke.

When it was time to leave, Cromwell sent a groom to bring Gondomar around to the front door. Jane Whalley was there, to bid him farewell. She was taller than he had supposed when sitting beside him at table. She wore an embroidered cap over her blonde hair, a different gown than she had worn at dinner. Her smile was warm, and she curtseyed. He bowed and smiled back.

"God speed you, Father Williams," she said.

"Until we meet again," he replied with another bow, and mounted Gondomar, tipping his hat to her.

"That would be Christmastide, I'm thinking." She smiled more broadly and waved.

Roger thought about Christmas all the way back to Otes Hall.

December 1627: Christmas at Otes

Christmas came soon enough. Roger and Gondomar continued their travels in Essex and London as the days grew shorter and chillier. By mid-December, the weather had turned cold enough that Roger welcomed a respite from his rides. He had a whole week at Otes before Christmas Eve, a chance to catch up with his duties as Chaplain. Christmas fell on a Saturday that year, so he would be preaching in the chapel for Christmas Eve on Friday, as well as Christmas Day, and the Sunday following.

The great house bustled with preparations. Lady Masham had determined to celebrate Christmastide with a ball for her family and friends, in spite (or because) of the fact that her husband was still imprisoned at Marshalsca. In fact, all her relatives at Barrington Hall were invited to come celebrate the season with her — except for her father and mother, who were still at Marshalsea. It would mean a full house, but "I won't let the King punish our family any more than he has, by ruining our Christmas," she said.

Roger was pleased to be part of this defiant celebration. Certain customs came with Christmas, of course, that troubled his Puritan sensibility a little — but he brushed those aside. They were celebrating Christmas for the cause; if the celebration was a little flamboyant, so be it. (Once the Church was truly reformed, there would be time to purge the paganism from Christmas, and from secular life as well.)

This was a God-fearing household, and Lady Masham wanted it to appear so, "About the dancing . . ." she began, "I would not have it said that we keep a debauched house. What sort of dancing would be acceptable?"

Roger thought a moment. "If the reputation of the house is in question, I should think the wine and spirits should receive the most attention. Debauchery has more to do with drunkenness than with dance, I think."

"So you would not constrain the dancing?"

"A little constraint would be in order, but country dances like reels and allemandes, where the partners are changing all the time, should be no problem. A man and woman may hold hands without scandal: so long as they do not embrace, I think there is no harm in it."

Lady Masham nodded and smiled. "As for the beverages?"

"Ale serves better than wine, wine better than brandy. It is the servants who are most prone to irregularities, in my experience."

"Quite so. Ale for the servants, wine for the family. Thank you for your advice, Father Williams."

In January, on Twelfth Night, the Mashams and the Barringtons were out in full force. They feasted in the early evening to the accompaniment of a dozen hired musicians. Roger found himself seated next to Jane Whalley. She wore a blue satin gown that matched the color of her eyes, her blond hair done up in braids tied up in a glittering comb, her neck bare, a pendant hanging across the low-cut bodice. He tried not to stare. Across the table sat Mary Bernard, also dressed in a formal gown, this one of dark green velvet. Her hair was up, as well. Some sort of bejeweled pin held it all together. She smiled. He smiled back. His own dress was plain by comparison, as befit a man of the "cloth" — black velvet doublet and trousers, white stockings.

Jane reached under the table and took his hand, startling him a little. Mary must have guessed what had happened because she giggled a little when he flinched and covered her mouth. Jayne spoke softly in his ear, " I suppose your ears must be burning this evening, Father Williams."

"Eh? How's that?"

"All the ladies have been talking about what a fine figure you cut this evening. I hope you have come prepared to dance."

Not quite what he had anticipated. True, there were not that many single men present. And dancing with Jane Whalley was definitely on his list of things to do this evening, but he was already torn between that intention and his responsibility as a religious figure to set a proper example. The thought that he might be the object of discussion for a group of women, like a fatted calf at a butcher's auction, was unsettling. He wasn't sure what his duty was: dance with as many women as possible, maybe? And keep an eye on his "flock," of course, lest they overindulge, and embarrass themselves, or fall into mortal sin . . .

After supper, the house servants cleared away the dishes, while the musicians assembled in the great front hallway, with its great staircase and galleries on the upper floor. When they were ready, it was time for the dancing to begin. They began with a minuet — a stately procession of couples. As it happened, Jane Whalley appeared at Roger's right, just as the music began. She smiled and gave him her hand. The next few hours were a blur: he must have danced with dozens of women through the gavottes, the reels, the round dances. Mary, Dorcas, and Elaine were familiar to him; several others had to be introduced to him. Lady Masham took a turn once or twice. One woman in particular stuck in his memory —

Jane Whalley. She was graceful, joyous, intoxicatingly charming. He scarcely had time to catch his breath from one dance partner to another, but he always seemed to come back to Jane, smiling Jane, laughing Jane. He quite forgot about the rest of his responsibilities. The world was reduced to this moment, this place, this woman; the universe sang with this tune and tempo as it surely had always done. This moment was the only one that mattered.

The ladies seemed to understand this intuitively; for Roger, it was a revelation. When the music stopped, it was as if something delicate and spiritual had departed. When it resumed, it was like a refreshing breeze that energized his weary feet. In such a state, he could believe that anything was possible — as long as there was music.

The music stopped, and the ball was over. The guests retired; the servants were left to clean up. Roger stood for a few moments in the hallway, feeling his weariness at last. He was drained, yet relaxed. There was a small postern door off to the side of the main doorway; he stepped outside for a moment to clear his head. It was chilly. He took a few breaths and stepped back inside.

On his way to his room, he passed Mary Bernard. She smiled and curtseyed, then giggled. "I apologize for doubting your stamina, Father Williams. The ladies and I had a wager among us as to which of us could dance you off the floor. You were overmodest about your skills, I think."

"I was blessed with willing partners," he said, "I have rarely enjoyed dancing so much."

"I think all the ladies would say the same," Mary replied. "It is all too rare to find a willing partner, still rarer to find one that embraces the music the way you do."

"In truth, I think the music embraced me this evening. I do not recall dancing like that before."

"Truly? You seemed at home with it tonight. I think I saw a side of you that I had not seen before. A side unexpected from a man of the cloth." Roger started at the remark; Mary wondered if she had been over-familiar. Perhaps she had crossed a line . . .

He recovered. "Perhaps a chaplain should be more decorous than I was tonight. Have I set a poor example for my flock?"

"That was not what I intended to say. I only meant that you seemed more like part of us this evening — not . . . set apart as much."

"Set apart?"

"I fear I have said too much. I meant no offense."

"No offense is taken. I am curious to know what you mean. How have I set myself apart?"

Mary hesitated. Then, "There is usually a reserve about you. Some might take it for arrogance, but I do not think you to be an arrogant man. You seem always to be in control — as if there is some great hound within you that you keep chained up at all times. You never let it loose, for fear of what it might do."

"You think me ambitious. I do not deny that."

"There is more to it than ambition. I suppose that you must have curbed your tongue as well as many of your private feelings when you were in service to Sir Edward Coke."

Roger stiffened a little, then nodded. "Then, and many times since. It is a servant's place to be invisible except when his presence is required, and silent unless he has some pertinent information."

"But you are not like other servants I have known. A good servant is faithful and obedient; little more is expected of them. Servants can be simple or silly; their masters tolerate it with laughter. But you have held yourself apart from that, somehow. It is as if you wish to be recognized as a different sort of man altogether."

She saw his shoulders sag a little. Even in the dim light, she saw something small and vulnerable in his eyes. He nodded, "You have named me, Mary Bernard. I do indeed long to be more than a servant. What that might be, I cannot tell. I hope that God has something more for me, but when I look at the path ahead, I see only closed doors. I have no land or title. I lack the aptitude for business. I have my education and a calling to the priesthood, but no way to fulfill that calling, except for the protection of the Masham family. My life is forfeit if that protection should fail; it seems that I have nowhere to go from here — ever.

Mary heard a tone of desperate resignation in his voice. "I did not realize you were so unhappy here," she said.

"Unhappy? Nay, on the contrary. My life here is the happiest I have known. All of the household are precious to me. The Mashams have been like a family to me. And I am part of a great cause — the likes of which few men are given a chance to be part of!"

And yet the great hound is still there, thought Mary to herself, *and it howls at night . . .*

Roger continued: "I have indeed learned to guard my thoughts; it has been the secret of my success. I have risen far in the world — farther than my own father would have imagined. It may be that I have risen as far as I ever shall — that is an unfamiliar idea to me. I am ambitious, no doubt. And prideful, at times. May God in his mercy teach me humility, and may the lessons be not too painful." He chuckled.

Mary chuckled and smiled. "That is a prayer for all of us, I think. Sometimes, I fear that my pride and ambition are so strong that God will have to visit me with some disaster that will break my heart, to humble me."

Roger looked at her soberly. "Pray, not so. Humility is less about the breaking of the heart than it is about the surrender of the will. May God give us all tender hearts and obedient minds." He excused himself with a bow and a smile.

Mary returned to the bed chamber she shared with Elaine and Dorcas. They had company this evening; Jane Whalley was also to sleep there, as it was too late to return to Barrington Hall. None of them was sleepy; the excitement of the evening still lingered.

"Where have you been?" asked Dorcas.

"Just now, I was speaking with Reverend Williams," said Mary.

"We were speaking about him, as it happens." Elaine and Dorcas giggled.

"He wasn't lying about his dancing," added Elaine.

Mary nodded. He was more than he appeared to be, that one.

"Jane fancies him!" reported Dorcas.

"I think all the ladies fancy him," said Mary.

"No, I mean she *really* fancies him. Set her cap for him, I'd say."

"And what if I have?" asked Jane. "He's as good a catch as any."

Mary looked at her. "You realize that his prospects are . . . constrained ? No family property to speak of, no money apart from what he has earned?"

"I imagine a man as charming as he will find his way to fortune. He has the patronage of the Masham family behind him."

"But his presence in this house is because he could never find employment as a parish vicar, or any one of higher position in the Church — his convictions disqualify him."

Jane shrugged. "His convictions are not that different from my father's. I believe Papa will like him. A lot of men trim their convictions to fit the times they live in. A man will make sacrifices for the woman he loves."

"And does he love you that much?"

"Not yet. But he is a wonderful dancer. Who knows what may come of that?" Elaine and Dorcas giggled again. Mary had to smile. *Who knows, indeed.*

March 1628: The Cockpit

By early January of 1628, King Charles decided he had made his point about the forced loans. As a conciliatory gesture, he released the seventy "gentlemen" (they had never been charged with any crime) so that they could return to their families — the Parliamentary elections were coming, and he believed that these men, now chastened, would be among those elected.

He was half right. All seventy of the men he had jailed were elected to seats in the new Parliament. They were not chastened by their experience; they were grimly determined to make it impossible for Charles or any other king to impose forced loans in the future.

They had other aims, as well. They intended to enforce the observation of *habeas corpus* for all English subjects, even before the Court of High Commission. They were equally determined to prohibit the King from detaining any of his subjects without charge or imposing martial law, except in times of a declared war, and to reiterate the rights enumerated in *Magna Carta*. Some, of course, were still determined to impeach the Duke of Buckingham for all his failures and peculations, but many recognized that such a demand would probably simply force the King to adjourn Parliament, as he had done years past.

The election returned many men whom Roger knew to Parliament. Sir Edward Coke was among them, as well as his son Clem. Sir William Masham was elected also, along with Oliver Cromwell, his nephew, and Sir Francis Barrington, his father-in-law. The majority of the 'Seventy Gentlemen' were elected to the House of Commons that year; the rest to the House of Lords. Far from being cowed by their long incarcerations, they were resolved to press forward.

In early March, Sir William Masham prepared to relocate to his house in London. He would take servants with him, of course, though the London House was staffed anyway.
"You'll be coming along too," he announced to Roger. "Expect to do some traveling, but I will need you in London."

Roger was excited at the prospect of returning to the liveliness of London. He would have a chance to see his family again, of course. More than that, he foresaw that Events of Great Import were about to occur, and he relished the chance to bear witness to them. This would be a Parliament like no other in his experience: united, grimly determined to have their way with an uncooperative king (was there any other kind?). He hoped to see his old mentor, Sir Edward Coke, and his son Clement. He was not their peer by any means, but he felt that he was more their comrade than their subordinate. Did they not share the same vision and the same cause? He had labored long in their service; now the fruits of that labor would be harvested. He would celebrate the feast with them.

A whole cavalcade was assembled at Otes Hall. Sir William and his retainers, along with his manservant, Roger, and a few others, to begin with. They were joined by Oliver Cromwell with a couple of servants of his own. Then Sir Francis Barrington arrived, accompanied by his own retinue and his son, Sir Thomas, who had also been newly elected. By the time they were ready to leave for London, they were thirty strong: Roger imagined groups of men like this on all the highways leading to London on that morning, powerful men, determined men, men who would contend for the Law and proper government. He was certain that the King had no understanding of what these men were resolved to accomplish; Roger smelled victory.

They were greeted on the streets of London as they rode into the city. The gentlemen and their retainers rode in front, and Roger rode to the rear, mounted on Gondomar; he had a good view of the crowd lining the streets. He recognized a good number of the throng — men and women whom he had worked with before: people entrusted with gathering information useful to the cause, spreading the word among the general population, and shaping the public mood. They had done their part in encouraging this display of popular support for the new Parliament, but the support was genuine — mostly driven by popular hatred of the Duke of Buckingham and his ilk, but also by genuine admiration for the steadfastness of the seventy "gentlemen" that Charles had imprisoned.

The latest scandal that outraged the citizenry concerned one Dr. John Lambe, an advisor to the Duke. Dr. Lambe declared himself to be a man of special gifts — an astrologer, a "conjurer" ("sorcerer", according to his Puritan detractors), advisor to the wealthy, and powerful. As an advisor, his track record was no better than the military exploits of the Duke of Buckingham would suggest. As a practitioner of the "black arts", he was feared by some and destined for hell according to others. This was not an auspicious time to be known as a witch or sorcerer, however powerful his clients might be. Worse, he had been convicted of raping an eleven-year-old servant girl, one Jean Seager, just the previous year. His execution was delayed through the efforts of the Duke and the King (who apparently valued his advice), and Lamb dropped out of public sight, but the case festered in the public imagination. What sorceries might Dr. Lambe have performed upon the King? What crimes might the Duke and the King be covering up? Was the whole government under the control of the Devil? Who could rescue England from the demonic power?

A parliament could. A parliament composed of upright, Christian men — Puritan men, men who could discern the demonic influences, and expunge them from the kingdom. Such was the word on the streets, in the pubs, and especially in the secret conventicles where the non-conforming and Puritan believers congregated. The stage was set for a Holy War. The men on horseback would lead the charge.

Parliament convened on March 17, 1628. Roger Williams was fortunate to gain occasional access to a gallery above the hall; seating on the main floor was dedicated to the members and their servants. From there, he could listen to the speeches, the arguments, the turmoil of the next few months.

He paid particular attention to the words of his old mentor, Sir Edward Coke. Edward Coke was now seventy-six years old — lean and gray, still erect, looking to Roger like nothing so much as an old, battered fox — or maybe a wolf. Many supposed him to be in his dotage; when he rose to speak, their suppositions were refuted. Over the weeks of debate and maneuvering, he emerged as the voice of implacable reason.

Many members of the House of Commons sought a path of conciliation. They hoped that the King might be persuaded to acknowledge their traditional rights if they reassured him of their loyalty: they sent soothing messages to the palace, praising his wisdom and graciousness; affirming their willing submission to his rule. Coke said nothing about this approach at first; he was willing to wait for the disillusionment that he was sure would be coming. Privately, he said, "These men think to woo the King with flattery; they will find him a cold-eyed shrew, determined to guard his honor — that is, his power and prerogative."

At first, things seemed to go well. Parliament approved five separate subsidies to fund the King's government (contingent upon finishing their other business), and he responded with warm letters of appreciation. He was grateful for the money, and they should trust in his grace — as their loving sovereign — to always honor and protect their rights.

It was Coke's time to speak. "Grace," he said, was not the remedy for the issues at hand. "We are not asking for grace — we are demanding our rights! Anything that the King 'gives' us by grace can be withdrawn at a whim. These rights are ours by birthright — they are not given by this sovereign or any other!"

There was debate about which rights were at issue and how best to guarantee them. The King's party argued that his word should be all the assurances that Parliament should require, insisting on any more than that was to imply that King Charles was a liar, that his word could not be trusted.

That put a point on it; a point that Parliament hesitated to press. Everyone understood that Charles could dismiss this Parliament, as he had others; the only leverage they had was the subsidies, which they had not finally approved, and the hope that they might grant Charles his tonnage and poundage. They would have to tread carefully.

Coke and his allies were willing to risk it. For the next several days, speaker after speaker rose to recount in detail the cases in which the King had failed to uphold their rights: the forced loans were an illegal form of taxation, prohibited in *Magna Carta;* the King had compounded that violation by imprisoning those who refused to pay or collect his illegal tax, even to the point of suspending *Habeas Corpus;* various commissions established by the King (such as the Court of High Commission) had been allowed to arrest, torture, and execute the King's subjects without charge or trial. The Duke of Buckingham had threatened to lodge his soldiers in private homes across London (the better to keep an eye on its citizens, presumably); all these, Parliament insisted, were violations of their fundamental rights as Englishmen.

The King did not admit that this was so. He granted that *Habeas Corpus* ought to be honored in most cases, but insisted that "Reasons of State" permitted him to ignore that right: some offenses were so heinous that they must be kept secret . . .

"Reason of State lames Magna Carta!" Coke responded.

Day by day, the debates continued. The King's spokesmen did their best to persuade the Parliament to drop the whole business. Always lurking was the threat that the King might simply decide to adjourn the Parliament, or simply imprison members he deemed threats, by 'Reasons of State'.

Day by day, Roger could tell that the King's spokesmen were losing ground. Parliament was beginning to resent the implied threats. The House of Lords was more favorably inclined to the King's point of view, but Sir Edward Coke appeared before them on behalf of the Commons and began to win them over. (Not a few of the Lords had been incarcerated over the forced loans; most of the rest had had to pay them.)

A man's liberty, Coke argued, was his property — the most personal of his properties, and the one possession that even the poorest Englishman could claim. If the government or its various commissions could deprive a man of his property without charging him with a crime or bringing the charge to trial, then he had no rights at all.

Roger was unable to be in chambers every day. The Mashams kept him busy delivering messages to various of their allies in the city and the countryside. Roger was among those reporters who made sure that speeches in Parliament were made public on the streets of the city, through word of mouth, or in the printed broadsheets that appeared each day. Naturally, the information was sifted and filtered to present Parliament's achievements in the most positive terms. He also carried correspondence back to Otes Hall and Barrington Hall at least twice a month. Barrington Hall was his favorite destination, or rather, Jane Whalley was. He caught himself thinking of her in all his idle moments, and other times as well. Her boldness and irreverence charmed him; her smile haunted him. When she took his hand (which she contrived often to do), there was a thrill that stayed with him long after she was out of sight.

Otes now felt like home to him; the Masham family and its servants were his flock, entrusted to his care by God for their instruction and nurture. It was a trust that he took very seriously. Each of them became precious in his heart.

The visits to Barrington Hall became precious for a different reason. The exchange of news and correspondence required him to stay in the manor house overnight, which meant staying for supper, which meant time with Jane Whalley. She had a habit of appearing at his side whenever he had a spare moment. It was delightful. She was delightful — lovely, attentive, laughing. It was clear that she wanted to be with him. More and more, Roger wanted to be with her.

By early May, Parliament had chosen its remedy. It would do no good to pass a bill that would eliminate the Court of High Commission and impose some sort of penalty upon the King's servants who might choose to ignore writs of *Habeas Corpus*: The King would never consent to such a bill. Edward Coke had a solution: Parliament should pass a petition that would clarify the rights they claimed and request the King's consent to abide by it. This Petition of Right would not have the legal force of law; it would be akin to a lawsuit before the royal court. If the King consented to it, it would be like a judicial verdict — a verdict from the highest court in the land, one that could not be overruled. "A precedent," said Coke," that will be part of the law of the land for all time." It was a peculiarly lawyer-like solution to the problem, and many members of Parliament had been trained in the Law.

By early June, King Charles' patience was exhausted. He appeared in person before Parliament. The Petition of Right was read aloud in his presence (his allies in the House had already made him familiar with its contents). He declined to accept it. Two days later, he sent a message that they must finish their business by June 11, and consider no new business, and especially no attacks upon members of his government. On the 5th of June, he ordered that Parliament cease debate on any issues at all.   There was silence in the House of Commons for "some while". Then a merchant adventurer, Sir Nathaniel Rich (cousin to the Earl of Warwick), stood and declared, "We must speak now, or forever hold our peace!" It was a humorous remark, but his intent was serious. If the King could silence the Parliament with a simple command, there was no point in any of the work they had done, nor any reason for their existence as a body. They were indeed like the witnesses to a wrongful wedding — a wedding of unmitigated power and privileged corruption. They had a duty to speak, to call the thing what it was.

Commons defied the King and voted to adopt the Petition of Right. The House of Lords followed suit. Two days later, the King appeared in Parliament again. The Petition was read. The King uttered the words *"Soit droit fait comme il est désiré"* —   the traditional French phrase that signaled the King's consent to any Parliamentary action. Shouts of triumph erupted in the chamber, and the celebration was echoed on the streets of the city. Bonfires shone brightly in every direction that night.

For Roger, the thrill of victory was intoxicating. He had cast his lot with the forces of law and liberty and won. All things now seemed possible. He had come into his own at last. Even marriage seemed possible. And there was one person in particular whom he wished to marry.

Coke's enthusiasm was more measured. There was nothing in the Petition that could compel the King to abide by it; his royal prerogative was untouched. The best that could be said about it was that it was now part of the great body of Parliamentary acts that must be considered part of the law of the land. The King might ignore it, but his magistrates were bound to respect it, and every lawyer in the Kingdom could cite its authority when arguing a case; every judge on every bench would have to apply it to their decisions. In that sense, it was the crowning achievement of Sir Edward Coke's career — a lawyer's victory. His thoughts turned to his manor at Stoke Poges. Rest was what he longed for now.

The euphoria on the streets of London did not last long. In a matter of days, broadsides were circulating which pointed out that the Duke of Buckingham had emerged unscathed from Parliament's deliberations. The popular mood turned sullen. On the evening of June 13, Dr. John Lambe emerged from his obscure lodgings to attend a play. His appearance was reported, and a mob greeted him as he emerged from the theater. Lambe tried to flee, but his 83-year-old legs could not carry him far; he was stoned to death in the street.

Lambe's death was a shock to the King's circle of advisors, as well as his Parliamentary opponents: a sign that there could be more trouble ahead. Street violence was common enough in London, but this had implications that reached up to the King himself.

"I fear we have gone too far," said Sir William Masham to Roger.

"How's that?"

"Stirring the passions of the common folk against the Duke was a key part of our strategy, was it not?"

"Aye, so it was."

"I'll shed no tears for that rascal Lambe," said Masham, "but we may have done the job too well. A man who spurs his horse must be sure of his grip on the reins, lest he find himself in the ditch."

Roger nodded. He knew far more than Sir William or any of his peers about the organizing of public opinion against the Duke in London — he had labored in that vineyard for longer than any of the Mashams or their friends were aware. He knew many of the clandestine printers and rabble-rousers personally; he was as much a part of their world as he was of the world of his patrons. Lambe's stoning was a step he had not anticipated. Had he been playing with a fire that was now out of control? He and his peers had been feeding fuel to that fire for more than a decade — he had no idea about how to dampen those flames, now that their cause was reaping success.

Sir William was right. If the horse had "got the bit in his teeth", as they say, the rider could only hold on as best he could — the destination and the duration of the ride were up to the horse. Such was the risk of cultivating public opinion to serve a political purpose: once the government appeased the people's will in one matter, there was no telling what the next demand might be.

Over the long haul, of course, the aristocrats had the advantage. Public opinion was fickle, the commoners were preoccupied with the struggle for mere survival. The ruling class could wait them out, secure in their wealth, their ancestral lands, and even if necessary, their military force.

Roger was glad to count himself on the side of his patrons; he would find his own place in their world and enjoy the security and prosperity that was their birthright. Still, he felt some sympathy for the common folk — they toiled long and hard, yet enjoyed so little of the world's comforts, and even less of the power to do anything to improve their lot.

Sir William was looking at him as if expecting a reply. "I suppose every horse must be bridled, else chaos would ensue," Roger offered.

"Exactly so. A horse without a master is of no use to anyone."

Roger nodded. The horse, of course, might be of a different opinion. It remained to be seen whether this particular horse could be bridled.

Parliament still had not granted King Charles his tonnage and poundage. Later in June, it granted him five subsidies, then "rose" for the summer, so that members could return to their homes until September. The months of wrangling had been a strain for everyone, especially Sir Francis Barrington. The Mashams and the Barringtons took their time on the journey northward, resting as necessary. They reached Otes Hall on the afternoon of the second day. The returnees were greeted with enthusiasm at Otes, but Sir Francis was determined to press on to Barrington Hall: "Time to sleep in my own bed," he said. His voice sounded weak to Roger. Lady Masham's face showed concern, "Why not stay the night with us, Papa? I can have Wallace drive you home in a carriage in the morning."

"Nonsense!" replied Sir Francis. "If the day comes that I cannot ride my own horse, you can put me in my grave!"

Roger volunteered to accompany Sir Francis to his manor that afternoon. They got Sir Francis a fresh horse — Gondomar still had plenty of journey in him. With luck, Roger would be back at Otes for supper. Oliver Cromwell agreed to travel with them, too.

They arrived before suppertime, as the shadows lengthened in the warm afternoon. Sir Francis's arrival was greeted with shouts from his servants, as Lady Joan rushed to embrace him. Jayne Whalley was there as well. She curtseyed and smiled at Roger. He felt an involuntary twinge. He could not help smiling back.

Oliver Cromwell was invited to stay for supper. Roger prepared to return to Otes, but Jane stepped forward and took hold of Gondomar's bridle: "Stand down, Father Williams. Bide with us a while. Surely," she turned toward Lady Joan Barrington, "you have earned a place at our table!"

Lady Joan pursed her lips but nodded her consent.

At supper, Jane sat at Roger's side. The mood was festive, though Sir Francis's eyes were dull with fatigue. The servants saw him up to bed as soon as the meal was over. Lady Joan turned to Roger and said, "I suppose you're expecting to spend the night with us, as well?" There was a distinct chill in her tone.

"Your ladyship's offer is most generous," replied Roger with a bow, "but if you will grant me leave, I am expected at Otes this evening."

Jane interjected, "Do not trouble yourself with Reverend Williams, my lady. I can see him off." She gestured with a nod of her head to the stairway, where Sir Francis was still slowly making his way upstairs. Lady Joan nodded and turned her attention to her husband.

Jane took Roger's hand as they walked to the stables. "I can find my own way, you know," he said.

"I think you may need some help, finding your way in the darkness, she replied, as she moved closer to him. It was dusk by now, but not dark yet. "Now that your business in London is finished, I suppose that you will not have reason to visit us here as often . . ." It sounded more like a question than a statement.

Roger collected his thoughts. "I suppose I may have to find some excuse or other. One that will be acceptable to Lady Joan."

Jane fastened her blue eyes on his. "What has Lady Joan to do with it?"

"This house is hers. I think I have nearly outworn my welcome here. If I wish to continue seeing you, I must have some pretext."

"*If* you wish to see me? Is there doubt about that in your mind?" She gave him a sly smile.

"There is no doubt in my mind; I would see you every day if I could."

She laughed softly. "I was right when I said you needed help finding your way. How could you have arrived at this place without my help?"

Roger was at a loss for words. She came to his help again; she turned her face up to his and closed her eyes. He put his arms around her waist and kissed her.

"I shall write you letters," he said at length.

"Letters!" She giggled. "I must be a very plain woman if a kiss makes you think of writing letters."

He shook his head, smiling at his awkwardness. "I only meant that I can get a letter to you, even if I have no reason to be here in person. There is much I would say to thee, more than can be said in a short visit."

"Then I shall await your letters," she said. "Speaking of short visits, you must be on your way. People will gossip if I am away from the house too long."

They both understood that a foundation must be laid before an official courtship could be initiated — particularly since Roger's prospects were so doubtful. If he had his own parish, with the security that such a position entailed, it would be different. But such a position would not be available to him until the hierarchy of the Church of England was utterly reformed, or until his reputation was completely rehabilitated. Neither of those events were on the horizon.

News came to Otes Hall on July 3 that Sir Francis Barrington had died in his sleep. Lady Joan Barrington was devastated, embittered. His life and her happiness had been sacrificed to a cause; a cause she had sympathy for, but none of the passion that had compelled her husband and so many of his relatives to put their lives and liberties at risk. The cost to her family had been high — too high. Others had gotten off cheaply. It galled her to think that the benefits of her family's sacrifice, if any, would be enjoyed by others who had chosen to avoid confrontation. She had hope of happiness with her beloved for the last few years of her life. She had been robbed of that happiness. The King had robbed her. The cause had robbed her, as well.

August 23, 1628: Portsmouth

With Parliament in recess, the King was free to conduct the government as he saw fit. The Duke of Buckingham saw an opportunity to redeem his reputation: a military victory would silence his critics in Parliament and might loosen the purse strings when Parliament reconvened in the Fall. He began the process of assembling and training an invasion force in Portsmouth, on the English Channel. The destination was France, as it had been several times before: the Huguenot fortress at La Rochelle was under siege by an army of 30,000 men, commanded by Louis XIII's chief minister, Cardinal Richelieu. Buckingham aimed to break the siege by opening the harbor at La Rochelle with the Royal Navy.

On the morning of August 23, the Duke left his hotel after breakfast and was surrounded by a crowd of admirers and supplicants. A man forced his way through the crowd and stabbed the Duke in the chest. Buckingham cried "Villain!", took three steps, and collapsed.

His assassin was John Felton, a veteran army officer and survivor of Buckingham's previous military disasters. Felton was quickly apprehended and made his motives clear: "I have avenged the thousands sent to their deaths in France by this callous, incompetent pretender. I have prevented him from wasting the lives of thousands more."

King Charles was devastated by the loss of his lifelong companion; thenceforth, he would rely on advisors who were just as ambitious, but less inclined to compromise than Buckingham had been.

As for Felton, his deed was widely acclaimed by Buckingham's enemies. The Privy Council was anxious to torture him to determine whether he had accomplices. Surprisingly, the magistrates in charge of his case refused to approve such treatment.

Felton's trial did not take long; he was convicted and sentenced to be hanged to death. On the streets of London, broadsheets circulated insisting that Felton was guilty of no crime at all, but merely the instrument of justice for the true criminal in the case — the Duke of Buckingham. (Some compared him favorably to Brutus, the assassin of Julius Caesar.)Toasts to Felton's health were offered in pubs across the city (one celebrant was arrested and sentenced to have his ears removed for such a toast, but the sentence did nothing to intimidate his peers). The death of Buckingham was widely regarded as the judgment of God upon a man who had turned, like old King Manasseh, away from the worship of God, to serve the demonic spirits (under the influence of his sorcerer, old Dr. Lambe). It was justice — and with justice, there was hope for a better future.

John Felton's remains were not buried after the hanging. The King and his advisors decided to send a message to the citizens of Portsmouth. His remains were transported there and publicly exhibited, as an example to any who doubted the government's ability to punish those who might raise a hand against the King's favorites.

The message was not received as intended. Bouquets of autumn flowers appeared at the place where his remains were hung, then votive candles. The sheriff's men were ordered to remove them, but more appeared each night. It became a shrine. The only way to put a stop to it was to bury his body in secret, lest his gravesite become a destination for pilgrims.

When Parliament reconvened in September, the battle lines were more starkly drawn than ever. Buckingham, for all his posturing and maneuvering, had been a sort of buffer between King and Parliament: playing both sides of the game had been the secret of his survival. Now the buffer was gone. Charles now understood the depth of distaste that many of his subjects held for his government. Parliament would not be satisfied with anything less than strict adherence to the points in the Petition of Right; Charles had no intention of subjecting himself to the humiliation of being called to account by any Parliament on any matter at all.

It soon became apparent that the King was no more likely to abide by the Petition of Right than to abide by any other promises he had made. He would continue to collect his poundage and tonnage without legal authority. He had learned a lesson about forced loans and incarceration without cause, but that was a tactical adjustment - He conceded not an iota of his royal prerogative to Parliament. He would avoid the expense of war by making peace with France and Spain. He would sell titles and property to supplement his revenue. He would economize, though it galled him. He would call no more Parliaments.

March 1629: Love's Labors Forfeit.

Lady Joan Barrington was in no mood for foolishness. Her heart still ached for the loss of her beloved husband, and she was bitter when she thought of the years that they might have had together — if not for those months in Marshalsea, and those years in Parliament. The King was mostly to blame, but she did not hold her husband's friends and allies faultless. The heady sense of triumph that had followed the adoption of the Petition of Right had dissipated in the months since — everyone now realized that the King was no more willing to be bound by the Petition than by any other promise he had ever made; Sir Francis had spent the waning months of his life on a hopeless cause. The Petition was a bitter legacy, as far as Lady Joan was concerned.

The letter she had just received was an insult added to injury. Roger Williams, Chaplain at Otes Hall and one of the men who had accompanied her husband to London, was proposing marriage to her maid-in-waiting, Jane Whalley.

It was an outrageous proposal. The Rev. Williams was overreaching himself, to put it mildly. He had no property to speak of, no ancestry worth mentioning, nothing to recommend him at all, except a kind of genial manner, and gratitude from the family for his service. He was 'well-liked': that much had to be conceded, but it really wasn't much at all, compared to Jane's pedigree, her beauty, her breeding.

She should have seen it coming, she supposed — all those visits throughout her husband's last days, and since; probably a pretext to court Jane Whalley — duplicitous. The man was ambitious, in the worst possible way.

Successful management of a manor like Barrington Hall involved understanding each person's proper place and responsibility. It was like a farm, really — the swine in their pens, the sheep and cattle in the pasture, the chickens in their coop. This man was like a fox: wild, sly, predatory; not in any case to be trusted, no proper place for his ilk anywhere in her world. She would put a stop to his conniving right now. She was bereft of her beloved husband, and men like Roger Williams now threatened his legacy. It was up to her to defend it, and defend it she would.

She would begin with a letter of sharp rebuke to her daughter at Otes Hall.

L ady Joan's rejection of his suit fell on Roger like a load of stones. "I will go to Barrington Hall to plead my case," he said to the Mashams.

"Nay, you must not do anything of the sort," said Elizabeth Masham. "My mother's mind is firm on this matter. You can only embarrass yourself — or worse — if you speak to her directly. I am sure that you would not be welcome in her house; her servants will turn you from her front door."

"Then I will write to her," he said.

Lady Elizabeth shook her head. "I will write to her. You must contain yourself and be patient."

"Do you think there is hope you can change her mind?"

"We will see. Contain yourself. Be patient."

Roger was distraught and humiliated. The rest of the household noticed his distress, and the reason for it was soon general knowledge. Most of the servants kept a respectful distance from his visible anguish. His preaching suffered.

S ix weeks later, the Mashams summoned Roger into the drawing room. "Please, be seated," said Lady Elizabeth. Roger sat. "I have news that you should be aware of," said Lady Elizabeth.

Roger held his breath. Surely this was about Jane Whalley.

"My mother's mind has not been changed. I am sorry to disappoint you."

"So Jane and I are relegated to limbo?"

Lady Elizabeth gazed at him with tender eyes. "Jane Whalley was married last week. She is now Mrs. William Hooke, wife of the Rev. William Hooke."

Roger struggled to make sense of what he was hearing. "I know the man," he finally croaked, "sound fellow. Good reputation." There was a ringing in his ears, he felt lightheaded, short of breath.

"Please do not imagine that this represents any diminishment of the esteem you hold in this family," said Sir William. "We have only the highest appreciation of your service to our family and indeed, to this nation. Your position is secure with us as long as you live. As for my mother-in-law, I have no explanation for her behavior." He looked at his wife.

"She is a dowager," said Lady Elizabeth. "Ever since my father's death, she has been preoccupied with the family legacy. She pays more attention to title and pedigree than she once did."

Roger nodded and struggled for words. "Please excuse me. I am not feeling well." His head was throbbing. He went to his room. That old woman had dashed his dreams and ruined his life and Jane's as well. What ruthless power had she used to force Jane into a marriage against her will — for certainly, Jane would never have broken her promise, unless forced to . . . He would write a letter to Lady Joan Barrington. He would strike her conscience at her weakest point. Perhaps she would repent of her crimes against love.

It took two hours to write the letter. Then he delivered it to the steward, who would see that it was sent to Barrington Hall. His headache was worse; he felt feverish. He went to bed.

In the morning, he awoke drenched in sweat, his head throbbing. He was unable to get out of bed. His absence at the household devotions was noticed, and servants found him in his room, half-conscious. A doctor was summoned from several miles away and did not arrive until afternoon. By this time, Roger was drifting in and out of consciousness, babbling incoherently at times. "His condition is dire," said the doctor. "It is some sort of sweating sickness. You must try to cool his fevers with damp cloths and warm him when he has chills. I hesitate to bleed him because he thrashes around so. Try to get him to drink something. There is little more you can do for him. He is young, and that may improve his chances. He will either get better within a day or so, or he will not recover at all. Has he family that should be notified?"

The Mashams admitted that they had no idea how to reach Roger's family, who were in London somewhere — too far away to be of any use. Lady Elizabeth assigned servants to watch him and attend to his fevers and chills. She asked Mary Bernard to keep an eye on him too: "See that they take good care of our chaplain," she said, "and keep me informed of his condition." There was little reason to suppose that the servants would be negligent in their duties: Reverend Williams was beloved by the whole household. But they were all quite helpless; nothing to do but watch and wait.

The night was long. Roger was in and out of sleep, tossing and turning. Mary stepped into his room before she went to bed and found a maidservant named Rebecca nodding off in a chair near his bed, a single candle lighting the room. She woke Rebecca and dismissed her for the evening, then took her place. Rebecca's face showed fear and disappointment: "No better, I'm afraid, ma'am", she said. Roger grew quieter as the night wore on. Mary decided that he was either getting better or slipping away. A useless situation to report; an observation that applied to everyone — *we will either live, or we will not* — a physician's infallible prognosis, a prophet's sure prediction. Somewhere in the night, Mary fell asleep.

When she woke, sunlight was seeping into the room. The place was reeking: Roger had soiled himself in the night. His eyes were open. "Good morning, Reverend," she said.

"If it is morning, then it is a good one," he croaked. "How long have I been like this?"

"You have been in bed since the day before yesterday."

"Has it always smelled like this?"

"We changed the linens yesterday. You had a mishap in the night."

He chucked weakly. "A mishap. Aye, that will explain it. My humiliation is complete — my spiritual condition and my physical state speak with one voice."

Mary stood and summoned servants to clean up the mess. When they had finished, she went back into the room and opened a window to let in some fresh air. Servants would be on hand to help him with the chamberpot; she would see to it that he got some broth and drank some water.

It was afternoon when a letter arrived from Barrington Hall, from Lady Joan. Lady Francis read it and was shocked to discover that it concerned her Chaplain. The Reverend Williams had sent a scathing letter to her mother, and Lady Joan did not spare her outrage in reply. Roger Williams was dead to her and would be roasting in hell if Lady Joan had anything to say about it. Lady Francis decided that her chaplain was in no condition to discuss the matter. She could guess what his letter had contained, and why. The best option was to plead mental incompetence due to a fevered brain and beg for forgiveness. That could wait for a few days.

News of the exchange of letters got out and became a topic of discussion. Everyone sympathized with Roger's reasons for writing the letter, and a few were pleased to think that Lady Joan's arrogance had been called out. But everyone agreed that he had overreached himself. No servant or hireling, however misused, could ever presume to rebuke his betters. It simply wasn't done. Whatever punishment he received was only to be expected.

The Mashams and Oliver Cromwell besought Lady Joan to forgive him. In the end, she grudgingly did so. It was generally assumed that Roger Williams had learned his lesson. He had — but it was not the lesson that they supposed.

It was three more days before Roger could take solid food; a week before he was steady enough on his feet to leave his room. Even then, he was not strong. He had lost weight, his face was pale, his eyes sunken. He would sit for the greater part of every day, near a fireplace, if the day were chilly.

Often, Mary Bernard would sit and talk with him for a while. It seemed to her that the reserve that once characterized their relationship had been lowered somehow. Maybe it was him: she had seen him at his weakest and most vulnerable, so perhaps he was less guarded with her. Or, maybe it was her — nothing diminishes a man's image like being seen lying in a pool of his own filth. In any case, she found him less intimidating. One day, she asked a question, not knowing whether he would answer it or not. "What moved you to write that letter to Lady Joan Barrington? Did you really think to change her mind?"

"It was bitterness, pure and simple. I believed that I deserved to be treated better, and I lashed out in spite when my pride was wounded."

"It must have wounded your heart as well."

"Aye. But a wounded heart, when it is pure, throws itself upon the mercy of God; it does not turn to spite. It was Pride that led me to presume that my learning, my labor, and my character had earned me a place among the highborn. I mistook the esteem of men for the approval of God. I once knew better; ambition confused me. God has humbled me, and I must return to the narrow path."

"The path of humility? How can you be certain that you are on it?"

" A cruel irony, that. A man who thinks himself humble is not. As long as he believes he has attained any virtue, he is ruled by Pride." He was back to his old way of speaking now: pedantic, preachy. Mary took it for a sign he was recovering.

"So our spiritual progress must always consist of recognizing how little progress we have made?"

"That is very perceptive," he said. "It is our destiny to live in our moral incompetence. That realization must be the foundation of true humility. A hard lesson, humility. My health ruined, my heart broken, my life nearly forfeit. I suppose I should thank you for seeing me through this illness, though I cannot say that my bitterness is yet healed. It still stings."

"Humility is less about the breaking of the heart than it is about the surrender of the will," she said, "or so I have been told."

He smiled ruefully. "I have heard the same. All my bitterness is simply Pride dressed up as self-pity. A truly humble Christian has no more business with bitterness than a man who curses the dark because the sun has gone down. *The Lord hath giuen, and the Lord hath taken it: blessed be the Name of the Lord.*"

"That is from the book of Job," said Mary. "Do you now count yourself among the ancient saints?"

He looked at her with surprise, then laughed — at himself. "See how easily Pride creeps back! I put it out of my house by the front door, and it finds its way back through an open window. Pray for me, that God will not let me be tested as Job was."

She nodded her head and chuckled. The somber tone of their conversation was broken.

"I admit to one nagging question that I dared not ask directly. Perhaps you can speak to it."

"What's that?"

"I wonder if my suffering is out of proportion to what Jane felt. I take no satisfaction in thinking that she may have suffered as much as I; I hope that the whole business was easier for her."

Mary looked at him. He seemed sincere. If so, his heart was on the mend. She had no specific knowledge of what Jane had gone through, though her experience of Jane Whalley suggested that she was the sort who landed on her feet. Plenty of tears, no doubt, but *"weeping may abide at euening, but ioy commeth in the morning"*, as the psalm said.

"A woman like Jane has fewer options than you may appreciate," said Mary. "She is free-spirited and bold, and her feelings for you were genuine, I believe. But in the end, a woman must choose a life that is possible, not one that is based on wishes and dreams. Her dowry was not large enough to secure the fortune of her family by itself; she needed to marry a man with means of his own."

"Meaning that she would not follow her heart into poverty with me."

Mary shook her head. "Jane is not the sort of woman who could wear poverty for a lifetime without losing that confidence and charm that you so admire."

Roger reflected on her words. His dreams of marital bliss with Jane Whalley had been based on the assumption that her desire to be with him would overrule any other considerations for her — that was certainly how he felt about her. He had little sense of what other desires or expectations might have lain in her heart . . .

"I have been a fool, then," said Roger with a sigh, "prideful, overreaching, and worst of all ignorant. A worthier man would have measured his resources against his Lady's need and curbed his ambition, to do the honorable thing.

"You were a man in love," said Mary. "Heedlessness is the way of that condition." It was a bold thing to say, she realized. Perhaps an overreach. Most likely his heart was still with Jane Whalley . . .

He made no objection to her remark, merely nodded. His eyes said that his thoughts were elsewhere. At length, he spoke: "I have had time to reflect upon my life because of this illness . . ." His voice trailed off. Mary waited for him to continue.

"The path I have followed is the path of vanity. It is as the Preacher of Ecclesiastes has said - *'I returned, and I saw under the sun that the race is not to the swift, nor the battle to the strong, nor yet bread to the wise, nor also riches to men of understanding, neither yet favor to men of knowledge: but time and chance cometh to them all'*. I fancied that my learning, my devotion to God, my earnest service to my betters, my cleverness, and self-restraint would allow me to ascend to a place of honor and privilege among my betters. I see now that was a deception from the Evil One.

No matter how well I perform my duties, I will never be one of *them*."

"One of whom?"

"One of the blessed and powerful. One of the noble and privileged. I have risen as far as I ever shall; from here, there is only falling or decline. My ambition is shown to be what it is — the idolatry of Pride."

Mary asked, "Is every effort to improve your lot a sin, then?"

Roger shook his head. "Not every effort. Only the efforts that rise from pride and ambition - which are most of men's efforts — vanity, as the Preacher says. The efforts that seek to do the will of God — feeble and foolish as they may be — are pleasing to him, and he rewards them according to his pleasure. It may be his pleasure for his servants to labor in obscurity or even reproach. I have yearned for anything but that, and so my Pride has ruled me. I am resolved to find the path of true humility: I will seek the praise of men no more."

It was a striking claim, thought Mary. One might even say an ambitious one.

July 1629: Sempringham

By midsummer, Roger's recovery was as complete as it probably would ever be. He had regained the strength and energy lost during his illness and was able to return to his duties, which once again involved a lot of travel. His morale was another matter. He had always seemed a man of modest attitudes; no one who met him would have thought him arrogant or puffed up with pride, but those who knew him best noticed a change. He was as polite and agreeable as ever, but there was a certain reserve about him — "like a cat that got its tail stepped on," as the steward said, "always keeps one eye open, even when it's asleep." The servants in the house understood. All of them at one time or another had received a rebuke or harsh correction for presuming too much — the humiliation was simply part of the job. They sympathized with Rev. Williams: he couldn't really be blamed for overreaching (a young man may do many foolish things for love), but the outcome was all too predictable. A lesson learned, a chastened servant. If anything, they felt it made him a better spiritual guide for them: a man who understood their lives; one of their own.

The Masham family was careful not to dwell on the matter or even mention it in conversation. Things had been more or less patched up with Lady Barrington, who was still mourning the death of her husband. She was still the matriarch of the family, but her day was passing. The next generation continued to respect and admire the Rev. Williams. He was welcome at their table, and in their conversations. Most important of all for Sir William Masham, he was an indispensable conduit of communication.

Roger was called to Sir William's library one July afternoon:

"There is a conventicle called for this summer. A great many influential men will be in attendance," he announced.

"Do these men have names?"

"They do, but it is best that they be not named, for now. They will be discussing matters of great import, matters concerning the condition of the Church of England, and the persecutions that we are subject to."

"And you want me to attend, and report what I hear?"

"We want you to attend and ensure that our views are heard."

"In what capacity?"

"As a minister of the Word."

"Surely there are other, more prominent ministers who could attend such a gathering."

"Indeed, there are. And they will be in attendance. But we need someone there who will speak for us."

"I do not understand . . . "

"Famous preachers make their reputations (and their livings) by inspiring and arousing their listeners. We need someone at the meeting who will preach reason and prudence. This event is far too important to allow some visionaries to lead it off on some prophetic crusade. Lives are at stake here. Wealth and prosperity are at stake: a great deal of wealth; quite probably the prosperity of us all."

"Under those circumstances, I would have thought you would be in attendance, my Lord."

"I shall attend. But I will not arrive when you do. We must avoid the impression that you are attending as part of my entourage, or anyone else's. You will be there on your own reputation."

"My reputation?"

"Do not be over modest. You are widely traveled and respected. People know you to be trustworthy and reasonable. Your preaching is much admired. More than that, they know you are versed in the political realities of our times. Preachers will speak as they are inspired, but you have risked your freedom, even your life, for the cause we serve. Many at this conventicle value deeds over words. I can speak for my own interests, but others will do the same. You can bring a spiritual perspective to these matters, and that could well tip the balance, other things being equal. You will also be in a position to transmit what you see to other parties — and your reports will not be treated as mere self-interest, because you are known to be a man of integrity, and you have no financial stake in these matters."

No financial stake. That was true enough; it described his position quite succinctly. Evidently, some of the attendees would have some financial interest. That was a clue to the purpose of the meeting . . . "When should I plan to arrive in Sempringham?" he asked.

Roger rode north on the highway to Lincolnshire astride Gondomar alone, as agreed with Sir William. His destination was Sempringham Hall in Lincolnshire. It was several days journey from Otes Hall, so he had plenty of time to reflect. It felt strange to undertake a journey of such length without the "cover" of some powerful patron or other. Stranger still to imagine fraternizing with some of the most powerful men in the kingdom as a man on his own reputation. He had known some of these men for years, but most of them had not known him — he was always the servant of one or another of them — beneath their notice, virtually invisible to the rest. How could they accept him as a peer, even in this unique setting? He was in no sense their equal, as Lady Barrington had so plainly and painfully established (the sting of that reminder still haunted him). Yet, in this moment of crisis, he had been invited to meet with these men, join in their project, perhaps even contribute his own views and counsel.

His recent acquaintance with humility suggested that silence might be his proper contribution to their work, but the fact that he had been specifically invited to attend suggested that there was some purpose in his being here — on this day, on this road, heading for this destination. He would assume that it was God's purpose until proven otherwise. God's purpose was anybody's guess.

Sempringham Hall was the ancestral home of Theophilus Clinton, 4th Earl of Lincoln. It sat on the site of an ancient monastery, which had been dissolved during the reign of Henry VIII. The Clinton family acquired the property and tore down the buildings; in some cases, using the stones from the old monastery to construct their new manor. The new house was large and splendidly decorated: some said it rivaled Hampton Court Palace. The countryside 'round about was flat, almost featureless. It had been fenland once — marshland — now drained and cultivated, fertile.

The first of the attendees Roger met he encountered on the road to Sempringham. They were clergymen, both famous men. John Cotton had acquired a reputation as a stirring orator, celebrated for his preaching about the regenerative work of the Holy Spirit in guaranteeing the salvation of the elect. For Cotton, there was little a believer could do but wait for the Spirit to perform his work on the believer's soul. It was a gentle form of Puritan teaching, much like the landscape that they were riding through, thought Roger. Cotton's career had been a model of success for a Puritan preacher; he had served as vicar at the same church in Boston, Lincolnshire, for more than a decade, despite pressure from the Court of High Commission in London. John Cotton had friends among the local magistrates and was on good terms with the Bishop of Lincoln — although his theology was decidedly non-conformist. When confronted with the contradictions, Cotton was pleasant, accommodating, agreeable. In private, he went his own way.

Thomas Hooker was scarcely less renowned, though his preaching tended to emphasize the necessity for each believer to "prepare" for the work of the Spirit through upright behavior and good deeds. Hooker was therefore more confrontational in his opinions, not only in criticizing the moral failures of others but also the structural inadequacies of the institutions of government. As a result, Hooker ran afoul of the authorities from time to time. His life and livelihood were less secure. He had been forced out of his position as lecturer in Chelmsford. He had found obscurity as a schoolmaster in Little Baddow, a village several miles from there. Roger found that he agreed with Hooker's views more than those of Cotton. Roger had more first-hand experience with the corruption of government than either of the others; his adult life had been preoccupied with "preparing" to reform it. Something about Cotton's ease with the convoluted pathways of his ministry felt like accommodation.

The three of these men had this much in common: their very livelihoods were under assault from the Court of High Commission. Without the protection of powerful patrons, they would all be unemployed, probably in prison, possibly dead. More than coincidence had brought them to this particular place on this day.

Cotton rode a solid-looking dappled gray mare. Hooker's mount was smaller, more skittish. Roger noted with some satisfaction that neither horse was a match for his own Gondomar. The quality of a man's horse said something about the magnitude of his influence — or the influence of his patron, in Roger's case. Both men outranked him in age and reputation, but his horse said he was to be taken seriously. He was bold enough to address them as peers, even to criticize them mildly for their willingness to conform outwardly to the rituals of the Church of England. Both of his companions seemed to be annoyed with him.

No matter, Roger was not here to ingratiate himself with these men. He represented other men, other interests.

The men assembled at Sempringham came from across the kingdom. The priests excepted, all of them were men of rank and influence in England. Some, like Richard Rich, Earl of Warwick, had decades of experience investing in projects in the New World. From New England to Virginia, to the Caribbean, even as far as South America. The Earl and his family had been involved in obtaining the royal charters for the plantations in Virginia and New England, including the failures at Roanoke and Popham. They had lost money on some of these projects, but they found others that returned a tidy profit. This next project was by far the most ambitious that they had supported, and the accumulated lessons of their past failures were to be applied.

Others, like John White, mayor of Dorchester, had experience and lessons of a different sort to bring. White had been the leader of a bold and apparently successful social experiment. In 1613, the town of Dorchester had been largely destroyed by a fire. John White led the rebuilding effort. It was not enough to replace the buildings that had been destroyed; the entire community needed to be reconstructed along moral lines, he said. This was the opportunity to apply Puritan principles to the construction of a new society — free of the corruption that had earned God's judgment, a beacon to the whole of England, a model of what a truly Christian society looked like. It was to be a "New Jerusalem", where righteousness and justice would be the norm. It was not a society that had much use for aristocracy, or even royalty: tradesmen and merchants formed its backbone; hard work provided the muscles and sinews.

Skeptics were forced to admit that Dorchester became a better place, though perhaps a bit boring. Notable among their achievements was their remedy for poverty. When Henry VIII dissolved the monasteries and friaries ninety years ago, the multitudes of poor who had literally depended on those institutions for their daily bread were cast loose, to find what subsistence they could. Some died of starvation, exposure, and disease. The most fortunate of the survivors found employment as servants to the wealthy and powerful; others found their way into cities like London, where they could beg on the streets. They were the first to die in a plague year, yet they continued to breed more of their kind — landless, unskilled, uneducated, and always at the brink of death. Parliament passed laws requiring that all of them work, but did little to create jobs for them. They persisted from generation to generation, a community of doubtful loyalties, drunkenness, petty crime, and disease: a lurking rebuke to the pretensions of English society.

The citizens of Dorchester resolved to answer for this glaring injustice in their midst. They imposed taxes on themselves to build a brewery with public funds, whose profits were dedicated to the needs of the poor among them. It was an inspired choice — whatever the economic conditions, the brewery made a profit. All the able-bodied poor were employed and housed, their children enrolled in school, and there was plenty of ale in Dorchester.

It was not a utopia. A few refused to work and found that sympathy was in short supply — begging for alms became more difficult, even frowned upon. A brewery was not the ideal place of employment for any man who tended to drink to excess. But a poor man or woman in Dorchester was far better off than their counterparts in any other part of England. The crime rate dropped. Illegitimate births declined. Church attendance increased. As one observer reported, " . . . *thus knowledge causing piety, piety breeding industry, and industry procuring plenty.*" Other towns began to copy Dorchester's example. The Puritans were on to something.

More to the point, the Dorchester experience was a model of how to construct a society from the ground up. They knew what sort of people were needed to have success, and how to find them (fortune-seekers and ambitious aristocrats need not apply). They knew what the cost of building such a society was, and how long it would take (no one would get rich quickly in this enterprise; any who was not looking to work was not welcome).

Dorchester had undertaken one more bold venture: they had made an effort to transplant their success to New England. Five years previously, they had sent a group of men and women to establish a settlement at an old saltworks on the shores of New England, miles north of the Plymouth Plantation. The project had struggled through two winters, and the Dorchester men had eventually abandoned the site in favor of another somewhat farther south, at a place they called 'Naumkeag'.

The Naumkeag plantation struggled also. But they had a good harbor and tillable land. Most importantly, they had John White and the city of Dorchester. Dorchester sent 50 more settlers, with sufficient food and livestock. They also obtained a royal charter for this new plantation, and they sent a governor: none other than John Endicott — the same John Endicott that young Roger Williams had met so many years ago, in the library at Hatton House. Roger remembered the conversation and the questions he had asked Edward Coke afterward. His intuitions were confirmed.

Naumkeag was renamed to 'Salem'. This very spring, Dorchester had sent five ships with more than 350 more people to Salem, along with livestock. Salem was now more populous than Plymouth Plantation.

Among the merchant adventurers at Sempringham was Sir Nathaniel Rich, Parliamentary member from Harwich. He remembered Roger: "You were once secretary to Sir Edward Coke, were you not?"

Roger nodded. He remembered Nathaniel Rich; surprising that Rich had apparently noticed him, so many years ago . . .

"I have many fond memories of Hatton House," said Rich, "Lady Hatton set a fine table. The King was pleased to knight me there, one evening — you might recall it?"

Roger shook his head. "I must have been otherwise occupied that day." In fact, Roger knew that the King had dined at Hatton House only after Sir Edward Coke had been forced to vacate the premises: Roger would have been sleeping at Serjeants Inn in those days . . .

"Come, look at this," said Rich. "You will no doubt appreciate this more than the usual cleric, due to your association with Edward Coke. It is our new charter."

Roger looked the charter over. He recognized the language; much of it was Sir Edward Coke's handiwork. He had seen similar language before. This one had a peculiar twist: the affairs of the plantation would be administered by a Board of Governors, wherever they might decide to meet. A minor point, but it gave the plantation a certain amount of autonomy: the board of the company did not have to meet publicly (out of sight of the government, perhaps?), nor at any specific location, whether in England or elsewhere. Roger wondered if this was an oversight on the part of the King's lawyers. It was certainly no accident that the loophole was there. The name of the Company was to be "The Massachusetts Bay Company."

"How came you by this?" he asked.

"This is but a copy of the original; the official version is in a safe place," said Sir Nathaniel.

"I mean, how is it that these lands have come into the possession of the Company?"

"Title was obtained from the 2nd Earl of Warwick, my cousin, who paid the King for it."

"And how did the King get it?"

"It is his by claim. Claim of discovery by John Cabot, Martin Frobisher, John Smith, and others."

Have no other kings laid claim to this land?"

"Ah. I see your point. Yes, the Spanish, the French, and the Dutch have all laid claim to these shores at one time or another. That is why the King wants to populate the place. We lawyers have a saying: 'Possession is nine-tenths of the Law'. Of course, the French and the Spanish have laws of their own. Gunpowder and steel must serve to uphold our claim."

Roger nodded. A practical approach. But, "Do not the natives of this place have a claim upon it?"

"They are savages. Quite innocent of notions like land titles and boundaries. The dominion of the King actually gives them some protection; as his subjects, they may appeal to him for justice, and he is obligated to defend them against attacks from the French or the Dutch, for instance."

Roger nodded. So the peoples of that place were savages — like children, really. A fertile field for the gospel, perhaps.

Nathaniel Rich began to relate the details of the settlement plan that the Board of Governors had prepared. "Previous efforts in New England have been modest by comparison," he said. "The investments have been too small — both in money and in people — to guarantee success. We have learned valuable lessons from those efforts, but now it is time for a greater effort."

The scale of the plan was impressive. A fleet of twenty ships. More than a thousand emigrants. The attention to detail even more so. "We won't send cattle or hogs until the settlers have cleared enough pasture to feed them and provide enough fodder to see them through the winter," White explained. "The same with horses or sheep. We already know that wheat, oats, and barley don't grow as well in the soil of New England as the Indian corn does, so there won't be flour for pie crusts or bread for the first few years. People will have to get used to eating what the land can produce. They will have to live in hovels at first — like the Indians do. We will send saws and sawyers with the first shiploads, so that they can begin building proper houses. We will have to send along enough food to sustain them through the first few winters. The number of new arrivals each year will exceed the amount of food that the earlier arrivals can grow. It may be ten years before the investors realize any profits from our plantation."

"Where will you find so many willing to go?" Roger asked.

"We have more volunteers than we can accept," said Rich. "It is clear now that the King will not be bound by the Petition of Right. His new Bishop of London is free to arrest and torture whom he will; *Habeas Corpus* has no force before the Court of High Commission. Men like yourself are his particular prey, but all men of conscience are at risk if they stay in England. We must be selective: we need men with practical skills for the building of our 'New Jerusalem' — craftsmen, farmers, fishermen. Fugitives from the government are of no use to us unless they can do some vital work. And of course, they should be married to sober, hard-working wives: women who know how to raise children and run a household."

The remark about marriage stung Roger just a little; the wound was still fresh. Truth to tell, sober and hard-working was not a description that would have applied to a woman like Jane Whalley, in any case . . .

Rich continued, in a lower tone: "Of course, we will need vicars. There are plenty of men who are seeking a safe haven from the Bishop of London's fury. We will take only the best — men of sterling reputation. Men like yourself." Rich was looking directly into Roger's eyes. Roger said nothing.

"The vicars will be well provided for," continued Rich, "an ample salary, a large house; no less than three servants will be provided. And there will be land. Lots of land. Hundreds of acres of it, for the right man."

Land. The foundation of prosperity and rank for a man and his family. The difference between men of power and the landless majority. That would draw plenty of eager volunteers, Roger reflected.

Rich saw that he had piqued Roger's attention, and pressed the point: "From what I have heard, it was lack of land that hampered your aspirations not so long ago. A substantial landholding could remedy that."

There it was. Apparently, his humiliation was the stuff of gossip by now. The worst of it was that Nathaniel Rich was right about the importance of land. Who knew? If he had brought his suit for Jane's hand as a substantial landowner, things might have gone very differently . . . He nodded. "Alas, I think the offer of land comes too late for me."

The purpose of his meeting, Roger realized, was to satisfy all the major figures in the Company that their preparations were on schedule and complete, that no detail had been missed. The names and capacities of the ships in their "fleet" were enumerated. The numbers and abilities of the first wave of emigrants were reported. They set a target date for departure: March 1st, 1630. They would be heading for Naumkeag (now renamed Salem), where John Endecott was presiding. Among the emigrants would be a new governor: a wealthy lawyer named John Winthrop.

The whole enterprise seemed to Roger like some great, massive beast that had been stirred to life; slow-moving but overpowering, like a rising tide. Nothing would be able to stop it.

At the end of all the reporting and reiteration, John Winthrop stood to address the assembly. He had a vision to expound, a vision of a New Jerusalem, in Massachusetts. It would be founded on Christian love, dedicated to true worship, and disciplined in obedience to the Word of God. It would be a safe haven from the persecutions that true believers were plagued with. The only thing that could prevent its success was a dearth of men and women to inhabit it.

"This venture cannot prosper without godly men and women to hazard their lives upon it. I challenge every man in this room to join this enterprise by pledging to emigrate to New England. If you do not believe that this is the only answer to the persecutions that our King has laid upon us, then find such relief as you can elsewhere. I and mine will find a future in New England."

His remarks were met with approval. His enthusiasm was undeniable. But, as Roger looked around the room, he saw some faces that were noncommittal. Not everyone welcomed the challenge to emigrate.

The business of the conventicle was nearly finished. It remained to end the meeting on a note of inspiration. John Cotton, eminent preacher, was invited to address them. Cotton had caught the spirit of the moment; he preached long and energetically about the folly of any man seeking his own way, when the way of the Lord had been made clear:

"We must not be like those Israelites who wanted to turn back to Egypt on the shores of the Red Sea: God's deliverance is for those who live by faith!" It was an inspiring message. Roger could tell that many men were moved by it. But not everyone was comfortable with the implication that emigrating was the only godly option . . .

Sir William Masham spoke up: "We have another Minister of the Word among us. I would hear what he has to say before we adjourn." He pointed to Roger.

Roger knew what he was supposed to say when his turn came. His patrons had no intention of fleeing to New England; they reckoned that their titles and wealth were sufficient to protect them from the Bishop of London and the Court of High Commission. In any case, their ties to their ancestral lands would keep them in England. For men like John Winthrop, there was no such protection, nor any such tie.

It was imperative that diverging prospects not lead to a divergence in purpose for the men here assembled. The emigrants needed the support of the wealthy and aristocratic men as much as they were needed, if the enterprise was to succeed. It would not do for one group to prosper by abandoning the other. Roger needed to articulate a calling for those who would remain that was at least as righteous and noble as the calling of those who were leaving.

"In the book of Ezra," he began, "We see that it was the hand of God that enabled the Jews to return to Jerusalem. First, ' *the Lorde stirred vp the spirite of Cyrus King of Persia, and hee made a Proclamation*' that permitted them to return. We see that the Lord has done the same thing in our own time, for how else would a King who hates us all so relentlessly approve a charter like the one we have, unless God himself had moved his heart?" Murmurs of "Amen" sounded around the room.

"Secondly, we see that not all the people returned to Jerusalem at first, but their brethren '*strengthened their handes with vessels of siluer, with golde, with substance, and with cattell, and with precious thinges, besides all that was willingly offred.*' This, too, is our experience — not all will be able to go to New England, but all have a share in building the New Jerusalem, and the generosity of those who will stay behind will make it possible. The light that shall shine from that place will be for all the nations, as it is written in the book of Isaiah, '*I will also give thee for a light of the Gentiles, that thou mayest be my salvation unto the end of the world.*'"

Roger caught a glance and a nod from Sir William Masham. He had fulfilled the purpose for which he was in attendance. But he was not finished yet. "Remember that the Kingdom we seek is not of this world. The true Jerusalem is the one that must come down from Heaven. Labor as we must, the fruit of our labors must always remind us of the splendor that was lost, as it was when the Jews laid the cornerstone of their second temple. The Land of Promise is not for those who seek comfort and safety, but for those who know that they have no other home in this world, and will dare to claim the birthright of God's covenant. All of those who labor with us have a share in that birthright."

More nods, more "Amens". Puzzlement on some faces. They were not sure what he meant. Roger was not sure himself. But he was sure that the "New Jerusalem" would not be the utopia that some were hoping for.

Afterward, John Cotton approached Roger. "You spoke well and wisely," he said.

"As did you," Roger replied, " a most inspiring message."

Cotton nodded. "And I detected an element of pragmatism in your speech, a proper seasoning for a dish of inspiration." It was a compliment, and Roger acknowledged it with a slight bow of his head.

Cotton continued, "Are you bound for New England with the rest?"

Roger shook his head. "Not with the first sailing. I have employment here that holds me for yet a while. It would stretch my finances to pay passage so soon as next March."

"It is the same with me," said Cotton. "There is work in England that I must finish. Still, I think Governor Winthrop made a strong case, don't you agree?"

Roger nodded. "Indeed, he did. I pray God will bless him in the New World, not least because the day may come when his New Jerusalem may be a refuge for men like me."

"Quite so," replied Cotton, "*For in the time of trouble hee shall hide mee in his Tabernacle: in the secrete place of his pauillion shall he hide me, and set me vp vpon a rocke.*"

That pretty much said it all: New England was a refugee of last resort, but need for refuge might come sooner than anyone supposed.

"They tell me you are not married," said Cotton, changing the subject suddenly.

"That is true," admitted Roger. His failings as a suitor were apparently on everyone's mind these days.

"You should remedy that deficiency," said Cotton. "A man of your gifts needs a helpmate. And there should be children, lots of children. '*and God said to them, Bring forth fruite and multiplie, and fill the earth, and subdue it, and rule ouer the fish of the sea, and ouer the foule of the heauen, & ouer euery beast that moueth vpon the earth.'* That much we can do with or without the New Jerusalem."

A pragmatic argument, wrapped in a spiritual shroud. Or maybe the other way round.

Roger rode back to Otes with Sir William, his relatives, and their servants — no reason to maintain the illusion of his independence, now. There was a brief shower on the first morning that muddied the road, but the sky soon cleared, and a fresh breeze carried the aromas of ripening harvests on either side. Roger felt he had crossed some sort of threshold in the path of his life. All that lay behind him was . . . behind him, now.

November 1629: Wedding

Roger returned from Sempringham with a changed mind. He had been invited to attend by the sort of men he had served all his life; aristocratic and wealthy men who trusted him to represent their interests. He had validated that trust. He had played the game by the rules — their rules — and discovered that the rules did not favor men like him. The aristocrats he had served valued his service and were pleased to call him their ally, but they would never consider him their peer. At Sempringham, he had spoken for their interests; they expected no less. Time to consider his own interests.

The doors to wealth or title were closed. So be it. There were other opportunities that an industrious man might take advantage of: opportunities that were not available to his patrons, precisely because of their social rank. The example of men like John White and John Winthrop was an open doorway to another way of life: a life that neither his patrons nor their adversaries understood. That way was risky, unproven; but it led to a world where title and tradition, and royal prerogative were reduced to trivialities :

'But they shall sit euery man vnder his vine, and vnder his figge tree, and none shall make them afraid: for the mouth of the Lorde of hostes hath spoken it. For all people will walke euery one in the name of his God, and we will walke in the Name of the Lord our God, for euer and euer.'

Roger would seek his destiny on a different playing field.

There was another change in his outlook, as well. It might have been the remarks of John Cotton, or just the presence of so many other men with families of their own, but Roger decided that he needed a wife. Not just any woman would do: he needed a mate who could assist him in his new life, strong, courageous, even daring. It went without saying that she should be pious, sober, virtuous, and industrious. He realized with a start that Jane Whalley was none of those things. Charmed as he was by her, she would not have made a good wife for him: Lady Joan's rejection of his suit was actually a blessing. Roger felt some bitterness seep out of him. He concluded that the whole painful business was an act of God's claim upon his life.

He set about looking for a wife. In his travels, he had met many eligible young women. He thought he had made a good impression on nearly all of them, so the pool of candidates was large. In practice, he knew very few of them well enough to form an opinion of their compatibility with him or their receptiveness to a courtship. This was no accident: the world in which he lived assumed that the parents' generation would best make such assessments. In Roger's case, his parents would not be involved, but he was sure that the Mashams would act as surrogates if he asked them to. He chafed a bit at the idea. If his destiny was to live in the new world, a world where aristocrats and patrons were irrelevant, then his choice of a life partner should not be dependent on the judgments of the old one. But there seemed to be no alternative.

There were a few young women whom he knew quite well: he was their pastor. In particular, Lady Masham's ladies-in-waiting, Dorcas, Elaine, and Mary. He was still a suitor without any estate other than his books and his talents. But he believed that the Mashams held him in high regard. Maybe that would be enough.

He prayed about his need for a wife on many days. One night, he awoke from a dream with a start: He had dreamed of Mary Bernard, who appeared to be in distress. She was standing in the midst of the sea, on a rock or sandbar of some sort, the waves were rushing about her feet. The water was rising. She looked at him with imploring eyes as if asking for help. The water looked deep. He looked around for anything to reach her with . . . and then he woke up. It seemed to him a sign from God. It was also fraught with complication. It seemed a violation of his vocation to court a woman whom he was pastoring. The only ethical thing to do was to declare his interest as soon as possible. Speaking to Mary might put her in an awkward position; he would have to ask Lady Masham for permission to initiate a courtship first. If she said no, his position at Otes would be at risk. He did not relish the prospect of being rejected a second time.

In the event, Lady Masham was pleased with his request. Pleased that he had come to her first, pleased that there was a suitor for Mary Bernard who — plainly put — had reached the age where it would be difficult to bestow her. She had no large dowry, and since she was not related to the Mashams by blood, it was unlikely that Lady Joan Barrington, the family matriarch, would veto the match. She called Mary into the sitting room and closed the doors to give her the news.

"A man has asked for permission to court you," she said. No reason to beat around the bush.

Mary took the news in for a moment. She had always supposed that this moment would come, but she was still surprised when it did. It was the sort of announcement that threw her world into disarray. "May I know the man's name?"

"It is the Reverend, Roger Williams."

Mary caught her breath. She sorted through her memory of the last weeks for any clue in his speech or demeanor that would have indicated his interest. She found none. No flirtation, no innuendo, no longing looks. Perhaps she had mishcard. "Arc you sure that he is the one?"

"Quite sure. What do you say?"

Mary focused her thoughts on practicalities. "I am twenty years of age, and there are not that many prospects hereabouts," she said.

Lady Masham nodded. At least the girl was realistic about her prospects; it spared the need to belabor the point. "And you could do worse than the Reverend Williams. He is not bad looking, as men go, and he is a congenial man — probably not the sort who would prove overbearing as a husband. What are your reservations?"

"I had hoped for more passion in the man I would marry, a man who could inspire more passion in me. He is, as you say, a congenial man, but I doubt whether congeniality is enough to bind us together."

"Congeniality is of more worth in a marriage than you suppose," said Lady Masham, "but I take your point. There is something calculating about him. I do not mean that he is deceptive or disingenuous; he has a genuine honesty that seems sweet, or even naive. But his discourse is all reason and rationality. He behaves as if that is all there is to him. Whatever passion there may be in him, he keeps buried. You would have to plumb the depths of him to find it (if it is indeed there at all: some men are simply bland and shallow). You might be disappointed with what you find there."

Mary nodded. That was indeed the question. What lay beneath the congeniality?

"You will never have as much say over your future as you do right now," Lady Masham continued, "the man has asked for your hand: you have the right to question, to negotiate, to extract concessions. Once you are wed, your power will be of a different sort — more dependent on his goodwill."

Mary nodded again. "It seems a bit... mercenary to speak of negotiations and concessions. What assurance is there that promises made today would be kept tomorrow?"

"Say not so," Lady Masham insisted. "The time to negotiate is now. As for promises, they are only as good as the integrity of the one who makes them. But I do not think you have much to worry about in this case: Reverend Williams has proved himself a man of his word many times; he will keep any bargain that he makes if it is possible to do so.”

There is that, said Mary to herself, *I know him to be a man of honor.* “I shall speak to him,” she said.

Lady Masham nodded and added, “Best you have your negotiating points in mind before you do, and stick to them. Remember that he has permission to court you. I will not agree to matrimony without your consent.”

Their next meeting was a bit awkward. It was early October; the weather was mild that day, and they walked together in the flower garden. By this time, nearly all the servants in the manor house knew something about their business and were discussing it in whispers. Mary looked for a way to start the conversation. She chose a direct approach: “Lady Masham has spoken to me of your . . . initiative,” she said.

Roger nodded. “I am curious to know your mind on the matter, if you would care to tell me,” he said.

“I have questions,” she said, “but before I say anything else, I should acquaint you with my expectations for married life. It may save us both a good deal of time.” That came out a bit colder than she intended. Perhaps it sounded harsh to his ears. Nothing to do but plunge ahead now . . .

Roger was looking directly at her and smiling — on the verge of a chuckle, perhaps. He nodded, inviting her to continue. In truth, he was relieved that she was taking the conversation in this direction. He was much more sure of himself speaking in practicalities. The language of courtship was unfamiliar to him; perhaps because so many of his entanglements with young women had been on their initiative, not his. Talking of feelings was the last place he wanted to start.

Mary took a breath, gathered her words. “My requirements are not onerous,” she began, “I do not expect to marry a man of great wealth or influence. It would not suit me to marry a title. I do expect a measure of comfort and security. I will not marry a pauper, nor a man who makes his living through underhand or covert means. Fidelity is a given. I also expect honesty and intimacy, as befits a lifelong partnership."

Roger smiled again, then looked away. "Surely you are aware that my service to the Masham family has often been 'covert' or even 'underhand'. Am I disqualified thereby?"

Mary shook her head. "The service you did was noble. But such is the work of a young man unencumbered by a wife. A married man must see to his family. I do not wish to marry a man who is destined to spend his life in prison — what would be the point?"

Roger inhaled slowly. A practical approach, indeed. "If I could promise myself that I shall never see the inside of a prison cell, I would. But in these times, nothing is certain. My "success" thus far — if that is what it is — has come from obscurity; I am simply too unimportant for the government to bother about. I am not sure that will be the case in future. I can promise that I will do everything in my power to avoid the fate of Sir Francis Barrington."

Mary was a little taken aback at his frankness. At least he was aware of the perils he faced . . . She turned the conversation back to him: "You have said nothing about what your expectations would be."

"You may think me frivolous, but I have not given that much thought," he replied. "Fidelity, of course. And . . . intimacy. Mostly, I should hope for companionship, for a trustworthy partner, a family. I will not conceal from you that others have urged me to find a wife and to withdraw from covert and underhand activities. I might as well tell you that there is financial advantage for me if I find a wife."

"Financial advantage? You are misinformed if you think I will fetch a large dowry!"

He laughed out loud. "Nay, not that sort of advantage. I have been offered the chance of employment in New England. With a salary, and land — lots of land. Enough land to make a family secure."

"But you would have to live in New England to claim it."

"Aye. But with enough land, a man may live where he likes. There are plenty willing to be his tenants."

So. He had plans, this one. Hard to blame him for his ambition. "So you mean to join the ranks of the landed gentry? I thought you had renounced such aspirations."

"I am not decided on that course. I simply wanted you to know that I am not without prospects — it was you who spoke of comfort and security."

She caught a twinkle in his eye. She relaxed a bit. "You have said nothing about why you think I would make a good wife," she pointed out.

Ah. Time to say something charming. "You are a handsome woman," he began. Feeble. "I know you to be modest, temperate, prudent, trustworthy. You have all the qualities that a man would seek in a wife." True enough, but hardly the stuff of a love sonnet. "I think we would make a union that would glorify God." He was a priest, after all; had to mention the spiritual nature of what he was suggesting . . .

Mary looked at him with raised eyebrows, half smiling. "Go on, say more. Say something about your heart, your feelings. Do you have feelings for me?"

He appeared to be taken aback by the question. "I feel great respect for your character. I feel gratitude for the way you nursed me when I was ill. I feel at ease in your company."

Not the feelings she was asking about. "I will set you a harder question. On the day you came to Otes Hall, a certain woman was mentioned. Unless I am mistaken, you had feelings for her once. Tell me about Frances Coke Villiers." She saw that the mention of the name had struck him deeply; he was at a loss for words.

Roger had not expected the topic to come up so soon in the courtship. Might as well face it. "When first I met Frances Coke, I was dazzled by her beauty (as so many men have been). She was to me like a goddess; I desired nothing more than to be in her presence."

"And she rejected you?"

Roger shook his head. "She befriended me, confided in me; ultimately, she sought to use me. I was unable to be what she wanted me to be. I failed her."

So that was it. Mary understood the man, now. His earliest experience of passion with a woman had failed so miserably that he had spent all his years since avoiding it . . . until Jane Whalley caught his affections, and that led to failure, as well . .

"Did she flirt with you? Play with your heart?"

He nodded, smiled. "Flirted, yea. Some women cannot help themselves, I think. I do not blame her for that — she was young and did not know her power. As for playing with my heart, I think she needed to test my trustworthiness more than anything. I do not blame her for that either. She was raised to assume that men like me exist only to serve her needs, and to imagine that affiliation with her beauty and wealth was fair payment for that service. I could not sell myself that cheaply, however enthralled I was with her."

Mary struggled to digest what she was hearing. He had escaped a trap by the narrowest of margins, yet he was not bitter. It was a side of him that she had noted before, but not truly appreciated. His eyes showed his . . . regret? guilt? Hard to say. He had learned to mistrust his passions — now she understood why: his was an orphaned heart, no place to call home. She felt an impulse to comfort him, but didn't know how.

They saw each other every day, usually in the course of their duties. But they also found time to be alone together: the household servants made an effort to give them time and space for each other, even as gossip and speculation ran rife.

Roger explained his interest in New England: not merely the opportunity to become a landowner, but more importantly, a chance to be part of something new — a community where righteousness was valued, where kings and bishops and commissions were too far away to make trouble. A New Jerusalem.

Mary acknowledged the appeal, but "The building of that place is hardly begun. The first fleet will not sail until next spring. I would rather abide here yet awhile, where my family and friends are. Promise me that you will not force me to leave them, unless we are in peril." Roger nodded and agreed.

He was not so different from her father, she decided. A man who would labor in the vineyard of the Lord, hoping for a bountiful harvest, even as time — that great thief — numbered his days. That was a life she could embrace. She agreed to marry him.

In November, they received news that Thomas Hooker had been arrested by the Court of High Commission. He had withdrawn from preaching to become headmaster of a school in a small village called Little Baddow. Surely he would find safety in such obscurity. It was not so. His friends posted bail for him, and he disappeared. John Cotton also disappeared.

Another famous person had disappeared, also. Frances Coke Villiers had been accused of adultery (before the Court of High Commission, due to her high social rank). She had not been a cooperative defendant; she refused to take the Ex Officio oath, on advice of her father. She insisted that the magistrates had no authority to make her testify against herself, and referred to them publicly as "cuckolds". Found guilty, she was sentenced to pay a fine and make a public confession of adultery. Instead, she took refuge with the Ambassador from Savoy. Although the house was surrounded by constables, she managed to escape to France with her son, whom she still swore was heir to the Villiers fortune.

Roger and Mary were wed on December 15, 1629, in the chapel at Otes Hall. Mary's father, Richard Bernard, performed the ceremony. It was a simple one—no ring, no wedding attendants—as Roger and Mary desired. (The bishop and the High Commission had no jurisdiction here.) Roger's mother, brothers, and sisters traveled from London to attend. Afterward, the Mashams hosted a feast for all of them; family and household servants all together.

November 1630: The Way of the Sea

I have news," said Sir William. His face said that the news was unwelcome. Roger and Mary joined him in his library. Lady Masham was waiting for them there. "The King has moved against us again," said Sir William, "He has commanded that the name of every household chaplain in the kingdom be delivered to the Court of High Commission."

Mary was puzzled. "Why would the King need their names?" There was something vaguely sinister about the demand, but what was the King up to?

"This comes from Bishop Laud of London," said Sir William. "The King is merely doing his bidding. Laud intends to arrest all these men. They will recant their faith, or face the consequences."

"Consequences?"

"Torture. Death in prison. Execution, perhaps. Laud has made his intentions clear enough."

Mary felt a chill. She looked at Roger; his expression was hard to read, but she could tell that his mind was fully engaged.

"That means that I can no longer be your chaplain," said Roger. "If I am no longer a chaplain, then my name need not be reported. Perhaps I can find employment as a schoolmaster somewhere in the area."

"Thomas Hooker tried that; they came for him anyway."

Roger nodded. Hooker had been arrested, posted bail, and fled to Holland just last year. "As it happens, I speak Dutch. I do not relish the thought of living in Holland, but I suppose I could find a way to make a living there." He gave Mary an apologetic look.

"If Holland is truly where you wish to go, I can arrange safe passage there for you," said Sir William. "However, there is another possibility that I think you should consider."

"Which is?"

"New England. You would be most welcome in Massachusetts Plantation. You would not have to struggle to make a living."

"You mean that we would hide until the summer when a ship to New England is available?"

"There is a ship available now. *The Lyon* is docked at Bristol and will be sailing for Massachusetts very soon. I know the captain, and can ask him to delay until you are on board."

Mary was feeling overwhelmed. He world had just been turned upside down, and these men were discussing the implications with the detachment that they might apply to a discussion about the relative merits of two horses.

Lady Masham noticed her distress. "We need time to digest this . . . bitter morsel that the King has served us."

"Time is in short supply," replied Sir William. "Bishop Laud intends to move quickly."

Roger turned to Mary. "If I flee to Holland, you do not have to come with me — at least not until I find employment. The Bishop has no reason to trouble you."

Mary felt her cheeks getting hot. "I am your wife! *'whither thou goest, I will goe: and where thou dwellest, I will dwell: thy people shall be my people, and thy God my God.'* Do not dare to think that I will remain here when you leave!"

Lady Masham smiled and looked at her husband.

"In that case," said Roger, "New England is the place that we are more likely to find a friendly welcome and a secure home. It will mean a long and perilous sea voyage, but God will deliver us, else all our plans are vain."

"Well spoken," said Sir William. "Wallace can escort you and your property to Bristol with one of our carts. You can be gone before anyone misses you. The Massachusetts Plantation will be delighted at your arrival."

"How much can we take with us?" asked Mary.

"You will have to be selective. The ship will not be crowded with passengers, but the hold will be full of supplies for the plantation. Your clothes and personal items must be sufficient. If it appears that you are moving a whole household of stuff, it might arouse suspicion."

Mary sighed. Just as she was getting her home fully furnished, she would have to start all over again. She hoped that they had good carpenters in New England.

Sir William stressed the urgency of their situation: "You dare not delay. The ship will not wait forever, and once the agents of the High Commission find you, it will be too late for anything. You can write farewell letters to your families. I will see to it that they are delivered, once you are well on your way."

They left early the next morning, with only what they could take with them — some of Roger's precious books, their clothing, a chest with some bed linens, some cooking and eating utensils. Their furniture, so patiently acquired, had to be left behind. It was barely daylight; fog obscured Mary's view of everything but the looming gray silhouette of the manor house. Sir William and Lady Masham were there to see them off; Dorcas and Elaine were there too, of course. Most of the rest of the household staff were unaware of their departure: a careless remark might yet betray the Williamses to their pursuers. They had more than 100 miles to cover before reaching any place that could be considered remotely safe.

"God speed you both," said Sir William. Lady Masham nodded her agreement, Elaine and Dorcas began to cry. Mary embraced them before climbing up to the seat on the wagon. No carriage for them: nothing that would suggest they were people of means. Their team of horses was sturdy enough, but not the sort that would be remarked upon in passing or be remembered half an hour later. Roger, Mary, and Wallace were dressed plainly for the same reason. Fortunately, the rough woolen cloak that Mary was wrapped in was warm, she thought; the fog was chilly. It would be a long and bumpy ride. They would take the highway southwestward for short distances, then turn off to take side roads for a while, to look like local people on their way to some village or other. It would take longer, but blending into the landscape was the key to a safe journey.

By mid-morning, a raw breeze came up and swept away the fog. Blessedly, the wind was at their back. The sun peeped through the clouds, and their mood lifted. "We'll be heading toward London today," volunteered Wallace, "Then we'll veer a little farther west, to Windsor. Probably spend the night in some village between here and there. After Windsor, we'll head west toward Winchester, as if we're making for Portsmouth. Before we get that far, we'll turn westward, through Newbury or Andover, on back roads. That should confuse anyone following us." Roger nodded. Mary had heard of these places, but had only a dim sense of how far away they were.

"Four days to the seacoast then?" Roger suggested.

"Maybe five. Depends on how many detours we take," said Wallace.

Roger had little to say for long periods of time. Mary tried to make up for it by keeping up a conversation with Wallace. Wallace had worked for the Mashams since Mary first came to live with them. He was not a stranger, but he related many details of his life that she was unaware of. Some of his stories were funny — Mary had to laugh. Even Roger smiled, though he said little.

They found lodging in a small village not far off he highway the first night, as Wallace had said. The following day was chilly but sunny, and they made good progress, passing west of London. Wallace was visibly relaxed: "The journey toward London was the riskiest part of this trip," he explained, "The farther from London we are, the harder it is to catch us." Roger nodded but said little more.

Late on the second day, Roger seemed to grow more attentive. Wallace noted the change. "You recognized this road?"

"Aye," Roger replied. We are near Stoke. I rode this way with my mentor, Sir Edward Coke, when he was confined to his estate."

"Confined?"

"The King declared that he could travel no more than six miles from his home, so we traveled the same roads often. They accused him of treason, but he was acquitted, in due time."

"What has happened to the old man?"

"I believe he lives at his manor in Stoke Poges these days. Not more than two miles in that direction." Roger nodded his head to the left. "I would visit him to bid a final farewell, but circumstances will not allow . . ."

Mary saw the pain in his eyes. She took his hand. "He was dear to you, wasn't he?"

"Aye. More like a father to me than my natural father. A great teacher. A great man, to tell the truth. I am blessed to have known him."

That evening, after supper, Mary spoke of Sir Edward again. "You could send him a letter," she suggested, "no doubt he would be grateful to hear from you again."

Roger shook his head. "I do not know what to write. I am sure that he will learn of my exile as soon as that becomes public."

Mary sighed. "This is a grievous time for both of us. I fear I may never see my father and mother again, nor any of my siblings or friends; whatever God's plan for us, the loss of so many that I love is hard to bear. Is it the same for you? You have hardly spoken these last days."

He bowed his head and sighed. "It grieves me sore to be leaving England," he admitted, "I have never lived anywhere else, and I never intended to. It is a bitter thing to be exiled from one's home. And yes, I have said nothing about it, because I do not know what to say. If my silence has added to your grief, I beg your forgiveness."

Mary nodded and said,

> *"By the riuers of Babel we sate, and there wee wept, when we remembred Zion.*
>   *Wee hanged our harpes upon the willowes in the middes thereof.*
>   *Then they that ledde vs captiues, required of vs songs and mirth,*
>   *when wee had hanged vp our harpes, saying,*
> *Sing vs one of the songs of Zion.*
>   *Howe shall we sing, said we, a song of the Lord in a strange land?"*

Roger smiled sadly. "Even so, we shall have to learn to sing in our exile. It is as the time of Jeremiah: he prophesied that the exiles should settle themselves in Babylon:

> *"Buylde you houses to dwell in, and plant you gardens, and eate the fruites of them. Take you wiues, and beget sonnes and daughters, and take wiues for your sonnes, and giue your daughters to husbands, that they may beare sonnes and daughters, that ye may bee increased there, and not diminished. And seeke the prosperitie of the citie, whither I haue caused you to be caried away captiues".*

At least he was speaking to her, if only in Bible verses - at least a word of hope. Mary felt something relax inside her. Whatever the future held, it was not so different from what God's people had been through before. God could make a way for them again. Too soon for despair. She prayed for courage.

Late in the afternoon on the fourth day, they came at last to Bristol, nestled in a valley beside the River Avon, hemmed in on all sides by hills. Bristol was an important seaport — with no apparent access to the sea. As a first-time visitor, Mary was mystified at the proliferation of ships of all sizes moored at the docks just downstream of the city; There seemed to be no purpose for so many vessels crowding such a small river.

Wallace had an explanation. "There is a gorge downstream which cuts right through yonder hills to the sea. You cannot see the ocean from here, nor can you see Bristol from the ocean. The hills protect the city from the worst of the storms; the fortifications at the gorge deter invaders - a protected place, is Bristol. Many have found refuge here."

Wallace drove the wagon down to the docks west of town and pulled up near a line of ships. "Wait here," he said. He got down and approached some men on the dock, then returned to his seat. "*The Lyon* is just down the wharf a way," he reported. He pulled up near a ship further down the line and shouted, "Ahoy, the ship!"

"What's yer business?" came the reply.

"Cargo for *the Lyon*," said Wallace.

A sailor appeared at the rail, walked down the gangplank, and spoke with Wallace in hushed tones. Then he turned to Roger and Mary, still seated on the wagon. "Best ye come with me," said the sailor, and led them aboard ship. "Cap'n wants to see ye," said the sailor. They were led to the captain's cabin, to be greeted by "Captain William Pierce, at your service." Roger bowed and Mary curtseyed. From this point on, the captain was their master.

"I am pleased to see you," said Pierce."We have been awaiting your arrival and will be sailing as soon as possible. The mate will show you to your berths. I insist that you stay below decks, out of sight, until we are well away. Your luggage will be brought to you below decks."

On the afternoon of December 1, 1630, *The Lyon* slipped her moorings and rode the river current seaward with the outgoing tide. It was as Wallace had said: she passed through a narrow gorge with looming forts overhead, and out into the broad estuary where the River Avon meets the River Severn. A northeast wind filled her sails, and soon she was headed toward the westering sun and the open sea. Roger and Mary watched England and Wales recede in the wake, then turned forward for a view of the sea — cold, gray and windblown. Mary shivered a little at the sight.

Roger put his arm around her and spoke: "The sea is before us; Pharaoh's host is behind us. God will make us a way through the sea to safety, and our enemies dare not follow us."

"But there can be no return for us", Mary said to herself. She was reminded of a song her mother had sung to her many years ago.

> 'The water is wide, I cannot get over,
> Nor have I wings to fly.
> Give me a boat that can carry two
> And both shall row, my love and I . . .'

Historical Note:

This is a work of fiction. Though many of the characters in this story are real people known to history, my depiction of their characters and personalities is the product of my imagination. I have relied on the work of professional historians to provide a framework for my story, and though they cannot be held responsible in any way for my creative tale-telling, it is only fair for me to acknowledge their assistance in what I have written. Readers who may wish to perform a "reality check" on my efforts, or simply want to know more of the "real" story, are invited to consult these sources:

- Catherine Drinker Bowen's (award-winning) biography <u>The Lion and the Throne: The Life and Times of Sir Edward Coke</u> is a fascinating account of the life of one of England's greatest jurors, and includes a number of details about Roger Williams.
- John M. Barry's <u>Roger Williams and the Creation of the American Soul: Church, State, and the Birth of Liberty</u> (another award winner) covers much of the same material from a different angle, though it focuses primarily on Roger Williams's later life (which will be the subject of a later book by me, God willing).
- Like many people, I have come to rely on the online world for information and have gleaned many ideas from sources like Wikipedia or Encyclopedia Britannica (online). A browser search on any of the major characters in this

book will open a window to all sorts of interesting things, nearly all of which, alas, I could not make room for in this book.

About the Author

A.L. Porter is a child of the 50's, a "boomer," etc. and a history buff and storyteller who especially likes stories that explain something about who we are and how we got here. His writing incorporates his love of history with his family genealogy - his ancestors actually lived through the events of this book.

9 798889 282209 1